THE REFUGE

MARVELLE ZOLLARS

Inspiring Voices®
A Service of **Guideposts**

Songs (in public domain): Up from the Grave He Arose -- words and music by Robert Lowry The Old Rugged Cross -- words and music by George Bennard

All Scripture quotations are from the Holy Bible, New International Version

Inspiring Voices books may be ordered through booksellers or by contacting:

Inspiring Voices
1663 Liberty Drive
Bloomington, IN 47403
www.inspiringvoices.com
1-(866) 697-5313

ISBN: 978-1-4624-0139-0 (sc)
ISBN: 978-1-4624-0138-3 (e)

Library of Congress Control Number: 2012937618

Printed in the United States of America

Inspiring Voices rev. date: 04/20/2012

SARA

The battered old taxi rattled down a wide country road, raising a billowing cloud of dust that obliterated everything in its wake. The ancient car's inadequate air conditioning system added to the racket but provided very little respite against the heat. As they barreled down that pitiful excuse for a roadway, a large sign came into view.

"Stop! Stop right here!"

Startled, the driver hit the brake with unexpected force, hurling his passenger forward against the seat that separated them. He gazed at wide emerald eyes in his rearview mirror, seeing an angry hauteur that he had seldom encountered in one so young.

"W-what's wrong?" he asked timidly.

"I want out right here," the girl stated with certainty as she reached for the oversized suitcase that lay in the seat beside her.

"You're gettin' out *here?*" he asked incredulously. "But, ma'am..."

"How much do I owe you?" she asked, interrupting his protests and flinging her long auburn hair away from her striking face.

"Uh, well, it's a good long ways from the bus depot clear out here..."

"How much?" she asked again, her impatience quickly changing into extreme annoyance.

"Uh, that'll be $12.50," he answered, a note of apology in his voice.

She tossed a twenty dollar bill onto the front seat with careless negligence and wrenched open the door on her right. It shrieked with resistance as she pushed it wide. She began to drag her heavily packed bag across the seat, then noticed that the driver was busily counting out her change and shook her head with disgust.

"Use that money to get some oil for this door," she shouted as she slammed it shut and waved him on.

Finally fed up with her rudeness, he stomped on the accelerator and took off with a roar, leaving "her highness" coughing and spluttering in the suffocating blanket of dust his spinning tires spewed forth. Fuming with rage, the young woman squeezed her eyes tightly shut and tried not to breathe until some of the horrid dirt began to settle.

When she finally dared open an eye, she saw a dingy world come slowly into focus. Lush vegetation filled the ditches, but it appeared to be a sick yellowish color. Leaves, completely covered with the fine dust that seemed to hang forever in the air, drooped listlessly. And the heat! She felt as if she had stepped into the very jaws of hell.

She looked down at her expensive clothing with dismay. She had worn long sleeves this late August morning against the chill of autumn that already permeated the beautiful valley in Montana where she had been born seventeen years ago. The deep green of her western style silk shirt now nearly matched her tan slacks, and her favorite boots struggled to peak through the sand on the road. She furiously brushed the grimy dirt from her clothes as she surveyed this totally foreign place that was called Oklahoma.

Where in the world were the *trees?* What few she saw, dotting the flat countryside, were of some unknown variety and looked very different from the lofty pines and firs and tamaracks that covered the mountainsides near her home. The area seemed utterly remote. She half expected to see a band of renegade Indians appear suddenly on the horizon to come tearing across the prairie toward her.

She sighed and wiped the perspiration from her forehead, which was already turning red in the blistering sun. She had never felt such scorching heat in all of her life! She thought wistfully of the new snow that she had noticed only this morning on the mountain tops above Missoula, as her plane had lifted into the big, astonishingly blue sky that Montana is famous for.

She gazed at the large sign on her right that announced her arrival at this obscure destination.

WELCOME
TO
THE REFUGE

In You, O Lord, I have taken refuge;
let me never be put to shame... (Psalm 31:1)

The young woman wrinkled her brow with distaste. She realized that she was going to have to put up with a lot of religious nonsense in this place. But that *had* to be better than confronting her father—or that witch, Caroline!

She reached for her heavy bag that was now coated with the ever-present grittiness of this place. The copse of large trees that surrounded her new home seemed much further away now that she stood alone on this gravel inferno. The retreating cab was but a dirty smudge on the horizon.

She thought fleetingly of another taxi in a faraway city, and the ride that had somehow changed her destiny. That had brought her with unmistakable verity to this unknown place. As she began to walk wearily toward the beckoning spot of green in front of her, she remembered with remorse the beautiful wooded valley that she had left behind.

Whenever Sara Franklin thought about her childhood, she saw it in two distinctive chapters, rather like the *BEFORE* and *AFTER* pictures she sometimes saw in magazine advertisements. But, unlike the illustrations of dingy, unpainted houses, or drab, unattractive women without makeup, her *BEFORE* was bright and beautiful, a full-color portrait of love and laughter. No, it was in the time *AFTER* that torturous summer day that her life had changed forever. The world she had always known had come crashing down around her in an avalanche of heartache, and had become a daguerreotype of pain and loneliness and rebellion.

Sara was born to Laurie and Lance Franklin, loving parents who had taught her to respect them, to respect God and His creation, and to respect herself. She had lived the early years of her life in an unpretentious farmhouse just to the northeast of Missoula, Montana. Rattlesnake Creek bordered their property on the east, and beautiful Squaw Peak, sparkling white in winter and a soft smoky blue in summer, looked down upon their small tree-covered acreage with benevolence. Her father owned a modest lumber mill and "farmed" their forested land with care, always replacing the harvested trees with seedlings that would preserve the beauty and value of the land, as well as protect its wildlife.

Sara learned to ride almost as soon as she had walked, and her first love had been her little mare, Nellie. She and her mother had explored every nook and cranny of their picturesque valley, riding almost daily through the thick forests and along the numerous streams that rushed from the snow-covered peaks above.

Life had been good, with none of the luxuries of great wealth, but abounding in the joys of discovery and the warmth of love and security. Until the summer that she had turned nine, and that one day that had started innocently enough, only to end in a terrifying nightmare of sudden pain and sirens, and the desperate finality of death.

The details of that day had been permanently etched in her memory. She could still see the soft wash of pinks and lavender in that early morning sky as the sun had inched its way above the rugged peaks rimming Hell Gate Canyon. It promised to be a fine August day. The air was crisp and cool as she hurried to the barn to check on the baby raccoon that she and Mama had found down near the creek the day before. The tiny animal had clearly been abandoned, and was near starvation.

She had cradled the little ball of fur in her hands all the way home, and then Mama had helped her force a few drops of warm milk down the poor creature's throat. Later that night, the little raccoon, which she decided to name Bandit, had swallowed the milk with a bit more enthusiasm.

Sara was delighted to find Bandit much stronger on that morning, as he eagerly accepted the dropper full of warm milk and then nuzzled at her hand for more. She held him and cuddled him for some time, then rushed back into the house where Mama had a stack of pancakes and a pitcher of hot maple syrup waiting for her.

"Bandit's better today, Mama," she shouted as the door slammed behind her. "He drank all of his milk and begged for more!"

"We'll give him another dropper full in a couple of hours," Mama answered with a glad smile. "It's better not to rush these things."

"I know," Sara answered amiably. She and Mama had nursed many wild things back to health, always returning them to their natural habitat when they were restored.

"Wild creatures need to be free," Mama had said many times over the years. "It's a sin to keep them confined." Sometimes Sara wished she was a creature of the wild, free to roam as she pleased every day of her life, instead of being cooped up in a stuffy old schoolroom most of the year.

Summer had always been her favorite season, so she gulped her pancakes and fresh orange juice quickly, eager for that day's activities to begin. She knew that after she fed Bandit again, she and Mama would saddle the horses and ride up to Daddy's mill. They would take a giant stack of sandwiches and a big jug filled with lemonade with them to his office and they would all enjoy lunch around his comfortable old desk. Sara loved the sounds and smells of the mill, where a thick carpet of fine sawdust covered every inch of the ground and gave off a most pleasant aroma.

The day had passed as many other such days, in an easy camaraderie with nature, as she and Mama hunted for wild strawberries and picked a large basketful for their supper, and then, on a whim, followed honey bees to a hollow stump deep in the woods that was full of fine comb honey. They had marked the spot so that they could return the next day, prepared to gather some of the sweet nectar.

They arrived home just before sunset, tired and hungry and happy. Sara took both mares to the watering trough for a refreshing drink, and then on to the barn, where she brushed and curried them. She then fed them their supper before going inside to help Mama set the table for their own meal. Daddy would be home soon.

Later, as they all sat around their supper table, chattering about the day's events, Mama had suddenly gasped and dropped her fork with a clatter. She clutched at her head in obvious agony as Daddy jumped to his feet in alarm.

"Laurie! What's wrong?" he shouted with concern.

"My head..." Mama managed before she collapsed in his arms. He gathered her up and carried her quickly to the sofa. He shouted at Sara, who still sat at the table, as if paralyzed, "Call 911! And *hurry!*"

Sara finally broke out of her terrorized trance and rushed headlong to the phone. And then there had been the sirens, and the serious-faced medics, and the interminable trip to the hospital. And the waiting, and the unbelievable fear, and the mysterious words from the doctor about an aneurysm in Mama's brain and the possibility of prolonged unconsciousness.

Mama had never awakened. After three days in a deep coma, she lost hold of the frail thread that had connected her to this world, and Daddy wept as he told Sara that Mama had gone to heaven. Grandma and Grandpa came from Helena, and all the aunts and uncles and cousins drove in from everywhere, and somehow Sara got through the whole ordeal of the funeral and that awful juncture when they lowered Mama into the ground. But Sara's heart froze within her at that moment, her life forever changed.

Sara's ninth birthday fell on the last Saturday in August, exactly ten days after her mother was buried. Her daddy, a tall, rugged individual, cried like a baby as he handed her presents down from a closet shelf.

"Here, sweetheart," he sobbed. "Your mother... She... she bought these before..."

Sara opened her gifts with a heavy heart, loving the beautiful new riding boots most of all, because she knew her Mama had searched diligently to find exactly the right pair. There had been no birthday cake, of course. No one wanted a cake made by anyone other than Mama. They decided to go out for pizza, but neither she nor Daddy was hungry, and so they picked aimlessly at their food and returned home in silence.

The days that followed found Sara increasingly alone. Her father buried himself in his duties at the mill in an effort to overcome the cloud of grief that threatened to overwhelm him. He hired a woman to come during the daytime to see to the cooking and cleaning, and, Sara knew, to keep an eye on her also. But it hurt her so badly to see someone new in Mama's kitchen that she had avoided the house as much as possible.

Lance Franklin, who had always had an interest in forest conservation, began spending hours alone in his study, searching for every scrap of information or any new research in the field. He experimented with the new ideas on his own land, and soon captured the attention of the University of Montana's School of Forestry. The attractive campus became his second home as he collaborated with research stations that studied every facet of forestry conservation and wildlife.

And his hard work and tireless hours of experimental cultivation paid off, monetarily, at least. Increased profits from his small mill, along with a modest life insurance benefit from his wife, allowed him to nearly double the size of his holdings during the next two years. But at a cost that he failed to notice.

For Sara had become the loneliest of little girls, spending her summers roaming the trails that she had explored with her mother, and her winters in school during the daytime, and then locked in her room at night. Her grades fell gradually from A's and B's to B's and C's, and her long reddish-blonde hair that Mama had always kept in carefully braided pigtails hung in tangled disarray. Her companions, for the most part, were the animals of the forest and her mare, Nellie.

On Sara's eleventh birthday, Daddy proudly presented her with a beautiful, high-spirited mare which she named Ginger, because she was exactly the color of the ginger snaps her Mama had always baked at Christmas time. Daddy explained that she had sadly outgrown little Nellie, and that he thought she deserved "a real horse" since she seemed to spend the majority of her time riding. Sara hugged her father with a fierceness that surprised him, not only because she loved his wonderful gift, but also because it was the first time he'd really seemed to notice his daughter since the death of his wife.

It was on a bright morning a few days after Sara's twelfth birthday that she rode Ginger up to the site of her father's greatly expanded lumber mill and saw, to her surprise, two very expensive looking cars parked in front of his new office. She didn't want to interrupt her father and his visitors, so she went in search of Jim Marshall, the new mill foreman.

She found Jim out in the lumber shed, helping two young fellows stack a load of newly cut 2x4's. He looked up at her with a warm smile, his kind eyes beaming with pleasure.

"Mornin' Miss Sara," he said, stopping to wipe the perspiration from his face. That's a fine lookin' saddle you've got there. Looks brand new!"

Sara slipped out of her new saddle and onto ground covered with wood shavings and sawdust. Ginger snorted her displeasure at this interruption in their morning ride, stomping her foot with impatience. Sara laid a soothing hand on the mare's neck and said a few calming words before she answered Jim's query.

"Daddy got it for my birthday," she said proudly. Their newly acquired prosperity may not have brought her any more of her father's attention, but it had certainly been responsible for an increase in her worldly possessions. "What's going on down there, anyway?" she asked with a glance toward the office buildings.

"I'm not rightly sure," Jim answered, following her gaze. "Some fancy politicians, I reckon."

"Politicians! But why? What do politicians want with Daddy?"

"I think your Daddy's gotten the attention of a lot of people lately, what with the work he's doing at the university and this fine, modern lumber mill of his," Jim answered reflectively. "I wouldn't be at all surprised if they asked him to run for public office."

Sara was stunned by his words. Her father, in politics! Things had certainly changed since her mother's death three years ago. She left the sounds of the roaring saws behind as she rode off into the woods, deep in thought. She let Ginger take them wherever she wished, and soon the rushing sound of Rattlesnake Creek filled her ears. The mare loved drinking from its icy waters, fresh from the high peaks to the north, so Sara let her have her head, knowing the sure-footed horse would follow the most direct path to the water's edge.

Ginger suddenly snorted with surprise, then shied at an unexpected movement in the rocky underbrush of the creek's bank. The head and shoulders of a boy appeared above the thicket that had hidden him until he straightened at their unexpected approach. Sara pulled Ginger to an abrupt halt, and stared into the sky-blue eyes of an exceptionally good looking young fellow, who appeared to be not much older than herself. Neither spoke for a long moment. Then the boy flashed a quick, shy smile and said softly, "Hi!"

Ginger, apparently having decided that the stranger posed no threat to them, stepped forward and lowered her head for a refreshing drink. Now nearly abreast of the boy, Sara let her eyes flit from his bare chest to the fishing pole in his hand, and then back to his sun-baked body. She saw that he was taller than she had at first supposed, and very thin, and there was something about the play of muscles along sturdy arms and shoulders that made her squirm slightly in her saddle and drop her head.

Instantly, the boy reached for the faded blue tee shirt that lay on a rock near his feet and quickly slipped it over his head. Sara felt her cheeks grow warm, not because of the naked torso that she had just observed—after all, she had practically grown up in a lumber mill and had seen many shirtless men—but because this wiry young fellow with hair the color of ripened wheat had so easily read her thoughts.

To cover her discomfort, she glanced again at the pole in his hand and asked nonchalantly, "You catchin' anything?"

A happy smile brightened his face as he bent and lifted a stringer full of gleaming rainbow trout from the swirling water. "The Lord's been good to me today," he said gratefully.

The Lord? Was he referring to God? Sara found the thought somehow unsettling.

"*You* cast the line and reeled them in, didn't you?" she asked.

He nodded. "Sure. But He provided the fish," he answered simply, meeting her gaze with steady blue eyes that held no guile.

Sara had gone to Sunday school and church as a youngster, when Mama had been there to see to it, but this easy familiarity with the Lord was foreign to her. Wishing to change the subject to something more comfortable, she asked, "What's your name?"

"I'm Ross. Ross Marshall." He glanced with appreciation at her well-bred mare and expensive trappings and added, "And you must be Miss Sara."

She stared at him with unabashed astonishment. And then his name registered in her confused mind. Ross *Marshall*. "You're Jim's son?" she asked incredulously.

"That's right." He reached for his battered tackle box, as if preparing to leave, and Sara reined Ginger back from the water's edge. He noticed how the single thick braid of hair that fell almost to the girl's trim waist glowed like burnished copper in the morning sun. Her face, even shaded by the wide brim of her western hat, appeared to be every bit as pretty as his pa had described. He suddenly found himself asking, "Why don't you come up to the house with me? My mother would love to meet you, and so would Becky, my little sister. We could clean these fish in no time! Do you like fresh trout?"

He blurted all of this in a breathless rush and she found her mouth watering in spite of herself. When she hesitated, he added apologetically, "I mean, if you don't have to be somewhere else for lunch. Will your father be worried about you?"

She thought about that for a moment, knowing full well that absolutely no one would be the slightest bit worried about where she was. Her father was much too involved with his rich political friends, whoever they were, and no one else even cared. She gazed at the soft spoken boy standing below her and answered frankly, "No. No one will worry. And fresh trout sounds really good! I... I'd like to go, if you're sure your mother won't mind..."

He flashed another brilliant smile. "She'll be tickled. Come on!" he said as he filled the upturned bucket he'd obviously been sitting on with icy water from the creek and lowered his fish into its depths. He began to move upstream.

"Do you want to ride with me?" Sara asked courteously.

Ross shook his head. "Naw, I'll just walk. It's not far."

"Then I'll walk, too," Sara decided, and she promptly dismounted to walk beside her new friend. They chatted amicably as they moved slowly down a narrow path through tall trees. Ginger followed sedately behind them. Pine needles cushioned their steps and wild rose bushes crowded the edge of the trail. Bobolinks and wild canaries flitted above them in a joyous cantabile of song.

As they approached the small farm which was nestled in a clearing at the foot of the mountains, Ross explained that the house and outbuildings had been a part of her father's newly acquired timberland. As foreman of the mill, his father was allowed to use it for their home. A couple of milk cows grazed placidly in the grassy pasture behind the barn and a shaggy collie came bounding from somewhere in back of the house to greet them.

Snorting with displeasure at the approach of that exuberant animal, Ginger tossed her head and nearly pulled the reins from Sara's hand. Ross quickly quieted his dog, with a soft but stern command.

"Sugar! Stay down, girl," he said, fondly rubbing the collie behind her ears and then giving her a quick hug. The dog licked his hand, sniffed curiously at the bucket of fish, and then reached her cold nose to briefly touch Sara's hand in greeting. She then bounded back to the front porch of the house where a young girl had appeared.

Struck by a sudden thought, Sara asked, "How old are you, Ross?"

"I'll be fourteen next month. And you?"

"I'm twelve," she answered absently, her thoughts clearly elsewhere. "It seems strange, but I don't remember seeing you around school."

"I don't go to school. At least not in town. My ma is home schooling Becky and me," he answered candidly.

"*Home* schooling? You mean you go to school *here*? But... is that legal?" Sara asked with disbelief.

"Sure. Lots of people do it now, especially Christian families. We study the same as you, and take tests to be sure we're learning everything we need. I am testing a full two years ahead of those my age in public school. Ma says I'll be ready to take the GED in a couple more years," he replied with pride.

"Isn't that like graduating—at the age of *sixteen*?" Sara stared at her companion with unabashed amazement. "But what will you do then?"

"I can enroll at the university. Since we're so close, I can still live at home and help with the milkin' and the gardenin' and the mowin' and everything, just like I do now."

Sara struggled to digest this unexpected piece of information as they drew near to the porch. Mrs. Marshall had joined her daughter to welcome them. Sara noticed that Ross's mother and Becky, his sister, also had sandy colored hair and sky blue eyes, but the females of the family were petite, while Ross shared his father's lean lankiness. And they were warm and open, showing Sara a genuine friendliness that she responded to eagerly. It reminded her of a closeness that she hadn't experienced since the death of her mother.

The day flew by with surprising swiftness, and Sara was included in their daily chores as easily as if had she been a part of this family. She ate hungrily of fish from the stream and sliced tomatoes, fresh lettuce and corn on the cob, all from their garden. A freshly baked cobbler, made with apples picked from their own sizable orchard, completed a most delicious meal. Even her tall glass of milk had come from the cows she'd seen near the barn. It was a simple life, filled with joy and laughter, and centered around God. And Sara found herself oddly reluctant to ride away from it at sundown.

School started at the end of August, and early in October Sara's father announced his plans to enter the race for State Representative. The seat from their district was to be vacated at the end of the present session, and local political leaders had strongly urged him to become a contender. They felt that he would not only represent the interests of the lumber industry, but also of the proponents of forest conservation.

And then, soon after the new year began, Lance divulged plans to begin construction of a new home. Sara couldn't imagine leaving the only house she'd ever lived in, but he argued that he had found a prime building site in town. It was near Waterworks Hill and would be much more accessible to the university and to the local political leaders and other dignitaries who were backing his campaign. The view, he added, would be spectacular, overlooking beautiful Greenough Park with Sara's beloved Rattlesnake Creek meandering through it. Looking further to the south, he explained, the range of view would include the magnificent sweep of the Clark Fork River. And towering above the river was Mt. Sentinel. The attractive buildings of Montana State University's campus clustered at the foot of the mountain and marched on up its steep, grassy slopes.

Even though Daddy joked that it was about time they used some of that lumber that his mills turned out every year for themselves, Sara had the uncomfortable feeling that this new house was to be more of a showplace than a home. She guessed that it would become just a pretentious object of prestige where he could entertain his wealthy new friends lavishly. She thought the house they already had was plenty good enough, and asked with some petulance, "So what do you plan to do with this place, just abandon it to the pack rats and the rattlesnakes?"

"Actually, I was thinking of letting your friend Ross and his family move over here. It would be a step up for them, and now that I'm away most of the year, I'll be hiring an assistant for Jim at the mill. That would open up the Marshall place for the new man. Besides, you're going to need a place to keep Ginger once we move into town, and since you're practically living with the Marshall's these days anyway, that would seem to be the ideal place."

Ginger! It had never occurred to her that she would have to leave her beloved mare! How could her father do this to her? She hated the new house already, and they hadn't even poured the foundation yet. She stormed and pouted and sulked for a solid week, and then, as had become her habit over the past few months, she went to Ross and shared her tumultuous feelings with him.

"Oh Sara, I wish I could help you somehow," he said in his quiet way. "I know that that place has always been your home, and must hold a million memories of your childhood and your mother and..."

Sara suddenly burst into tears, all of the old heartache and pain assaulting her with devastation. And then she felt his strong young arms enfold her in a compassionate embrace. A surge of warmth engulfed her, and she surrendered to his caring gesture that somehow helped to fill the awful void of loneliness that had become so much a part of her life.

As she rode home that evening, she looked at their farmstead with new eyes. She couldn't imagine living in some fancy mansion in town, away from the familiar call of the meadowlarks and the sweet smells of wild columbine and Rocky Mountain laurel. She tried to imagine Ross living in her house, maybe even sleeping in her room! She remembered the feel of his arms as he had held her gently that afternoon, and again felt an unfamiliar warmth flow through her.

They moved into their new home late in September. Lance Franklin was chosen during the November elections to serve as congressman, representing the state's richly forested areas west of the Continental Divide. A surge of vehement tears and angry protestations from Sara finally convinced her father to rent a small pasture, complete with a warm barn, so that she could keep Ginger close by. The small acreage was within easy walking distance of their new house, so Sara spent little time in that palatial dwelling that they now called home.

Lance also engaged an older couple as live-in caretakers of his new domain. Joe and Mary Wilson were kind and open-hearted, and Sara liked them in spite of herself. They tended the house and its extensive grounds with diligence, and gave Sara a sense of security that had long been absent. And Sara, herself, grew lovelier every day, emerging from the tall, gangling awkwardness of adolescence into the tall, graceful elegance of young womanhood.

Her father began grooming her to act as his hostess for the grand parties his newly acquired status would call for, and often invited her to accompany him on his many trips to Helena, their state capital. He gave her unlimited funds, and encouraged her to buy "pretty, feminine things, for a change," and to have her hair professionally styled. And gradually, she became aware of a difference in her own status—at school, in her childhood haunts in Missoula, even with the Marshall's.

Although Ross remained her steadfast friend, Becky, who was growing up herself, often gazed wistfully at the older girl's pretty clothes. Because even the "old things" that Sara had saved back for her riding attire were better than anything Becky had ever owned. And when the blossoming young beauty donned her best, heads turned with appreciation, and due respect was shown.

Sara learned with heady intoxication that she now possessed a great new power. While Joe and Mary treated her much as they would a granddaughter, sometimes offering advice or gentle reproof, Sara realized that she was ultimately in command. Even her father, on the rare occasions when he was present, deferred to her wishes. And, filled with her own sense of self-esteem, she grew willful and demanding.

The months flew past. Lance took to politics like a duck to water. He was hardly installed in the State House of Representatives before Montana's elite began pushing him for a seat in Washington. His spiraling career was heady stuff indeed, and he campaigned with an enthusiasm and a warm friendliness that brought him instant popularity. In a whirl of activity that left Sara breathless with pride for her father, she saw him move from a local political arena to the much more highly esteemed national level.

But then he had had the audacity to bring Caroline into their lives. He just appeared one day, home for the Christmas recess, with no warning at all that he would be accompanied by the exquisite junior senator from Colorado. And at sixteen, Sara could only look at the petite brunette with horror and suspicion. How dare this beautiful stranger interfere in a world Sara had finally managed to conquer! And how could her father, who had never, to Sara's knowledge, looked upon any woman other than her own mother with love, cast such adoring eyes upon this creature.

Sara rose early the next morning, and dressed in her oldest jeans and a thread-bare shirt that needed ironing, and started out for the edge of town and her horse. She rode for a long while in the woods along the Rattlesnake, ending, as usual, at the Marshall's. She helped Ross shovel out the cow shed and then replace manure soiled straw with a fresh warm bed for the cold winter nights they were now experiencing. Reluctant to return to a home that now housed her supposed rival, she stayed on to help him with the milking. Having finally mastered the art, Sara found a deep contentment in resting her head in that hollow between Red's warm flank and the roundness of her belly, and listening to the steady swish-swish of milk as it filled the pail between her knees. Ross's old radio provided a backdrop of soft music, and Sara's distressed heart was soothed.

It was long past dark when Sara mounted Ginger for the return trip to town. Ross insisted upon walking with her as far as the barn, and then helped her to unsaddle and feed Ginger. Since it was only a short walk along well lighted streets on to Sara's home, Ross left her there, squeezing her hand in a brief show of encouragement and then disappearing into the night.

At a few minutes after 8:30 Sara, smelling strongly of horse flesh and sweat and manure, pushed open their heavy oak door and entered the foyer of their sumptuous dwelling. She was greeted by the surprised stares of her father and Caroline, along with Chuck and Margie Dawson, who were apparently evening guests. Sara knew that Chuck held some important post at the university, and Margie had been her third grade teacher.

She heard Caroline ask in a faint voice, "What is that *smell*?"

And her father's reply, "That, I'm afraid, is my daughter."

The look of horror and revulsion in the woman's eyes as they traveled from Sara's tangled mass of auburn hair to her mud splattered boots brought a small, satisfied smile to the girl's face as she bent to remove the offensive footwear.

Joe appeared out of nowhere, hand extended, and said, hastily, "Here. I'll take those boots out back and give them a good cleaning. I'm sure you're anxious for a warm bath and a change of clothes."

Sara once more surveyed the group gathered comfortably around a roaring fire, then squared her shoulders and lifted her chin as she marched resolutely toward the stairs. As she moved up and out of sight to those below her, she heard a loud guffaw burst from Chuck. He chortled, "I do declare, Lance, if that girl doesn't get her nose down a notch, she's gonna' drown the next good rain we get!"

Sara seethed as she soaked in a hot tub of fragrant water. She wanted more than anything to just retire to her room for the night without facing any of them again, but she was hungry, and the thought of an egg and bacon sandwich and a cup of hot chocolate drove her back downstairs an hour later. She saw with relief that their visitors had gone, and she would have gone straight to the kitchen had her father not called out to her.

"Sara! Come join us. We've just been talking about you," he said.

She stopped short, and then entered the luxuriously furnished living room and perched on a chair as far as possible from the couple reclining on the sofa. She saw at a glance that Caroline was curled intimately in the crook of her father's arm, her ebony hair catching highlights from the fire like a sleek black cat. "Caroline was just telling me about a private school for young ladies such as you in Boulder, Colorado. She feels that it might do you good to associate with other girls of your class and..."

"My *class*?" Sara interrupted incredulously. "And just what is *my class*?"

"Perhaps your father has made a poor choice of words," Caroline offered soothingly. "Miss Priscilla's Academy for Girls is a finishing school for young ladies who are entering 11th grade, and continues their education through graduation. It is a beautiful school located at the foot of the Colorado Rockies, and offers such amenities as riding and skiing. You would learn the social skills necessary to young women of your cl... uh, your station."

Sara was shaking her head even before Caroline finished. "No!" she shrieked. "NO!! I will not go to some *Finishing School*! I have a plenty good enough school right here!"

"You must think of your father's political future, Sara," Caroline continued condescendingly. "Members of the press are always watching, and that scrutiny will increase as the next election grows closer."

"Caroline feels that your close association with the Marshall's, who are, after all, our hired help, would be looked upon as somewhat inappropriate," her father continued. "At a private school you would meet other young girls of high ranking families. We feel you would learn a great deal besides the standard studies offered in public school."

Sara jumped to her feet, having heard all she intended to hear. "Oh, *we* do, do *we*? Well, *I* feel that my school and my friends are *my* business, and *I* tell you that I am staying right here!" She stomped off to her room, her hunger forgotten, slamming the door with all of the vehemence that she could muster.

She used every wile imaginable over the next few months in an effort to dissuade her father and his precious Caroline from their proposed plans. But her tears and her temper tantrums, her pitiful pleading and prolonged pouting were all of no avail. And, when the couple announced their upcoming wedding, set for late August, she gave up entirely and sulked away the remainder of the summer.

Two days after her father married again, in Missoula's social event of the year, Sara rode her beloved Ginger to the Marshall's where the mare would be left for the winter. She sobbed as she buried her face the Ginger's soft mane, and then sobbed some more as Ross, who had been her closest friend and companion for the last four years, but who was apparently not good enough for her anymore, held her in a fierce embrace.

He whispered brokenly, "It's only for a few months, Sara, and the time will go fast, I promise. I'll take good care of Ginger, you can be sure of that. And I'll be right here when you get back."

As the girl clung to him with desperation, he added through tears of his own, "You'll not be alone, Sara. God will be there with you. Bless you, girl."

Miss Priss's Abomination for Girls, as Sara liked to call it, was horrible. Just as she had known it would be. Maybe *because* she had known it would be. In truth, she had to admit that the grounds were beautiful. And she loved to ski, a sport she had never before had the opportunity to try. But the girls were snobs, and her teachers were prissy old maids with absolutely no sense of humor.

In the classroom she was taught American History and English and Proper Etiquette. In the dormitory where she lived, she was taught by her high class peers to smoke and to swear, and the various intricacies of sex. She, who had never even been kissed, was ridiculed for having her virginity intact, and was encouraged to share in the filthy stories and disgusting language of those around her. She remembered that Ross had told her that God would be there with her, but she couldn't imagine His presence in such a place. Slowly she became one of them, taking on the superficial veneer of the very wealthy.

But she said good-bye to her classmates in the spring with little emotion and no intention of ever returning, even though she knew that she was bound for a home that now included Caroline, her new *stepmother*! The thought made her grow cold.

To her intense relief, Caroline was in Colorado visiting friends and family when she arrived home. Her father met her at the airport and took her to lunch, but left her soon after, amid profuse apologies, to attend an important meeting. She immediately changed into comfortable old jeans and implored Joe to drive her up to the Marshall's to see her mare. He hesitated, knowing full well that her father would not approve, but he had never been able to resist Miss Sara when she begged him for a favor.

The Marshall family, with the exception of Jim, who was at the mill, as usual, came rushing out of the house to greet her. Sara sent Joe back to town, hugged her old friends with joy, and then headed straight for the pasture behind the barn. Ginger, who had obviously been well tended, was sleek and shiny, and nickered eagerly as she galloped toward the fence where Sara waited with Ross and Becky.

That night Sara pulled out the old milking stool and joined Ross in his chores. The radio serenaded them like old times, and Sara felt a sense of deep contentment enter her heart. She let her eyes linger on Ross as he stood with his pail full of milk. He would be nineteen years old in a few months, and she saw that his shoulders had broadened and that his face had taken on a new look of maturity. He smiled at her tenderly, and she felt something stir deep within her.

The balmy May night was breathlessly still, the blue-black sky lit with a million stars. As they left the darkened barn, Sara gazed at the spangled heavens and grasped Ross's hand to halt his slow stride. She remembered a favorite spot from her childhood and tugged at his hand.

"Come, I want to show you something," she urged softly.

He followed her without question to a small cow shed beyond the barn. It was open-fronted, and was covered with corrugated tin on three sides, as well as on its sloping roof. The front stood higher than Ross's head, but when they went to the back side, they found it low enough to easily climb upon. Sara scrambled up quickly and lay flat on her back, with her face to the stars above. Ross lay down beside her and gasped at the glorious spectacle that awaited him.

"I used to climb up here on summer nights when I was a small child and pretend I was sailing alone on an endless sea with only the stars to guide me," Sara breathed. "I was sure that those friendly lights would guide me to the handsome prince, and the exciting life that was to be my destiny."

Ross chuckled softly as he cast a quick glance in her direction. "I guess I'm a pretty poor substitute for a handsome prince. But that sky is truly the handiwork of God. Personally, I can't think that life gets much more exciting than this."

"Ross, have you ever kissed a girl?"

Surprised by her unexpected question, he turned to see that she was watching him closely. "No, Sara, I can't say that I have."

She laid a hand softly against his cheek and moved ever so slowly, until her lips brushed his. The feather-like touch of his warm breath acted as a magnet, pulling her mouth once more against his. Heat swept through Sara's body, bringing with it a heightened awareness of the young man at her side. She thought of the stories she'd heard during the school year of the sexual escapades of girls no older than herself and suddenly longed to understand, to feel, to experience firsthand.

As if the thought prompted the action, she rolled against him, her hands feverishly exploring his body, her mouth smothering his sudden protest. A passion she hadn't believed was possible washed through her as she slipped her hand beneath his shirt and felt the heat of his bare skin. She vaguely sensed his effort to pull away from her once again, but she yanked first at the buttons on his shirt and then at those on her own.

When she pressed her firm young torso against his, he groaned his surrender to this girl that he had loved since that long ago day along the banks of Rattlesnake Creek, when she had walked into his heart once and for all.

And then it was finished, and she realized with some consternation that Ross was weeping. "Sara," he sobbed brokenly. "I'm sorry. I'm so sorry. Oh, God, please forgive me!"

"Ross! What's wrong with you?"

"Oh Sara. Don't you see? What we have just done is *wrong!*"

"So nobody's going to know! It doesn't matter, Ross."

"Yes. it does matter! It matters a great deal. Because God knows! And we have sinned against Him."

Suddenly angry, Sara jumped down from the shed. "God's not going to tell anyone, is He? Just forget about it! It doesn't matter, I tell you."

And with that she stomped off to fetch her saddle from the barn and then called for Ginger. She saddled up and rode away into the night, leaving Ross on his knees beside the old cow shed, praying to his Father for forgiveness.

It turned out that Ross was right, of course. That few minutes of exploration and ecstasy proved to matter very much indeed. When Sara learned with horrified dismay that she was pregnant, she vacillated between fear and fury. She blamed Ross for... for, well for just being *right*, when she'd been so sure that he was being silly. And she blamed his God for letting this happen to her. She'd been certain that God would allow this one small indiscretion to go unnoticed, and now it appeared that He intended for the whole world to know.

But the whole world must not know! Most of all, her father must not know. His image must be protected. And she knew that the all-important press would have a heyday with this savory little tidbit. So what was she to do?

She hadn't seen Ross since that awful night more than two months ago. At first she'd stayed away out of embarrassment and anger at his unexpected reaction to their love-making. And then, when Caroline returned from visiting her relatives, she had hardly let the girl out of her sight, as if suspecting some sign of rebellion. And now she knew that she could not possibly face Ross with the truth. And so Sara found herself alone in her terrible dilemma.

The more she thought about her predicament, the more she thought about the possibility of having an abortion. She hadn't known anyone who had had an abortion before going to Miss Pricilla's, but the girls there had laughed at her innocence and assured her that "everyone was doing it these days." School would be starting again soon, and arrangements had been made for her second year at Miss Priscilla's. She knew with certainty that she could not go back there in her present condition. She must make a decision, and make it very soon.

When Daddy asked her to accompany him to Helena so that she could find some new things for school, she believed the fate of her unborn child had been decided for her. She would have the perfect opportunity to find an abortion clinic in the city, and thus get the whole thing taken care of away from the inquisitive eyes of friends and family. Her careful planning almost came to naught when Caroline announced that she would make the trip with them, but at the last minute her stepmother decided to attend the meeting at the governor's mansion with her father instead of shopping with her.

They dropped Sara off near the busy downtown area, and she waved goodbye to them with a pocket full of money and a credit card, scared out of her wits at what she had determined was her only choice. She walked to a nearby pharmacy and searched their phone book until she found an address in an unknown section of the city, and then hailed a taxi.

The shabby young driver glanced at her in askance when she gave him her destination, but drove off without a word. She guessed that he had probably been there before, and shivered with dread.

Sara watched as well-kept city streets gave way to a gradually declining neighborhood, her feelings of foreboding increasing as the area became cluttered with debris, the buildings unkempt. When her driver pulled up in front a derelict old office building and stopped, waiting for her to pay the fare and exit his cab, she found that she could only stare with dismay at the trash-filled doorway and the unpretentious sign above that announced the confines as being The Women's Clinic of Abortion. At a sharp look from the man behind the steering wheel, she reached for her purse on the seat beside her, then suddenly noticed the remnants of an old newspaper, left behind by some unknown passenger.

Her eyes were drawn to the headlines on the front of a magazine supplement, called *Mainstream*. Bold lettering proclaimed the very large and extremely attractive house pictured below it as: *THE REFUGE*: A Christian Alternative to Abortion.

"Hey, miss! You gettin' out?" the driver asked impatiently.

Sara tore her eyes away from the picturesque dwelling on the magazine's cover to look again at the dreary scene out her window. And she knew, without understanding how she knew it, that she couldn't walk into that disgusting place and let strangers have free rein with her body. And, in realizing that, she knew that her only other option lay before her in that forgotten magazine.

"No. No, I... I've changed my mind. Just take me back downtown. Take me to Chloe's Boutique on First Street."

Sara picked up the wrinkled pages that described a "beautifully rambling old home near Bartlesville, Oklahoma, where women can find Christian direction, warm understanding, and medical care during an unplanned pregnancy." She carefully folded the article and shoved it to the bottom of her purse.

And now she needed to concentrate on getting "some nice new things," because everyone must be convinced that she intended to return to school as planned.

Sara trudged the last few steps of her long journey, and then set her heavy suitcase down beside her as she gazed through gates flung wide in an unspoken welcome. Lettering on the archway over the entrance assured her that she had reached *THE REFUGE*. Her expensive silk shirt now clung to her with a tenacity that bordered upon the ridiculous. Perspiration streamed off her sunburned face and dripped down her neck.

She grabbed up the burdensome luggage at her side and moved gratefully from the hot, dusty road into the shade of huge trees that bordered a well-kept lawn. She felt the coolness of an unexpected breeze touch her skin and tugged the damp fabric of her blouse away from her body. The mist from a nearby sprinkler reached her blistered face, and she felt refreshed.

The peaceful scene entranced her. Tiny spots of errant sunlight squeezed through the leafy canopy overhead and puddled in the grass, giving the effect of deep green velvet, spatter-painted with gold. But it was the great white house that drew her attention. It somehow reminded her of a huge ocean liner afloat on an emerald sea.

She slowly opened the clasp of her purse and dug into its depths until she found folded sheets from a magazine, wrinkled and worn from much handling. She stared at the picture of this rambling structure that had always seemed to her to beckon with open arms, and lifted her eyes again to its stately beauty. She walked toward it with sudden determination.

She stood at the door for a long moment and then, gathering her courage about her, she thrust her chin into the air, lifted her hand, and knocked sharply.

When the door finally opened, she found herself face to face with a small, trim woman with softly curling hair and a kind smile. Sara surveyed this petite lady, who somehow reminded her of her grandmother, and decided in that moment that she should have no problem at all in manipulating her.

She tossed her head with arrogance and stated calmly, "My name is Sara Franklin. I've decided to give your place a try."

TOM

⚬

T om yanked off his glasses and rubbed his eyes wearily. He sighed, and gazed with distaste at the spectacles in his hand. Just one more sign of middle age! Not that he was that old, but there was something about approaching sixty that made you stop and think. And here he was, embarking upon another great journey in his life. But, he had to admit, it was, without a doubt, the most exciting and the most thoroughly frightening assignment yet to be set before him.

His eyes fell on the name plate that adorned his cluttered desk. It proclaimed him James Thomas Logan, Vice President, Division of Marketing, American Trucking, Inc. But, as impressive as that title sounded, he knew that his most recent endeavor as founder and head of The Refuge, although a much more humble position, had given him the most profound happiness that he had ever known.

And the most apprehension, he thought with a wry chuckle. He looked down at the half-finished speech that he was trying to write for the upcoming quarterly meeting with other American VP's. He had been working fruitlessly for most of the afternoon, and knew that part, at least, of his lack of success had stemmed from his divided attention. For he was deeply concerned about the financial status of his newly opened home for young women facing an unplanned pregnancy.

When he and Amy Anderson had opened The Refuge last June, he had hoped that the unexpected publicity from an article in *Mainstream*, a Sunday magazine supplement included in many of the area's larger daily newspapers, would spark the donations needed to help him provide a warm, comfortable and fully staffed Christian refuge for young women and their babies at no cost to them. For that was the only way, he felt, to provide an atmosphere that saw each individual, regardless of her prior circumstances, as God saw them. As being completely and totally equal.

But the costs seemed to mount steadily, and the donations, although generous, had come slowly. Here it was August already, and the east wing that had been set aside for the birthing rooms and the nursery still lacked many of the medical instruments and supplies necessary for safe delivery. And Gretta, one of four young ladies who had moved in when the center opened late in June, was due to deliver in September.

He tossed his glasses onto the desk and stood, stretching his aching muscles, then moved to the window across the room. The luxury of his office was lost on him as he stared unseeing at the street beyond his window, late afternoon sunshine dancing off the windshields of vehicles as they sped past. He frowned in sudden irritation at his lack of faith. Hadn't God seen them to this point, meeting and overcoming their needs and frustrations and fears as only He can? After all, the whole idea of opening that grand old house for young women who needed "a refuge" had seemed just some preposterous notion in the beginning, and he, Tom Logan, the most illogical choice for its forming and founding. But his Savior had most assuredly led him here, and he had needed only to accept the will of his Father. What a joyous journey it had become!

The sudden shrill ringing of his telephone interrupted his musings. He reached for the receiver, wondering who would be calling him so late on a Friday afternoon.

"American Trucking, Tom Logan speaking."

"Daddy?"

"Jenny! Hello, Jenny," he said with sudden joy. "Is it really you?"

"Yeah, Dad, it's really me," she replied softly. Tom heard the smile in her voice. "How are you, Dad?"

"I'm fine, Jenny, just fine! It's so good to hear from you! Are you okay?" He'd made it a point to speak with his daughter at least twice a month, although much of the time it was only briefly, and he was the one who had made all the calls. It had been that way ever since those awful days when his marriage had begun to crumble around him and everything he had held dear was torn from his grasp.

"Yes, I'm okay. Dad, I got a letter from Crystal a couple of months ago, after her article was published in *Mainstream*. She sent me a copy of it and told me all about her trip to Bartlesville and her talks with you. I was really surprised. I hadn't heard from Crystal since college and..."

Jenny's voice over the line had grown gradually softer and then faltered, and Tom knew she was remembering that time when she'd had the abortion, and the terrible distance that had already grown between the two of them had slowly become an angry chasm of misunderstanding and harsh words. He had finally come to his senses, of course, and gone to her in abject apology, but he had never been able to regain the closeness he'd had with her when she was "Daddy's little girl."

He spoke now to cover her momentary emotion. "Crystal did an excellent job for us. That article has been instrumental in bringing us some much needed support for our efforts here."

"Dad, do you suppose I could come and see it—The Refuge, I mean? It looks really beautiful in the picture and, well I just can't seem to quit looking at it, and I just wondered..."

"I would like that more than you can know," he answered gently. "Of course you can come, anytime!"

"Would next weekend be all right?" Her voice sounded eager now, and excited. "I... I don't have anything planned, and I get off work at three on Fridays. I thought I might come that evening, uh, that is, if you don't have other plans..."

"That sounds great! I'll take you out to the finest restaurant in town— or to Pizza Hut, if you'd rather," he said with a happy chuckle.

"Uh, I think I want to get really dressed up and go someplace nice," she said, sounding very much like the little girl he'd once thought he could never lose. How carelessly we take our loved ones for granted!

"Good," he answered, striving to control emotions that threatened to unman him. "I will call for reservations and do my best to make myself look presentable. I can't have you feeling ashamed of your old Dad!"

"Oh, Dad!" she laughed merrily. "You always look wonderful!"

"Thank you, Jenny. You are very kind. Why don't you plan to come here to the plant first and I'll show you around, and then we'll go out on the town. Will you stay with me at the apartment or would you like for me get you a room downtown?"

26

"I... I think I would like to stay with you, if you don't mind," she said shyly.

"I don't mind. The spare bedroom is small, but comfortable enough. I'm just so glad you're coming, Jenny. I love you..." He broke off, unable to continue.

"I'm glad too, Dad. And I love you, too. I'll see you next week!"

He wasn't sure, but he thought he heard a soft little kiss as she broke the connection. Just like old times!

Tom replaced the receiver and leaned back in his chair with a satisfied smile. Maybe, just *maybe,* his prayers were being answered. At last! For losing his daughter had caused him nearly as much heartache as losing his wife, and the two together had all but cost him his soul.

It had started many years ago, just how many, he wasn't sure. But slowly he had begun to realize that Joyce, his partner and his friend, the mother of his children and the love of his life, was showing unmistakable signs of unrest and discontent. He had thought at the time that she had somehow become bored with her life as homemaker and caretaker of their two children. Jimmy and Jenny were, after all, growing up and becoming more and more independent of her care.

He had suggested that she return to school and finish the degree that she had abandoned so many years before to become his bride and then the mother of their children. And she had done so, happily, but, as she grew more and more involved with her new life, she had moved further and further away from him and the life they had shared for more than twenty years. A life, he still believed, that had abounded with joy and love and devotion.

And as his wife slowly but surely began to desert him, she had taken Jenny with her, for they were very close as mothers and daughters should be. He wondered later if Joyce had deliberately turned his daughter against him in an effort to alleviate her own feelings of guilt, or if Jennifer, finding herself suddenly in a position where she felt pressured to "take sides," had turned naturally to her mother.

And then, in a new environment of unexpected freedom and permissiveness, Jenny had dropped her Christian friends one by one and had begun running with a much wilder crowd. She began dating anyone and everyone who asked her out with careless abandon. And Tom had watched in helpless agony, unable for the first time to reach his daughter. His calls were refused, his letters unread, his prayers, it seemed, unanswered.

When Joyce had demanded a divorce, and then remarried a few months later, he had gratefully accepted an assignment to head up the marketing department of American Trucking's newest branch in Chicago. It was only when his son Jim, his sole friend and confidante at that time, had called from college the weekend before Tom was to move, that he had learned that Jenny had gotten pregnant and subsequently had had an abortion.

And so Tom had run away, on a bleak autumn day five long years ago, in total despair, to a new job and a new life in a new city. He knew he was running away from the shame of his failure as a husband and father, from his pain and his heartache. He was, in truth, running away from God.

Tom had found Chicago cold and wet and windy. But he had arrived there in a dark mood, and with a frozen heart that even the hottest summer sun would have failed to penetrate. He quickly and completely immersed himself in his work, shutting out the rest of the world with a vengeance. The deep faith that he had carried in his heart since his childhood failed him. As Sundays came and went, he found it easier to hide away in his small apartment, buried in statistics and sales reports and endless paperwork, than to venture out in search of a place to worship.

His fellow workers and the young sales staff that served him found him fair and honest to deal with, but stern and aloof, making them unwilling to form any kind of personal relationships with him. All of them, that is, with the exception of Tony Bryant, an exuberant young African American whose exceptional sales ability had kept him consistently at the top of the sales team. His unfailing good humor and friendliness occasionally brought a small smile to Tom's face.

On an unseasonably cold Friday afternoon in early April, Tom found himself wrapping up Tony's quarterly appraisal with an unusually warm commendation.

"You have proved yourself to be a first-class sales representative with an unprecedented record in our company. You have shown impeccable character and a truly unflappable good nature, and I must tell you that I am proud of you," Tom said with frank appreciation.

Tony received the words gratefully, knowing full well that they were rare words indeed, coming from a man who had always set the highest of standards, not only for his staff, but for himself as well. He smiled broadly and answered with sincere humility, "Thank you, boss. I couldn't ask for a greater compliment."

Tom gazed at the lanky young fellow sitting with quiet composure in front of his desk and felt an unaccustomed stirring somewhere within him. He stood abruptly, signaling an end to the meeting.

"Well, I would imagine you are anxious to get out of here and on with your weekend," Tom said briskly, extending his hand toward the younger man for a friendly handshake.

Tony slowly moved to his feet and accepted Tom's hand in a warm, firm grasp. "As a matter of fact, I am looking forward to this weekend in particular," he said. "You see, my family always has a big get-together for Easter, and this year will be no exception. Will you be seeing your family as well?"

Tom knew that Tony had asked this last innocently, but was unable to stop the brief look of hostility that crossed his face. He hadn't even realized it *was* Easter this Sunday and he was uncomfortably aware that he had no family at all to spend it with.

He stammered with uncharacteristic vacillation. "I... No, I... I have lots of work to get done..."

"Mr. Logan, I don't want to be impertinent, but you seem so... so *lonely*. I... my family and I would be most honored if you would join us for worship on Sunday morning." Tony spoke the words with such undisguised sincerity that Tom was momentarily taken aback.

"Uh, no... that is, I don't think..."

Tony broke in with quick words of reassurance. "I know I'm black and you're white, and it's true that our minister, Brother Seth, is also a black man, but we have many white brothers and sisters that worship with us, and I'm sure that you wouldn't feel uncomfortable there..."

Tony had spoken with breathless urgency, as if it somehow really *mattered* to him that Tom join them in their Easter Sunday morning worship. Tom stood quietly, looking into dark eyes full of entreaty. He had attended a worship service of some sort, in some place or another, every Easter Sunday of his life, he guessed, and he suddenly knew in his heart that he didn't want to quit now. He nodded slowly.

"All right. Where..?"

"We meet at ten o'clock, and I would be more than happy to pick you up at your place at about 9:30. There will be a huge feast afterwards with the best home cooking you've ever eaten, but I'll be glad to bring you on back home if you'd rather," Tony said with enthusiasm. "Will that work for you?"

"Yes," Tom said softly. "That will work just fine."

With a huge grin that was nothing short of radiant, the young man turned and hurried from the room.

The small Baptist Church was typically crowded for the Easter worship service. Tony spotted his young wife, along with the rest of his family, down near the front of the sanctuary. He gave her a brief smile and a wave of his hand, then slipped, much to Tom's relief, into a pew near the back of the church. Tom let his eyes wander over the gathering crowd, happily decked out in their new spring attire. They greeted one another as they intermingled with many hugs and warm smiles.

The service began with the joyous sound of many voices raised in songs of praise and adoration. Tom was content to just sit and let the music swell around him for a time, and then, without realizing just when it happened, he found that he had begun to sing along, his clear baritone voice harmonizing with the purity of Tony's tenor next to him.

The sermon, delivered by Brother Seth Walters, focused on the death and resurrection of Christ, as did virtually every sermon in every church everywhere on this Easter morning, Tom supposed. He had heard it all many times before, but somehow, the anguish of the message failed to touch him as it had in the past. His mind flitted aimlessly. He thought of Joyce with a stab of pain and quickly turned his attention elsewhere. He squirmed restlessly, and then winked at a small boy who had turned to stare at him, a stranger in their midst.

His attention was caught again by Brother Seth, who had stepped ponderously down from the podium and now stood near the front row of pews.

The old minister began to speak quietly and with deep emotion.

"We dwell extensively on the death and resurrection of our Savior at Easter time, and that is good, of course. But I try to think about my Lord and his terrible suffering in those dark hours before his death every day of my life."

He paused, his eyes touching briefly on various faces before him. Then, in shame and remorse, he dropped his eyes to the floor in front of him and continued, "Because I know that with every unkind word that escapes my lips, with every deception, no matter how slight it may seem to me, with every angry thought that enters my mind, I add another thorn to my blessed Savior's crown."

He raised his head again and a shaft of sunlight streaming through stained glass caught and held a tear that rolled slowly down his cheek. His voice, though thick with emotion, grew stronger. "And I know in the very depths of my heart that if I had been the only man standing at the foot of the cross on that day, mocking Him and scourging Him, that He would have lifted His eyes to heaven and shouted, *Father, forgive Seth Walters! He doesn't know what he's done!*"

He spoke those last words with a roar that rang and echoed in every corner of the room, his eyes raised, one hand flung toward heaven. There was absolute silence in the church. Every eye was riveted on the speaker, every ear straining to hear his next words, spoken so softly that Tom leaned forward in his seat in an effort to hear.

"And then He would have died—for me alone. He would have done it all, just for me!"

He ended with a muffled sob, tears now streaming down his wrinkled old face. Tom blinked furiously as his own eyes filled, and then realized as he glanced surreptitiously around him that many of the congregation were weeping openly. He would have staked his life at that moment on his conviction that what he had just witnessed had been no Easter service theatrical, but the heartfelt words of a true man of God.

Tom slowly became aware of the low voice of an unseen woman, which settled upon the silence of the room. She began to sing with haunting eloquence.

> *Low in the grave He lay, Jesus, my Savior!*
> *Waiting the coming day, Jesus, my Lord!*
> *Vainly they watch His bed, Jesus, my Savior!*
> *Vainly they seal the dead, Jesus, my Lord!*
> *Death cannot keep his prey, Jesus, my Savior!*
> *He tore the bars away, Jesus, my Lord!*

The voice that had begun softly grew steadily stronger and finally ended in the fullness of triumph. And then, as if on cue, the worshippers surged to their feet as one and joined the woman in a glorious shout of praise.

> *Up from the grave He arose*

they sang in unanimous affirmation.

> *With a mighty triumph o'er His foes.*

Tom, also on his feet now, let his voice join the others in unashamed abandon.

> *He arose a Victor from the dark domain,*
> *And He lives forever with His saints to reign.*

Shouts of "Praise God" and "Thank You, Jesus!" and "Hallelujah!" were heard over the magnificent chorus of jubilant voices. They sang with great thanksgiving and in such marvelous harmony that it seemed to Tom to be a chorus from heaven above.

> *He arose! He arose!*
> *Hallelujah! Christ arose!*

The song ended on a mighty note of triumph. Tom, the tears now rushing freely down his face, turned with some embarrassment, to glance at Tony standing beside him. The younger man saw in that moment what had happened in Tom's heart and, without another thought, flung his arms wide.

The two men, no longer separated by status or age or any other such unimportant trivia, embraced with joy and love. The hands of those around them reached out to squeeze an arm or pat a shoulder or give a friendly clap on the back, welcoming this stranger as their brother in the Lord. Inside of Tom, a heart that had turned to stone now swelled and grew and throbbed, and finally burst wide open.

And the Spirit of God came rushing in.

On a fine day nearly two months later, Tom's secretary, Janice Jackson, looked up to see an elderly gentleman come striding purposefully through the door of American Trucking's Chicago office. The thought that he might be a man of the clergy never once entered her mind, for he was dressed quite casually, in an open-necked cotton shirt and khaki pants, which were cinched around his sizable middle with a worn leather belt.

As he approached her desk she noted that his large, square head was crowned with a mane of tightly curled hair that was both the color and the consistency of steel wool. Bright eyes behind wire-rimmed spectacles danced, as if with some secret mischief.

"I'm lookin' for Mr. Tom Logan," he announced with no preamble. "Am I in the right place?"

"Yes, Mr. Logan's office is right down that hallway, the first door on the right," she answered, pointing him in the right direction. "If you'll give me your name, I'll announce you."

"I reckon I can announce myself, thank you," he said, not unkindly, as he marched toward Tom's door. He gave two sharp taps on the door, and entered.

Tom looked up with surprise, then rose to his feet and extended his hand in one fluid motion. A glad smile replaced the astonishment on his face as he greeted the older man, "Brother Walters! Hello! Please, have a chair."

"I'd be mighty pleased if you would just call me Seth. Can I call you Tom?"

"Of course. Can I get you something to drink?"

Seth, who had ignored the invitation to sit down and had, instead, moved to the window, turned and regarded his host candidly. The plaque on the door had told him that Tom Logan was not just any employee here, but, it appeared, the head of the whole show. However, that had never detoured him from his purpose before, and it didn't stop him today.

"It's a wonderful day out there," he said with a careless gesture toward the window. "Far too nice to be cooped up in here. Would you care to join me for a short walk?"

Tom glanced at the pile of work on his desk, then tossed his glasses into the middle of it with a grin and reached for his suit jacket.

"You won't need that where we're goin'," Seth said dismissively, and led the way back out the door he had so unceremoniously entered a few moments before.

Janice stared at the pair of them as they passed her desk and then left the building together. The old black man, lumbering along in his baggy clothes and scuffed brown shoes, was a full two inches shorter and a good many inches broader than her boss. And, as usual, Tom was impeccably dressed, in well-tailored navy slacks and a crisp white shirt. She was just wondering at Tom leaving the building without his jacket, when she saw him yank his tie loose and unbutton the collar of his shirt. Her mouth dropped open in amazement.

Outside in the bright sunshine of a picture-perfect day, Tom sighed with pleasure and turned to his companion. "Where we goin'?" he asked without caring.

"Doesn't matter," Seth replied with a grin. "But it's high time we got to know each other!"

Tom couldn't have agreed more. His admiration and respect for Seth Walters had grown steadily as he sat, Sunday after Sunday, listening with rapture to the fine old preacher speak words of wisdom. It seemed he never failed to capture his audience completely. Tom had not spent another Sunday morning alone in his apartment since Easter, and had grown to love his new Church family. But he was not prepared for his minister's next words.

"I've watched you over the past few weeks, Tom, and I know there's been some changing goin' on in your heart. But God keeps whisperin' to me that there's somethin' inside you that's causin' ya a heap o' pain. I thought mebbe we should do some talkin' and prayin' about it."

Tom looked at Brother Walters in astonishment. No one, not even his co-workers here in Chicago, knew the particulars of his private life. For he considered it just that, his private life. And now Seth seemed to be asking for details, painful details that Tom had buried deep within him in an effort to hide from the shame and the unbearable agony.

A part of him wanted to be angry at this intrusion, but he could find no guile in the eyes that met his steadily. And so he admitted sadly, "Yes, that's so. I... I lost my wife, that is, she... she left me. I... we... we're divorced now."

The words came out with great difficulty, sticking in his throat. But he continued, "I didn't think it was possible to love another human being like I loved her... still love her. I don't know what I did... why..."

He swallowed the tears that threatened to strangle his speech, and then spoke with mounting passion, "And you're right, I can't seem to get over it. No matter how hard I work or how many problems I face during the day, I still wake in the dead of the night and stare at the ceiling and try to understand. And it hurts so much..."

He ended with a muffled sob, unable to go on.

They had reached a park of some sort, and Seth laid a gentle hand on Tom's arm, urging him to sit on a nearby bench. Children squealed in childish laughter, birds rejoiced in gay song at the coming of yet another spring, a siren wailed somewhere in the distance. But Tom heard only the softly spoken words of his friend.

"Pray for her, Tom. Not that she be returned to you. That would be a selfish prayer and would serve no purpose. But she's certainly worthy of your prayers—for her well-being, her happiness, her salvation. And an honest prayer, asked in sincerity, never fails to bring a blessing to the one who uttered it."

Tom sat with his head in his hands for a long moment, then slowly straightened and nodded with understanding. "I'm sure that's true," he said slowly. "But then there's the anger and the bitterness that just overwhelm me at times, with no warning at all. Times when I suddenly remember that I have given her every ounce of love that I ever possessed, and she has just thrown it away like so much garbage! She's gone merrily on her way, happily married to some other guy now, gone, apparently without a thought to the years we had together, the children we had together, the *fun* we had together! I know that I wasn't always the perfect husband, that I sometimes spent hours at work when I should have been at home, that I didn't always show her how much I loved her. But I was *true* to her always! And I trusted her to be true to me. How could she have done this thing to us?"

Tom spoke with vehemence and not a little outrage.

And so Seth answered with measured calmness. "You feel that she has sinned against you. And rightly so, I suspect. But I'm sure that you would readily admit that you, too, sinned within the confines of this marriage. However, your sins seem quite small compared to hers, am I not right?"

Tom stared at the old man in silence, not sure where Seth was leading him.

With a sigh of deep compassion, Seth spoke again. "I don't claim to know the mind of God, but I believe we humans see sin in quite a different light from the way God looks at it. We want to compartmentalize it, putting the really bad sins, like murder and adultery, over here in one pile, and then a stack of lesser sins, like petty thievery and lying, over there, and then, finally, the little bitty ones like "borrowing" the company stationery or stamps for our personal use and gossiping about our neighbors, in yet another pile over yonder. But I believe that God sees sin as just that—sin. Every shape and form of it looks the same to Him. And that makes it the great equalizer of mankind. Because we all sin. And He forgives every one of us if we will just let him."

Tom sat quietly for some time, pondering those words, as the late afternoon sun worked its own special magic on tense, frayed nerves. The face of his daughter Jenny appeared briefly in his mind's eye. Relaxing visibly, he finally spoke softly, "And we, too, must forgive."

Seth slipped an arm around Tom's shoulders. "Are you ready to pray about it now?" he asked.

Back at the office, Janice locked the door and started for home. When five o'clock had come and Tom still hadn't returned, she'd wondered again at his odd behavior, but it certainly wasn't any of her business where he went or who his friends were.

She walked briskly, her high heeled shoes making a sharp clicking sound against the sidewalk as she moved down the street toward the parking lot where she had left her late model Honda that morning. As she passed the small park that city fathers had refused to give up to the industrial community around it, she glanced, as she did every evening, at the children playing there. Except during the most inclement weather, they gathered there daily to play until darkness or hunger or parents called them home.

And then she stopped "dead in her tracks," as her granddaddy used to say. For she couldn't believe what she saw. There, on a park bench, in broad daylight, sat her boss and that old man. And it looked for all the world like they were deep in prayer.

Tom stumbled along an overgrown pathway through deep forest, and the sounds of unseen birds screeching overhead and unknown beasts crashing through the trees urged him to even greater speed. He was lost, and afraid. Suddenly, he saw a clearing ahead, and sunlight streamed through an opening above.

As he rushed toward this wonderfully bright oasis, he became aware that a woman stood in the center of it, on ground that was slightly raised, a small grassy hill. She was facing away from him, her head bowed, and he thought that she was weeping. He stopped, reluctant to intrude upon her grief.

As he stood there with uncertainty, the forest around him became suddenly silent, and he heard a voice calling in desperation, "Help me! Please help me!"

He moved then, thinking that the woman had cried out for assistance. But, when she noticed his presence and turned, he was amazed to see that it was his daughter Jenny standing there, and that she was large with child.

He stopped again, in his confusion, and once more heard the wailing voice, "Help me!" It was then that he realized that the voice he heard was coming from within the womb of this woman, who had the face of his daughter. Her babe was calling to him with urgency, and he did not know what to do.

A movement from the edge of the clearing caught his attention, and he turned and saw with horror that a huge, ugly beast of unknown origin crouched there, as if waiting for some anticipated happening. The scene before him made him think of a verse in Revelation, and he spoke the words aloud, '... and the dragon stood before the woman which was ready to be delivered, for to devour her child as soon as it was born.'

The words seemed to frighten the creature, for he shuddered, and then retreated a short distance into the trees. At the same moment, as if sensing an unexpected reprieve, the woman turned and fled headlong into the thick forest. Tom looked sharply at the retreating back of his daughter, then at the beast cowering in the thicket, and, with sudden decision, he turned to follow Jenny.

He ran blindly, pursuing only the sound of her flight through the dense undergrowth. And finally, without warning, he found himself at the edge of yet another clearing, this one much larger. It was a beautiful spot with an old, rambling house sprawled amidst brightly blooming flowers, lush green grass and large trees. He stopped, incredulous, and stared at the peaceful scene. He could see no sign of life, and decided that Jenny must have entered the house.

He walked slowly toward the building, seeing as he grew closer that it was incredibly big—a mansion, really. The only sounds he heard were the chirping of happy birds and the soft gurgling of a small stream somewhere. He noticed a sign above the door as he reached up to knock, and then was immediately diverted when the door swung open to reveal a throng of young women. They were all scurrying about, laughing and chattering gaily. Apparently, no one saw him in the doorway, and so he entered and called out, not at all loudly, "Jenny?"

The girls gave him no notice, but when he spotted Jenny in the corner of the large room, he rushed to her and said, a bit louder, "Jenny!" The young woman who turned to face him was very pregnant, but, he saw with some regret, she was not his daughter. Then he was sure that he saw her across the room, coming through a doorway from another part of the house. He hurried in that direction, only to find yet another who, again, was not the one he sought.

He began to feel some panic, as he approached one after another of these women, who, he realized with amazement, were all in some stage of pregnancy, only to find that none of them was Jenny.

His alarm mounting, he cried out with urgency, "Jenny! Jenny! ..."

"Jenny! Jenny!"

Tom came awake with a start, the sound of his own voice hanging on the air. His heart pounding, he struggled to tear himself out of the dream that remained as vivid in his mind as if he had just watched the whole thing played out in some horror film. His hand moved involuntarily to the telephone beside his bed, and then stopped as his eyes came to rest on the clock. Three ten. Common sense finally overruled an overwhelming fear that his daughter was in some danger, and that she needed him desperately.

He took a deep, steadying breath and reason returned. Jenny would never forgive him for calling at this hour, and all because of some silly dream. But it still seemed so frighteningly real. He wondered, briefly, if God had sent the dream to him in an effort to reveal some hidden message, or, perhaps, to inflict a punishment upon him.

He finally slept, restlessly, and then awoke a few minutes before six, feeling troubled. He called Jenny as soon as he felt certain she would be awake, finding her safe and well, and more than a little perturbed that he had interrupted her as she hurriedly prepared to go to work. And then he rushed off to his own job, tired and out of sorts.

Three weeks later the dream was back. It was exactly the same, as nearly as he could recall, until he reached the house where he had searched with futility for his daughter. He again read the name above the door, and then immediately forgot it in the bevy he found inside. As he rushed about in search of the woman who was Jenny, he suddenly heard someone call his name.

"Tom Logan!"

Tom whirled around and noticed for the first time a stairway extending down into the large parlor. A woman, dressed in a long white dress or a gown of some sort, stood about halfway down the stairs, and she spoke again, "Tom! Who is it that you seek?"

"My daughter, Jenny! Have you seen her?"

"Of course. She is here. She does not wish to see you now, but you need not worry about her. She is safe here. Come, let me show you."

The woman seemed to glide down the remaining steps. As she came closer Tom was astounded to see that it was Amy Anderson who had spoken to him and who now beckoned to him to follow her. She moved to a window and pointed to the edge of the clearing. Tom saw, to his utter dismay, that the horrible creature again stood there, poised and waiting. He recoiled in fear and said with urgency, "I must find Jenny and take her away from here!"

"No, the beast cannot reach her as long as she remains in this house," Amy said with conviction. "Look, and you will see."

She pointed toward the forest again, and Tom saw then that a great ditch, somewhat like a moat, separated the animal from those who dwelt in this house. "Will you keep her here, safe in this place? When I found her, she was alone in the forest."

The woman shook her head sadly. "I cannot keep her here if she wishes to go. It is a decision she alone can make."

Tom felt an unbearable sorrow at the woman's words and began to weep, sobbing uncontrollably...

A convulsive sob tore from Tom's throat and wrenched him out of the dream's powerful hold. The certainty that God was trying to reach him was so strong that he slipped from his bed and knelt in prayer.

Please, Father, show me the meaning of this dream. Open my heart in understanding and give me the courage to follow Your will.

It was a few minutes after nine when Tom heard a familiar tap on the door of his office, and, without looking up from the monthly sales report he was working on, he said, "Mornin' Seth! Have a chair."

The two men had become great friends over the past several months, and Tom had grown used to these impromptu visits. Janice had learned to stop the elderly man only when Tom was involved in an important meeting.

"Is that somethin' that can't wait?" Seth asked, pointing to the report Tom held in his hand.

"Nope," Tom answered without hesitation. He glanced at the stack of unfinished work on his cluttered desk, but pushed it all aside and leaned back in his chair. Seth's visits always proved fruitful, and Tom was especially glad to see his friend this morning. "Something special on your mind?" he asked curiously.

"Well, I'm not sure," Seth answered, pulling off the shapeless old cardigan that he had worn against the autumn chill on this bright October day. "You see, I was talkin' with my Father this morning, as usual, and he told me that something was troublin' my friend Tom. I thought mebbe you needed to talk about it."

Tom grinned, shaking his head with wonder. "And, as usual, our Father was right! Seth, do you believe God speaks to us through dreams?"

Seth studied his companion closely for a moment. "God certainly used many methods to speak to our forefathers, dreams being a prominent one. It's my opinion that He uses whatever form of communication that will best get our attention. You've had a dream, then?"

Tom nodded. He began to talk, the images of the dream coming to him with remarkable clarity. Seth listened without interruption as Tom told of his feelings of fear as he wandered, lost and alone, in a deep forest, and then of his encounter with the woman who was really his daughter, Jenny. He described the ugly beast and his certainty that the creature intended harm to his daughter's unborn child.

The old man's attention seemed to sharpen as Tom spoke of his flight through the trees in pursuit of his daughter, only to find that she had disappeared "into a great, white house that sat in a wonderfully peaceful meadow filled with warmth and beauty."

"As I reached the doorway of this magnificent dwelling, I saw a sign above the door," Tom continued. "I read the words, but then immediately forgot them when I entered a great room filled with young women, all of them, to my surprise, expecting babies. I searched and searched, but I could not find Jenny. I awoke calling her name."

Seth stirred in his chair. "Your daughter, Jenny. Is she expecting a child?"

Tom shoved one hand through his carefully combed hair, leaving it slightly mussed, and stood, moving to the window. He answered slowly, "No. No, she's not." He turned suddenly toward his beloved minister, blurting out the words he'd been unable to say until now. "Seth, I've told you about my wife, Joyce, and the terrible times we went through, but what you don't know—or maybe you *do* know, for that matter," he acknowledged with a slight smile, "is that shortly after my wife remarried and Jenny went off to college, my daughter got pregnant. I knew nothing about it until after she'd gone and had an abortion. I was sick with shame and anger, and I never even spoke to my daughter for the next six months or so. Not, in fact, until after you and I had our talk in the park that day, and you made me see that her sin was no greater than my own."

Tom had begun to pace the small confines of his office as he spoke these tortured words. He stopped before his mentor and spoke again, with anguish, "Seth, I forgave her, only to find that she couldn't forgive me. Oh, we held each other and cried and prayed together, but there is a space between us still that was never there before. And I have to wonder if this dream is God's way of punishing me."

Seth shook his head slowly. "No, I don't believe He works that way. But I do think that He has somethin' in mind, some path He intends to set you upon. Have you had the dream again?"

"Yes. Last night. It was the same dream, except that it continued on. As I hunted in vain for my daughter, I heard someone call out my name. I turned to see a woman, dressed in white, standing on a staircase. She told me not to worry about my daughter, that she was safe as long as she stayed there in that house. She led me to the window and showed me that the beast was still waiting, but that a deep ditch prevented him from entering the clearing and the mansion that stood in the midst of it.

"I asked her to promise me to keep Jenny there, so that she would be safe, but the woman said that she could not keep my daughter there if she wished to go. I awoke with tears in my eyes. I felt the unmistakable presence of the Holy Spirit and I immediately began to pray for understanding. It would seem that He has sent you here today to give me some answers!"

"Have you been able to remember the words on the sign above the door?" Seth asked, unexpectedly.

"No. I have tried and tried, because they seem to be important, somehow. But I can't remember."

"And the woman on the stairs, does she have any special significance, do you think?"

Tom began to pace once again, traveling the same path from desk to window and back. "Actually, I recognized her," he answered with some bewilderment. "Her name is Amy Anderson and she has been a dear friend of mine for many years."

Seth raised a shaggy eyebrow in surprise. "Tell me about her," he said quietly.

Tom began to speak again, haltingly at first, then more smoothly, as he recalled the friendship that had begun years before when he was a struggling marketing rep in American Trucking's Kansas City office and she a brand new dispatcher in the Tulsa branch. They had known each other only as voices on the telephone, he explained, but she was embroiled in a loveless marriage with an alcoholic husband and had gradually turned to him in a desperate need for support. Amy's husband left her for another woman soon after she and Tom had become acquainted, he continued, leaving her with two teenage daughters to raise alone. An older son, Jonathon, was away at college at the time.

Tom related the whole story, omitting nothing. He admitted that, after meeting Amy for the first time some months later, he was staggered by the realization that she was in love with him. He was dumbfounded, and his first reaction had been to turn away completely. He avoided talking to her, even though the very nature of his job required some contact. But after praying extensively about the situation, he came to understand that he was hurting another human being needlessly. For she had never once given even the slightest hint of her feelings for him. Only her eyes had given her away, and he knew in his heart that she would never become an obstacle in his relationship with his wife.

He had come to love Amy as a dear friend as the years passed and they continued to work together. He rarely saw her, but spoke to her often on the phone after she was promoted to Controller and he was asked to assume a management position in the Kansas City Market Center. It was a short time later, he explained to Seth, that he became aware of the slowly growing rift between himself and Joyce. When it became apparent that the problem was a serious one, he had told Amy good-bye and had not spoken to her for more than four years.

"I saw Amy one time, after the divorce was final and I was about to begin my duties here in Chicago," Tom remembered. "In my despair and loneliness, I held her briefly, and then I told her good-bye again. I know that she loves me, but the ties that once bound me to Joyce in marriage still have a hold on me, and I simply cannot return Amy's love in a way that would be fair to her."

Seth grunted as he rose from his chair and took Tom's place at the window. He stood there for some time, deep in thought. Finally he turned and began to speak. "Let us assume that the beast in your dream represents abortion. And your daughter, when you came upon her, was apparently struggling with indecision. The child within her, however, seemed to see you as a possible savior, and cried out to you for help.

"And then your daughter deliberately led you to this great white mansion where she, and others like her, had found care and protection. I am sure that our Lord hates the beast abortion just as you and I do, and I believe that He is preparing you for some role in this battle. Just what that role may be is not yet clear."

Seth moved to where Tom now sat at his desk and reached for the younger man's hand. It's time to pray," he said, as he sank, with some difficulty, to his knees.

The next several months found the two men in constant study and prayer and heated discussion, as they sorted through the symbolism and significance of every facet of Tom's dream. More and more, Seth was convinced that Tom was being led to provide his own "great, white mansion" for girls in need of it, as a direct counter-option to abortion. As the services of abortion clinics became more easily accessible, he argued, that option had become an easy out for an increasing number of young women, and the need for a Christian alternative was great.

"I agree with your premise," Tom stormed. "But I can't believe *I'm* the one to do this!"

"Why not you?"

"Because I know nothing about caring for pregnant women!"

"Then find those who do and ask for their help!"

"But that sort of thing takes a lot of money!"

"Money is not the issue here."

"It is if you don't have any!"

"God never asks us to do a job without providing us with the means to accomplish it."

"But why *ME*?"

"Why not?"

And then word filtered down from American Trucking's higher echelon that Tom was being considered for an unprecedented promotion.

It was rumored that Bill Johnson, president of the company since his father died several years ago, would soon name a successor to fill his secondary position as Vice President in charge of Marketing. Bill had held that office since his father had formed American Trucking, Inc. some thirty years ago, when the senior Johnson had appointed each of his five sons to leadership roles.

No one, outside of the immediate family, had ever held such a position within the company, and Tom was astounded that he was being considered. When he mentioned the possibility to Seth, the old man had merely smiled and nodded his head, as if he had known all along.

"And I suppose a job like that brings with it a mighty sizable paycheck," he commented nonchalantly.

"I suppose so," Tom agreed.

"Probably more than enough to renovate a big ole house into a pretty decent 'great white mansion' for a few unfortunate young ladies, I would imagine."

"Probably. Maybe I could get Amy to run it for me," Tom mused.

"It seems pretty obvious that she is to be a part of this," Seth answered, encouraged that his friend seemed at last to be considering the idea. "These girls will certainly need someone to mother them."

"I keep feeling that this mission, however it turns out, is to be some sort of redemption for both Jenny and myself, a cleansing, if you will, and, hopefully a renewal," Tom confided. "I just hope that I am up to the task."

"I can do all things through Christ," said Seth with a broad smile, quoting Philippians 4:13. "And now that you have finally accepted that there is, indeed, a task to be done, I believe that God will reveal exactly what He wants from you."

And, as if the wise old man had prophesied it, the dream came back that very night and left no lingering doubt in Tom's mind that it was he who had been chosen to carry out God's plan. And that God expected to lead him every step of the way. For the dream once again extended into more detail.

When the woman in the long white gown saw that Tom was overcome with sorrow, she laid a hand softly on his arm and spoke gently, "Tom, the girls have prepared a great feast in your honor. Come, your daughter waits for you."

Tom followed as Amy led him into a huge dining hall where a large table was already laden with many platters and bowls full of food. The young girls were busily putting fine silver flatware and crystal goblets at each place around the table. He looked anxiously for some sign of his daughter, and then he noticed a cradle on the far side of the room.

He was drawn to the tiny crib and peered inside to see a perfectly formed child there, sleeping. A door opening nearby drew his attention away from the infant, and he saw with gladness that his daughter stood before him. It was immediately apparent that she had given birth since he had last seen her, and, pointing down at the sleeping baby, he asked with joy, "Is this your...?"

He broke off suddenly, seeing a terrible sorrow wash over her face. She shook her head and glanced toward the window. Tom followed her gaze to where the odious creature he had seen earlier still reclined at the edge of the forest. He knew at once, with an unexplained certainty, that she had been drawn by some secret fascination, and, caught in the pangs of childbirth, had surrendered her babe to the power of the beast.

An immense sadness filled Tom's heart as the beckoning hands of the other girls bade him sit at the table. Amy sat beside him and then began to beg him to stay with them. "We have many needs here, Tom. And the beast grows larger every day. Soon he will be able to leap across the ditch and we will no longer be safe. Please, stay and help us to build a high wall that no evil can penetrate."

At her words, the girls stopped their chatter and the room grew strangely silent. And, in the stillness, he heard a multitude of tiny voices imploring, "Help us! Please, help us!"

He knew, of course, that it was the unborn babies who spoke to him, and he rose to his feet and moved to the head of the table where his daughter still stood. She held out a hand to him, and he took it in his own. She turned to the others in the room and spoke with pride. "This is my father."

Tom awoke. The omnipresence of the Holy Spirit filled the room. Tom reached for his Bible and let it fall open in his hands. His eyes were drawn to the scripture before him:

> *In you, O Lord, I have taken refuge;*
> *let me never be put to shame;*
> *deliver me in your righteousness.*
> *Turn your ear to me,*

come quickly to my rescue;
be my rock of refuge,
* a strong fortress to save me.*
Since you are my rock and my fortress,
* for the sake of your name lead and guide me.*
Free me from the trap that is set for me,
* for you are my refuge.*
Into your hands I commit my spirit;
* redeem me, O Lord, the God of truth. (Psalm 31:1-5)*

Tom reached for the telephone without a second's hesitation. When Seth answered sleepily, after the fourth ring, he heard Tom's jubilant voice ringing across the line.

"I remember the sign above the door to the great mansion!" Tom shouted with joy. "It is called *THE REFUGE*."

The harsh buzzing of his intercom line jerked Tom back to the present with an unpleasant jolt. He glanced at his watch as he reached for the phone. Five o'clock, *already*! Who in the world..?

"Yes?"

"Mr. Logan! I wasn't sure you were still here! I was just about to close the switchboard when Mrs. Anderson called for you. Shall I send the call back?"

"Yes, Cathy. By all means," Tom answered.

Seconds later Amy's quick, breathless voice came across the line, bringing a smile to Tom's lips as it always did. "Tom! Thank goodness, you're still there. I can't believe I managed to catch you before you left the office!"

Her speech was still as soft and youthful sounding as it had been all those years ago when she'd joined American Trucking in Tulsa as a dispatcher. Her voice had always reminded Tom of the well-modulated tones of a flute, adding a musical quality to every word.

"I'm afraid I was doing a bit of wool-gathering," he admitted. "In fact, I was so deep in thought that the phone gave me quite a start! But you sound rather flustered. Is there some problem at the house?"

"Well, we had an unexpected visitor this afternoon. Although 'visitor' is really not the correct word. She just appeared out of nowhere and announced that she had come to stay!"

"She? A young girl, alone?" Tom frowned, as thoughts of the possible trouble that could come from harboring a runaway teenager crowded his mind.

"Yes. A rather remarkable young woman, I must say. I opened the front door to find her standing there, entirely alone and with no visible means of transportation. And when she calmly explained that she had just arrived from Montana, I couldn't hide my surprise!"

"But, her parents. Do they know where she is? You know that we must contact them if she is a minor," Tom admonished carefully.

"Yes, I know. Actually, I was hoping *you* might notify her father— her mother, it seems, died when she was only nine years old and she isn't exactly enamored with her new stepmother. Tom, her name is Sara Franklin, and her father is Lance Franklin, U.S. Representative from the State of Montana!"

"Oh, no!" Tom groaned, seeing his problems mounting steadily. "Do you realize the bad publicity he could generate for us if this isn't handled properly?"

"Yes, Tom, I know," Amy answered quietly. "And there's more. Sara is supposed to be settling in at this very moment at Miss Priscilla's Academy for Girls in Boulder, Colorado, where her stepmother, Caroline, is from. And Caroline, who happens to be a Senator, by the way, is a very unpleasant woman, if you can believe Sara. The girl begged—no, she *demanded* that we not tell them of her whereabouts or of her condition. She's only three months pregnant and, so far, no one has even suspected.

"But, of course, they'll find out soon enough, whether we contact them or not. I explained to Sara that it would be much less painful for her if we just tell them up front where she is, rather than having the police descend upon us some night to drag her off in chains, so to speak. And we don't have to tell Mr. Franklin that his daughter is pregnant, although you and I both know it won't take many minutes for him to come to that unfortunate conclusion."

Amy sighed with the magnitude of the situation. Tom asked in her silence, "And where is her father? Did you get a number where we can reach him?"

"Yes finally. It seems they are in Washington D. C., looking for 'a swanky place to live that will properly reflect their *class*'—Sara's words, not mine—and she says they probably won't even realize she's not where she's supposed to be for a month or so! She eventually gave in, after I told her she would have to go elsewhere if she refused to follow our regulations. But the only number she had was through her father's office in D.C. This family doesn't appear to have a close-knit, loving relationship, to put it mildly!"

Tom hung up the phone a few minutes later, the scribbled note containing Lance Franklin's telephone number clutched in his hand. He had known there would be times like this, when the answers didn't come easily.

And Amy had sounded completely exhausted, he thought reflectively. When he'd asked her to act as housemother for The Refuge upon her retirement from American Trucking last year, it hadn't occurred to him that he would be placing such a tremendous burden upon her. It wasn't fair that she had to shoulder so much of the responsibility on her own. But there just hadn't been available funds to hire any help. Except for Sam, who was Amy's dearest friend and who had agreed to manage the business end of things for them, Amy was pretty much on her own with her brood of young girls.

And he worried about them living alone in that big house, six females with no man about to offer any semblance of protection. As soon as it was even remotely feasible, he must hire a man to act as caretaker of the grounds and as a sort of "guard of the manor" should trouble arise. And they needed a woman to cook and keep house, thus relieving Amy of those duties, although the girls were required to help.

As Tom once more stood at his window, watching the sky soften into the haziness of evening and the windows along the street come alive with light, he bowed his head and spoke with his Father.

Dear Lord, show me the way. Give me the means, or maybe just the wisdom, to find some much needed help for our home. I know that You already have the answers that I need. I just open my heart to You for Your blessed guidance.

BEN

Aslashing rain beat against the fragile walls of the large packing crate. Ben shivered against the unseasonable coldness of a wind-driven onslaught, thankful for this crude measure of protection, meager though it was. He pulled a threadbare blanket closer and buried his face in the warm coat of Molly, his faithful companion. The ragged spaniel whined softly and reached a long pink tongue to Ben's hand in a mutual affirmation of affection. They both would fare far worse on this horrendous night without the comfort of each other.

Ben thought of the long winter nights ahead with dread. This packing crate that he'd managed to drag all the way from Clarkson Appliances to this spot beneath an abandoned bridge on the outskirts of Bartlesville would provide scant shelter against the frigid temperatures that the next few months would bring.

A tear trickled down his cheek unbidden. How could he have come to this point? A mere five years ago had seen him living in splendor, much in demand as one of the top selling Christian recording artists in the country. The money had seemed to flow in an unending stream from concerts and albums and churches who vied for his appearances as guest soloist. His pure tenor voice had soared with unparalleled richness. And so had his bank account.

He'd spent with abandon, buying first an outlandishly expensive automobile, and then that house that had been one of Oklahoma City's finest. And, of course, he'd had to staff that huge monstrosity of a dwelling, and furnish it lavishly. And every performing artist knows that you need an abundance of designer clothing. The list had just continued to get longer and longer as his popularity had increased.

It hadn't always been like that, of course. Back when his beloved Libby had been with them and he'd been just an ordinary music instructor at the New Hope Academy, he'd had to give private voice lessons on the side just to scratch by. They'd managed to send their three youngsters to New Hope, but only because he'd been on staff and they'd gotten reduced rates.

He shivered as a sudden gust of wind slammed against the plywood box that he now called home. Sheets of cold rain battered the flimsy structure and began to seep inside through cracks that hadn't been apparent before. He realized that he was going to be miserably wet and cold by the time this night ended. But it was still August, he consoled himself, and tomorrow would likely bring back the hot winds that would dry his clothes, as well as his humble abode, in no time. And if not tomorrow, then, hopefully, the next day.

After all, he had no place to go now. No appointments or class schedules or recording sessions. Just his job at the church. But that wasn't until Saturday, when he cleaned and straightened and swept walkways and polished pews as happily as if it were his very own cherished home. Sometimes he pretended it really was his. And since he'd found that old mattress in the basement storage room, he'd managed, secretly, to make it his home for one night out of every week.

Ben thought it was ironic that his only source of income now was from a church. Because that was where it had all started so many years ago. In church. Singing. Even as a very young child, his voice had been noticed and praised, and he had begun singing solos for special programs at the tender age of five. By the time he was thirteen, he knew his life would be music. It had to be. He had knelt before that old altar in the little country church he'd grown up in and vowed to spend his life praising his God in song.

Even his love for Libby could be traced back to that old church. They had met in Sunday School and he'd thought that she was the prettiest girl he'd ever laid eyes on. He'd been ten years old at the time, and she only eight. When he was always chosen to be Joseph for the Christmas pageant because he was the best singer, she'd stood with the rest of the angels and glowed with pride at his fine voice.

He realized with a pang that she had never lost that glow of love and pride where he was concerned. He, and their children. She'd always been there for all of them with gentleness and quiet support and deep devotion. Never thinking of herself. And that was probably why she'd let the pain go on without complaining until it was too late to save her. For hadn't the doctor explained that it wasn't the gall stones that had killed her, but the intense pain that had sent her into a state of shock? Pain that she had chosen to ignore because their son Johnny had had a school play that night and she knew that he was to sing his very first solo.

And because he, as their instructor, was involved in every detail of the program on that evening, Ben hadn't even realized Libby was suffering until he came home late that night and found her already in bed. She, who had always waited up for him until he managed to tear himself away from his endless duties at the school and to come home to share the evening's triumphs and trials with her, had gone on to bed without him! He'd been just a mite miffed, he remembered, until he'd seen the agony in her eyes as she writhed against unbearable pain.

He and the boys had very nearly drowned in the sorrow that enveloped them after her untimely death. But they'd struggled on, one day at a time, and they'd made it somehow. And then one day Ben realized that he'd managed to finish what he and Libby had started on the day that little Benny was born. Their sons were grown and gone, fine young men with lives and careers and families of their own. And he was totally and inescapably alone.

It had been during that time of loneliness when his job at the school had become unbearably tedious. The income no longer mattered to him. He had no one to spend it on except himself, and he had very few needs. It slowly dawned on him that the time had finally come when he might pursue his childhood dream of becoming a recording artist—of singing praises to his Master on a much grander scale than an occasional solo at his local church.

The Churchmen, a quartet of men singing in wonderful harmony with himself as their lead vocalist, had made an immediate impact on Christian music charts. They began touring the country and soon their concerts were a guaranteed sell-out. In just five short years the group had three of the top ten Christian hits as their own, and they managed to keep at least two of their recordings in that coveted group for a period of nearly six months.

Life had been incredible, or so it had seemed then, Ben mused as he tried to move his cramped body to someplace away from the steadily dripping water and found that it was impossible to do so. He had marveled that he was being paid astounding amounts of money to do what he had always before done for free. Sing. With The Churchmen, or as a guest soloist. Even his church choir had paid him for his occasional visits back home. It hadn't even occurred to him to refuse the money which, without a doubt, could have been spent on more worthy causes. After all, he was a star, wasn't he?

Ben stirred again, remembering with shame his sudden downfall from those glorious heights. Molly whined at his apparent restlessness and touched his cheek with her warm tongue.

"I'm sorry, girl. I just get to thinkin' 'bout it all, and then I get stirred up all over again. I feel so bad, knowin' that I was to blame for everything. After all, it was *my* voice that gave out, or mebbe it was just my poor ole ears that let me down. I don't know, but I do know that me an' the boys would still be singin' today, and livin' high on the hog with never a worry 'bout keepin' warm or dry, if I could just sing like I used to!"

He remembered how embarrassing it had been when he had begun missing his high notes—just a mite off pitch, he'd been. He, who had always been praised for his perfect sense of pitch, his unerring ear for the closest harmony, seemed to have lost both. Why, he'd been the one who'd always heard any little discrepancy during their rehearsals and quickly pointed out the missed note.

At first he'd attributed his occasional dissonance to a loss of hearing. But he'd gone to one specialist after another, and all had found his aural skills to be normal. He would never forget the recording session that went awry after six tries at a successful cut of *How Great Thou Art*. He'd stomped out in fury when Will, their able producer, had finally lost patience and told him to go home and practice some more or they'd just have to find a new tenor for the group.

He'd tried to maintain his luxurious lifestyle even after The Churchmen disbanded, hoping for a miracle. Where was this God he'd been singing about anyway? Surely He would restore the voice that had sung His praises to the world in such grandeur! But somewhere in the far reaches of his heart, Ben suspected that God might, in fact, be trying to tell him something. He admitted that he could have shared his sudden wealth with those less fortunate, that he had been far too quick to feed his own selfish pleasures. And so he promised God that he would do better if only he were given a second chance.

But it appeared that God wasn't looking for a deal. Ben finally sold his fine house and his fancy car, but neither was paid for, and so he salvaged very little cash from the sale. When it became evident that he would lose the lease on his small apartment as well, he fled from Oklahoma City in shame.

A sharp clap of thunder startled him from his reverie. He huddled even closer to Molly and pulled the dirty blanket that he had found in someone's trash can over his head. He thought about praying, but found himself somehow unworthy to approach his Father. He sure hoped Libby couldn't see him now.

The rain stopped sometime before dawn and Ben fell into a deep sleep. He awoke to bright sunshine, his body so stiff he could hardly move. The morning was cool and he shivered in his sodden clothes. The sandy stream bed that had been dry most of the summer now carried a lusty little creek that sang merrily as it scurried along towards places unknown.

Ben retrieved the old suitcase that he kept hidden in a hollow underneath the concrete lip of the unused bridge. All of his worldly possessions now fit easily into that one small bag, and he reached inside to pull out his other set of everyday clothes. He had also kept a good suit, complete with white dress shirt and tie, and a pair of leather shoes for "special occasions," such as a possible job interview that might lead back to a more normal lifestyle. And he was glad he had something dressy to wear now that he worked at the church for Jonathon. He could spiff up in his nice clothes on Sunday mornings and no one would ever be the wiser.

Ben followed Molly down to the gurgling stream and quickly washed in the chilly water, then replaced his soggy clothes with dry ones and proceeded to wash out the dirty set. He was thankful for the little stream of water. Now he wouldn't have to sneak his dirty clothes into a restroom somewhere and rinse them in the sink that was never big enough to do the job properly.

He spread his laundry to dry over the branches of thick bushes that surrounded his little haven, and then stretched with pleasure. The exercise, along with the warmth of the sun, had eased the cricks out of his back and neck, and he found himself surveying his "home" critically. He had been lucky to find this deserted road with its sandy creek bed meandering under a sturdy bridge. He could see that the roadway had led straight into town in years past, until they put in that big shopping center with its pretty landscaping and curving streets. Why, if this road were to keep on goin' today, it would run smack dab into that fancy grocery store and out through one of those little specialty shops that sold women's dresses or antiques or some such.

Not that he had anything against the mall. No siree! If he was careful, he could spend most of a day unnoticed within its confines. If nothing else, he could join the "walkers" that made innumerable trips up and down the hallways in search of exercise. And there were many and varied food shops where he could get a cup of coffee or a sandwich. As long as he kept on the move and didn't visit every day, the security people paid him very little mind.

At the moment, a cup of coffee sounded very good indeed. He decided he'd walk to McDonalds and try to find a newspaper lying around somewhere. He never gave up looking at the help wanted ads, just in case. But very few people wanted a has-been musician for anything, and so his hopes of getting more than some yard work or a janitor's job were slim to none. After all, he couldn't very well show up for work in the same clothes everyday and hope to keep his secret intact.

And he just couldn't bear for anyone to know that he had nothing—no home, no car, nothing. He thought, for the hundredth time, as he walked down a back street, then around the block and into McDonalds from the side entrance, that he'd made a mistake coming to a small place like Bartlesville. It wasn't easy losing yourself in a town this size, but he'd wanted nothing at the time but to escape from his life in Oklahoma City. And then he'd stumbled onto the cleaning job at Central Community Church and, in the middle of a frigid winter, he'd had no heart for moving on.

He found Molly nosing around the trash bins when he stepped back out into the street with his coffee and the want ads in hand. They walked slowly back towards their hideaway, enjoying the clean smell of rain-washed air that carried just a hint of fall. Today was the first of September and Ben knew their days under the bridge were numbered. As secluded as it was, they would need more shelter during the winter months. Although he had saved every penny he could from his wages, he was afraid he wouldn't have enough for even the cheapest car available before the cold winds forced him inside.

"We jest can't get through another winter like last year, Molly," he said to the buff colored dog at his side. "Tryin' to hide in empty garages and sneakin' around the bus depot in hopes of gettin' a few winks of sleep while the guards are off havin' coffee. I swear I aged at least ten years in those three or four months."

Ben saw Molly's ears come to attention and grinned, thinking she must really be paying attention to his ramblings. Then she took off with a yelp, hot on the trail of a frightened young cottontail. He chuckled, hoping she would capture her prey. For *he* surely couldn't afford to feed her!

He found a sunny spot to spread out his newspaper and began to scan the ads. The vehicles were all completely out of his reach, as usual. He sighed. A car with a heater and just enough gas to run the engine for an hour or two during the long cold nights would make the upcoming months so much more bearable! Maybe there'd be a job opening somewhere if he just kept looking. Somewhere warm, he hoped.

He knew he could escape to the Shelter where other unfortunates gathered for a hot meal or a night's sleep if things got desperate enough. But he hated to go there. He just couldn't bear to equate himself with those down and out bums! He remembered that one lady who went there and helped to cook and clean up sometimes, and knew that she, like himself, was too proud to beg. What was her name? Helen! That was it. Helen, who sat over in the corner and read her Bible when she wasn't helpin' out somewhere. He somehow admired Helen, and wondered how she had come to be where she was. Which was no different from where he, himself, was, of course.

Ben heard a rustling in the brush and looked up. Molly came loping up the grassy slope, carrying the bunny between her teeth, a proud smile on her face. Ben looked at the dog with some envy. She, at least, had honestly earned her dinner!

Ben awoke early on Saturday as usual, anticipating the day ahead. A heavy gray sky promised rain. The air was still and muggy and very warm. Ben and Molly had slept on the old blanket, spread near the sandy stream bed, as they had nearly every night of the summer. He was glad to see that a small trickle of water still ran beside them, making his morning ablutions much simpler. He quickly washed and shaved, then combed his sparse head of hair and changed into fresh clothing.

Rev. Gardner, or Jonathon, as Ben had been instructed to call him, would not be expecting him for another hour yet, he knew. And yet his eagerness could not be curbed. Ben commanded Molly to stay, grabbed his old suitcase, and started for town. He would while away the next hour or so over a cup of coffee and a newspaper, until Jonathon finished with the elders' breakfast and returned to his office.

Ben knew that other folks wondered why he carried a suitcase to work with him, and sometimes he was required to explain this odd behavior. His reasons varied with the situation, but usually he could just pass it off as carrying his "tools of the trade," such as gloves and special cleansers or gardening implements that he might need. Of course, an inspection would have revealed soiled clothing that he would launder wherever possible and his only set of dressy clothes, along with a few personal items.

He never left the suitcase out of his sight for more than a very short time even now that he had found this secluded spot. He had learned the hard way that nothing was safe in this world where there were no doors to lock, nothing that he could call his own. But those first cold months after he had arrived here had taught him many lessons that he'd had no need to learn before.

He'd searched diligently during those dark December days and finally found an ancient garage huddled at the rear of an empty house. The dwelling had obviously been the victim of a fire, but the garage, which opened onto the alley running behind the property, had escaped the flames. Weeds and bushes that had grown up around it very nearly obscured it from view. It was the perfect hiding place, he had thought at the time, although the droppings on the dirt floor told him that he would be sharing it with some unwelcome companions.

He'd had to work for some time just to get the small side door open, but he didn't want to disturb the old wooden slab that had served as the overhead door. There were many cracks in the rough walls, and the roof leaked badly, but with time and patience he'd managed to cover the biggest of the gaps with cardboard, making his abode a fair shelter against the cold winter winds.

And then he'd set about furnishing his "home." He dug through the trash of the very rich, searching for the treasures of the very poor. A heavy woolen blanket that was frayed on the edges but exceptionally warm, and a dirty old pillow, piled on top of a sizable stack of cardboard, gave him a rather comfortable bed. A discarded metal pail became his stove after he spent some of his meager savings on a bag of charcoal briquettes and made himself a fire. The smoke drove him out into the cold that first night, so he learned to take the pail outside until the fire had burned down to red-hot coals, and then, if he set it near the door, which wouldn't shut completely anyway, the draft would suck out the worst of the smoke.

An old piece of plywood laid across the top of a sturdy box gave him a table of sorts, and he found that he could keep most foodstuffs fresh during those frigid winter days. Yet, he lived in constant fear. He never approached his new home without checking in every direction to make sure he was not observed, and he only dared to make a fire on the darkest and coldest of nights for fear the smoke would be seen and he would be discovered.

And then, on a mild day in April, he left the garage early in the morning to do some yard work for an elderly widow he had happened onto the day before. He'd been walking down the street when he had noticed the old lady struggling with a heavy hose that was still stiff from the winter cold. He'd stopped and offered assistance and, after looking him over carefully, she had opened the gate to her yard and gratefully accepted. He'd ended up moving a large planter and then filling it with several bags of moist potting soil, and the woman was so pleased she'd asked him to return to help get her garden and flower beds in order. She'd be glad to pay him, she explained, and would feed him a nice hot dinner in the bargain. He hadn't been sure which appealed to him the most!

But he had returned to his garage that night to find it in shambles. His blanket and pillow, even his pail of charcoal, were gone. Every bit of food had been taken and, most disastrous of all, his expensive warm coat, which he had worn all the way from Oklahoma City and which had literally kept him from freezing to death during the winter days that followed, had been stolen. He had fled the place immediately, fearful of imminent discovery. How thankful he had been that he had decided on that morning to take his suitcase with him so that he could wash up his clothes, sure to be soiled by the day's labor. He never again left his old bag behind.

A few drops of rain began to fall now as he neared the shopping mall. It was early yet, and few shoppers were in evidence. He decided to duck inside and get a cup of coffee at the little canteen that catered to the early morning crowd of "mall walkers," as he called them. If he was lucky, the shower of rain would end by the time he returned to the street for his walk to Central Community Church.

The sun was playing hide and seek with racing clouds when he emerged from the mall a half hour later. If the sun managed to win out over those sulky clouds, it was going to be a mighty sticky day, he thought, as he wiped away the perspiration that had already formed on his upper lip. But, regardless, it would be a good day. And, if he continued to be fortunate enough, a good night, with a hot shower and a clean bed, as well. Since one of his duties was to arrive early on Sunday morning to unlock the building and turn on lights and air conditioners or heaters, as the case might be, no one would question his presence, dressed, as he planned to be, in the respectable clothes of respectable people.

As usual, Ben arrived at the church before Jonathon, and, also as usual, he sat quietly on the bench near the side entrance and waited patiently. Jonathon hurried up the walk a few moments later, carrying a foam box that Ben knew would contain the leftover sweet rolls and donuts from their breakfast. Jonathon always handed the box to Ben with a smile and invited him to "take them on home, as there is no sense in wasting good food!" And Ben always thanked him graciously and set the treat aside to move quickly to his duties. His job, he was sure, depended upon Jonathon's never knowing he had no home to go to.

He worked happily all through the day, vacuuming and dusting and straightening hymnals until the sanctuary was gleaming. Then on to the restrooms and the kitchen area, and finally to the children's classrooms. He loved cleaning these rooms the most, as they were decorated cheerfully with brightly colored flowers and friendly beasts, and sprinkled liberally with Bible verses. When he finished inside, he swept the walks and carried the trash to the giant receptacle at the back of the parking lot.

He knew the teenagers would be arriving soon for their Saturday Night Songfest and he needed to be gone when they arrived. They met in the basement, where they laughed and sang and studied together, ending the evening at about ten o'clock with cookies and punch or soft drinks. They, along with their adult leaders, always cleaned this area completely before they left, and then locked the building behind them. But Ben had the key that Jonathon had entrusted to him in his pocket. He waited patiently for the last light to be put out and the last car to leave the lot, and then silently re-entered the building and crept through the darkened hallways to the basement stairs.

Once he reached the bottom of the stairs, he felt his way to the door of the little storage room located off the back hall. There were no windows in those rooms located at the rear of the church basement, as they housed only the furnace room, the storage room, and two shower rooms that opened off the big gym area where the teens regularly met. A small concession stall at the far south end of the back wall provided a refrigerator, a sink and limited cupboard area, and was more than adequate for the group's needs.

Since Ben always waited until after eleven to return to the building, he relaxed slightly. It would be rare, indeed, for anyone to need inside the church at that time of night. He remained alert, of course, but was able to enjoy his one hot shower of the week. He shook out his good suit and shirt and hung them from a pipe running overhead on hangers that he had found in a box of junk in the corner. He then washed his dirty clothes in the deep vat that served the shower room as a sink, using hot water and a bit of detergent. It was the only time he felt that his clothes got really clean, and he always breathed in the sweet, soapy smell. He had found a wire line in the furnace room where he could hang them to dry overnight.

Ben whistled a little tune as he went about these homey chores, feeling a security that he never found anywhere else. When he had finished, he found a soft drink in the refrigerator, tossed a quarter into the cash box, and sat down to enjoy the sweets that Jonathon had given him that morning.

It was the first food he'd eaten that day, and he devoured every morsel. Finally, clean and fed, he spread a blanket over the mattress that he'd pulled out from behind a stack of boxes and, switching off the overhead light, lay down thankfully for a comfortable night of rest.

It seemed that he had just dozed off when the distinct click of a door opening startled Ben awake. His fear was so great that he nearly cried out. He strained to see in the pitch black of the little storage room. Suddenly the door swung open and the form of a man was silhouetted by bright lights in the gym. Weak, and shaking with fright, Ben managed to push himself up into a sitting position, his panic now a full blown monster.

He saw the man's arm reach ever so slowly for the light switch. He blinked in the sudden brightness of the room. And, with a horror too great to be borne, Ben found himself staring into the surprised eyes of his pastor and boss, Jonathon Gardner.

JONATHON

❧

A sense of unease had dogged his steps the whole evening. While he was bathing two-year-old Daniel, a chore he always enjoyed, and even later as he tucked his son into bed with the usual hugs and kisses, the prayer he whispered as he held his child close, the last minute drink of water, and one more goodnight kiss.

And now, as he tried to relax and enjoy the Chuck Colson book he was reading, his worries returned to distract him. Sunday evening was normally Jonathon's favorite night of the week—his Friday night, so to speak. His work week started on Tuesday, if he was lucky, and culminated with a full day on Sunday. It was a night to relax and to enjoy with his wife Julie and their young son—a night to reflect over the week just past and to get prepared for the one upcoming.

Julie, who was expecting their second child in March, perched on the arm of his chair for a few moments, obviously tired from the day's activities. They had both gotten up early that morning in preparation for the short service at The Refuge, and had ended tonight with a fellowship meeting for the young marrieds here at the house. She pleaded exhaustion, and he gave her a warm kiss and sent her off to bed.

Once more he opened his book, and once more his unrest stole his attention. Ben's face, working convulsively with obvious fear, stared back from the page in front of him, and he closed his book with a sigh. What in the world had that old man been doing there in that cramped little storage room anyway? He'd asked himself that question a hundred times during this day, but a satisfactory answer had not been forthcoming.

He knew he should have stayed and confronted his janitor last night when he'd had the chance, but Ben had shown such remorse and embarrassment that he'd just backed out of the room, advising the other man that he was more than welcome to stay where he was, and not to worry about it. But, although the church key was on his desk this morning as usual, and the lights turned on and the doors unlocked, Ben, himself, was nowhere to be seen. And Jonathon was very much afraid that he would never see the man again.

And, although Ben had proven to be the best janitor they'd ever had at Central Community Church, finding another was the least of Jonathon's worries at this moment. For no matter how many times he examined his impressions from last night's encounter, the only logical explanation for Ben sleeping in the church basement on a discarded old mattress on the floor, instead of in his own home, was that he had no home. And that realization left Jonathon shattered.

He'd come straight home last night and pulled out the application form Ben had submitted when he came for the job interview last winter. And, of course, there was no address, no phone number. Only his name, Ben Smith. Jonathon remembered Ben saying something about his having just moved into town, he'd have to let him know later about a permanent address. And he'd thought nothing more about it.

What bothered him the most about this sad situation was that he, Jonathon Gardner, minister of Central Community Church, had known and had actually had in his employ for the past six months a man who, unless he was very badly mistaken about it, was in dire straits indeed. And he had done *nothing*, had not even questioned Ben about his life or his needs.

Ben had told him that he was a widower of many years and that his three sons were grown and gone. He had assumed that the man was quietly retired and that the weekend job at the church was just something to do in his idle time. How could he have failed another human being so completely? Ben—always smiling, never complaining.

And now, in all likelihood, he had disappeared, and Jonathon would never be able to explain that he didn't mind at all that the old man had borrowed the mattress in the church basement for an occasional night's rest. That he was more than welcome to stay there *every* night if he wanted.

That certainly the two of them together could find him steady employment that would pay for a small apartment somewhere and three meals a day.

Maybe, just *maybe* Ben would be back on Saturday as usual. But Jonathon feared that he had seen the last of Ben Smith. For there would be no records at the utility companies, no mailing address at the post office, nothing that would give him so much as a clue as to the whereabouts of a homeless man wandering the streets. He would check at the Shelter, of course, but he knew in his heart that Ben wouldn't be there.

He dropped his head into his hands and asked a special blessing for his friend, Ben Smith.

Jonathon spied his mother kneeling in the flower bed north of the house as he drove up the driveway and through the gate to The Refuge. He could see that she was hard at work, cleaning the bed of weeds and dead foliage. He tapped on the horn a couple of times, and she looked up with surprise.

When Amy saw who it was that approached, she smiled happily, always pleased to see her son. She wondered what brought him there so early on a Monday morning. After all, today was supposed to be his day off. Maybe this was just a social call, but she doubted it.

Jonathon stepped out of his car as Amy stood and stripped off her gardening gloves. She called a glad, "Good morning!" and watched her tall, dark-headed son stride purposefully toward her. He looked thin, she thought, as she always did. Too thin. She wished he would slow down and eat properly.

"Hi, Mom. You work way too hard, you know that, don't you," Jonathon scolded as he gathered his mother in a warm hug.

"Sometimes it feels like I don't work nearly hard enough!" she answered with a laugh. "At least I never seem to manage to keep up with everything that needs to be done. Tom brought his daughter Jenny here to meet me on Saturday afternoon, and while we got acquainted and toured the house, he mowed the lawn. Doesn't it look pretty? Only now the flower beds just look that much worse!"

"We've got to figure out a way to get you some help out here, that's all there is to it," Jonathon said, and, as the words were being spoken,

Ben's face came to his mind again, and an idea began to form. Ben would love puttering around this place, keeping the yard and flowers neat and trimmed, and helping with the heavy work inside. He could even live in one of the servant's cottages that now stood empty behind the big house! Jonathon almost spoke in his excitement, and then remembered that Ben could very well be gone from them forever.

He realized that his mother was speaking again as they moved toward the back door. "... and the girls are upstairs cleaning their rooms. They will be down for their lessons in about twenty minutes. Can you come in for a cup of coffee?"

"Sure. I need to talk to you for a few minutes about something I've been thinking about," Jonathon responded as he held the door for her. He could hear the distant hum of the vacuum cleaner running somewhere upstairs. He knew that the girls were required to help with the cleaning and cooking, and that Sam, bless her heart, had taken over all of the ordering and shopping in addition to her role as business manager. But the task of overseeing and mothering and teaching, as well as planning the meals and the activities for the girls, was already too much without adding the outside chores that his mom had assumed.

"How are the lessons going?" Jonathon asked as they walked past the oversized dining room table, already laid out with books and study guides and paper.

"Well, we're really just getting started. But I believe that the home school curriculum is going to work well. Gretta, who graduated just before she came here in June, is the only one who has finished her high school studies. But she joins the other girls every day, working on correspondence courses in Home and Family, and Child Psychology. We will know more later, of course, when the testing begins and we can see how well the girls do in comparison to their counterparts in public school."

Amy poured a cup of coffee for her son and a glass of juice for herself and pointed to a plate of bagels. "Help yourself, Jonathon. Sorry, we don't have donuts. The girls would prefer that, of course, but Dr. Cameron keeps a close watch on their weight and insists on good nutrition, so I try to plan a healthy diet for them."

"You're doing a wonderful job, Mom," Jonathon praised as he settled into a comfortable chair and took a sip of his coffee. "But I wanted to talk to you about my work here. I'm afraid that the short service early on Sunday mornings is not accomplishing much. I always feel so rushed to get over to Central for the services there, and the girls always look as if they're still half asleep. And I well know that mornings are not a pregnant woman's best time of the day!

"How would you feel about an afternoon service? We could take as much time as we needed, and maybe make it more of a study session than just a worship service. I was thinking of calling it our Sunday Session and, in addition to our normal worship activities, we could begin a sort of lecture series in which the girls would be encouraged to take an active part."

"I like that idea very much, Jonathon!" Amy responded, enthused. Her bright blue eyes sparkled with anticipation as she considered his suggestion, and then enlarged upon it. "The girls would love to have a morning to just "sleep in" and we could meet at about one, say, for a real Sunday dinner, followed by your study session. I'm sure the girls would be more than agreeable, and I think they would benefit greatly from it."

"Good! I'll begin making plans for it then, and we can start this Sunday. By the way, who is the new redhead I noticed last week?"

"Sara! Sara Franklin, fresh from the mountains of Montana! And what a challenge she has been!"

"A trouble maker?" Jonathon asked with raised brows. "I noticed a bit of hostility in her eyes, now that you mention it, but I guess I attributed it to the early hour. Tell me about her."

"Well, she just sort of dropped in out of nowhere and announced that she had decided to stay. She's the daughter of a congressman, a *wealthy* congressman, I might add, and she has literally rebelled against every rule we have here. When I told her that she would have to store all of her expensive clothing in the basement and wear the walking shorts or slacks and tee shirts that everyone else wears here, she threw quite a tantrum! She viewed the common bathroom which she would have to share with the others with disdain, and demanded a private bedroom. Which she got, as it happens, but only until another girl comes to join us. When that happens, there will be a battle to end all battles, I'm sure." Amy shook her head wearily and Jonathon once again felt a pang of worry for his mother. She was such a *little* thing, and he saw an ever increasing number of silver hairs mixed in with her soft brown curls. She was supposed to be retired now, but it appeared that she was working harder than ever.

"It sounds like this girl could use some counseling, or maybe just a good spanking!" Jonathon countered with a grin. The sound of footsteps on the stairs and voices raised in girlish chatter announced that it was time for lessons, and he rose to go. "Hang in there, Mom," he said as he set his coffee cup on the tray and reached to give her another hug. "And don't worry about these things. I'll take this tray to the kitchen on my way out the door."

"Thank you, son. I'm so glad you stopped by. Give my love to Julie and little Daniel," she added as she opened the door of her office and headed for the dining room.

Jonathon said a quick good morning to the girls and then set the breakfast things on the kitchen cupboard as he hurried to the back door. His mother's dirt-covered gloves, lying on the porch where she had dropped them, reminded him again of Ben. Why couldn't he have thought of recommending Ben for the job of caretaker here before? A snug little cottage to live in, good food, and pride in a job well done would have made all the difference in the world to the man, and would have solved a multitude of problems for Tom and his mother. Oh, the wonders of hindsight!

"Come back to us Ben!" he muttered under his breath as he stepped into his car and buckled his seatbelt. "Let us show you that we *do* hold to the Christian love and values that we profess. Please, don't let us be too late!"

On Saturday morning Jonathon hurried to the church, the white foam carton in his hand, as usual. He hoped the elders hadn't noticed his scattered attention, his rush to finish the meal and go. As he rounded the corner of the building and headed for the side entrance, his eyes sought the bench where Ben had always waited for him without a hint of impatience. It was empty. His steps became leaden, his heart heavy.

He glanced at his watch and saw that it was, indeed, early. Earlier than he had ever gotten back, he thought with a small ray of hope. Maybe Ben would still come. Maybe.

He went to his office and began working on his first Sunday Session lecture for the girls at The Refuge. He'd decided to make love his subject, something every young girl thinks about a good share of the time, he thought, and so he might have a chance at snaring their attention. Then, if he was careful, he might be able to steer their thoughts away from the lusty human kind of love that they would all be familiar with and get them to thinking about a higher, more Godly kind of love.

Jonathon looked up at the clock every five minutes or so until he finally got immersed in his work and forgot about Ben and the time and his worries. He was jotting notes and checking scripture in earnest when a movement at the door brought his head up with a jerk.

"Ben! Come in!"

The old man hovered in the doorway hesitantly. Fearing he was ready to bolt at any moment, Jonathon called again, gently, "*Please*, Ben. Come in and have a chair."

As Ben stood there, uncertain, Jonathon studied the man closely for the first time. He saw a small man, short of stature and thin. Very thin, Jonathon realized with a start, almost emaciated. He was probably slowly starving to death, and no wonder! Ben held his battered old cap in his hands and Jonathon noticed that the man was nearly bald, his sparse hair graying but neatly combed. The light gray eyes that finally met his were alert and intelligent, and Jonathon decided that the man was probably several years younger than he had at first thought. He was suddenly sure that this man was nowhere near retirement age.

Although his apprehension and discomfort were very apparent, Ben moved slowly into the room and sat in the chair that Jonathon had indicated. His eyes on the floor, he mumbled softly, "I... I'm so sorry, Jonathon. I never meant..."

"Ben, this church is here for whatever need anyone may have of it. If you need a place to sleep, then you are more than welcome here, *anytime*."

"No, I... I had no right, sneakin' in here without you knowin'..."

The other man still spoke to the floor and Jonathon urged quietly, "Ben, look at me."

The sad gray eyes were filled with tears when Ben finally raised his head to meet Jonathon's gaze. "Ben, why didn't you tell me, let me help you? I feel so badly about all of this," Jonathon said with anguish.

Ben's head dropped back to his chest. "I couldn't... I'm so ashamed. I... I thought you wouldn't want me here if you knew..."

Those words stung the very soul of the young minister. Was that the image he portrayed to the impoverished? He spoke sorrowfully. "Why would you think that, Ben? What have I done that makes you believe that I would have turned away from your need?"

Ben heard the pain in Jonathon's voice and lifted his head in a quick denial. "No, no. I wasn't blaming *you*! You've always been more than kind, and I really have enjoyed my work here. It's just... I'm so... so *ashamed*..."

"Ben, you keep saying that. What is it that you're so ashamed of?"

With a look of utter astonishment, Ben spoke, as if to a child who had asked an absurdly simple question. "Why, of... of *everything*! I have no home, no money... Any self-respecting man should be able to put a roof over his head and food on the table..." He finished with such remorse in his voice that Jonathon was taken aback.

"Are you also ashamed of Jesus?"

"Jesus! Why, no. No, of course not. Why would I be ashamed of Him?"

"Well, the scriptures tell us that Jesus was also a homeless man. That he hadn't even a pillow for his head."

Ben stared at Jonathon for a long moment, then dropped his head once more. When he finally brought his eyes up to meet his pastor's, they were unwavering. A small smile played about his lips as he answered, "You know, I spent the better part of my life singing about my Jesus, and I never once thought about that!"

"Do you mind telling me about your life? About what happened to bring you here?" Jonathon asked hesitantly.

The other man sighed, and shook his head. "No, for the first time, I don't mind. I see now that I must, in fact, if I'm ever gonna get any self-respect back again."

And so he began to talk. About his early life and his musical talent. A talent that he later misused, he admitted, and then lost, along with everything else.

After his long recital, Jonathon sat quietly for some time, trying to digest the incredible tale. When he finally spoke, he asked with curiosity, "How could I have known you for all this time and never once even guessed at the truth? You don't... you've *never* looked as I would have supposed a man in your plight would look."

Ben grinned. "I guess I owe that fact to Helen."

"Helen?"

He nodded. "When I stumbled into the local Shelter that first icy cold night, hungry and half frozen, Helen took care of me. She found a warm blanket and made some scrambled eggs and hot coffee—a regular angel of mercy she was. I found out the next day that she was just as penniless as I, but that she helped out at the Shelter on a regular basis. I tell you, that woman could fix a delicious hot meal out of whatever happened to be available, and sometimes it wasn't much, believe me! But, anyway, Helen told me somethin' that I've never forgotten. 'Ben,' she says, 'Always remember to keep yourself clean, and to walk tall. Cause if you slink around in the dirt with the dogs, people will treat you like one!' And I believe that bit of advice has helped me more than about anythin'."

Jonathon nodded his agreement and made a decision he'd been toying with for the past several minutes. Maybe he was going out on a limb, but he felt he had to speak now. "Ben, I know a man who is looking for a full time caretaker for a large estate in the country. Although the salary would be rather low, I believe the job comes with living quarters and three meals a day. Would you be interested in talking to this man about such an arrangement?"

Ben's eyes widened in amazement. "Well, yes! Yes, I *would*!"

"Fine. I'll call Mr. Logan today. If he's interested in meeting you and can come by here this evening, would you be willing to meet with us back here at say, seven o'clock tonight?"

"Oh, yes! Thank you, Jonathon. I..."

"And now," Jonathon interrupted with a grin, "you'd better get to work! Because if *you* don't clean this place today, *I'm* going to have to do it!"

A wonderfully wide smile spread itself across Ben's face as he jumped to his feet. "You bet, boss. I'll get right to it!

Jonathon told the whole story to Julie as they drove out to The Refuge for Sunday dinner with Amy and Sam and the girls. In the back seat young Daniel prattled endlessly in his excitement at going to see "Gamma." It was a beautiful fall afternoon and Jonathon's heart was full as he spoke of the meeting between Tom and Ben the night before.

"I expected Ben to be overwhelmed by Tom's presence—you know how imposing Tom seems until you get to know him. But Ben just stood there, straight and tall—even though he's way shorter than Tom—and talked to him as an equal. I swear, the man dropped about ten years off his age between the time he crept into my office yesterday morning and the time we met together again last night! It's amazing what a bit of self-esteem can do for a person."

Jonathon glanced in his rear-view mirror as he spoke, and saw that Tom and Ben were conversing like old friends in the car following theirs. Tom had insisted that his new caretaker join them for dinner today so that he could meet Amy and Sam and get a look at his new home. After they had completed all of their business with Ben last night, he and Tom had driven out to tell Amy of the arrangement, and then had worked most of the night readying the vacant cottage for Ben's use.

"And Mom was just great!" Jonathon continued in his enthusiasm, sending a sidelong grin toward his wife. "I wasn't sure how she would react to our taking in a man from the streets, so to speak, to live right there on the premises. But she said that any man that had sung with The Churchmen, which had been her favorite gospel group for years, couldn't be bad. She commented that it seemed that Ben needed us as badly as we needed him, and so it must certainly be an answer to our prayers.

"And even though we insisted she go on to bed and let us clean the cottage, she kept popping in with a picture that would look just right in the living room, and a rug to lay by the bed, and then a few dishes from the kitchen so that Ben could have a late night snack if he wanted to."

Julie finally squeezed a word in, asking quickly, "But what about furniture? Surely that cottage has been empty for years!"

"Tom and I are going to load up some things from Mom's house in town. The furniture in the spare bedroom and the couch and chairs in the basement aren't being used for anything now anyway and will work just fine for Ben."

"When does he plan to move in?"

"The sooner the better, of course, given the circumstances. We hope to have everything ready for him by tomorrow night."

They pulled into the drive and parked beside the beautiful mansion. Jonathon saw Ben's smile of appreciation as he got his first glimpse of the spacious grounds that were soon to be entrusted to his care. Jonathon crawled out of the car and opened the back door to retrieve Daniel, who was screaming, "Gamma, Gamma, Gamma!" and then he walked around the car to open Julie's door. They waited while Tom parked his car, and then the other two men joined them to walk slowly to the back door.

"This is truly a sight for sore eyes!" Ben exclaimed as he looked around with joy. "How did you ever find this place?"

"This house was built in the early 1900's," Tom explained, "by a close friend and business associate of Frank Phillips, or so I am told, at least. Frank, in case you don't know, founded Phillips Petroleum and was an early day banker and oilman here in Bartlesville. If you think *this* place is grand, you should see *his* home in town!"

"Come in, come in!" called Amy from the kitchen as the group entered the big glassed-in porch at the rear of the house. Savory smells of chicken frying on the stove greeted them, and Amy, flushed from cooking, turned with a smile. Daniel squirmed out of his Daddy's arms and ran to his Grandma with a happy squeal.

At that moment a tall, attractive woman entered the kitchen from the dining room to join Amy. Jonathon proceeded to make introductions.

"Ben, I'd like you to meet my Mom, Amy Anderson, and this gorgeous redhead here is Sam—Samantha Sanders, our business manager and right hand. Ladies, this is Ben Smith, who will begin his duties as the caretaker of this humble estate very soon. If we pass inspection today, that is!"

They all greeted one another warmly, and Julie immediately pitched in to help the other women get the food to the table. The huge bowls of mashed potatoes and gravy set Ben's mouth to watering. This was going to be a feast the likes of which he hadn't seen for some time! He wondered if Amy could make gravy as well as Libby used to, and decided that it was unlikely, but he just couldn't wait to find out for sure.

As the group gathered in the dining room, the girls filed in from upstairs. They were all neatly dressed in their cotton slacks and oversized tee shirts—all, that is, with the exception of Sara. She had donned a pair of the knee-length shorts, which she had rolled up until they were virtually hidden beneath the huge tee shirt she had chosen, and she was barefoot.

Jonathon saw the quick frown that touched his mother's face as the girl tossed her long auburn hair away from her face with a look of defiance. But Amy turned to the group and said calmly, "Ben, I would like you to meet our girls. They are Gretta, Sandy, Jamila, April and Sara." She laid a gentle hand on each shoulder as she presented them, and then she nodded toward the table, indicating that all was in readiness for their meal.

The girls sat at one end of the huge table, surrounding Daniel, who was their little darling. The adults gathered at the other end. They all joined hands as Jonathon said a quiet blessing and then fell upon the food like a pack of hungry wolves. The girls hovered over Daniel, filling his plate and helping him with his drink, as they chattered gaily among themselves.

At the other end of the table Amy addressed Ben, unable to suppress her curiosity any longer. "Jonathon says you sang with The Churchmen! They have been favorites of mine for years, but I don't remember a Ben Smith in the group."

Ben took a bite of the tastiest fried chicken he'd ever had the pleasure of eating and shook his head slowly, "No, not as Ben Smith. You see, I was born John Benjamin Smith and grew up as little Johnny Smith, my Dad bein' *big* Johnny Smith. But when I went to Nashville to try to get a start in the recording business, they were aghast at such a common name as John Smith. So I became John Benjamin to those in the music world."

"You're *John Benjamin*?!" Amy asked with amazement.

"Yep. Imagine me twenty pounds heavier and with that ridiculous hairpiece they made me wear, and you'll see that I am," Ben answered with a small smile.

"John Benjamin has the most beautifully pure tenor voice I have ever heard in my life," Amy announced to those around her. "I can't believe I'm sitting at the same table with him!"

"Well, I *used* to have a good voice, that's true," Ben answered sadly. "But no more. I just can't seem to hit those high notes square on the mark anymore and I have trouble hearin' the harmonies, so I don't sing much now. Least not loud enough so's anybody can hear me."

Sam, seeing the old man's anguish, asked quietly, "So how does it happen that you're in Bartlesville?"

"I'm really not sure. You see, I never planned on coming here. When I left Oklahoma City that morning with nothing but what I could carry in my little suitcase, I thought I'd just head on up I-35 to Wichita, or parts beyond, mebbe. I was sure I could get a ride from someone and was hopin' to get there by night.

"But the cars and trucks just kept on whizzin' by, without a glance in my direction. And I thought about the many times I had done the same, with no concern at all for those poor sods waving their thumbs along the side of the road. I walked all day with just one short ride—a guy in a pickup that took me mebbe twenty miles 'fore he turned off to go on home.

"I slept that night in a dry culvert, so cold I thought for sure I'd die right there. I started out early the next mornin', hungry and cold and hopeless. I walked until my feet gave out and I had to rest, and then I walked some more. Late that afternoon a guy drivin' a big cattle rig stopped and picked me up. His heater blastin' hot air on my feet felt like heaven, and I fell asleep with him talkin' away 'bout how he was on his way to pick up a big load of cattle. I guess he may have told me where he was headed, but I was too tired to care.

"When he shook me awake it was dark, and he told me we were about ten miles from Bartlesville. I stumbled on into town around eleven that night, cold and footsore, and I just decided to stay. But I was thinkin' as I sat in church this mornin', with a new lease on life, that mebbe it was God brought me here."

He took a big bite of mashed potatoes smothered with gravy as he finished this long recital, and added with a grin, "And after eatin' this wonderful feast, I'm pretty well sure of it! Nobody I've ever known, 'cept for my Libby, and mebbe Helen, can come close to this kinda' cookin', Miss Amy!"

Amy smiled at the compliment and asked with a mischievous twinkle in her eye, "And who, pray tell, is Helen?"

Ben chuckled. "Well, I have to tell you, Helen is about the sweetest angel I've had the privilege of comin' across. When I practically fell into the Shelter that first night, Helen was there. She jumped up and got me a warm blanket and fixed me some scrambled eggs and coffee. First food I'd eaten in two days! I found out the next mornin' that she was just as homeless as I was, but she'd taken it upon herself to help others like us as much as possible.

"She'd sit in the corner and read her Bible to anyone who'd listen, and she always managed to find somethin' to cook for dinner. She can make the best meals out of the least groceries of anyone I've ever met!"

"And this Helen is homeless?" Amy asked with mounting interest. "And she can *cook*? Tom, I think we need to talk to her, also, don't you?"

"Why, yes, we probably should!" Tom answered as he thought of the possibilities. "Ben, do you think Helen would be interested in that other cottage out there, and a job cooking and helping with the cleaning of this monstrous house?"

"I guess I can't answer for her," Ben stated, "but she'll be at the Shelter at noon tomorrow as usual, I'm sure. Why don't you ask her yourself?"

Excited at this new possibility, Amy and Sam began discussing what furniture they could scrape up between them to furnish the second cottage. Ben slowly savored the last of his cherry pie and sat back with a sigh.

"So, how do you feel about joining this happy family, Ben?" Tom asked quietly.

"I would be most proud and happy to do my very best for you, Tom. But I do have one request."

Tom quirked an eyebrow in surprise. "And what's that?"

"Well, I was wonderin'... Do you think I could bring Molly with me? I've been thinkin' 'bout it, and I just can't bear to leave her."

"*Molly?* Who is Molly?"

"My little dog, Molly. She and I have been together for some time now, and I must say, she's been a lot of comfort to me."

Amy, who had heard the last of this exchange, said quickly, "Of course you can bring your little dog, Mr. Smith!"

"Please, call me Ben," the old man begged, and then added with some embarrassment, "But Molly—I... I think she might be in a family way. Are you sure that won't be a problem?"

Amy laughed gaily. "No, Ben. That won't be a problem at all. In fact, she'll fit in quite nicely around here!"

Ben looked at the group with bewilderment as they burst into laughter, and then glanced at the five pregnant young women chattering away at the other end of the table. Suddenly understanding, he grinned sheepishly.

"Yeah, I guess she'll fit in just fine, won't she?"

The girls had all gathered in the south parlor, where they were accustomed to meeting for their Sunday worship service, by the time Jonathon entered the room, carrying his Bible and a small cup of water. Amy and Julie slipped in behind him and softly closed the door. He silently blessed Sam for insisting on doing clean up duty in the kitchen and listening for Daniel in the event he woke from his afternoon nap before their Session ended. With Tom and Ben busily examining the grounds and the cottage that would be Ben's new home, his mother and his wife were now free to relax and enjoy the afternoon service.

Jonathon surveyed the small group, noting with some satisfaction that Sara was now dressed in dark slacks and wore sandals over her bare feet. He was continually amazed at the quiet control that his mother maintained with these girls of such diversified backgrounds. He took a deep breath, wondering where to begin. He decided to plunge in and hope for the best.

"How many of you have been in love?"

The girls looked at him with open astonishment. This certainly wasn't what they had expected! Gretta and April raised their hands shyly. Sandy blushed and then, with a shrug, raised hers also. Jamila stared at her hands, which were tightly clenched in her lap, and Sara met his eyes with such hostile defiance that he despaired of ever reaching her in any way.

"I want us to talk about love and its many forms today," Jonathon continued undaunted. "The love between a man and a woman is probably the kind of love that you think about the most, but I want you to consider other kinds of love as well. Can anyone give me an example of another form of love?"

There was silence in the room for a few moments, but Jonathon waited patiently, hoping for some interaction from among the group. Finally Sandy ventured, "Well, I love my parents and... and my brother, I guess."

There were some smiles of understanding at her obvious reluctance to admit to loving her brother, and Jonathon grinned along with them, relieved that they were warming a bit to the subject. "So we have the love we feel for our families, a love between parents and their children. And, of course, this is a very important kind of love, but one that feels somewhat different from the love you might feel for a boyfriend or a husband, right?"

They all agreed, and he saw that he finally had their attention. All of them with the exception of Sara, at least, who managed to convey quite clearly that she had no intention at all of joining in this nonsense. He decided to ignore her completely and to proceed.

"Can you think of any other kind of love?"

They thought about it some more, then Gretta spoke hesitantly, "What about our friends, our pets even?"

"Of course. We have friends that we feel very close to, and pets that are almost like family members. And we love them with yet another kind of love."

April raised her head and spoke for the first time. "I think that we should love God, too."

"By all means! And do you believe that the love you feel for God is different from the others we have mentioned?"

They all thought that it was, and suddenly the room was abuzz with thoughts and ideas. Jonathon caught his mother's eye and saw that she shared his joy at the seeming success of their little venture. He decided it was time to move to a deeper level.

"And what about the love God feels for us? Do you think that it is the same kind of love that we know, or is it on a different level altogether?"

"I think it's different, 'cause God is different..."

"He sure wouldn't love us like we love our boyfriends..." They all giggled at the thought.

"Maybe it's sorta' like a mother loves her baby..."

Jonathon let them explore these ideas for some time, then surprised them by saying, "I believe the love that God feels for us includes every kind of love that we can experience. Now I'm not talking about lust here, but honest, unselfish love. I'm going to tell you a story that I hope will illustrate my premise."

They looked at him with expectation as he began.

"Once upon a time," he started with a grin, and they tittered in their amusement at his use of this fairy tale beginning, "there was a young girl named Hannah who lived in a city far away from here. She was a beautiful young lady of, let's say... about nineteen years of age, and she lived with her parents and one younger brother in their modest but very comfortable home.

"Her family was by no means a wealthy one, but her father was the town's only doctor, and so in this year of 1888 in a growing community far to the north of here, she enjoyed some social prominence and was well known by everyone.

"One chilly morning as Hannah walked briskly down the boarded walkway that would today be a sidewalk, toward the small shop where she sold fine dresses and hats to the elite ladies of the city, she halted suddenly at the sound of a tortured moan. She wrapped her long woolen cape more closely around her against the sharpness of the early morning wind as she searched for the source of that eerie cry.

"She was about to move quickly on down the street so that she wouldn't be late opening the shop, when she again heard the unmistakable sound of someone in obvious agony. Thinking the groan had come from somewhere in the street, she moved cautiously to the edge of the boardwalk, only to find a man face down in the gutter below her.

"Wrinkling her nose with distaste, she assumed that the old man was intoxicated and had fallen in his drunken state into the mud and slime at the edge of the street. She was on the verge of turning away when she noticed that the coat he was wearing, filthy though it was, looked somewhat like the coat worn by her own father. And then he cried out again, 'Help me! Could someone please help me?'

"A sudden pang of fear shot through Hannah's heart as she wondered for one terrifying moment if this poor man could actually *be* her father, fallen in the street in the darkness of pre-dawn as he trudged home from an exhausting night of trying to save a life somewhere. But of course it wasn't her Papa—hadn't she just left him sitting at the breakfast table, quietly reading the morning news? She felt quite silly at her unfounded fear, but she edged closer to the street in an effort to get a better look at the creature below her.

"At that moment the man made a feeble attempt to raise his face out of the filth and he cried out again in obvious pain. Hannah surveyed the slime and the puddles of dirty water and the deep mud that filled the gutter at her feet, and she knew without a doubt that her fine leather shoes and the long skirt of her dress would be ruined beyond repair if she should step down there. But she'd already dallied in her indecision long past the time for opening the shop, and something in her heart wouldn't allow her to just walk calmly down the street, pretending that she didn't know full well that this man was in desperate need of assistance.

"And so Hannah made a very crucial decision at that moment. Although she didn't know it at the time, that decision would have a great impact upon her. It would, in fact, change her life. She clutched at her long cape and the voluminous folds of her dress and the petticoats beneath it in a vain attempt to avoid soiling them, and she stepped off the curb.

"She screwed up her face in disgust as she felt the cold wet mire soak immediately through the soft leather of her best shoes, but she noticed now that the stranger wore the clothes of a gentleman, not those of a beggar of the street. And she also saw that he had some sort of wound to his forehead which was bleeding, making the mud around his face a deep dirty red.

"Forgetting her fine attire, she stooped to her knees and spoke for the first time. 'Sir, can I help you?' When he didn't respond, she bent lower and was surprised to see that, instead of being an old man, as she had supposed, he was actually much younger, possibly near her own age. But he now lay so absolutely still that she feared that he might have bled to death from his wounds.

"Now Hannah was the daughter of a doctor and was not squeamish about blood and sickness, having seen much of it in her short lifetime. She reached to push her fingers inside the collar of the man's shirt and was gratified to feel a weak pulse. She now sat fully in the oozing filth around her, but her attention was so completely absorbed in her attempt to help the young man at her side that she gave it no thought.

"Finally the poor man stirred and groaned again, and Hannah managed to slide an arm underneath his neck and turn his face to where she could examine the gash on his forehead. She pulled at the edge of her petticoat until she found a relatively clean space which she used to wipe the grime from his face and out of his wound. She spoke again, more urgently, 'Sir, you need help. Do you think you could stand if I were to assist you? My house is not far from here, and my father is a doctor.'

"The man slowly opened his eyes and focused them with difficulty upon the beautiful young woman who apparently meant to save him. He tried to answer, but his voice was so weak that Hannah laid her head in the mud beside his in an effort to hear. 'Yes, help me, *please*,' he whispered, and Hannah smiled into his eyes, for there was not a hint of liquor on his breath and, now that she had wiped most of the mud and grime from his face, she saw that he was quite handsome.

"Together they struggled up out of the gutter and, with her support, the young man was able to stand, albeit rather shakily. With a supreme effort on both their parts, they were able to step up out of the mire and onto the boardwalk that would lead them to warmth and care.

"Now you can imagine the spectacle they made, stumbling together down the street, covered from head to toe in the slime from the gutter," Jonathon continued with a grin at his audience, who was now completely captivated by his tale. "But Hannah was a strong girl and she was able to give the weaker man the support he needed to get him to her house. Once there, her family rushed to his aid, her brother helping him upstairs to a bedroom, and her father grabbing his medical bag to tend to his wound.

"While the men tended to the stranger upstairs, Hannah washed the filth from her hair and her body and changed into fresh clothing. Then she and her mother busied themselves with preparing a hot, nourishing breakfast. When the young man reappeared some time later, bathed and dressed in some of her brother's clothes, his head neatly bandaged, Hannah stared at him in wonder. He was indeed a fine looking young man, and when he smiled at her in gratitude, her heart melted.

"Still weak from loss of blood and hunger, the young man said little until he finished eating the hearty meal they had set before him. Strengthened by the food, he settled back in a comfortable chair near the warmth of the fire and began to speak. He confessed that he had left his home and his family several years ago in search of riches and excitement, but had fallen in with some bad company and had strayed from the Christian values that he had been taught as a child. When he finally realized that he had left the only real source of riches and excitement when he turned his back on God and his loving family, he decided to return and try to find his childhood home.

"'I arrived last night to find a city that seemed larger and somewhat different from the one I remembered,' he told her. 'I stopped for a bite to eat and perhaps a bit of information about my parents, only to learn that my mother had died a year ago, broken-hearted by my long absence, and that my father was overcome with sorrow. I rushed headlong into the street, wanting only to find my father and to ask his forgiveness. But the walk was slippery from the falling rain and my eyes were blinded by my tears. I fell into the street, hitting my head on the edge of the boardwalk. I must have laid there unconscious for several hours.'

"He gazed at Hannah for a long moment and then said quietly, 'Thank goodness you were kind enough to come to my aid. Otherwise I would surely have perished there in that rank gutter.'

"The two of them chatted together beside the warm fire, becoming friends. She learned that his name was Samuel and that he was the son of a very close friend of her father's. When he again expressed his desire to find his father, she eagerly offered to lead him to his home. And so they once again walked out into the damp coldness of the morning, but with a newfound joy in their hearts.

"Samuel's father welcomed him with open arms and tears of gladness. He forgave his son, of course, as all good fathers do, and then welcomed Hannah as the daughter he had always wanted when she became Samuel's bride some months later. And, as you already know," Jonathon ended with a wide smile, "they all lived happily ever after!"

The girls giggled again and clapped in their appreciation of his entertaining tale. He bowed low, much to their delight, and then added with seriousness, "In this story Hannah made a very important decision that changed the whole course of events, not only for her but for Samuel as well. What was that decision?"

"When she decided to help him?"

"That's close, but not quite it."

"When she stopped, even though she was in a hurry to get to work?"

"No, that was important, of course, but still not the ultimate decision."

They looked at him in confusion and he stated emphatically, "I believe the one decision that she made that changed both her life and his, was the one to step down off that curb. It was only when she brought herself down into the mud and muck that he was mired in that she began to forget her own obligations and appearance, and started to consider and to care about his plight. It was only then that she was able to see him as a person worthy of being saved, instead of the drunken bum that he had appeared to be as she viewed him from the walkway above.

"And, if you'll remember, the lower she positioned herself, the more respect she gained for him. And, in doing so, she was finally able to give him the help and support he so badly needed. Once he realized that he was no longer alone in his misery, he summoned the strength to rise out of the gutter and move toward a better life."

Jonathon saw that the girls were beginning to understand the full import of his little fairy tale. He decided to go one step further. "I believe when we sin, as we so often do, that we must look to God very much like Samuel looked to Hannah when she first spotted him sprawled in the filth of the street. And I also believe that God wants all of us to behave as Hannah did when we see another human being in need. For Hannah demonstrated all of the forms of love that we talked about earlier.

"She stopped at a cry for help because she felt compassion. She knelt in the mud to offer support and friendship. She led a lost soul to shelter and safety. She fed him and listened to his confession of wrongdoing. And then she took him by the hand and gently guided him home to his father and the forgiveness he so desperately sought. Finally, she joined him in matrimony for a lifetime union of Christian service. And she did all of this out of love.

"Not the perfect love of God. But a Godly love, never-the-less. An all-encompassing love that is striving toward that perfect love that is described in our Bible in John 3:16. If you've ever been to church you probably know that verse by heart. Let's say it together."

For God so loved the world, that He gave His one and only Son, that whoever believes in Him shall not perish, but have eternal life.

Jonathon let his gaze fall on each girl in turn, noticing that they all joined him in reciting the scripture. And, finally, as they spoke the last few words in unison, he turned his attention to Sara. He saw, to his amazement, that, although her eyes were cast downward, she too had joined in the words they spoke. As though sensing his perusal, she suddenly raised her eyes to his.

And he saw in one fleeting glance eyes that were unguarded. Eyes that mirrored loneliness and uncertainty and something else... Sadness, he thought, somewhere in the far reaches of her heart. And he knew as he gazed upon the beautiful young woman with all that glorious red hair, that he must reach out to her, even if it meant ending this ever so successful Sunday Session on a sarcastic note. He spoke quickly before he could change his mind.

"Sara, what do you think that verse tells us about the love of God?"

At the sound of her name she ducked her head once more, and he saw a slight flush touch her cheeks. The room was absolutely silent, as if all in it were holding their collective breath. Sara was silent for so long that Jonathon began to despair of her responding in any way at all. And then she slowly raised her head and said in a clear, quiet voice, "I think He... well, He *really* stepped off the curb, didn't He?

AMY

Amy was pleased as punch. She smiled broadly as she took a deep breath, savoring this sun-drenched September day. She was actually taking a walk! She felt like a woman of leisure, so long had it been since she'd had the time—or the *energy*, for that matter—for taking a walk. What a difference an extra pair of hands can make!

And Helen O'Hara had proved to be much more than just another pair of hands. That sprightly little creature just seemed to be everywhere at once, spreading cheer, smoothing ruffled feathers, bringing giggles of delight. And busy every minute! It seemed that whenever Amy climbed the stairs to gather laundry, Helen had been there just ahead of her. And after they finished one of her delicious meals and Amy tried to help with the clean-up, Helen shooed her out of the kitchen, insisting that she and the girls would do just fine. And they did, too!

For Helen had an undeniable talent for making work into fun, and the girls were now involved in every aspect of keeping their home running smoothly. Helen was a firm believer that young girls needed to learn how to perform domestic duties if they were to become mothers and homemakers themselves. And that they needed to understand that it wasn't always easy, or necessarily rewarding, for that matter, but that it could always be fun if they had the proper attitudes.

The change in the girls had been astonishing! Even Sara! There was less squabbling to be heard now, and much more laughter. And instead of viewing their housekeeping chores as just that—*chores*—they seemed to be taking some definite pride in keeping the beautiful old house shining.

Amy sighed with pleasure. She gave a lot of the credit for this amazing improvement to Helen. But she knew that Jonathon's lecture on Sunday had truly touched these girls as well. Especially Sara, she thought again, with gratitude. For Sara had finally seemed to become one of the group, and not just because she happened to live in the same house with the others. There was a new unity, a *togetherness* that hadn't been apparent before, and Amy felt that each of the girls had made an effort in that direction.

And it had all happened so fast! First Ben, and now Helen, here by nothing short of a miracle. Amy chuckled aloud as she thought of Jonathon's recounting of their meeting at the Shelter on Monday. He'd described the look of astounded surprise on Helen's face when Ben walked calmly through the door, accompanied by Tom and himself. And how, once she'd collected herself, she'd just as calmly invited them all to sit down and have dinner. He'd been about to refuse, he said, when Tom thanked her politely and proceeded to seat himself beside the scruffiest looking bum at the table, and then to begin a friendly conversation with the group. Jonathon had laughed uproariously at the memory of Tom in his expensive business suit, immaculate, as usual, visiting comfortably with Bartlesville's lowliest, as if they were colleagues at a company luncheon.

Finally, satisfied that Helen's cooking was everything Ben had promised it would be, Tom had asked Helen if he might have a word with her in private. She had blushed like a school girl and had led him to the tiny kitchen at the back of the room. There Tom had praised her fine meal, and then had asked her who was in charge of the establishment. She'd called the elderly couple who lived in an upstairs apartment to come down and join them. When the feeble pair entered the room, looking very little more prosperous than those they cared for, Tom had shaken their hands with dignity and had explained that he was looking for a cook for The Refuge.

"You would never have known that this was anything less than a cordial business arrangement between associates," Jonathon had explained concerning Tom's handling of the matter with the elderly couple. "Tom just quietly asked them if they would mind if he offered employment to Helen, who was obviously their very fine cook. They said, no, of course not. They would miss her, but they were very happy for her. And Helen had said yes, she would love to cook for his 'houseful of girls,' and had quickly blinked back her tears. The fact that she was homeless and penniless was never even hinted at, and her gratitude was obvious."

And then Jonathon had continued, his voice becoming soft and rough, "As we were about to leave, Tom reached into his pocket and pulled out a roll of bills that would have choked a mule, and handed them to that poor old couple. He thanked them for an excellent meal and promised that he would be back. You could see that he was deeply moved by the poverty of these people, and I believe that he sees Ben and Helen and the others as a sort of out-reach mission for The Refuge."

Amy smiled as she recalled her son's next words, and the odd glow in his eyes as he spoke them. "Tom's a mighty fine man, Mom," he had said fervently, and she wondered now if there had been a deeper meaning behind his words. Her heart did a little dance as she walked slowly down the quiet country road. Yes, Tom was a fine man and, although she had never confessed it to Jonathon, she had loved Tom Logan for a very long time. There'd been a time when she had longed to marry him, but as they continued to work together in the running of The Refuge, she had come to the conclusion that the possibility of that ever happening was remote.

For it was obvious that Tom still loved Joyce, although they had been divorced for nearly ten years now. How awesome it would be to be loved like that, Amy thought wryly. A love that nothing could kill, not even the knowledge that his former wife was now happily married to someone else.

The foreign sound of a vehicle intruded upon the singing of the birds and the chirping of the insects that had so far been her only companions. Amy looked up to see the dirty red four-by-four that she recognized as belonging to Chet, their rural mail carrier, barreling down the road toward her. She returned Chet's friendly wave and cheerful grin as he flew past her and then stopped at their mailbox. And she knew she'd best be getting back to the house. Doc Cameron would be coming soon for the girls' check-ups, and tonight was the night for their Lamaze classes.

She turned reluctantly, drinking in the splendor of the afternoon. There were hints in the surrounding landscape that autumn was quickly approaching—a touch of gold in the trees that bordered the yard, and the swelling buds of the chrysanthemum bushes that nestled beneath the edge of the wide front porch. Ben's neatly kept yard would soon be ablaze with the brilliant colors of fall.

Amy stopped at the mailbox and pulled out a pile of sale bills and advertisements and one official looking letter. She studied the return address. Social Services Division, Chicago, Illinois. They usually received this kind of letter only when a girl was being referred to their home. But, from Chicago? She frowned, then hurried back into the house, more than a little curious.

The mouth-watering smell of something chocolate baking in the oven greeted her as she walked through the front door. She shook her head with a small smile. Helen was apparently baking—*again!* The girls loved it, of course, but Doc was going to have a fit if they'd all gained ten pounds! She would have to speak to Helen, who was of the opinion that expectant mothers were eating for two and needed to be fed that way!

Amy glanced with pleasure at the glowing hardwood floors, and then saw that a gracefully arranged bouquet from the flower gardens now crowned the dining room table. She caught a glimpse of her reflection in the hall's full-length mirror as she hurried past, and quickly smoothed her wind-blown hair. She was dressed casually, in the same kind of attire that they provided for the girls. Today she had chosen black slacks of a soft cotton knit, topped with a pale pink tee shirt which she had belted with a gold chain around her trim waist. Her cheeks were slightly flushed from her walk, her blue eyes sparkled with a healthy vigor, and her naturally curly hair framed a pleasant face that was altogether too youthful looking for her years.

As Amy closed the door to her small office, she inhaled a fresh lemon scent that told her that Helen had been there during her absence, polishing her old oak desk to a high gloss. Early afternoon sun streamed through lace curtains that covered wide double windows, giving the comfortable room a golden glow. She sank gratefully into the high-backed chair at her desk and quickly opened the letter from Chicago. She scanned the typewritten message and saw that they had indeed been asked to take another girl. Very little information regarding the young lady was included; only that she was in her second trimester of pregnancy, that she was nineteen years of age, and that she had recently lost her husband in a fatal shooting.

Amy slowly absorbed these facts and wondered if the newfound peace they were enjoying was soon to be shattered. Because this new inhabitant would, by necessity, be sharing Sara's room and Sara had made it abundantly clear that she did not intend to share her room with anyone. Amy had patiently tried to explain the merits of their "buddy system" where roommates not only shared a bedroom, but also became partners in their Lamaze exercises. Each provided support to the other, and that culminated during the birth itself. But Sara had brushed it off with a disinterested shrug.

Amy frowned as she tried to decide how to best approach the headstrong girl with this piece of news. But the sudden clatter of running steps in the hallway and a sharp knock at her door brought her out of her musings with a start.

"Miss Amy! Can you come quickly?" a breathless voice shouted through the closed door. Amy jumped to her feet with alarm. She flung the door open to see Sandy's agitated face, her eyes dilated with excitement.

"Sandy! What is it?"

"It's Gretta, Miss Amy! Her water's broken, and I think she's in labor!"

Amy rushed from the room, followed closely by the flustered young girl, who, although nearing her own due date, moved with remarkable speed. The letter that had so completely occupied Amy's mind a scant moment before now lay forgotten on her desk.

They were all sitting quietly in the front parlor, grinning like so many Cheshire cats, when Tom bolted through the front door at ten-thirty that night. He'd returned from a business meeting in Kansas City to find an urgent summons on his answering machine, and had dashed back out into the night without even stopping to check his mail. He came to a sudden halt just inside the doorway, and his eyes jerked from Amy to Jonathon to Sam, and then settled on Dr. Cameron.

Taking a deep breath, he finally retorted, "Well, whatever the emergency was, I'd have to say, from the pleased expressions on your faces, that it must be well under control now."

At that, they all began talking at once. Unable to decipher much beyond the fact that someone had given birth, and that they were all highly satisfied with the events of the evening, Tom raised both hands in a gesture of surrender.

"*Please*! One at a time! Amy, would you just start at the beginning and tell me what's happened?"

With a huge grin, Amy answered, "Oh, Tom! It was so *awesome*! Gretta's water broke at a little before two this afternoon..."

"And Doc Cameron drove in the driveway about two minutes later, like he had a premonition, or something..." Sam broke in.

"And by the time I got here, they had Gretta comfortably settled into the new birthing room, with a nurse from the hospital in attendance!" Jonathon added.

"It all worked like clock-work!" Dr. Cameron put in. "I had everything I needed, right where I wanted it, and that in itself is an amazing feat. As you know, we had just sort of pieced that room together with odds and ends of equipment whenever it became available!"

"And Sandy was just marvelous!" Amy finally managed to say, once again in control of the conversation. "She led Gretta through the breathing process with perfection, cheering her on and giving her the most wonderful moral support. You'd have thought she had been through childbirth a dozen times, instead of just expecting her first!"

At that moment Helen appeared in the doorway, holding a tiny pink bundle in her arms and surrounded by four giggling girls and one bemused gardener.

"Mr. Logan, we would like to present Megan Michelle, The Refuge's newest resident. She and her Mama are doin' just peachy!"

Amy tapped softly on the door to the birthing room and stuck her head inside. It was just after nine, and she knew that Miss Simmons, the nurse from Memorial who had spent the night with Gretta, would be getting anxious to go home. A peaceful scene greeted Amy's eyes as she glanced around the room and noted that little Megan was nestled close to Gretta's breast, nursing hungrily.

She smiled at Miss Simmons, who was changing the linens in the small crib, and asked, "And how is the new mother doing this morning?"

Gretta blushed, and grinned down at the infant in her arms. "I'm doing just great! Isn't she the most beautiful baby you've ever seen, Miss Amy?"

An overwhelming joy flooded Amy's heart and tears threatened to overflow from her bright eyes. This was truly the epitome of their mission at The Refuge, and she answered with deep emotion, "Yes, Gretta, she most definitely is. And I am so proud of you. You have proved yourself to be a strong, self-sufficient young woman, and I am sure that you will be a wonderful mother to Megan."

Gretta flashed her a look of pure gratitude and replied with honest humility, "I have a lot to learn about mothering, Miss Amy. I'm lucky to have you to help me."

"I... all of us will be here for you anytime you need us," Amy promised. "And now we must let Miss Simmons go home and get some rest. And, as soon as that young lady is finished with her breakfast, Helen and Sam and I will help you get a warm shower and into some clean clothes, and then we're going to move you and your daughter downstairs into your new room!"

Amy turned and kindly thanked Judy Simmons as the young nurse left the room, and then perched on the edge of Gretta's bed. "I hope you don't mind sharing this sweet baby with all of us," she said as she caressed one tiny fist. "She will be a very important learning tool for the other girls as they await their own deliveries. I am so pleased that you have decided to stay with us for your full six-week child-care allotment."

"Oh, sure. It will help me, too. I still have two more weeks of training in beauty school before I can begin giving haircuts and perms for money. But I should be able to get a place of my own within six weeks. I was wondering, though, if I could ask a favor..."

"Of course. What do you need?"

"Well, once I'm on my own, I'm gonna' have to find a babysitter for Megan. Do you suppose she could stay here during the day at first? The other girls would watch her, I'm sure, and I'd just feel better, knowing who was taking care of her..."

"That's a splendid idea! I am a firm believer that girls who are comfortable handling a newborn are much less likely to give up their own babies. And the duties of mothering are far less stressful for those who've had some experience beforehand. We'd be delighted to have her!"

"I don't know how to thank you, Miss Amy. You... everyone here has been so kind to me..."

"I'll tell you what! You get that beautician's license and I'll let you cut my hair!" Amy said with a laugh as she reached for the now sated infant. She placed the tiny bundle back into the crib. "And now I'll go get the girls started gathering your things together, and we'll get you cleaned up and settled into your new quarters."

Amy left the room with a smile. They had decorated the west wing of the old house for new mothers and their babies, thus keeping the noise of crying infants away from the other girls during the night. She knew that the expectant mothers would be anxious to help with the newborns during the daytime, but she felt that they needed to get their rest. She or Helen would be on call for night duty when and if the new mothers needed them.

Amy ducked into her office to get the paperwork for Gretta to submit to the hospital so that the birth could be properly recorded and a birth certificate issued. Her eyes fell on the letter from Chicago that lay where she had dropped it the day before, and she knew that the next business of this day must be a call to that office. And, if arrangements were made to accept this new girl, as they most probably would be, she must then face Sara with the news.

Help me, Lord. I'm gonna' need it!

Sam was diligently entering the past month's expenditures onto the computer in front of her when her door suddenly flew open and a furious voice interrupted her concentration.

"I have never in my life shared a room with *anyone*, and I don't intend to start *now*!" the shrill voice spat out. "I'll pay whatever you want..."

When Sam continued her task without any notice of this outburst, the angry girl spoke even louder, asking belligerently, "Did you hear me? I said..."

"I didn't hear you knock," Sam interrupted calmly, still staring determinedly at the figures she'd just input into their data base.

"I... I didn't knock," the girl spluttered with surprise.

Sam finally turned her attention to the raging redhead who had so rudely addressed her. She sat quietly for some moments, perusing the agitated young woman with interest. How amazing were the similarities between the two of them! For Sam, herself, had once possessed the same fiery temper, the same flashing green eyes, the same obstinate stubbornness, even the same long-legged loveliness of this young girl who stood, fuming, before her.

At last she spoke to the girl, in a very quiet and deadly serious tone, "If you wish to speak to me, I would suggest you go back out that door, shut it quietly, and then knock, as any properly brought up young lady would do."

The emerald eyes flashed dangerously, but the girl turned without another word and returned to the hall, shutting the door behind her. In a few moments, Sam heard a soft tap and grinned to herself. She waited a full minute, then stood and opened the door.

"Yes?"

"Hello. My name is Sara Franklin. Could I please have a word with you?" This was said with such forced politeness that Sam had to clench her teeth to keep from smiling.

"Certainly. Won't you come in and have a chair?"

Sara brought her chin up just a fraction, green eyes meeting green eyes steadily. The two were of nearly equal height and weight, but Sam's auburn hair had deepened to a rich reddish brown over the years and was now cropped short. The younger woman nodded almost imperceptibly and sat, straight-backed, in the offered chair.

Sam returned to her seat at the desk and asked quietly, "What did you wish to speak to me about?"

"I have just been advised that a new girl will be arriving within the next week or two, and it seems that she will be assigned to share my room. I prefer living alone and am prepared to pay whatever amount is necessary to retain that arrangement," Sara answered, matching the older woman's dignified manner to perfection.

"You don't have enough money to buy that privilege."

"And what do you know of my financial status?" A hint of her earlier anger touched Sara's voice.

"Absolutely nothing. And I have no desire to learn of it. But however much money you may have, it won't buy you any favors here."

"What do you mean?" Sara's tone became a shade more strident in her obvious frustration. "Surely you need money to run a place like this. I could give you quite a lot, as a matter of fact, and it would benefit both of us."

"No. We accept no money from the girls we help. That way everyone is treated equally here. Why do you think you are required to wear the same clothing, share in the same chores? I'm sure Miss Amy went over all of this when you moved in. If you had no intention of obeying our rules, why did you stay?"

For the first time, Sara dropped her eyes to her lap. "I don't know. I... I guess I thought it was better than getting an abortion." She raised her head and continued with some vehemence, "But maybe I was wrong! My father seems to think so. He has been trying to persuade me to leave here and go to some 'very secluded and very private place' that Caroline has picked out for me. I'm sure it's very posh, too, in keeping with our *class*!"

The girl had spoken these last words with such bitterness that Sam was momentarily silenced.

"And who is Caroline?" she finally asked.

"My dear stepmother!" Sara ground out between clenched teeth. "I came here in the first place to try to avoid the scandal that would taint her impeccable record in Washington—hers and my father's. All my father seems to think about these days is his political career and his fancy new life and his beautiful new wife!"

"So why don't you go to this posh place and let them kill your child? After all, you've just come barging in here, trying to buy some special privileges from me. It would seem that you fit very nicely into their lifestyle!"

Sara jumped to her feet and fairly yelled her denial, "*NO!* I am not like them! And I don't want to go to that place and let those snotty people touch my body! I'll stay here and share my stupid room first!"

Sam stood and faced the girl once more. "Of course you'll stay," she said lightly. "Because it would ruin all your plans if you gave in to your father's wishes now, wouldn't it?"

"And just what is *that* supposed to mean?"

Sam stared into Sara's flushed face without speaking for a moment. Then she turned and sat again at the desk. "Sit down," she commanded quietly.

She waited until Sara had obeyed, and then answered the girl's question softly. "I think you want to have this baby in order to punish your father. After all, you have his full attention now, don't you? I think that you've never forgiven him for ignoring you while he pursued his 'rich new life and his beautiful new wife,' as you so aptly put it. But you know what else I think? I think you might do this unborn child a favor by aborting it now, instead of using it as a weapon against your family."

Sara stared at Sam in open-mouthed astonishment. The woman's harsh words had singed her very soul, and she was unable to respond. When she dropped her head into her hands in surrender, Sam asked gently, "And the father of your child? Who is he?"

Sara remained silent for the space of several seconds, then slowly raised her head. "His name is Ross," she said dully.

"Ross. And what does Ross think about this child?"

"I… I never… He… he doesn't know."

"So is Ross a stranger, then? A 'one night stand,' I believe they call it."

"No. He… he's an old friend from my home."

"A friend? And you've chosen to keep his child a secret? Tell me about Ross."

Sara's eyes took on a far-away look as she remembered her childhood friend. When she began to speak her voice was curiously soft. "I've known Ross Marshall since I was twelve years old. I lived on a small farm then, and he lived only a couple of miles from my house. After my mother died I was very lonely, and so the Marshalls sort of became a second family to me. I… I spent a lot of time there, me and my mare Ginger."

She sighed and looked up at Sam expectantly. When the older woman remained silent, she continued, "I helped Ross and his sister Becky with their chores, and then Mrs. Marshall would always set a place at the table for me, just like I was one of her kids. I guess I had more fun at the Marshall's than I'd had since I rode the trails with my mother so many years ago.

"Anyway, Ross taught me to milk the cows, and I remember sittin' on that old three-legged milking stool and singin' along with his radio while we squirted milk in a swish-swish rhythm that followed the music. It was so peaceful there! One night after we finished Ross danced with me, right there in the barn. We had to watch out for the cow droppings on the floor, and we were swatting at the mosquitoes, but it was... I'll never forget it."

Sara finished with a smile, and Sam saw a softness in the girl's eyes and a glow on her cheeks that told her all she needed to know.

"You love him, don't you?"

Sara's head came up with a jerk, a deep red flushing her cheeks. "Love him? No! No, of course not. He's the son of the foreman at my father's mill. No, I don't..."

"The foreman's son? Oh, I see. That makes him quite beneath *you* then, doesn't it? Certainly not worthy of your love!"

Sara looked at Sam with a mixture of confusion and budding anger. But Sam continued caustically, "Make up your mind, Sara. First you tell me you're not like your father and Caroline, who obviously have some misguided sense of *class*, and then you casually dismiss the father of your child because he's the son of hired help. So where are *you* in this picture, I wonder?"

"I... I didn't just 'casually dismiss him.' I didn't tell him b-because I just couldn't, that's all. We... we only did it that one time, you see, and he, well he was really upset. I kept tryin' to tell him that it was okay, that it didn't matter, but... but he insisted it *did* matter to... to God. When I left him that night he was cryin' and prayin' and askin' for forgiveness. And so I... I just couldn't face him when I found out... when I got pregnant."

There were tears on Sara's cheeks when she stopped speaking. Sam stood without a word and walked around her desk to where the girl was now slouched in her chair. And then Sam knelt on the floor and slipped an arm around Sara's quivering shoulders.

"Sara, you have answered my question. Because your words have just placed this young man head and shoulders above all of you. And now you need to go back to your room and begin preparing for the young lady who is to become your roommate. For she will need your support and friendship, not your condescension. And when you have finished with that, I'd suggest you get down on your knees and pray that Ross Marshall will be able to find *you* worthy of *his* love. Because you and your baby are going to need it!"

"I have a special announcement before we start this week's Sunday Session," Jonathon said as the girls got settled into comfortable chairs. He noticed that Ben had slipped in and sat in a straight-backed chair near the door. Understanding that the gardener wouldn't want attention focused on himself, Jonathon refrained from inviting the old man to move closer. Nevertheless, he was greatly pleased that Ben seemed to be enjoying every facet of life at The Refuge.

"Julie, would you please come up here with me?" Jonathon asked. His wife blushed shyly and gave an almost imperceptible shake of her. But the girls began clapping and cheering her on, and she finally got to her feet and moved to join her husband at the front of the room. The look she gave him clearly informed him that she would get even with him later for this unexpected surprise.

Undaunted, Jonathon placed his arm about his wife's shoulders and announced with a big smile, "Julie and I are proud to tell you that we are expecting our second child in March."

This news was greeted with even more cheers and shouts of approval. Jonathon knew that the girls already viewed Julie as a sort of role model, and that they loved her dearly. She somehow represented all that they wished for themselves, and the fact that she, too, was pregnant only heightened their affections.

She ducked her head with embarrassment and started to return to her seat, but Jonathon tightened his arm around her, holding her beside him as he spoke softly in her ear, "I'd like you to stay here with me today. Do you mind?"

Julie stifled the protest on her lips as she saw that he was serious in his request and shook her head with a shrug. "No, I guess not..."

"Thank you," he murmured with a gentle smile, and then he turned her cheeks to crimson once again when he planted a tiny kiss on the very end of her nose.

The girls giggled with pleasure, and the mood was set for the topic Jonathon had chosen for his lecture.

"Last week we talked in depth about love and its various ramifications. About stepping off the curb to place ourselves on an equal footing with others so that we might really see them and their needs. And then about offering our hands and our hearts in support and love.

"This week I would like us to look more closely at the love between husband and wife and how we go about finding a partner that we can 'love and cherish til death do us part.' You've heard that phrase in wedding ceremonies many times, I'm sure. But what does that really mean? Is it just some fairy tale sentiment that rarely happens in real life? Is it possible for a man and a woman to find true love and happiness that can endure and grow deeper over a lifetime?

"Some of you—possibly all of you—probably have serious doubts about that. You've grown up knowing that the fairy tale ending—'and they lived happily ever after'—is just a way to end the story. But the Bible gives us some important instruction about finding our mates, and then tells us how we should treat each other in order to make marriages that not only will endure the hardships and hurts that we all encounter, but will flourish, and will provide strength and security and happiness for our families."

Amy surveyed the group from her seat near the back of the parlor. She had seen Sam slide through the door at the last minute, joining them today for the first time. She had expected her friend to take the vacant chair next to her own, but Sam had walked past her and settled next to Sara, supposedly to get a peek at the baby Gretta held closely in the next seat. But Amy had seen the look that passed between Sam and Sara, and the warm smile that Sam had flashed at the girl, and wondered again just exactly what had transpired between the two of them the other night. Sam had told her only that they "had talked" and that she felt that Sara would now at least make an attempt at being civil to her new roommate.

Her attention was brought sharply back to Jonathon's words as she heard him quoting from Ephesians. *"...so also wives should submit to their husbands in everything.* And then the writer tells husbands to love their

97

wives as much as they love their own bodies. In fact, he compares that love to Christ's love for the church, which He sacrificed His very life for."

Amy stiffened at his words. They were indeed Biblical, but she wondered at her son's judgment in addressing such a volatile subject to a room full of women. These girls were young, and pregnant by men who quite obviously hadn't, for one reason or another, accepted their own responsibility in the matter. And for any man—even one they respected as much as they did Jonathon—to stand there and tell them they must *submit* without question to the men in their lives could be fighting words indeed!

She saw that the girls were squirming in their seats, and the buzz of dissension which had started quietly began to increase.

"...so does submitting mean we have to do anything they tell us to do?"

"I submitted to a man once and look what happened to me..."

"...my mom says there's not a man on this earth that she would ever promise to obey..."

"...I know. My sister made them take that part out of her wedding vows..."

Jonathon let them chew on these thoughts for a time before taking control again. "Now there are some important things to understand here. Number one, you have not been instructed to submit to *every* man, but only to the man you take as your husband. And that man who becomes your husband has a very strict command given to him. He is to love his wife as he loves *himself.*

"If you think about it, that is very serious business. Because we men are very protective of ourselves. That's why we take our vitamins and buckle our seat belts. And that's why we always let our wives clean up any broken glass or other sharp objects..."

The hoot of laughter that followed those words considerably lightened the tension in the room. Jonathon continued quickly, "I wonder, would *anyone* deliberately bring pain or destruction to his own body? If you desperately wanted to get to the other side of a river but the only way to get there was to swim through alligator infested water, would you go? Probably not. The point I'm trying to make is that a man who loved you as completely as he loved his own body would be a man you could trust implicitly. Right? He would care as much about your well-being and comfort and safety as he did about his own."

The buzzing began again as the girls speculated on this premise. Finally Jamila asked the question that seemed to be upper-most in everyone's mind, "And where in the world are we gonna' find a man like that?"

The girls tittered in agreement. Amy held her breath. Sam raised a doubtful eyebrow. Ben perched on the edge of his chair, ready to bolt if things got out of hand.

And Jonathon turned to his wife with a smile. "I'm gonna' let Julie answer that question," he said calmly. "Because she has obviously managed to do just that, right? After all, I always insist upon cleaning up the broken glass at our house, don't I dear?"

Julie sent such a venomous look toward her husband that the girls again burst into laughter. But then she turned to them and said in her soft, shy voice, "Actually it *is* possible to find such a man, if you set your mind to it. And, much as I hate to admit it in front of him, Jonathon truly is that kind of husband."

The girls giggled again as Jonathon struck a cocky 'I told you so' pose and Julie deflated him with an elbow in his ribs.

Bolder now that they were talking to another woman, the girls began a barrage of questions. "But where are these men? How will I know he's really that kind of man? Do I have to marry a minister? Where did you meet Jonathon?"

"Well, you obviously don't find that kind of man without doing some serious looking," Julie responded. "But you don't have to marry a minister, either. I met Jonathon at a single's retreat sponsored by our church, which, I might add, is a *wonderful* place to find nice, single young men—all those handsome young preachers and Christian college students there, huntin' for a woman!"

She paused with an impish grin as her audience broke into amused applause. Then she turned serious as she continued, "But being a minister or a professed Christian doesn't necessarily make the kind of husband we're talking about. Jonathon is not a good man, or a good husband and father, just because he is a minister. He may have chosen to be a minister because he is a Godly man, but he could have chosen any profession and still be the kind of husband a woman can trust with her life.

"And he *is* a husband that I can submit to entirely and know that he will never intentionally make a decision regarding my life that will hurt me. Although he tells me that he loves me, and I know that it is true, it is not just because he loves me that I trust him. It's because he loves *himself,* and he loves his God. You see, any act on his part that would hurt me would be a sin against God. And a sin against God is going to ultimately hurt Jonathon. When you find a man who honestly and sincerely serves his Master, you will have a man you can joyfully submit your very life to. And I think you will recognize him when you find him."

The girls nodded solemnly. Amy sighed with relief. Sam sent Julie a broad smile of approval. And Ben settled happily back into his chair.

Sara trailed behind the others as they clustered around Julie. Dismissed from this latest Sunday Session, they all headed toward the stairs where Helen and little Daniel could be heard shrieking wildly as they engaged in some childish game. Instead of following the group, Sara headed for the back door and the beckoning sunshine of a warm autumn day.

She stepped out into the brightness of the afternoon and stood on the porch for a few moments before sitting down on the warm step with a sigh. Something about the way Jonathon had spoken to Julie during today's Session, maybe just the look in his eyes when he was near her, reminded Sara of Ross. He'd had that same gentle caring way towards her, she remembered with nostalgia. Maybe she *should* tell him about the baby—someday, at least. After all, he was a thousand miles away now, happily absorbed in his college classes with hundreds of pretty girls around him every day. She wondered if he had found someone special and had forgotten all about her. The thought was depressing.

Suddenly she jumped to her feet, disgusted with herself. Why should she care what Ross was doing? As she walked slowly along the back of the house, she heard soft whistling noises and looked up to see that Ben was already in the yard, busy with some chore in the big flower bed south of the house. She wandered to where he worked, and asked without any real interest, "Whatcha' doin'?"

Ben turned with a jerk, surprised by the girl's presence. He held the end of a long garden hose in his hand. "Oh, hello, Miss Sara. I was just tryin' to get this hose rolled up while it's still warm and pliable. The nights are startin' to get chilly, and there's nothin' harder to handle than a cold, stiff hose."

"Need any help?" she offered indifferently.

"Sure. If you'll get a hold of the other end there, mebbe we can get the kinks outa' this thing."

She obediently picked up the end of the hose, which was partially hidden under a twisted mess that looked vaguely like a long green snake, curled and ready to strike. She was surprised at the soft warmth of the sun-baked rubber in her hands. She looked up at Ben and was suddenly curious.

"So what did ya' think of Jonathon's lesson today?"

Ben stopped tugging at the hose and considered the girl's question. "Well, I thought it was purty good, as far as it went..."

"What do you mean?"

"Don't get me wrong," Ben said hastily. "Julie was dead right in what she said. But she failed to mention how the love of a good woman can jest sorta' make a man *want* to be a good husband. My Libby... well, she was always there for me, makin' me proud to treat her good. The first time I ever laid eyes on her, she was sittin' in church, listenin' to me sing. She had such an adoring look in her eyes, it made me want to sing even better, and she was only eight years old at the time!

"And she never lost that look til the day she died. I always knew I could count on her to be my best friend, and my biggest fan. And after the Lord took her... I remember searchin' the audience after my concerts, lookin' for her purty face. She wasn't there, of course, but I would see her anyway, smilin' her approval, clappin' louder than anyone. Least until I got big-headed with my own importance and began to believe I didn't need her, or anyone, anymore... Sometimes I'd still look for her face in the crowds that were cheering for me, but she wasn't there anymore..."

Ben's voice trailed off, lost in his sad memories. Sara stared at him, trying to make heads or tails out of his disjointed story. What in the world was he ramblin' on about anyway? You'd almost think that he'd been some sort of rock star or something! She shook her head in disbelief. Clearly this old man had lost his marbles!

101

She tugged at the resistant hose, dragging her end to the far side of the yard as Ben patiently straightened and smoothed and coiled its length from the other end. Inside, as the others scattered in various directions, Jonathon slid an arm loosely about his mother's shoulders and walked slowly down the hallway with her toward her office. Amy looked up at her son with pride, and exclaimed, "That was just wonderful, Jonathon! And Julie was *marvelous*!"

"Hey, I married her because she reminded me of you," he said, giving her shoulders a little squeeze.

Amy chuckled. "Flattery will get you anything! I have to admit, I was worried about the outcome of this Session there for a while. I've struggled a good part of my life with that 'submissive' stuff, but Julie showed me today that my real problem was in my choice of partners. First your father, and then Nick—such weak men, both of them! Hopefully our girls here will take this message to heart and choose more wisely than I did!"

"I don't remember much about my father, but you had little choice about becoming the rock of the family after Nick let alcohol ruin his life. Dani and Nicki and I owe a lot to you for providing the security and the strength we needed as we were growing up."

"Thank you, Jonathon. It was pretty rough at times, that's true. And I thought I had to carry the burden all on my own shoulders. I see now that submitting to a good husband is not unlike submitting to the Lord. A thing of joy, really..."

She let the thought hang there for a moment, then turned her attention back to Jonathon and said reflectively, "You know, it occurred to me as I sat in there today, that these wonderful lessons of yours are being somewhat wasted on such a small group. I realize that the girls are your primary audience, but I know that I, too, gained enormous understanding from you and Julie this afternoon. It's a shame we don't have room to invite others from the community to join us..."

"Well, maybe someday we can have a place..."

"Jonathon!" Amy interrupted excitedly. "Let's build a chapel, right here on the grounds! I still have the money I inherited when Mama died, and I can't think of anything I'd rather use it for. Or that Mama would appreciate any more! It doesn't have to be big or grand or anything. Just a small A-frame with huge windows... We can build it back in the trees beside that little brook. That's such a lovely, peaceful spot!" Amy's eyes were shining in her excitement.

"That sounds like a wonderful idea, Mom, but that money is yours. You need to think carefully..."

The sudden shrill ringing of the telephone brought their conversation to an abrupt halt. Amy moved to answer it.

"Hello... Tom! How nice to hear from you! Jonathon and I were just discussing... Oh, Tom, I'm so sorry. Of course, you must go... Be careful, Tom. You'll be in our prayers."

Jonathon watched his mother closely as her face changed from obvious joy to deep distress. She hung up the telephone and turned to him, her face pale, her eyes troubled.

"That was Tom. He said... there was a terrible plane crash this morning. Somewhere in Mexico, I think he said. Anyway, it seems that Joyce and her husband were on board. Her parents just called him from Kansas City. The official report states that there were no survivors..."

Amy moved slowly to the window and vaguely noticed that Sara and Ben were engaged in some project in the south flower bed. When she turned back to Jonathon, he saw the quiver of her lips. "Tom... he sounded so... so desolate..."

Her tears spilled over as Jonathon stood quickly to gather her into his arms. "Mom, I'm sorry. You... I've always thought... you care a great deal for Tom, don't you, Mom?"

Amy lifted her tear-filled eyes to her son. "Yes, Jonathon. I... I've loved Tom Logan for more years than I care to count. But, well, I've known for a long time that his love for Joyce was all-consuming. And it was very apparent in his voice just now..."

Jonathon struggled with the pain that he heard in his mother's voice. "Mom, this terrible tragedy today will take its toll on Tom and his children, there's no doubt about it. But God often brings blessings along with devastation. Maybe Tom will find the closure that he needs now from a relationship that realistically ended long ago."

"That may be true, Jonathon. Death brings with it a kind of finality that somehow lets us live again, I know. But since I have so totally immersed myself in The Refuge, I have realized that I no longer need the love of a man to make me feel whole. Does that make any sense?

"What I'm trying to say, I think, is that although the love and companionship of a good man would bring a certain happiness into my life, the outpouring of my love for the girls here, the giving and the supporting and the caring for them, has somehow supplanted my *need*, if not my desire, for that other kind of love."

Jonathon nodded. "Yes. Godly love as opposed to human love. It's a wondrous mystery. I always think of God's love as similar to water. The water that fills our lakes and rivers on this earth is gathered up by the rays of the sun in a process we call evaporation. Just as a heavenly light raises us to the heights of love, the sun causes moisture to rise and form clouds filled with life-preserving rain. And, just as the clouds in the sky overflow, letting water return to feed the land below it, our hearts, filled to capacity with God's love, then begin to overflow to share that love with others. And just as water always seeks the lowest places, flowing ever downward, we, too, by bringing ourselves down to the most humble of positions, become closer and closer to the perfection God desires.

"The very giving of that type of love overcomes our need to be loved in return. But, at the same time, it allows us to enjoy to the fullest the very kind of relationship we suddenly find we don't need. For loving, in its most perfect form, is always giving, and forgiving."

Amy nodded with understanding, a smile finally breaking through her tears. "We have an awesome God, don't we?" she said with wonder.

Outside her window, Sara and Ben had finally closed the gap between them, the hose now a tamed and docile loop hanging over Ben's arm.

"So, do you believe in love?" Sara asked curiously.

Ben gazed at the vibrant young woman, her head held high, her demeanor so assured, and he saw beneath that confidant pose a child's loneliness and bewilderment. He said with a kindly smile, "With all my heart!"

CRYSTAL

⌘

S he stared at the letter in her hand with wide-eyed, open-mouthed, full-blown, mind-boggling astonishment. Her eyes traveled once more to the top of the page. It was, indeed, addressed to her: *Ms. Crystal Atoka, Family Life Division, The Daily Oklahoman.* She reverently brushed her fingertips across the illegibly scrawled signature at the bottom. Neatly typed directly below it was the name that sent a fresh wave of excitement whirling through her: *J. Randolph Rawlings, Editor, Lifestyles Magazine.*

The message of the letter was short, and oh, so sweet. He'd read her "fine article" about The Refuge, which had appeared in the June 28th edition of *Mainstream Magazine.* He hoped that she would consider returning to Bartlesville, Oklahoma now that the center was in full operation, for a follow-up story to be published in *Lifestyles* early next year. They were planning a series of articles, he said, called *Options for the Unborn.* Included in the series would be real life stories about young women who had been faced with the facts of an unplanned pregnancy, and the decisions that they had made. They wanted to provide clear insight into the technicalities and procedures involved in a variety of choices, including abortion, adoption, and single parenthood, he continued, with an emphasis on the emotional impact on the young mothers. He hoped that she would accept this free-lance assignment. He felt she would need four to six weeks of in-house preparation, during which time she could observe and interview the young women as they prepared to give birth, and as they faced the momentous decisions regarding the future of the child.

She glanced at the calendar. It was late October, and Mr. Rawlings wanted copy before the end of the year! That meant she must decide *now*. But she'd made her decision already, she knew. It was, in fact, no decision at all, for who in their right mind would turn down such an offer! *Lifestyles* had hit the marketplace just over a year ago and seemed to appeal to every age. J. Randolph Rawlings was a no-nonsense publisher who was not afraid to address the real issues of today's chaotic world with honesty and a kind of "grandfatherish" perspective. She, herself, had devoured every single issue, marveling at the deep insight of his staff of writers and the home-spun simplicity and authenticity they managed to convey in every article. There seemed to be a kind of Christian goodness about the publication, without the "preachiness" that turned off today's young readers.

She felt a flutter of anticipation in her stomach. Was she capable of the kind of writing that would be acceptable to such a prestigious magazine? She guessed Mr. J. Randolph Rawlings must think so, at any rate. She remembered the animosity she had felt when LaKesha had handed her the original assignment to write about The Refuge. The lavish feature that LaKesha had written the week before about Oklahoma City's finest abortion clinic needed to be followed by something the pro-lifers would appreciate, and Crystal knew that she was delegated for this assignment only because LaKesha considered the job unworthy of her talents and had refused it.

And she had made the trip to the small town of Bartlesville with a distinctly negative attitude, she recalled with some amusement, expecting to find some old couple who were in the process of putting together a haphazard shelter of some sort for unwed mothers. How was she ever to make a name for herself as a journalist with second rate assignments such as this? She had graduated from Northeastern's School of Journalism with aspirations of making a difference in the world, of erasing some of the world's oppression and pain in some small way. And she had been sure that she would never get there with petty stuff like this!

But now it appeared that she couldn't have been more wrong in this assumption. She caught up her astounding letter in both hands and clutched it to her breast with a whoop of unrepressed joy. She remembered her initial interview with Tom Logan and knew that this would not only be the chance of a lifetime, it most likely would be an entirely enjoyable assignment. For, loath as she had been to write the original article, she had found herself pleasantly surprised, both by the renovation that was in progress on the outskirts of Bartlesville, and the people who were so enthusiastically involved in it. She was suddenly anxious to begin, to visit that wonderful old house again, now that remodeling was complete, and to see firsthand the work being done there.

And she positively could not wait, she thought with an impudent grin, to see the look on the face of her beautiful, arrogant boss when she was presented with this piece of news! LaKesha Gilmartin was without a doubt the most stunningly beautiful Afro-American woman Crystal had ever seen, and she knew that the head of Family Life used her petite, curvaceous body and her soft, sexy voice to every advantage. But Crystal had heard LaKesha's voice when it was raised in harsh criticism, had seen her luminous black eyes turn hard with anger, had heard the totally unlady-like expletives that spewed from her alluring mouth when her fiery temper was ignited.

And Crystal had also, in the past year since she'd joined the *Daily's* staff, been the victim of a racial prejudice the likes of which she had never before in her life encountered. A Native American herself, Crystal had expected a sort of mutual understanding between the two of them, a bonding of minorities, so to speak. But her boss had wielded her authority without mercy, giving Crystal only the dregs of the job, while LaKesha took for herself the attractive subjects, hoping, Crystal knew, to get the very kind of recognition that she had just received from Mr. Rawlings.

She still couldn't believe it! She must call Tom Logan immediately to make arrangements for an extended stay at The Refuge. She hoped she could actually live on-site so that she could become friends with the girls there. She would need that kind of working relationship, she knew, to be trusted enough for the girlish sharing of confidences that would make this story more than just good. It had to be great!

As she accessed her address book on the computer in front of her, searching for Logan, Tom, she remembered that day early last summer when she had first met him. So tall and dignified and good looking! She grinned to herself as she reached for her telephone. The next few months promised to be a most welcome change!

⸂⸃

That Tuesday, the first day of June, had dawned with spectacular magnificence. Clouds, resting sleepily on the horizon, had taken on brilliant hues of coral and gold and lavender as the sun climbed resolutely from her bed and chased them from her path. But Crystal had stared only at the road in front of her, disgruntled by the early hour and the miles that she must travel, and, most of all, by the futile story that LaKesha had pushed upon her. Her usually serene face was darkened by an unattractive scowl, which mirrored her mood.

But she was determined to arrive for her eight o'clock appointment on time. Nothing put a reporter at more of a disadvantage than tardiness, and she had smiled in spite of her peevishness when she pulled up in front of the offices of American Trucking Co. at exactly four minutes before the hour. She stepped out of her little Firebird, took a deep breath of pungent autumn air, and walked slowly toward the entrance of a surprisingly handsome building.

The chipper little receptionist pointed her to the door on her right, saying that Mr. Logan would see her immediately. Thank goodness! For, although she always made a point of being punctual herself, she had spent many precious minutes waiting to gain audience with others. She scanned the gold nameplate on the door, and was suddenly glad that she had taken the time, regardless of the early hour, to dress carefully. Mr. Logan was apparently a VIP here, and the opulence of her surroundings suggested that this was no shabby little company.

She tapped lightly on the door and, after only a moment, found herself gazing into a pair of brilliant blue eyes that were on a level slightly above her own. She was a bit surprised, since she had deliberately worn her three-inch heels that morning, which, in addition to her five feet eight inches of height, often gave her the advantage. She'd found that towering over a man sometimes made up for the disadvantages of her sex and her race, but Mr. Logan stood facing her as tall and as straight and as quietly in control as his title had subtly suggested.

She took in his carefully combed silver hair, his finely chiseled facial features, and his expensive navy blue suit in one sweeping glance, impressed in spite of herself. But she spoke in a well-modulated voice that betrayed none of her surprise.

"Good morning, Mr. Logan. My name is Crystal Atoka, and I'm here from *The Daily Oklahoman.*"

"Hello, Miss Atoka. Please come in and have a chair."

The words were spoken with an easy grace and a warm smile, and she seated herself in the comfortable chair he had indicated with a small measure of relief. Maybe this wouldn't be so bad after all.

She glanced up to see him gazing at her with frank admiration.

"You're American Indian," he noted without even a hint of condescension in his voice.

"Yes. I am Cherokee," she replied proudly.

"Where is your family home?" he asked with obvious interest.

"I'm from Tahlequah, Oklahoma. I graduated from Northeastern State University a year ago with a Master's Degree in Journalism."

"I spent a couple of days in Tahlequah several years ago when I attended a sales meeting there. It's an interesting town in a very scenic location."

"Yes. It is the capital of the Cherokee Indian Nation. My ancestors were among those who formed the Constitution for the new nation in 1840."

"Where was your ancestral home?"

"My grandfather, many times removed, was a prominent plantation owner in Georgia before the white man drove the Indians from their land," she answered truthfully, hoping that she wouldn't offend her host before the interview even got off the ground.

But Tom Logan gave a solemn nod. "The Trail of Tears."

"My people called it "The Trail Where They Cried," she said quietly. "Nearly one fourth of the Cherokee Tribe died on that long trek from Georgia to Oklahoma, from disease or starvation or exposure. We are proud of the mighty nation that we have managed to rebuild, but it will never again be quite the same."

Tom nodded again. "I have read extensively of your people. You have every reason to be proud. And I feel a terrible shame for the wrongs my people have done to yours."

She looked at him with honest approval. This man was no small-town geek, and she now found herself openly curious about The Refuge. She reached for her notebook and pen and looked up to find him once again studying her.

"You are very beautiful," he said softly, a simple statement of fact. He let his eyes wander from shimmering black hair, which framed a perfect oval face dominated by velvety brown eyes, to the fawn colored suit that molded her long, slender frame. Suddenly he saw twin black braids falling to her shoulders, a dress of soft buckskin, and beaded moccasins. An Indian Princess from a childhood picture book.

"I'm no Pocahontas!" she countered with an amused chuckle.

He gave a sheepish grin, flustered for a moment by her unerring insight. "I guess we'd better get on with the interview," he answered, indicating the pen poised above her notebook. "I want to thank you for making the long trip to Bartlesville for this story, and I hope that you will find our project as intriguing as I do. If you have the time, I would like to take you to our huge old house for a tour, and to introduce you to Amy Anderson, who is overseeing the bulk of the work there."

"I would like that very much," she said. "And I hope to take some pictures of the house, if you don't mind."

And so began the interview that led, first to publication in *Mainstream*, a coup in itself, and then to her latest assignment. And she had found herself caught up in Tom Logan's enthusiasm, in spite of herself. However, the depth of his commitment to this project remained an enigma to her until she spotted a gold-framed picture on his credenza. He had stepped out of the office to get mugs of coffee for both of them, and she had taken the opportunity to stretch her long legs and to examine her surroundings more closely.

The family portrait was no different from a hundred others she had seen gracing the offices of men she had come in contact with during the past year. But she bent to study it with interest. She'd learned that a man's family sometimes brought insight into the man himself, and she made a habit of examining any pictures she might discover. She realized immediately that she'd hit pay dirt with this one! Tom stood proudly, his arm around an attractive woman who was obviously his wife. The big, strapping young man at his side had to be the couple's son. But it was the young lady next to Mrs. Logan that caught her attention and held it. Jenny! Her roommate at Northeastern during her junior and senior years! The fact that her friend's last name was the same as Tom's hadn't even occurred to Crystal, and probably wouldn't have seemed important anyway.

But it was at that moment that the pieces began to fall into place. For she would never forget the day of Jenny's abortion. She had, in fact, accompanied her friend to the small clinic, and had sat uncomfortably in a dingy, dark waiting room while an unknown doctor performed the quick, vile procedure to Jenny's young body that had left the girl pale and desolate. Crystal remembered feeling queasy just sitting in that awful place, and the Jenny that emerged from its depths had lost forever the happy sparkle in her eyes. Crystal knew, without understanding how she knew it, that Tom Logan must have been unbearably hurt by his daughter's action.

He found her staring at the picture of his family when he returned with coffee and donuts a few minutes later. Crystal raised her eyes to his and spoke the thought that was on her mind. "I had no idea that you were Jenny's father," she said softly.

Tom halted midway across the room from her, an unfathomable look in his eyes. Finally, he asked, "You know my daughter?"

"We were roommates at Northeastern. I ... I was with her when..." Unsure of her ground, Crystal let the words hang between them.

Tom stared at her for a long moment, then deliberately turned to set the tray on his desk. He spoke without looking up. "You know... about the abortion, then."

"Yes." Her answer was barely audible. He turned slowly to face her, and she continued in a voice that was stronger, and full of compassion. "Your daughter was... is one of my very dearest friends. I believe she did what she did out of desperation, and shame. She felt that she had no other choice, as many young women in her circumstances do."

Tom nodded. "And abortion seemed to be an easy answer." He handed her a cup of coffee and indicated the plate of donuts, "Help yourself, Miss Atoka. I must apologize for not recognizing your name, but I... well, I knew very little of my daughter's life during that time. In fact, you probably know far more than I."

"She was determined that you *not* know, Mr. Logan. I think she was very confused and lonely, and I know she did many things that she was deeply ashamed of. But she always loved you..."

Tom sipped his coffee, then raised his eyes and stated frankly, "I hope that you will refrain from using Jenny's name in your article. Because my mission here is not a result of her abortion, although that certainly brought the issue to my attention. But, as much as I abhorred her action, I would never have even considered such a project as The Refuge if God hadn't stepped in and led me there."

He said those words with such conviction that Crystal was momentarily speechless. This interview was certainly not going as she had expected! But she answered him with the same kind of direct honesty, "I would never include Jenny's private life in this story unless you specifically asked me to, Mr. Logan. I hope that my desire to make a name for myself in the field of journalism will never push me to the use of sensationalism, or to an unnecessary invasion of privacy."

"I appreciate that very much," Tom answered gratefully. "And I will be glad to give you whatever information you need concerning The Refuge. Would it be easier to talk at the house where all of this will make more sense?"

"Yes, let's do that," Crystal responded happily. She rose from her chair and set her coffee mug back on the tray, then followed Tom with growing excitement. This just might result in a good piece of work after all.

The day flew by. Tom Logan and Amy Anderson were gracious hosts, and that *house!* She took picture after picture! She suddenly knew that she was going to be able to write a meaningful feature, possibly her best to date. For this project touched her heart as few had, and the deep commitment to making this an attractive, Christian environment for young women in need was obvious.

As Crystal reluctantly said good-bye to Tom late that afternoon, she spoke candidly, "Mr. Logan, I must admit that I came here today under protest. I felt that this assignment was just so much unimportant filler to satisfy some political need on the part of the newspaper. And I don't mean to sound disparaging about your mission here, but it just didn't seem to fulfill *my* mission in terms of meaningful journalism. I... I have this dream of somehow making a *difference*, of giving the world some deep insight that would lead us to a better understanding of human needs. And this seemed..."

"Like small potatoes," he answered with a grin. "Crystal, there are many missions in this world. But I challenge you to make a difference wherever you may find yourself. Not everyone speaks from the ghettos of New York or remote regions of Africa or the battlefields of a war-torn country. Truth and compassion are the real tools of the journalist. If one young woman chooses life for her unborn child as a result of the article you are about to publish, you *will* have made a difference!"

As she sat at the desk in her quiet office, Amy's eyes kept straying to the glory of the beautiful October day that beckoned from her window. As she tried to sort through the paperwork that always managed to pile up on her desk she heard a light tap on her door and called a cheery, "Come on in!" She looked up as the door opened, expecting to see Helen with today's menu in hand. But her heart gave a little lurch as Tom stepped into her office, a warm smile on his face. It was the first she had seen of him since his return from his former wife's funeral, and she was quick to notice the lines of stress and fatigue in his face.

"Tom. How are you?"

"I'm fine."

"You look tired."

She saw the flash of pain that momentarily darkened his eyes, and then he looked at her with a quick grin. "When I worked the Kansas City area years ago I had a grizzly old truck driver named Red who used to tell me at times that he felt like he'd been 'rode hard and put up wet!' That's pretty much how I feel today!"

Amy chuckled, and then asked softly, "And how are Jim and Jenny?"

"I believe they are doing all right. Jenny, especially, seems to have found a sort of peace now that it's all over. I guess we all feel that the chapter is finished, so to speak, and the book has finally ended."

Tom moved restlessly to the window, and then turned to her again and resolutely changed the subject. "What's the news here?"

"Well, we had another baby while you were away—you seem to miss them all, don't you! Sandy gave birth to a healthy boy last Tuesday in the wee hours of the morning after a long, painful labor. She never saw her child. The couple selected by the adoption agency picked up their new son with great joy that evening. And Sandy left us yesterday, after many tears and hugs and sad farewells, to return to her home. I pray that she will be okay."

"Was this terribly hard for you?" he asked gently. "I remember how devastated you were by Dani's decision to give her child up for adoption so many years ago."

Amy smiled. "Thank goodness my daughter changed her mind at the last minute! But in Sandy's case, adoption seemed to be the only reasonable choice. She is only thirteen, after all, and with an alcoholic mother to go home to, she knew that her child would be far better off in a warm Christian family. I met the young couple briefly, and they were positively radiant! I admit that I can now see the positive side to adoption that I was unable to understand when it was my own daughter and my grandson who were involved."

Amy looked up with a glad smile. "And speaking of Dani, I had a letter from her yesterday. She's finally decided to marry her cowboy! They are planning a spring wedding. She asked if she and Josh could bring Jerry and his two teenage daughters here to have Christmas with us! Do you suppose that would be all right?"

"Sure, it's all right. It's more than all right! Because my two kids want to come, too! Especially Jenny. She told me she has decided to return to school to pursue a degree in some area of social work. She mentioned again how impressed she was with our place here, and she is anxious to visit again. I believe she hopes to get involved in counseling young girls who have had very little Christian guidance."

"I am very glad to hear that, Tom. Jenny is such a sweet young lady, but I felt that day when she came here to visit that she was searching for a more meaningful direction for her life. She certainly has much to offer!"

"Yes, there's nothing like hard, painful experience in life to prepare us for understanding others," Tom agreed. "I'm very proud of both my kids, and mighty happy that they want to spend Christmas with their old Dad!"

"Oh, Tom!" Amy exclaimed with excitement. "Let's have a huge family Christmas for the girls! After all, they'll be separated from their own families, won't they. I'll invite Nicki and Mike and all of their brood to come, too, and, of course Jonathon and Julie and little Daniel will be here, and we can have a big Christmas tree with loads and loads of presents..."

Tom had to laugh at the girlish sparkle in Amy's eyes. And he suddenly knew that it was that childlike spirit that made the girls here love her so much. Made *everyone* love her! He decided it was time to tell her his big news.

"It looks like we'll be having yet another guest for Christmas!" he said with an air of secrecy.

Amy looked up curiously. "Really? And who would that be?"

"Do you remember Crystal Atoka?"

"Of course! That beautiful Indian girl who wrote the article that made us famous! Have you heard from her?"

"There was a message from her when I returned to the office yesterday. I spoke with her this morning, and she had some very interesting news. It seems she's gotten her first big break, and we're to be her subject!"

Amy looked at him with wide-eyed surprise. "She's doing another story? About The Refuge?"

Tom grinned, relishing the impact his next words were sure to have on Amy. "She's received a letter from J. Randolph Rawlings, editor of *Lifestyles*. He's asked her to write an in-depth feature about our work here for his magazine. It's to be published in the February edition."

Amy jumped to her feet in her excitement. "Tom! That's incredible! *Lifestyles* is the hottest thing on the newsstands right now! And what a wonderful opportunity for Crystal!"

"Do we have room for her to stay here for a few weeks, probably until the end of the year? She feels that living here with the girls would provide an intimate knowledge of their feelings and emotions, and would give the story greater authenticity."

"The decorators have promised me to have the final two rooms done by the end of next week. When will she be coming?"

Tom studied the calendar on Amy's desk. "Well, she wants to meet with all of us here on Friday to make final plans for her stay, but she mentioned that she had a few things to finish there before she could actually begin the work. I think we can be ready for her, and I'm sure that living right here will be an advantage."

"Oh, Tom, I am so excited! And Crystal is such a lovely girl! Did you say she's to be here on Friday?" Amy glanced at her appointment book with a small frown.

"Yes. Is that going to be a problem for you?"

"No, I don't think so. Kasaundra Lawrence, the new girl from Chicago, is to arrive that day, but I should be able to manage everything."

"Chicago! Another proof that Crystal's work has already put us on the map! I can't even imagine the kind of recognition an article in *Lifestyles* will bring to us," Tom said with awe. "God is surely giving us every opportunity to reach those who need us, as well as others who have the means and the desire to open centers just like this one. When good Christian care becomes as easily obtainable as abortions are, I believe we will have a fighting chance to overcome that evil practice.

"And that reminds me," he continued, his face suddenly breaking into a warm smile, "of the other reason that I came by here today. Jonathon tells me that you want to build a chapel on the grounds. Are you serious about giving your inheritance for such a project?"

"You make it sound much grander than it is, Tom. It's no enormous amount of money, by any means. But enough, I think, to construct a small, simple chapel for us to worship in. And, yes, I want very badly to do this," Amy answered with fervor. "I didn't always agree with my parents' 'fire and brimstone' type of philosophy, but they were deeply committed Christians, and I can't think of a better way to use this money."

"I couldn't be more pleased with your decision, Amy. And I think we should get started as soon as possible, before the weather turns bad. I'd like it to be ready for use before Christmas."

Amy's eyes danced with pleasure. "Do you really think that's possible? Oh, I can't wait! I have a vision of a rustic little A-frame sitting down in our woods, with a wall of glass behind the pulpit giving a panoramic view of that little brook and the trees and..."

"Let's go look! Do you have time?" The enthusiasm was apparent in Tom's voice, and his invitation to go outside on this gorgeous fall day was irresistible.

Amy grabbed her sweater from the back of her chair and followed Tom to the door, with a call to Helen that they would be back soon. An autumn nip in the air made Amy hasten to don her sweater, but bright sunshine put a glorious shimmer on the riotous color that surrounded them. They walked slowly down the little path that led into the thick forest of trees behind the house, waving to Ben, who was fighting a losing battle with the multitude of leaves that continued to fall into the yard.

Amy led Tom to the spot she had chosen, a bit off the path in a small level clearing near the stream. It was a peaceful scene, and they stood quietly for a moment, listening to the cheerful babbling of the little brook and breathing in the pungent smells of autumn.

"This place has always been special for me," Amy said softly. "It seems... I don't know... closer to God, somehow. I come here often to think, and to pray."

She looked up at Tom, then, and he saw the sheen of unshed tears in her eyes. She looked exceptionally lovely to him in that moment, the sun in her hair giving her an almost ethereal appearance. He had a sudden recollection of his long-ago dream, when she had stood on the stairs and beckoned to him to join them for a meal. And then had begged him to take care of them, to save them from the beast that hovered in the forest, waiting to devour them all. He realized with acute clarity that she had been God's instrument in that dream, leading him to understand the mission that he must undertake.

As Amy let her eyes wander again over the small plot of ground, envisioning a rustic chapel in the midst of all the beauty that surrounded it, she felt Tom's gaze upon her, and turned once more to face him. There was something inscrutable in his eyes that made her heart leap within her. She felt that he was staring into her very soul. That he was, perhaps, really seeing her for the first time.

She reluctantly pulled her eyes from his. "Do you like it?" she asked, feeling an unaccustomed shyness.

"It's perfect," he said softly. "I'll call a building contractor today to get started on the blueprints." He reached for her hand and squeezed it warmly as he added tenderly, "Thank you, Amy. Thank you for everything."

They turned back toward the house and walked slowly, hand in hand, through the trees. Amy was aware of a strange buoyancy, as if her feet hardly touched the leafy path beneath her. Her mind told her in no uncertain terms that nothing had changed between them. But her wildly beating heart told her that everything had.

Crystal, Tom, Sam and Jonathon were chatting amicably in Amy's office when she hurried in with an apology on her lips. "Sorry I'm late. But Mrs. Lawrence is now settled in, I hope."

"Did you say *Mrs*. Lawrence?" Sam asked with surprise. "Is this girl married?"

"Actually she's a widow, at the incredibly young age of nineteen," Amy answered with a sad sigh.

"What's her story?" Tom asked with interest.

"It's a sad one, I'm afraid. Kasaundra, or Sunny, as she prefers to be called, is pretty much alone in this world. Her father, a Negro, met and married her mother while serving our country in the Philippine Islands. Sunny apparently remembers very little about her mother, who, she says, was very tiny and very fragile. She died in childbirth, along with her third child, a son, when Sunny was only three years old, her sister just five. Two years later Sunny's father was killed in an automobile accident. At that time, Sunny and her older sister went to live with their grandmother, a woman she remembers as being warm and loving, but who had already raised eleven children of her own. The poor woman died when Sunny was only 15, and it is the girl's opinion that she literally worked herself to death."

Amy shook her head with sorrow. "Sunny left school at that time and went to live with her sister, who was already married and had two children. Sunny got a job as a waitress to try to help put food on the table, because, as she says, 'Josie's old man was always drunk, and then one day he just left and we never saw him again.' When Sunny met Noah Lawrence, she found the first real security she had known since her mother died. They married, and she had just learned that she was pregnant when Noah, a young black police officer, was killed in a racial riot in Chicago's slum district a few months ago."

As Amy paused in her story, Jonathon gave a quick nod toward Crystal, who had been writing furiously throughout this recital. He said with a grin, "Our reporter is already on the job!"

Crystal looked up with a jerk and glanced around the room self-consciously. "I hope you don't mind my taking a few notes now. This girl will be a human interest story all by herself."

"Of course we don't mind, Crystal," Amy said kindly. "I'm sure you'll get to know Sunny well while you're here. And then you'll understand, as I now do, why everyone's always called her Sunny. She's like a pretty little angel, so sweet and always smiling. But there's something very fragile about her also, and I just hope that everything will go well for her here. But, enough of that. We must not keep you too long, Crystal. Have you seen your room yet?"

"Yes. It will be more than adequate, thank you, Mrs. Anderson. I am just *so* pleased to be able to stay here in the house. I have been trying to persuade Mr. Logan to let me pay room and board, but..."

"Nonsense!" Tom cut in. "You will be working for your keep, and, believe me, the article you will be publishing will be worth more to us than any..."

At that moment the door flew open and Sara burst into the room shouting, "I will *not* share my room with that... that *half-breed*!"

She stopped midway into the room, and turned crimson as she realized that the office was filled with people. The others sat in stunned silence until Sam spoke up acidly, "I see that you still haven't learned to knock!"

Sara looked wildly around the room and stammered, "I... I'm sorry. I... I didn't know..."

She had started to turn and run from the room when Amy's icy voice halted her in mid step. "*Sara!* Sara, I want you to meet Crystal Atoka. She is here to write a feature story about The Refuge and will be living here in the house for the next few weeks. Crystal, this is Sara Franklin."

Sara turned slowly to look at Crystal, who stood and greeted her politely. "Hello, Miss Franklin."

Sara's eyes widened as she gazed at the beautiful young Native American standing proudly before her. "H-- Hi! Uh, I..."

And then she saw the same story from *Mainstream* that she'd carried with her all the way from Montana, lying on the desk where the group had been discussing it earlier. Her eyes fastened on the small portrait of the author, and then flew back to Crystal's face. "You... you're... you wrote that?" She asked haltingly as she pointed to the open magazine.

Crystal nodded, and then Amy stood and interrupted, "You may go now, Sara. I'm sure that you'll have an opportunity to get to know Crystal later."

Sara gulped. "Yeah. I... I'm s-sorry..." And then she raced for the door.

Twenty minutes later when the meeting ended and the group emerged into the hallway Sara was waiting in the shadows. "Miss... Miss Crystal, could I talk to you just for a moment?"

"Of course." Crystal sent a questioning glance toward Amy, who pointed to the parlor door, where the two of them could have some privacy. Then she followed the young redhead into the room and quietly closed the door.

Sara lifted her hand, in which she clutched her well-worn copy of *Mainstream*. "Miss Crystal, I just wanted you to know, I found this story in the back seat of a taxi in Helena, Montana, as I sat there, trying to get the courage to go inside an abortion clinic and let them kill my baby. As I read your words, I realized that I couldn't do it, that I must find this place, even though it was nearly halfway across the country from where I lived." She laid her hand on her bulging stomach and continued candidly, "This baby lives because of that story."

Tears jumped unbidden to Crystal's eyes as she remembered Tom Logan's words of last summer, "If one young woman chooses life for her unborn child as a result of the article you are about to publish, you *will* have made a difference!"

"Thank you for telling me, Miss Franklin. You can't pay a higher compliment to a journalist than that."

"And I... I didn't mean what I said in there," Sara stammered with embarrassment. "That was... was *awful*, and I'm sorry..."

"Sara, I don't believe anyone who hasn't experienced it can understand how it feels to be discriminated against, to be *hated*, even, because of something they have no control over, such as race or color. I truly hope that you will go back to your room and make every effort possible to see your new roommate as a human being such as yourself, a creation of God, a young woman who faces the same problems and has the same feelings and emotions that you have. Will you do that? For me?"

"Yes. Yes, I will," Sara answered solemnly. "I promise."

Crystal settled into her new environment with a minimum of fuss. Amy had apologized for giving her a room in the nursery wing, hoping, she said, that little Megan wouldn't awaken her when she cried in the night. But Crystal found herself immediately and completely captivated by the young miss, and she and Gretta hit it off from the very beginning. What an amazing courage it must take, Crystal confided with envy, to face the world alone with an infant to care for! But Gretta had shrugged it off with a smile, saying earnestly, "I could never have done it without Miss Amy and Mr. Tom. They made it possible for me to go to beauty school so that I can now earn my own way, and they—everyone here—has helped so much with Megan. I'll never in my whole life be able to repay them!"

And, gradually, Crystal gained the trust of the other girls as well, even though she was from the "skinny side of the house," as they laughingly called it, and they all continued to grow "fatter and fatter!" Sunny was all Amy had said she would be, bringing joy with her like an ever-present shadow. She had a tiny heart-shaped face with huge almond eyes. Her mouth seemed a bit large, but was perpetually curved into a joyful smile. It was only after she had watched the girl for some time that Crystal was able to detect the deep pain in her eyes, whether from a physical source or from the grievous loss of her young husband, she did not know.

And, Crystal realized as she observed and made notes and watched quietly from the sidelines, Sara also had seen the elusive suffering that Sunny tried so hard to mask. Thankfully, she had responded to it with a gentleness that surprised them all. As the days marched past, Sara seemed finally to come into her own. It was almost as if by willing herself to see Sunny as an equal that she was able to open her eyes to a new world around her. Those surface qualities that had seemed so important among her wealthy peers were now just so much dust in the wind.

An unusually strong bond began to form between Sara and Sunny. One that went far beyond the normal relationship between roommates. They were soon inseparable, and Crystal wondered if Sara had found the sister she had never had.

But there was something more. Sara, who was strong and healthy, apparently sensed in her friend a lack of strength—not weakness, really, but a physical frailty that brought to the surface her own childhood tendencies to care for anything that was hurt or broken. And so she became Sunny's protector of sorts, and in doing so, she began to emerge, for the first time, as a vital part of the group. Instead of shying away from her and her unpredictable temper as they had in the past, the girls now turned to her as their undisputed leader.

And through it all, Crystal observed and listened and enjoyed every facet of her new life at The Refuge. Most of all, she wrote, documenting emotional insights into the hearts of these young women—the fears and the hopes and the dreams that lie in the hearts of every girl everywhere, with one exception. These young ladies all carried a second life within them that would forever alter the course that they had set out upon.

It was in the midst of this whirlwind of laughter and tears, of highs and lows, of sudden bursts of energy followed by deep lethargy, of sharp voices raised in anger only to be dissolved moments later by a smile and a hug, that Crystal found a happiness she had never before known.

Sunny slipped quietly from her bed and tiptoed through the early morning silence to the door, and then moved quickly down the hallway to the bathroom where she was violently sick. When her retching finally subsided, she let her head rest on the cold hardness of the toilet bowl, willing her erratically beating heart to slow and the pain in her chest to ease.

"I thought I would find you here." Sara's sympathetic voice brought Sunny's head up with a jerk. "Let me help you."

Sara slipped one strong arm around Sunny's slight frame and helped her to her feet as she bathed the girl's flushed face with the cool wet washcloth she held in her other hand. "Thank you, Sara," Sunny whispered. "I didn't mean to wake you."

"I just can't understand why you're still battling with morning sickness after all these months when I hardly noticed anything at all, even at first! I sometimes wonder if this baby of yours will be worth all the misery he's put you through."

Sara had spoken lightly, in a joking manner, but Sunny's denial was quick. "No! Don't even think such a thing! My baby is worth *everything...*"

"Okay, okay. I didn't mean anything," Sara answered apologetically. "But have you thought about what you will do? I mean, after the baby comes. Will you go back to live with your sister?"

"No." Sunny spoke with certainty. "I will never go back there. Josie wrote me that her husband is back, and he's mean and hateful. He... he hit me once when I was there before, and when he gets drunk, which is most of the time, he slaps Josie and the kids around somethin' awful. I would never allow my child to live in that house!"

"I worry about you Sunny. All alone and so frail! It would be hard enough by yourself, but with a baby to care for and to support... Well, sometimes I honestly think you would have been better off to have had an abortion. After all, you were just barely pregnant when your Noah was killed..."

Weak as she was, Sunny's eyes flashed with anger. "Never would I have even considered killing this baby! Noah's child, that he was so proud and happy about! *Never!!* My grandma used to tell us that the Montgomery's always took care of their own, never shirking their responsibilities no matter how tough things got. I will give birth to this child even if..."

Sunny left the thought unfinished as the two of them trudged slowly back to their room. Once inside the door, Sunny turned to Sara and spoke with some urgency, "Sara, will you promise me to take care of my baby if something happens to me?"

"Don't be silly," Sara answered, shocked by her friend's words. "Nothing's going to happen to you! Once you have this baby all of this nasty business will be over with, and you'll be fine."

"Just promise me, Sara. *Please!*"

"Well, sure. I promise. I'll help you in any way I can. In fact, I think you should stay right here with me after the baby's born, so I can help you look after him." Sara grinned at Sunny with genuine fondness. "We'll stick together, you and me, okay?"

"Okay!" Sunny replied. And she smiled, as she always did, to hide the pain that once again sliced through her heart with blinding fury.

Amy stared out at the cold gray November day without really seeing the heavy dark clouds or the wind-whipped trees that were now stripped and naked. Her heart matched the dreariness of the morning as she recalled Dr. Cameron's words of the day before. He had stopped by her office after his weekly visit to the girls, a slight frown troubling his usually calm countenance.

"I'm worried about the Lawrence girl," he had said with no preamble. "I believe she has a degenerative heart condition. She tries valiantly to hide her pain behind that smile of hers, but I imagine she suffers a great deal. And I'm deeply concerned about the birth of this child."

"Do you think she's in danger?" Amy had asked with concern.

"I'm not sure. I wish there was some medical history on her, but she maintains that they were too poor for doctors, and she's probably telling the truth. Amy, I want to call in a cardiologist to have a look at her. But we may be too late. Because her heart may not stand the strain of childbirth, and I'm afraid we won't be able to put her under anesthetic for a Caesarean. In any case, this birth *must* take place at the hospital. We cannot take any unnecessary chances."

Amy turned now from the stark scene beyond her window and began to pace the confines of her little office, deeply saddened that such a sweet child had suffered so much. Not only the physical pain that Sunny undoubtedly faced on a daily basis, but also the loss of her young husband, and her parents before that. Was this child to fight so bravely through all of that only to lose her own life in childbirth? It was more than Amy could bear to think about.

She turned her thoughts to the young girl that would be arriving at any minute. Scarcely a happier subject! For the conversation she'd had with Charlotte's father a week ago had been anything but pleasant. Such scathing criticism for his weak, erring daughter! When Amy had learned that he was the minister of the small country church in a rural community south of Nashville where they lived, she had been appalled.

A sharp knock announced their arrival. Amy forced a smile to her lips and opened the door to a stern-faced man in an ill-fitting suit of shiny black gabardine. He met her smile with a scowl and interrupted her warm greeting with an abrupt introduction. "I'm Abner Brown and this here's my wife, Cora." He indicated the meek, sad-eyed woman that stood just behind him. A skinny young girl, whose head was ducked in embarrassment so that her long straggly blond hair covered her face, and who was most certainly his daughter, he ignored completely.

"Please, come in," Amy invited. As the girl stepped hesitantly through the doorway behind her parents, Amy laid a hand gently on her arm. "You must be Charlotte. Welcome to The Refuge."

Amy caught a quick glimpse of wide, dark eyes and a tiny tremulous smile before the unruly strands of hair covered them again. Charlotte was dressed cheaply, in a shapeless gray coat that covered an equally shapeless dress of dull blue. The girl was stick thin, with the obvious bulge at her waist the only curve she possessed.

Amy turned to Mr. Brown, who was saying in a harsh, hurtful voice, "Well, thar she is. She's all yours now, jist see thet she behaves. She's brought enough shame on my family and my church to last a lifetime. We want nothin' more to do with her."

"We'll take good care of Charlotte, Mr. Brown. And we will keep in touch with you and Mrs. Brown, to let you know how she's doing. When it's time for the baby to arrive, we'll give you a call. If you want to be here with your daughter when she gives birth, Mrs. Brown, we would be delighted to have you."

Amy looked pointedly at Cora Brown, who had spoken not a word. The woman flushed painfully, as her eyes darted uncomfortably toward her husband. "Well, I.."

"We're not interested in the child, Miz Anderson," Abner Brown cut in rudely. "You ken find somebody who'll take it off yer hands, I reckon. Anyways, we got to git goin' now. It's a fer piece on home."

And without so much as a glance at his daughter, the Rev. Abner Brown pointed his wife toward the door and the two of them vanished into the dark day. Amy realized after they were gone that she had been the only one who had referred to their child by her name.

Turning to Charlotte, she placed both hands on the child's shoulders. "We are very pleased to have you, Charlotte. If you will come with me, I will show you around our house and introduce you to the other girls. You will have a room to yourself until someone new arrives, and at that time you will have a roommate, just like everyone else."

Charlotte gave a small, shy smile, and Amy could not repress the urge to smooth the girl's hair back from her eyes. She pointed toward the stairs and took Charlotte's hand. "Are you ready?"

"I guess so." They were the first words the girl had spoken, and Amy gave her a warm smile. As they reached the top of the stairs, the telephone began to ring, and a moment later Helen called Amy to the phone.

"Tell them I'll be right there," Amy responded, and then looked at the young lady beside her, standing in the empty hallway. She made a quick decision and called out, "Sara! Can you come here for a moment?"

Sara appeared from a room down the hall, and Amy continued, "Sara, I have a phone call. This is Charlotte, and she has just arrived. Could you show her around and introduce her to the other girls?"

"Sure," Sara agreed, and, as Amy rushed back down the stairs, leaving them alone, she turned to the girl beside her. "What's your name again?"

"M'name is CharlotteMarieBrown," she answered in a small, shy voice, running the words together in the way southerners often do.

Doors up and down the hallway began to open as Sara called out, "Come here, everyone. Ah'd like y'all ta meet CharlotteMarieBrown," she said, in a perfect imitation of the other girl's distinctive drawl.

Charlotte turned beet red at the obvious parody of her speech. Sunny, seeing the girl's distress, immediately placed an arm around her and turned on Sara with vengeance. "Sara! Shame on you! You've hurt Miz Charlotte's feelings!" And as Sara looked on with shame-faced apology, Sunny proceeded to make the introductions.

Then, with an impish grin, Sara again took charge. "Hey, Charlie Brown, I'm sorry. Let's take a tour of the palace, shall we?"

Charlotte took in the circle of friendly faces around her and suddenly smiled. Charlie Brown! The more she thought about it, the more she liked it. Sara reached a hand to her, and she took it gratefully. It was warm and strong, and she felt oddly protected. It occurred to her that she was more at home in this strange new place than she had been *anywhere* for such a long time!

Sara snapped her American History book shut with such a violent crack that Sunny jumped with fright. Pushing her chair back from the desk where she had been studying, Sara jumped to her feet, grinning at Sunny's wide-eyed stare.

"Wake up, sleepy head!" Sara drawled to her friend who had been nodding over some dippy romance novel. It was the girls' study time, but Sunny had quit school long ago and had no interest in returning to it now. "It's too nice outside to stay cooped up in here," Sara grumbled. "Let's go for a walk, okay?"

"Sure," Sunny responded with her ever-present smile. She laid her book aside and rolled off the bed to follow Sara out the door and down the stairs.

It was one of those glorious Indian summer days that sneak into the damp chill of late autumn with an unexpected reprieve, and the girls walked out the back door and into the welcome sunshine of a perfect afternoon. They wandered aimlessly down the path toward the thick wooded area that followed their meandering little stream.

"This is the kind of day that Noah liked best," Sunny reminisced softly. "He always loved being outside..."

Sara looked at her companion with understanding. "You still miss him, don't you?"

"Yes. He was always kind, always thinking of me first."

"I guess he must have been a lot like Ross," Sara mused without thinking.

Sunny looked up quickly. "Is Ross your boyfriend?"

"I... no, not really... just a friend, I guess..."

"Come on, Sara," Sunny said with a twinkle in her eye. "*Someone* put that baby in there." She patted Sara's bulging tummy with a giggle and asked, "Could it have been this Ross?"

Sara blushed. "Yeah, but..."

"So are you gonna' marry him?" Sunny persisted.

Sara shook her head. "He... he doesn't know..."

"Ya mean you haven't even *told* him about his baby?" Sunny asked, aghast. "Why *not?*"

"I... I don't know. Nobody knows about it except my father and my stepmother. They would be furious if anyone found out. But I might tell Ross someday, I guess," Sara finished lamely.

"Well, if your Ross is anythin' like my Noah, he'd want to know, that's for sure. It's wrong to keep somethin' as important as that from him, Sara!"

Sara nodded with reluctant agreement. They had reached the busy little creek bed and Sara suddenly brightened. "Let's follow this stream and see where it goes!" she said, grabbing Sunny's hand with excitement.

Sunny looked at the tangled growth along the bank of the stream and hesitated. "Are you sure you wanna' do that? What if there's snakes or..."

Sara laughed merrily. "Come on, silly. I used to go explorin' with Mama all the time back home, and in lots bigger forests than this one!"

"Did you and your Mama ever get lost?" Sunny asked doubtfully.

"Sure. But we always found our way back home!" Sara answered with a careless grin.

Sara picked her way through the brush and trees and rocks that bordered the stream, breaking a path for Sunny who followed dubiously in her wake. A frog, startled by their approach, made a sudden leap and landed in the water with a loud plop. Sunny cried out in startled fright.

"Wh-what was *that*?" she stammered, clutching at Sara's arm fearfully.

Sara looked at her friend with some amusement, then suddenly pointed toward the thick tangle of trees ahead of them and whispered with mock alarm, "It's a *bear*! See it?"

Sunny gave the dark thicket a quick glance, her eyes wide with fear, and then turned abruptly back in the direction they had come from. Sara grabbed her friend's arm as her laughter pealed merrily through the small forest, scaring up a rabbit in the process. The sudden flight of the animal through dead leaves and bushes only heightened Sunny's alarm, and she cried out again.

Realizing Sunny's terror was very real, Sara slipped an arm around the startled girl and explained, "It was only a silly 'ole frog, jumping into the water, Sunny, and then we scared up a cottontail. There's no bears in this part of the country. I was just kiddin' you!"

Sunny finally relaxed and managed a shaky smile. "Are you sure? I... I guess I'm not much of an explorer. When I was growin' up in my grandma's little house, the only place we had outside was in the street!"

Sara stared at Sunny, trying to imagine the life she must have lived. "I'm sorry, Sunny. You see, I grew up wandering the forests and the mountains that surrounded our home in Montana. Mama and I rode our horses nearly every day, explorin' the animal trails and caves along Rattlesnake Creek. When she died I rode by myself, but it was never the same again..."

Sunny heard the sorrow and loneliness in Sara's voice and spoke softly, "Sara, you're so lucky..."

"*Lucky*?! How can you say that?" Sara exploded. "When my Mama died I lost my very best friend..."

"Oh no! Not lucky that you *lost* your Mama!" Sunny hurried to explain. "But lucky that you *had* a Mama like that! All the things you did, the places you've been... and the *memories*! I... I can't even remember my Mama."

Sara stared at her companion with new understanding. "You've lost everyone, haven't you? Your Mama and then your Daddy, your Grandma... and Noah, too! You must think I'm just a selfish, spoiled brat..."

"No, Sara, I don't think that at all. And I don't mean to sound like a cry baby. I have so many things to be thankful for..."

An unexpected gust of wind whipped through the trees and Sunny shivered, looking around with sudden awareness. "It must be gettin' late! Don't you think we oughta' be gettin' back to the house?"

"Probably so. I forgot all about the time! Are you cold?" Sara realized that the sun was quickly losing its afternoon warmth, and wished she'd thought to bring jackets. She turned and started hurriedly back along the path they'd broken.

"No, I'm all right," Sunny replied, panting in an effort to keep up with Sara's long strides. "We're not gonna' get lost, are we?"

"Not as long as we follow the stream," Sara called back over her shoulder. She moved as quickly as she could through the rough terrain, and then halted abruptly at a cry from Sunny.

She turned to see the girl crouched in the weeds, obviously in pain, her face pale. Sara ran quickly and knelt beside her. "*Sunny*! Are you all right? Is it your baby?"

"No," Sunny gasped weakly. "My chest... I... I just need to rest a minute..."

Sara looked around her, knowing that darkness would come quickly at this time of year. As soon as Sunny had caught her breath, she helped the girl up and, grasping her arm tightly, she led her slowly toward the path to the house. When they caught sight of the new chapel they knew they would soon be home.

"Do you suppose we could stop here for a few minutes?" Sunny asked breathlessly. Sara glanced at the unfinished building.

"Sure. Are you gonna' be okay?" She asked with concern.

Sunny nodded. They approached the entrance, pushed open the still unpainted door and looked inside. It was dusty, and cluttered with ladders and tools, but Sara noticed a couple of folding chairs along the back wall and guided Sunny in that direction.

Sara apologized contritely, "I'm sorry, Sunny. I shouldn't have gone so far! But your chest... what happened? Are you sick...?"

"No, not really. I mean... it's nothing new. I... I've had somethin' wrong with my heart for a long time... ever since I was a child. I usually don't even think about it..."

"You need to go to a doctor, Sunny!" Sara exclaimed with fervor.

"Yeah, I know. Doc Cameron said that, too. He's makin' me go see some fancy heart doctor next month. I don't want to, but I guess..." Sunny let her words trail off and leaned back, resting her head against the wall behind her.

Sara wandered aimlessly toward the front of the room, stepping carefully over and around pieces of trim board and buckets of paint. Late afternoon sunshine streamed through the large front window, providing both light and warmth. She contemplated her friend's words. How could she have been so stupid, dragging Sunny through the woods when she should have been resting comfortably in their room! She moved back to the girl's side, and saw with alarm that Sunny now sat with her eyes closed and her head bowed.

"Sunny! Are you all right?" she asked once again.

Sunny opened her eyes and smiled broadly, as she slowly came to her feet. "Yeah, I'm fine now. I was just thankin' the good Lord for givin' me a friend like you."

Sara stared at the other girl with wonder, tears clogging her throat. She, who had never before in her life been at a loss for words, was now quite speechless. And so she flung her arms around her very good friend, and gave her a huge hug.

As it turned out, Sunny never made it in to see Dr. Thurman, the cardiologist. The very busy doctor had finally agreed to squeeze Sunny into his full schedule on Monday morning, December 7. On the evening of December 6, at exactly 6:17, Sunny's water broke and an ordinary Sunday evening meal became one that none of them would ever forget.

Crystal remembered the time later because she had just glanced at the clock, and her reporter's trained mind had locked that little tidbit of information away, just in case. They were enjoying the last of their Thanksgiving turkey, which Helen had thoughtfully sliced and stuck away in the freezer for a cold, blustery evening like the one they were having, when Sunny rose from the table to pour herself another glass of milk. Her sudden gasp reached Sara, who was sitting next to her, as usual.

"Sunny! Are you okay?" Sara looked anxiously at her friend.

"Oh, my!" Sunny breathed, looking at the puddle at her feet.

Amy was up and at the girl's side in an instant. "It's okay, Sunny. Your water has broken. We'll call Dr. Cameron and get you to the hospital."

"The *hospital*?" Sara asked with sudden fear. "Why is she going to the hospital? Isn't she going to have her baby here, like the rest of us?"

Amy had been dreading this moment, had hoped to discuss it quietly with the girls before Sunny's labor began, but it was too late now. The child, who wasn't expected until early January, was apparently intent upon making an early appearance.

She turned to Sara and spoke quietly. "Dr. Cameron has asked that we bring Sunny into the hospital because she's had some health problems. He feels that everything will go smoother with a full staff on hand to help if need be. Now, will you go upstairs and pack a bag for Sunny to take with her?"

But Sara was shaking her head and clutching Sunny's arm with both hands. "If she goes, then *I* go! I'm her birth partner, and I'm not letting her do this alone!" The girl's voice was strident with determination, her wide eyes betraying her fear.

Amy wished with all her might that Sam was there with them at this moment. Sam seemed able to cope with this headstrong girl better than any of them, but she had been called to Wichita where her Aunt Ella lay dying. Amy was instantly ashamed of herself—Sam was where she was needed most right now, and she, herself, could certainly cope with a seventeen-year-old girl, no matter how stubborn!

Crystal, who had stayed silently in her place across the table, stood now and moved to where Sara still hovered over Sunny. "Let me help you, Sara," she said in a quiet calm voice that was nevertheless authoritative. "We can gather Sunny's things while Miss Amy calls the hospital. Maybe Dr. Cameron will let you attend to Sunny there."

Crystal's eyes met Amy's questioningly, hoping she hadn't overstepped her boundaries. Amy nodded quickly, obviously relieved that Crystal had taken charge. "Please bring some dry things down for Sunny to put on, as well as some towels, and I'll call Dr. Cameron. Sunny, you just sit where you are for now and try to relax. And the rest of you can help Helen clear the table."

As Crystal and Sara moved toward the stairway, Amy hurried to her office to call Dr. Cameron. Her next call went to Tom, who was, thankfully, at home. And then, after a moment's hesitation, she dialed Jonathon's number. She couldn't stop thinking of Dr. Cameron's words of warning, and she knew that she would feel better if she were surrounded by others who cared.

Sunny was feeling only a dull ache in her back, she said with a smile. The pain had started early that morning, she added, but she'd chosen to ignore it. They loaded her into the car, and, at the last minute, Crystal asked hesitantly if she might accompany them.

"Of course! You *need* to be there, actually," Amy answered, delighted to have a woman's company for the hours ahead that were sure to be long. Sara, who had stuck to Sunny's side like a burr, would be the only outsider allowed in the birthing room, Dr. Cameron had informed her, and then only if things went well. But the doctor knew that Sunny needed the support and encouragement of a birthing partner, and he had been impressed by Sara's sturdy strength and avid loyalty to her friend.

Tom and Jonathon were already visiting quietly in the hospital's maternity wing waiting room when the group arrived. Amy gave Sunny a quick hug, and turned to Sara with another. She then watched helplessly as they disappeared down the long hall, surrounded by white-jacketed nurses.

Sara pushed Sunny's wheelchair with a mixture of grown-up pride and little-girl anxiety. She'd shied away from hospitals since that horror-filled night when they'd whisked her mother away from her so many years ago. But this would be different. Sunny hadn't been struck with some mysterious ailment—she was only pregnant and about to deliver the baby she wanted so badly. Sara was determined to make things as easy as possible for this girl who looked so tiny and so fragile, and who never complained for a minute about anything.

By the time the nurses finished with their "prep," as they called it, Sunny was feeling some strong discomfort. Her contractions seemed to be concentrated low in her back, and Sara helped her to her side, and then massaged tirelessly, applying strong pressure when she felt Sunny tense with pain. It was several long hours later before the medical team finally put Sunny's feet into stirrups and urged to her to push with the pains. Sara's own back and legs now ached with fatigue, and one of the nurses asked kindly if she didn't want to take a break. She was, after all, pregnant with her own child, and it wouldn't do to get herself overly exhausted.

But Sara stayed by her friend's side with dogged determination. She remembered the Lamaze exercises they'd practiced and chanted over and over, "Breathe, breathe, push, push, push— relax, that's a good girl, you're doing just fine, just keep hanging in there!" But Sunny's strength was failing fast, and the team of doctors, which now also included Dr. Thurman, looked anything but pleased. Sara heard low voices, a murmured question, the mention of Caesarean, and then saw Dr. Thurman's quick but decisive shake of his head.

The atmosphere in the room was tense and hushed. Sunny's skin was nearly as pale as her own, Sara saw with dismay, and her cries of pain were now hardly more than whimpers. Dr. Cameron frantically massaged and pushed and reached for the infant's tiny body, using his own strength in every way possible to help the struggling girl. And then, after a particularly long and strenuous contraction, he glanced at the monitor that told the story of Sunny's erratic and weakening heartbeat and made a quick gesture to the nurse at his side. She laid a hand on Sara's arm.

"I'm sorry. You need to come with me now," she said gently.

Sara straightened her tired back with a jerk and turned wild eyes on the nurse. "*No!* I *can't* leave her now! *I promised*!!"

But Dr. Cameron flashed her a stern look, and the nurse quietly but firmly propelled her toward the door. All of the terror of her mother's death came crashing down upon Sara in that moment, and she suddenly tore her arm from the nurse's grasp and turned back toward Sunny's semiconscious form.

"*You can't let her die!*" she screamed hysterically. "*You've got to DO something! PLEASE!! DON'T LET HER DIE!!*"

And then nurses were on each side of her, forcing her to leave the room. She was sobbing uncontrollably, fighting those around her, loving Sunny with every ounce of strength in her young body. She felt the prick of a needle touch her upper arm and then drive home. As the door swung shut behind her, she heard a brisk command, "Get her to surgery now, or we're gonna' lose the child!"

"Come with me, miss. We'll find you a place to sit down," a kind voice murmured in Sara's ear. And then Sunny's bed came crashing through double doors, surrounded by the doctors and all of the medical paraphernalia that monitored and anesthetized and nourished the small form that lay motionless upon it. Sara watched in stunned silence as her dearest friend disappeared from view, and then her legs buckled beneath her and she slumped, unconscious, into the nurse's experienced embrace.

She opened her eyes some minutes later to see Amy's concerned face hovering over her, a cool, wet cloth on her forehead. She stared around her, disoriented for a moment, and then, remembering, she jerked upright, pushing Amy's arm abruptly away.

"Where is she? They took her away!! *What have they done with Sunny?*"

She jumped to her feet, as if to go in search of her friend, just as Dr. Cameron appeared in the doorway of the waiting room. He was gray with exhaustion and failure.

"We couldn't save her," he said in a low, defeated voice. "But her son will be fine, I think. We're watching him closely. There were some breathing problems at first, but he seems to be stabilizing nicely."

He then turned to Sara and laid a gentle hand on her shoulder. "I'm sorry, young lady. You were magnificent."

But the girl barely heard his words. She shook her head vehemently, tears coursing down her cheeks. "NOOOO—no, no, no!" she wailed with inconsolable grief. "They didn't even let me tell her good-bye! Just... just like Mama..."

Jonathon reached for her with compassion. "Sara, you did everything possible, you and the doctors and everyone. But Sunny's heart was weak, and she just couldn't do it. We need to think about her son now, to pray that he will..."

"And what good will prayer do *now*?" Sara flung tearfully. "Where was your God when Sunny needed Him? What kind of God would take a baby's mother and leave him an orphan? *I WANT NOTHING TO DO WITH A GOD LIKE THAT!!*"

Sara turned and ran blindly out into a cold December dawn, her world once more shattered by death.

Crystal hurried into Amy's office later that morning, unsure of why she had been included in their "summit meeting," as Tom had called it. The others were already there, Tom seated at the desk, and Amy and Jonathon in two of the three chairs gathered close. Crystal quickly took the third chair, noticing at once the subdued atmosphere in the room.

Tom glanced up with a slight frown and asked, his question obviously directed at Amy, "Have you heard from Sam?"

"Yes. She called yesterday to say that her Aunt Ella had lived only a couple of hours after she arrived there. The funeral is tomorrow. She had planned to come home and then return for the funeral, but Ella's sons begged her to stay and help with the arrangements. She should be home tomorrow evening some time."

Tom nodded, and then turned to more important matters. "I called you all here so that we could make some decisions concerning Sunny's death, and the child that we now have in our care. I understand that some of the arrangements for Sunny's burial have already been made."

Jonathon answered with an affirmative shake of his head. "Yes, her body has been taken to a local mortuary. I finally reached her sister in Chicago, who apparently has no money, and, while she expressed sorrow at her sister's death, she has pretty much left everything to us. She did ask that we send the girl back to Chicago for burial in the family cemetery, but we will need to bear most of the expense."

"Are we going to have a service here?" Amy asked quietly.

"I really believe we should," Jonathon answered reluctantly. "The girls, especially Sara, need that kind of closure, even though they may wish to avoid it. I would suggest a quiet service at the mortuary."

Again Tom nodded his agreement, and then looked at Crystal. "I asked you to join us today, Crystal, because we may very well receive some bad publicity concerning this unfortunate affair, and I would like your input. Only a brief announcement of Sunny's death will appear in today's paper, but some avid reporter will sooner or later realize that she was in our care and try to make something of it. How do you feel we can best avoid that?"

Crystal mulled the situation over for several seconds. "Well, Tom, I have always been of the opinion that one can best fight fire with fire. What if I were to write an honest and compassionate account of what has happened and take it to the local paper before anyone else gets a chance at it? After all, you have nothing to hide, since she was put under the best care available, and every precaution possible was taken."

"Yes! I like that idea," Amy said. "I am so thankful that Dr. Cameron insisted that she be taken to the hospital for the birth. Now no one can infer that her death resulted from second rate facilities or limited medical personnel on hand."

"Yes, I agree," Tom said. "Crystal, if you will put something together and take it in today, I would appreciate it very much. But you probably should mention something about the baby, also. Do we know where we stand there?"

Amy shook her head. "Sunny left no explicit instructions except that she did *not* want her baby in the care of her sister. She was so adamant about it that I took the precaution of having her sign a statement to that effect. And what a good thing, now that matters have turned out as they have. For, to my knowledge, her sister is her only family. At this point, I would say that the baby is completely in our care."

"Okay, just handle it as tactfully as you can, Crystal," Tom added. "I'm sure we can find adoptive parents for the child who will give him a good home."

Jonathon turned to Amy and asked with concern, "How are the girls handling this situation, Mom?"

"Most of them seem to be doing pretty well, but Sara is inconsolable," she answered sadly. "She has taken to her bed and refuses to see or to talk to anyone. We must do something to lift her spirits and get her up and about or she is going to endanger her own health and that of her baby. I just wish Sam was here!"

"Yes," Jonathon answered reflectively. "I think I will try to have a talk with her as soon as we have finished here. It occurs to me that we have our chapel all but ready for use, and it seems the perfect place for a special occasion once the sad business of Sunny's funeral is behind us."

"Oh, yes," Amy put in with growing excitement. "Tom, do you think we could have it ready for next Sunday's service?"

"I'll see to it," Tom answered emphatically. "And I think it should be something special, as Jonathon has suggested. What about a dedication ceremony? We could invite others from the community who may be suddenly curious about the work we're doing here. Do you think it would be appropriate for Crystal to include something about it in her story?"

"Yes!" Jonathon and Amy answered in unison. "Oh, Tom," Amy continued, "this is just what the girls need right now! And let's do something different—maybe a guest speaker, or..."

"I agree," Jonathon interrupted. "Do you think we could persuade your son to come and speak for the service, Tom? Doesn't he work with underprivileged kids somewhere?"

Tom smiled, obviously pleased at the suggestion. "Yes, he does, but his kids are a football team in an inner city school in Kansas City. Kind of a far cry from a group of pregnant girls!" he offered with a chuckle.

Crystal remembered the family portrait she had seen last summer in Tom's office, and bits of information about Jenny's brother filtered into her mind. She spoke suddenly, as a thought occurred to her, "Didn't Jim turn down some big offer to take on this coaching job?"

"Yes, as a matter of fact, the NFL was expected to draft him," Tom answered with pride. "He had just graduated from Michigan, and was still flying high from all the division championships and victorious bowl games. He drove all the way to Chicago to see me and to discuss his future. We spent a long weekend talking and praying about it, and he went back to announce that he would accept the coaching job at a school that could barely afford to pay him enough to live on instead of the big money and notoriety of the NFL. I was never more proud of anyone in my life!"

"I think you should ask him," Crystal said with approval. "He just might be able to offer the spark these girls need right now!"

"Yes, Tom, *do* ask him!" Amy urged. "And what about music? Could we do something special, do you think? We don't have a piano or anything, but maybe we could..."

"I think we should ask Ben to sing!" Jonathon blurted out suddenly.

Crystal gaped in surprise. Was he referring to Ben, the gardener? She saw a doubtful look cross Amy's face. But Tom responded with enthusiasm. "That's an excellent idea! It's time for Ben to crawl out of his shell and get back to his music."

Jonathon was nodding wholeheartedly. "Absolutely! I'll ask him today!"

And so the meeting ended on a much lighter note than it had begun. Crystal rushed to her room to write an article for the local newspaper and Jonathon headed out to see Ben, whistling as he went. A short time later, Jonathon emerged from the little cottage that Ben called home with a big smile on his face. He came into the house and headed straight up the stairs, calling as he climbed, "Beware! A man is about to invade your quarters!"

Jonathon found Sara's closed door and knocked sharply. He heard a muffled moan from inside and hollered through the door, "Sara! Get up and get dressed! I've got something to show you. And put on something warm. We're going outside!"

Inside the bedroom Sara looked sourly at the door. What in the world did Jonathon want with her? She called back insolently, "I don't want to get up!"

"I'll give you ten minutes! If you're not dressed and downstairs by then, I'm coming in after you!" Jonathon shouted relentlessly. And with that he turned and stomped noisily back down the staircase.

Sara thought about waiting to see if he really would break through her door, but curiosity got the better of her, and she crawled from her untidy bed and pulled on warm sweats and the biggest sweatshirt she could find. She couldn't believe how big her belly was getting! She looked in the mirror with a frown and quickly ran a comb through her tangled hair.

When she reached Jonathon's side a few minutes later, he turned with a grin and said with unmistakable mystery, "Come on. I've got a surprise for you!"

As he led her to the back door, he pointed at the rack of heavy coats. "Grab your coat," he ordered. "It's cold out there!"

And he wasn't kidding. The blast of wind that greeted them nearly took Sara's breath away. But it was oddly invigorating after the many hours she had hidden away in her room. The two of them hurried to Ben's door, and Jonathon knocked once, then pushed the door open. A chorus of yapping and whining reached Sara's ears, and she looked with wonder at Molly, Ben's faithful friend, who was surrounded by four—no, there were *five*—squirming, noisy puppies.

Sara dropped to her knees with a gasp. Soft wriggling bodies climbed all over her, touching her hands with warm, moist tongues. "Ben!" she squealed happily. "Why didn't you tell us you had puppies out here?"

"Well, I didn't want 'em to be a bother..." he said with a wide smile. "I've been busy buildin' a pen out back. Otherwise, the minute I let 'em outside, they'll be right in the middle of the flower beds!"

When Jonathon finally tore the girl away from the nest of puppies, he noticed that some color had returned to her wan face. "Let's go for a short walk!" he invited, and then asked, "Or is it too cold for you?"

"No, it's okay," she conceded.

They walked into the shelter of the trees, where they were somewhat protected from the icy wind, and on toward the new chapel. They chatted about the puppies and the fact that Christmas was only a couple of weeks away, and then Jonathon reached for the girl's hand and turned her to face him.

He spoke softly. "Sara, I know how much you loved Sunny, and how devastating her death has been for you. But I keep thinking about what you said about God. It's true that it is so much easier for us to believe in God when things are going well, but He teaches us many things through our pain and sorrow."

Sara stood with her head bowed, not speaking. Jonathon continued with compassion, "Sara, I just want you to promise me something."

The girl finally raised her eyes to his, and he saw her tears.

"Sara, will you do your best to look for some evidence of God in your life in this next week? Listen for Him to speak to you in some way, to give you some of the answers that you need so badly. Promise?"

She nodded sadly, and, without thinking, reached again for Jonathon's hand as they walked slowly back toward the house.

Helen hurried up the steps with a squalling baby cradled in the crook of her left arm, a warm bottle clutched in her right hand. She knocked twice, then pushed Sara's door open and unceremoniously entered the girl's room. She walked to the window and opened the shade, and the sudden onslaught of sound and light brought Sara out of sleep with an unpleasant jolt.

"Wha-at?" Sara blinked against the bright glare from the window, then ducked under her pillow in an effort to shut out the wailing of the child in Helen's arms.

But Helen grabbed the pillow away and said sternly, "No, you don't. Get up, Sara, and help us out a bit. This baby is ready for his breakfast, but the rest of us aren't going to get any if I don't get after it. I just plain don't have the time to sit down and feed a baby! And Miss Amy is plumb tuckered out. She's just heard from Sam again, and it seems she's to be gone for *another* night. Somethin' about her havin' to stay for the readin' of the will tomorrow. Maybe she'll inherit a fortune and we can hire some more help!"

Helen gave a short laugh as she placed the pillow against the head of the bed for Sara, who was struggling into an upright position. "And besides," Helen added with a note of gentleness, "Sunny loved you more 'en any of us. She'd want you to be carin' for her child, I reckon."

She bent to lay the hungry infant in Sara's lap and handed her the bottle of milk. "Here, put this in his mouth, quick!" she ordered with a grin.

Sara did as she was told, and was amazed at the tenacity of this tiny scrap of humanity as he began to suck greedily. She felt awkward and uncomfortable. He was so little! What if she dropped him or something! She opened her mouth to protest, but Helen had already disappeared down the stairs, and she was left to her own devices.

Sara squirmed until she had maneuvered herself into a better position on the bed, and then gingerly eased the infant up against her breast. Her arm just naturally curled around the soft, warm little bundle, and she felt a wide smile spread involuntarily across her face. He felt so *good*!

"Hey, little guy! You'd better slow down. Maybe you should burp or somethin'." She remembered that Gretta had always stopped in the middle of nursing Megan and placed her baby on her shoulder, patting her back until she gave a resounding belch.

Very carefully Sara removed the bottle, now surprisingly half empty, from the young man's mouth. He squirmed a bit in protest, but relaxed against her as she began to rub his tiny back. "You like that, don't you?" she whispered into one minuscule ear. He responded by stiffening his body momentarily and then releasing the most amazing belch she had ever heard. And from such a little guy! She giggled out loud.

He began to flail his tiny arms again and screwed up his face in the most awful frown. "Okay, okay," Sara crooned. "Here's some more milk. You're a regular little pig, aren't you?"

She felt oddly content as she gazed down at the suckling infant. She thought of Helen's words—'Sunny loved you more 'en any of us'—and a tear trickled down her face. And then she remembered Sunny's own words on that morning when she had insisted that Sara promise to care for her child. And she had promised, of course, but it hadn't occurred to her then that it might mean *this*! Maybe even *forever*. But she realized now that Sunny had indeed meant forever, if that became necessary.

She squared her shoulders with determination. If that was what Sunny wanted, then she would do it! She decided to have the child's crib brought here to her room today. She would take over now—after all, she no longer had a roommate. Who better to fill the empty spaces that Sunny had left, than Sunny's child!

Sara saw that the baby had relaxed his hold on the nipple and was now sleeping peacefully in her arms. She felt the glow of a maternal love spread throughout her body, and she bent to touch her lips to his sweet face and whispered, "I guess we'd better find you a suitable name, young mister! It will have to be Noah, of course, for the daddy you will never know. Let's see—Noah... how about Noah Franklin? Noah Franklin Lawrence!"

She smiled with the decision. Now, whatever happened in the future, he would always be part hers, would always carry her name.

Amy hurried to answer the jangling of the telephone in her office. It was amazing how much better a body felt after a good night's sleep! She hoped Sara wouldn't wear herself out caring for little Noah, but she knew that responsibility for the child had succeeded in rousing the grieving girl from her doldrums as nothing else could have. The flush of pride and motherly love had been apparent on Sara's face at breakfast this morning, even though she yawned several times as she ate.

Amy picked up the phone. "Hello?"

"Amy! How are you doing?" It was Sam! Amy grinned with fondness.

"I'm fine. I just hope you aren't calling to give me another excuse for staying away from here! I'm beginning to wonder if you're avoiding us!"

Sam laughed. "No, no. In fact, I can't wait to get back. And I'm so sorry that I had to be away at such a bad time for you. But I have the most astounding news!"

"What's happened?" Amy asked cautiously. Certainly Sam wasn't going to tell her of some event that would further prolong her return. She missed her so!

"Well, they read Aunt Ella's will this morning. And guess what! Aunt Ella has left her antique organ to *me*! Do you remember it?"

"How could I forget it? That organ caught my eye the minute we walked into your aunt's living room that night. It is one of the most beautiful pieces I have ever seen. And it's to be *yours*?"

Sam laughed again. "It appears that it is. But whatever will I do with it, Amy?"

Amy let her mind go back to the shopping trip she and Sam had taken to Wichita more than two years ago. Tom had just arrived in Bartlesville after four long years of silence and had called to ask her for a dinner date. All of the excitement of that time rushed back to her. Sam had insisted on the trip to Wichita "to get you a gorgeous new outfit," with an overnight stay at Aunt Ella's included in the plans. What fun they'd had! And Aunt Ella had been a sweet and gracious host, opening her beautiful home to them happily. The wonderful old organ that Sam had just inherited had stood proudly amongst the woman's other fine heirlooms, and Amy had thought upon seeing it that it really belonged in some church where its music would bring joy and peace to others.

She let her thoughts move to the little chapel in their woods where a very special service was being planned for this Sunday. "Oh, Sam!" she said with glee. "We have just the place for it!"

Amy hurried down the well-worn path that led to the chapel, her arms heavily laden with a huge Christmas wreath, a hammer and nails, and some fresh pine branches she'd gathered from their woods. She did *so* want the little chapel to look warm and festive for their first Sunday Session there! As she moved quickly through the silent trees, a sound reached her ears and brought her to a standstill.

She was sure she heard music, and she listened intently, trying to determine what it was and where it came from. She looked back at the house, but the sounds didn't seem to come from there, and then suddenly there was only silence, and she wondered if she had imagined it all. She started on down the path, but halted again with wonder. The beautiful strains of a hymn reached her ears, and she quickly identified the song as one of her favorites—*Sweet Hour of Prayer*.

And then she knew! The music was coming from the chapel—*someone* was playing that wonderful old organ! But *who*? She had despaired when, after the movers had so carefully installed the beautiful instrument, she had realized that they had no one at all who could play it! They could ask someone from town, of course, but how lovely it would be to have their own organist. Maybe Ben played, she thought with joy. After all, he was the real musician among them.

She approached the simple but picturesque structure and quietly pushed open the heavy door, laying her burdens on the floor in the vestibule. Then, taking care to make no noise, she eased open the double doors to the sanctuary. The beauty of the soaring strains from the organ brought a gasp of joy to her lips. She searched with eyes unaccustomed as yet to the sudden dimness of the room, striving to see who it was that had brought that silent old instrument to such glorious life.

Finally, she made out a small, yellow head, bent in concentration over the keyboard, long, unruly strands of blond hair completely hiding the face. *Charlotte!*

The music abruptly stopped, and the blond head jerked to attention. Amy realized with regret that in her surprise she had spoken the girl's name aloud. The frightened child jumped to her feet and stammered apologetically, "Oh, Miss Amy! I... I'm s-sorry... I shouldn't have..."

"No, Charlotte." Amy broke in hastily, seeing the girl's fear. "It's quite all right. It's just wonderful, in fact! You play beautifully."

Charlotte stood, rooted to the floor, and stared at her mutely. Amy moved down the aisle to the front where the girl stood trembling, and continued quietly, "I'm so glad to know that you play the organ, Charlie. Where did you learn to do it so well?"

Amy saw the girl's frightened features relax a bit at the use of her nickname.

"At... at home. I... I played for my father's church," Charlie stammered shyly.

Amy gazed at her thoughtfully. She noticed her unusual choice of words. Not "my church" or "our church," but "my father's church." She suspected that the Rev. Abner Brown not only ruled his household with an iron fist, but most probably "his church" as well.

"I hope you will agree to be our organist here at The Refuge," Amy implored. "It would be such a shame to have this beautiful instrument here in our chapel and no one to play it!"

Amy saw a brief smile behind the ever-present strands of long hair. Charlie gave a quick little nod and said softly, "Sure!"

Crystal lagged behind the rest of the group as they moved excitedly down the path toward the chapel. She gazed around her with wonder. The ceremony they had planned for this afternoon promised to be a special one, and their little forest was certainly dressed for the occasion!

For the unseasonably warm spell they'd been enjoying had broken late the day before, and a cold north wind had brought in heavy, gray clouds and much lower temperatures. As darkness approached, a steady, bone-chilling rain had begun to fall, and then, sometime after midnight, the sky had cleared and the temperature had plunged into the teens. The sun had risen this morning upon a dazzling winter wonderland of shimmering ice, and the gaily chattering group now walked through a virtual fairyland of breathtaking beauty.

The somber atmosphere in the house had lifted, as Jonathon had known it would, once Sunny's funeral was over and life returned to some semblance of normalcy. The girls had begun to talk about Christmas, which was fast approaching. Amy had announced that they would have a great celebration with a tree and presents and a huge feast. They were to be allowed a shopping trip and fifty dollars apiece to spend on presents for each other. Ben had suggested they search their own wooded acreage for the perfect Christmas tree, and the girls were delighted, and bubbling with excitement.

Crystal knew that today's service was supposed to open this happy and holy season on a joyful note, and she couldn't suppress her own feeling of excited expectation. The rustic chapel appeared suddenly through thick trees, and its bell tower, which housed the vestibule at its base, then rose upward in a majestically soaring steeple, was now ice-coated and blindingly beautiful against an azure sky. Someone was playing *Joy to the World* on the organ inside, and Crystal felt her heart lift with gladness as she joined the others in the open doorway.

She sat near the back where she could watch and listen and take notes for the last time. For she knew that she must compile everything she had gathered over the past weeks into a completed article and send it off before the week ended. There would be the normal changes and editing, she knew, and *Lifestyles* was sending their own staff photographer here next week for a shooting session. It was nearly over, and she was both eager to see her story actually appear in print, and sorry to have it all end.

The room seemed dim after the brightness of the day outside. Her gaze was drawn to the spectacular scene that was framed by the front window. Amy had planned wisely, she thought, for that view would be impressive at any season. A stir at the door behind her brought her attention to the back of the room, and she turned to see Tom enter, followed by a huge young man that could be none other than his son. The resemblance was astonishing; the same brilliant blue eyes, the same quick, easy smile, the same erect stature. Only his massive size, which literally dwarfed his father, who was no small man, himself, and a thick head of curly blond hair gave him his own unique identity.

The young man's glance swept over the group already gathered in the small sanctuary. Crystal felt his eyes touch her briefly, move on, and then skip back to her for a long moment. She was aware of a slight stirring somewhere deep within her as their eyes met. Did he remember her from some old snapshot of Jenny's, some snatch of conversation during which she was mentioned in passing? A touch of Tom's hand and his gesture toward the other end of the room drew Jim Logan's attention away from her, and she watched as he followed his father move to greet Jonathon and Amy who sat near the front.

Crystal noticed then, for the first time, that it was Charlie who sat at the organ, letting her fingers move effortlessly, or so it seemed to her, over familiar territory. The girl looked quite nice today, with her long hair pulled back and tied with a bright red bow at the nape of her neck. Crystal knew this transformation was largely the result of Sara's fussing over her, brushing the blond strands until they fairly glowed, and then begging Amy for some ribbon. The face that had emerged was plain, but graced with big beautiful eyes that were sometimes brown, then green, and, occasionally, highlighted with flecks of gold.

Crystal settled back and relaxed. The music was simple and soft, a soothing background of well-remembered carols. She saw Ben then, and gave a little gasp of surprise. She hadn't even recognized him in his dark suit and tie! He must be singing today, after all, she mused, and tried to reconcile in her mind the Ben who was their unassuming gardener, and this Ben who must have some musical talent—why else would they have chosen him to sing for this very special occasion?

Sam walked past her to join Amy in the front row of pews, and then she saw several well-dressed couples that she didn't know enter and take seats toward the middle. The room grew quiet, and she opened her notebook and prepared to write.

Sara squirmed uncomfortably. The levity of the day had somehow disappeared in the quiet confines of the chapel, the organ music only reminding her of Sunny and the funeral they'd all attended last week. She felt the melancholy mood of the past several days stealing back over her, and she wished she'd stayed at the house with Noah. Her arms felt curiously empty, her heart heavy.

She looked up as Tom began to speak.

"Good afternoon, ladies and gentlemen. I want to thank you for joining us here today..."

Sara let her mind wander aimlessly. She saw Ben, and a quick grin flitted across her face. He looked like another person, all dressed up like that! He must really think this is gonna' be somethin' special, she thought with wry amusement. And then she saw that Amy had risen to join Tom at the front of the church.

Tom was saying, "... would like to dedicate our new chapel in honor of your late parents, Walter and Jessica Lincoln. This plaque is to be placed above the doorway, proclaiming to all who enter here that this humble place of worship is called *The Lincoln Chapel*. It is my prayer that this service today, as well as all occasions to follow, whether they be joyous or filled with sorrow, will be blessed by God."

Sara saw quick tears gather in Amy's eyes as she accepted the gold plaque with a smile. She hoped this wasn't going to turn into a weepy event. She'd had more than enough of that lately to last her a lifetime! She saw that Tom was about to introduce the big guy who was a stranger to her, but who anyone with eyes in their head could see was obviously his son. So *he* was to be their speaker today! Some jock who looked like he belonged in a locker room somewhere! She thought of pre-game interviews with athletes who could scarcely form a coherent sentence. This could be a long afternoon!

But as Jim Logan began to speak in a quiet, husky voice that somehow didn't fit with his wide shoulders and thick, muscular neck, she found herself listening intently. He stood to one side of the speaker's podium, one arm resting casually where others might have stashed their notes, a dog-eared old Bible clutched in his other hand. His words, although hushed, easily reached the back of the room.

"When my father asked me to come here today and speak to you, my first thought was, 'What could a coach like me possibly have to say to a group of lovely young ladies like you?' After all, my speeches are usually given to a bunch of big, sweaty football players, and consist mostly of phrases like, 'You're gonna' have to wake up and look alive out there or those Bulldogs are gonna' have us for supper!'"

Sara grinned along with everyone else. She liked his smile and his easy good humor. And she thought it was neat that he had singled them out, she and the other girls, and addressed his remarks to them, even though there were many others in attendance as well. She listened as he continued.

"But the more I thought about it, the more I realized that, although I've never met any of you ladies before, there are some things that I actually do know about each of you. The most obvious fact, of course, is that you are all expecting babies. But, more importantly, you have each already made possibly the biggest decision you will ever make concerning your child's life. For you have decided to give your child just that—*life*. Otherwise, you would not be here today."

Well, that seems pretty obvious, Sara thought sarcastically. Was this to be a lecture on the evils of abortion, then? She thought again of Noah, and wondered if Helen had fed him yet. She should have just stayed there and seen to him herself! This was turning out to be as boring as she'd feared.

Jim was saying, "... maybe you never even considered abortion as a possible answer, but I'd be willing to bet that most, possibly even all of you, entertained that idea, at least momentarily. And then, for one reason or another, you decided to let your child live. Some of you may choose to raise your child yourself, possibly with the help of parents or others. Or you may feel that adoption is the best solution. But, regardless of these decisions, I also know something very important about your child."

Jim Logan paused. Sara wondered where he was headed. He continued, "I know as surely as I'm standing here today that God has a plan for your unborn child. He already loves your baby, and has already begun to shape his future. Whether or not you choose to take an active role in the rearing of your child, God will always be there."

Sara felt the anger begin to build within her. So what about Sunny's child? Did God have a plan for him, too? A plan that somehow overlooked the fact that both of his parents were now dead? And what about Sunny, herself? How could a loving God just snatch away her life before she'd ever even had a chance to hold her baby, or to show him how much she loved him? Sara all but jumped to her feet and bolted from the room, then heard her own name spoken and jerked her attention back to Jim's words.

"... Sarah, the wife of Abraham, Jochebed, the Levite woman who gave birth to Moses, and Mary, the mother of Jesus, are some good examples of women God chose to carry out His divine plan. Let's take a look at these women who lived so long ago, but who must surely have shared many of the same worries and temptations and frustrations that you face today.

"The Bible tells us that Sarah was barren, the most humiliating situation a woman who lived in those days could ever face. For giving her husband sons was the highest honor a woman could achieve. Daughters, too, of course, but especially sons. Sarah was so distressed that she sent her maid to sleep with her husband, so that he could have the child she hadn't been able to give him. But that wasn't God's plan. And, although He waited until the couple was very old—well beyond the normal childbearing years, the scriptures tell us—God appeared to Abraham and promised to give him a son through his wife Sarah, and to make him the father of many nations.

"Now when Sarah learned that she was to become pregnant after all those years, she laughed. After all, she was ninety years old! Whoever heard of a ninety-year-old woman getting pregnant? She'd begged God for a child back when she was young enough to conceive, and her pleas had been ignored. And now she was to have a child? It all seemed so absurd that she had actually laughed at God!

"But God didn't think it was funny. Sarah did, indeed, become pregnant. Now I want you to think about it for a minute. Think of all the reasons why you might have been tempted to have an abortion. Were you embarrassed and ashamed, afraid your friends and family would turn against you? How do you think Sarah felt, donning maternity clothes for the first time at the ripe old age of ninety? And morning sickness! Add seventy years onto how old it made *you* feel! Maybe you had other plans? Better things to do during these fleeting days of your youth than to interrupt it all with diapers and colic and two o'clock feedings? What if you were facing all of that at Sarah's age?

"Do you suppose Sarah considered abortion? For a minute or two, anyway? Now I realize they didn't have clinics to go to then, but those midwives were pretty smart. You can bet your bottom dollar they knew how to get the job done! But Sarah, like you, decided against abortion. After all, God was already mad at her for laughing at Him! She probably decided she'd best do as God wished. And so she bore Abraham a son, whose name was Isaac, and, as God had promised, she was blessed as the mother of nations and of kings."

Jim shifted his position slightly and thoughtfully contemplated his audience. Sara considered that other Sarah, whom she'd heard about, of course, in those long ago years when her mother was still alive and they'd read together from her Bible Story Book. She remembered the rest of it, too, when God had commanded Abraham to offer his young son as a sacrifice, and then had stepped in, just in the nick of time, as the Good Guys always did, and had saved the day, as well as young Isaac's skin. God certainly liked to do things in His own peculiar way! But then, if Sarah had given birth to her son in her youth like normal women, nobody would have even have noticed, would they?

She turned her attention back to Jim as he began telling, still without the aid of his Bible or any apparent notes, the story of the birth of Moses.

"We find a much different set of circumstances with the mother of Moses. She was, it would seem, happily married and delighted to find herself pregnant. But it happened that the pharaoh, who was a wicked man, had issued an order that all newborn baby boys were to be thrown into the Nile River, allowing only the girl babies to live. Now the baby that she bore was a fine boy, and she decided that she couldn't bear to drown her son, even if it meant giving him to someone else to raise.

"And, although you are not faced today with laws that would require you to kill your own child, you may find good reason to make that same decision. She couldn't ask an adoption agency to handle the details, but the scriptures tell us that she prepared a sturdy, waterproof basket for baby Moses and placed it among the reeds along the banks of the Nile River. And when Pharaoh's own daughter went there to bathe, she found the child, and, although she understood that it was one of the Hebrew children that her father had ordered killed, we're told that she felt sorry for the infant and took him for her own son.

"Just because Moses' own parents weren't allowed to raise him didn't alter the fact that, once again, God had a plan. And, even though Moses felt unqualified to carry out God's plans for him, we know that he became one of the greatest leaders of that time, saving the Israelites from the Egyptians and taking them to the Promised Land.

"And that brings us to a young girl named Mary, who lived in Nazareth. Mary found herself in a situation that very nearly mirrors your own. She was very young, possibly fifteen or sixteen years of age. And she had a boyfriend, a fine young man named Joseph. They were in love and planned to get married.

"And then one day Mary had a very strange visitor, an angel named Gabriel, sent by God. Gabriel told Mary that she was to bear a son—not just any son, but the Son of God. Mary was terrified and confused, as you might imagine. How could she possibly have a child when she was still a virgin? Gabriel assured her that the Holy Spirit would take care of all the details, for, as he said, 'Nothing is impossible with God.'

"But let's consider Mary's situation for a moment. She was unmarried and pregnant. Now she pretty much understood how this had happened, but what about her family and friends, and, most of all, her boyfriend Joseph? Can any of you imagine going home and trying to explain to your parents how this angel appeared to you, and now you were pregnant. But it wasn't because you'd been sleeping with your boyfriend, it was the Holy Spirit that had done it, *honest!*"

There was scattered laughter and Sara chuckled at the thought. But Jim hurried on, "And then she had to try to explain it all again to Joseph! He knew very well that she had told the truth when she'd insisted that she had never been sexually involved with *him*, and he loved her and trusted her, but she was, after all, pregnant. If *he* wasn't the father, *then who was?* But, regardless of any doubts he may have had, Joseph was a good man, and he wasn't about to abandon Mary in her time of need. He asked her to marry him and let him help her raise her child.

"And so Mary faced all of the challenges and frustrations and shame of being pregnant and unmarried, even though, in her heart, she knew she was acting for God. And if you think the stigma of the unwed mother is bad today, what do you think it carried in that time? Mary literally faced ostracism from her family and her community under the strict laws of the Jewish people. But Mary was a brave girl. And she knew that she had been chosen above all others for this most blessed honor. Gabriel had told her that she had found favor with God. She may not have understood, and she may have wondered how in the world she was going to deal with it all, but the Bible says she merely answered, 'I am the Lord's servant. May it be to me as you have said.'"

Jim Logan stepped down from the dais and spoke softly. "I have often considered the life of Mary, the mother of Jesus. She had to have known her Son was special from the moment of His birth, for she alone knew without a shadow of a doubt that this Boy truly was the Son of God. And yet he was just a Boy, who needed care and love and discipline. She and Joseph had other children together, but Jesus was *her* Son, hers and God's. And, although neither she nor Jesus made much to do about it, she must have felt a tremendous burden, and great pride, as she watched Him grow into manhood.

"She saw Him, even urged Him, as He performed His first miracle. She saw the crowds gather around Him, eager to hear His every word. And then one day she stood on a desolate hill at the foot of a cross, and watched as they crucified Him. Her Son, who was good and compassionate and loving, and who certainly did not deserve to die like that! Do you think she questioned God at that moment? Did she wonder how God could have turned His back on His Son, and on her, who had gladly borne the shame and humiliation in order to give Him life? She probably believed more than any of us that God truly had a plan for her Son, but she was forced to stand by, helpless, as God allowed evil men to mock Him, and then to kill Him.

"Little could she have known the marvelous scope of that great plan! For her Son died only to be raised again, to sit at the right hand of His

Father. To be the ultimate sacrifice for the sins of us all! To save the world!"

Jim began to pace slowly across the front of the small chapel. "I guess we all question the ways and the wisdom of God sometimes. His plans don't always fit in with ours. But then, they are, after all, *His* plans! And He's got one for each of us—for me, for you, for the babies that you carry. Regardless of the circumstances of your child's conception, regardless of who will act as his parents, regardless of his station in life, God has a plan. I implore you to look for it, and to let God guide you always. Bless you!"

Jim Logan quietly took his seat, and Charlie began again to play the organ. Sara saw, to her astonishment, that Ben had risen and had moved to stand near the podium that Jim had so recently left. Certainly he wasn't about to *sing*!! She stirred restlessly. Jim's words were still echoing in her head, and she felt confused and angry and uncertain. The quavering voice of their gardener reached her ears and she grimaced with disgust. This was horrible! She wanted to leave, but something kept her there, made her mind recall the words she'd screamed at Sunny's death. Had Mary felt that same way? Ben's voice, off key and uncertain, pushed into her consciousness again, intruding upon her thoughts.

On a hill far away stood an old rugged cross,
The emblem of suff'ring and shame,
And I love that old cross where the dearest and best
For a world of lost sinners was slain.

But Sara was unable to dwell on Ben's unsteady voice. Her thoughts were whirling madly in her brain. Was Jim Logan trying to tell her that Sunny's death had a reason? That, instead of God punishing her friend, it was somehow all a part of His plan? How could that be? And the child! An orphan! *Regardless of his station in life,* Jim had insisted. But if God did, indeed, have a plan for young Noah, who would be there to lead him, to help him find it? Sara tried to reject the only reasonable answer, but couldn't. *Promise me that you'll take care of my child if something happens...* Sunny's words. But she was expecting her *own* child, and had no plan, as yet, for *his* future! *Maybe God does...* whose words were those?

Sara was suddenly aware of Ben once more. Because, as she listened, she heard his voice become sure and strong, his words ringing wondrously to the very rafters. His eyes were closed, and on his face was a most rapturous expression. Sara saw Charlie look at him with surprise, and then she, too, appeared ecstatic.

> *To the old rugged cross I will ever be true,*
> *Its shame and reproach gladly bear;*
> *Then He'll call me some day to my home far away,*
> *Where His glory forever I'll share.*

And then Sara was there, too, in the midst of the angry cries, the shouted accusations. She was Mary, watching with despair as they put her Son to death. She heard her own words ring out, *I WANT NO PART OF A GOD LIKE THAT!* But those were *her* words, not Mary's, she realized. For, grief stricken as she was, Mary would not have, *could* not have turned her back on God. Because it had been God who had given Jesus to her in the first place, had allowed her the privilege of giving birth to Him, humble though it had been. And God *had* had a plan, a plan that had also included Mary. It seemed reasonable, then, that God must have had a plan for Sunny as well, and for Sunny's child. Did that plan also include her? Maybe.

> *So I'll cherish the old rugged cross,*
> *Til my trophies at last I lay down;*

Cherish? The cross? Why would you cherish an instrument of death? Because it had ultimately led to life? And did that mean, then, that she was expected to find meaning in Sunny's death? Joy, even? And if that was so, then *how*? *Through Noah, her son...*

> *I will cling to the old rugged cross,*

And then Sara saw it, like a lightning bolt across the sky. Like someone had written the words in big block letters, bold face, and pasted them on her brain. **SUNNY KNEW SHE WAS GOING TO DIE.** Had known it all along. And, knowing that, she had chosen to give birth to the child she carried, no matter the cost. *This baby is worth everything, even if...* Because she had loved his father. Because she loved her unborn child. She hadn't had her life snatched away at all! *She had given her life willingly—gladly, for her son.*

Sara felt a great weight lift from her heart. And then she remembered Jonathon's plea, "...listen for Him to speak to you in some way... Promise?"

Her eyes flew to the front of the room where she found Jonathon, sitting beside his mother in the front row. And then he slowly turned, as if some inner voice had spoken to him. He scanned the faces behind him until his eyes met hers. He looked at her intently, as if reading her heart. A great magnet began to pull at her, and Sara suddenly found herself in the aisle, unmindful of anyone in the room except for Jonathon, who now stood, with his arms outstretched, beckoning. She stumbled to him, tears streaming from her eyes, and felt his strong arms wrap around her with joy as Ben finished on a triumphant note...

And exchange it someday for a crown!

Charlie saw out of the corner of her eye that Sara was headin' for the alter. She was the organist, after all, and expected to keep an eye on everything that happened during a service. And she couldn't have been more pleased! Everything was turning out so much better than she'd hoped. Actually, she'd seldom seen things start so badly, and then end so well.

She'd sensed Ben's panic the minute he'd stepped to the podium. An accompanist just naturally feels those things, and she was instantly alert, ready to react to whatever might take place as Ben began his solo. He was only the gardener, for goodness sakes! What did they expect?

And it was worse than she'd feared. His voice was weak and wavery, his tones uncertain. In an effort to spare the old fellow more embarrassment, she did something she normally would not have done—she opened up the stops on the old organ and let its sure tones take over. Not completely overshadowing Ben's words, of course, she could *never* make herself go that far! But just enough to draw some of the attention away from the notes gone flat and the breaks in his voice.

At some point, about midway through the second verse, she thought, something happened. She was aware of a change, a strengthening, a sudden resonance in Ben's delivery that astonished her. He was no longer the lowly groundskeeper, staggering in his feeble attempt to sing for them. He was the soloist, an artist who was now performing with great skill.

She gradually softened the organ into the background once more, for it was there to provide depth and support only, not to lead, and she gladly let Ben's soaring words fill the chapel with glory. She couldn't stop the wide smile that she felt spreading across her face, for she knew that the music they were now creating together was nothing short of great.

And she'd been so afraid that the beautiful words spoken by Mr. Logan's son would be forgotten in a disastrous aftermath. That people would walk away, shaking their heads with sympathy for that poor man. Did someone say he was their gardener? Jim's powerful lesson would be lost forever. But there was Sara, responding. To Jim Logan's words? To Ben's powerful music? To God? Or maybe just the unforgettable combination of all three!

It didn't matter a whit! It was good. And she was now filling in what would have been an uncomfortable silence, broken only by the sniffling of those folks in the audience who'd started to cry at the beauty of it all. She played soft chords and arpeggios that would only add to whatever words Jonathon was sure to say at any moment now.

She saw him turn to his audience as Sara sobbed in his comforting embrace, and lift one hand. She cut the volume back to almost nothing and let his words fill the room.

"The angels in heaven rejoice with us today!"

Four very pregnant young ladies, sitting side-by-side in the third row, broke into sudden, spontaneous applause. It was contagious, and soon everyone in the tiny chapel was clapping wildly. Charlie pulled out all the stops and launched into a spirited version of *Victory in Jesus*. It was wonderful!

Ben couldn't stop smiling. He'd been scared spitless, more nervous even than that day when he'd sung in a recording studio for the first time. His knees had been so weak and shaky he'd thought he might just collapse in an ungainly heap on the floor.

It had been so bad from the very moment he'd opened his mouth and released that first sad note. He'd wanted more than anything just to run for the door. He should never have let Jonathon talk him into this! But Jonathon was such a good man, and had never asked a favor before, despite all the kindness he'd shown. Ben hadn't had the heart to refuse, but *now*...

He realized, after it was all over with, that he had been so mortified that he had simply turned off his mind to the dreadful spectacle that he was creating. He'd begun to concentrate only on the words of the beautiful old hymn, since he'd already completely destroyed the melody. And that was when God had taken control.

For Ben had been suddenly transported to another time and place, a desolate place called Golgotha. He watched his Savior, writhing in pain and humiliation, knowing well enough that He had the power to call a legion of angels to His aid, but choosing instead to suffer and to die a criminal's death. Ben saw the soldiers draw straws for his Master's few belongings, and he cried out as they thrust a sword through His side. And then, as though through a haze, he heard his own words...

> *For the dear Lamb of God left His glory above,*
> *To bear it to dark Calvary.*

Was that *his* voice, ringing strong and true once again? He closed his eyes and let the song's wonderful lyrics pour out, painting a picture of torturous trial ending in triumph, and knew that God had given him a miraculous gift. When he'd finally stopped listening to his voice and started to hear his words—a message that had always been meant to glorify God, and not himself—he'd been granted the return of his former talent. It was a miracle he would never forget, and he promised God in that moment to dedicate the remaining days of his life to His service.

He heard Jonathon's proclamation of Heaven's joy, and he once again closed his eyes. He saw them then, all of God's angels looking down upon this little assembly with great thanksgiving. And then he saw Libby, clapping and cheering the loudest of them all. She looked down at him and smiled.

Crystal put aside her pen and closed her notepad. Not only were her eyes flooded with tears, but she found she simply had no words for the depth of her feelings. The truth was, her hands had lain idle in her lap for some time now, so deeply immersed was she in the things she had just witnessed.

Sporadic clapping, undoubtedly started by Sara's friends, gradually grew into thunderous applause. She noticed that the people around her were getting to their feet, as if unable to stay seated any longer. A standing ovation for God! She stood with the others and wiped a hand across her face in an effort to clear her vision.

As she gazed at the tableau at the front of the room, Crystal saw Sara pull from Jonathon's embrace and look around her, as if searching for someone. When she found Ben, now standing at the end of the first row of pews, she started hesitantly in his direction, paused, and then, with a glad smile, met him halfway and moved into his outstretched arms. The look on Ben's face as he held the girl was indescribable. The most enormous smile spread across his countenance, and two tears escaped from tightly closed eyes to make twin tracks of wetness down his cheeks.

Crystal knew as she watched that her note taking was not quite finished, after all. For her writer's mind told her that there was yet another story here, if only Ben would agree to sharing it. Their hard-working gardener must have a history. That marvelous voice hadn't just appeared out of nowhere!

She saw then that Amy, still clutching the plaque that Tom had presented to her tightly in her arms, had moved forward as if waiting to speak to Sara. And there was Sam, right behind her! Crystal had often thought that there was a special bond between Sam and the tall, red-headed girl that looked enough like her to be her own daughter. And from the glow of pride and love on Sam's face, you'd think it was true, Crystal mused happily. She was glad. For Sara truly needed someone to mother her, she decided, despite the girl's confident air and her independent ways.

Crystal turned her attention back to Amy, and saw tears streaming down the woman's face. She knew that Amy shared her own feeling that today's service had been far more than a dedication. It had been a miracle. And then, as if noticing Amy's deep emotion for the first time, Tom suddenly stepped from the dais and went to her side, slipping an arm around her and pulling her against him in a quick, warm hug.

"When is that man gonna' figure out that he's in love with her?" Crystal asked herself wryly. She had known from the very first that Amy adored Tom, and why wouldn't she? Tom's such a *decent* man, she thought, and then amended that thought immediately. Honorable. Yes, that was better. She let the words flow through her mind. *Tom Logan is an honorable man.* She nodded her head even as a question jumped in on the heels of that statement. *And what about his son...?*

Her eyes flew to the young giant standing quietly to one side, his head bowed, his long arms meeting in front of his massive body, his well-worn Bible grasped gently in both hands. He looks like a Greek god, she thought with wonder, or a proud young warrior. She remembered his husky voice, the powerful words he had spoken with such tenderness and compassion. She noticed how the dark brown material of his jacket stretched over wide shoulders and strong arms, and how nicely it contrasted with his fair hair.

Behind him, in a panoramic view through wide windows, a pair of cardinals flitted in the icy boughs of an evergreen tree—a winter scene by Currier & Ives. And then they were gone, and the world beyond the windows became a dazzling holiday display at Saks Fifth Avenue, or the glittering confection atop a wedding cake.

Her eyes rested on him once more, and, as if sensing her perusal, Jim Logan lifted his head and met her gaze. Flustered, Crystal tried to tear her eyes from his, and found that she couldn't.

CHARLIE

❧

Charlie squeezed into the tiny back seat of Crystal's little red car, hoping that she and Brenda would both be able to fit. Brenda, who had moved into the house at the first of the month, was a big, stocky girl with a sour-faced look that seemed to speak of her thinking she'd got the short end of the stick somewhere along the way. Charlie was just grateful that the pert little Bette had arrived there before Brenda—otherwise she'd now be sharing her room with this altogether unpleasant girl. She hoped Brenda wouldn't spoil the day for them, since they'd all looked forward to this shopping spree with such eagerness.

She thought about Bette, who was riding in Sam's big black Cadillac for today's outing. Bette seemed such an odd name for such a lively girl. Not Betsy or Beth, just Bette—like something you'd do at the racetrack. She'd gotten used to the name, of course, and she could hardly believe her good fortune at getting the giggling, chattering Bette for her roommate, since the wildly talkative girl more than made up for herself never saying a word.

She gazed with envy at Sara and Crystal in the front seat of the car, laughing and talking with such ease, while she and Brenda sat in the back, silent and still as two posts. She looked longingly at Crystal's straight black hair, not stringy like hers, but the sort that swayed all in one piece when she talked. And *Sara!* Now there was a girl who obviously knew what she was about. So sure of herself and always knowing what was the right thing to say. Although Charlie *had* been a bit put out when Sara had made a point of doing something with her hair on Sunday. It had looked nice, she admitted to herself, all shiny and neat for a change, but she'd hidden in its untidy depths for so many years that she'd felt suddenly naked and exposed.

She'd forgotten all about it in the wonder of that afternoon, however. She let herself relive the whole thing again, now that she was safely surrounded by hair once more, and no one could see the silly grin that was inching across her face. It had been the highlight of her young life! All those years of practicing the piano and playing the organ for uneventful Sunday morning services had finally paid off. For hadn't she anticipated every unlikely incident, handling it all with a competence she hadn't realized she'd possessed?

She remembered Ben's words, spoken to her quietly as the others began to move toward the door. The stir that Sara had created had finally settled down to a pleasant hum of happy voices, and Ben turned to her in gratitude. "Thank you, Charlotte, for a very fine piece of work. I'll never forget the way you covered for me today. And I want you to know that you are, without a doubt, the finest accompanist I have ever worked with!"

She couldn't help but wonder how many others there could possibly have been, his being the gardener and all, but it was the highest praise she had ever received, and she was so very pleased. For she had been at her music since she was just a mite, thanks to her Mama standing up to Papa for once in her life, and letting her take piano lessons from Mrs. Harkey in town. Never once in all those years had anybody ever taken any special notice of her playing, except for the few words of encouragement she'd gotten from her teacher.

But wasn't that the way she'd wanted it to be? She'd always been a slight, pale child with fair hair and fair skin, and quiet as a mouse. Her large dark eyes had been her only redeeming feature, the only thing that anyone at all had ever even noticed. And she'd buried them behind a wall of unattractive hair long ago.

She'd known from her earliest existence that she was a disappointment to her Papa. But not until the day she'd overheard Miz Lucy and Miz Ella saying what a shame it was that the pastor hadn't got the son he'd wanted so bad, had she understood just why. No wonder Papa had always chosen to ignore her! When she thought of the rowdy group of boys in the churchyard after services, so loud and rambunctious, she could well imagine the poor comparison she must have made.

It had become such an easy thing just to disappear, even at school where her teachers had rarely remembered she was there. And when they did ask her to answer some perfectly simple question, she'd only stuttered and stammered so terribly that they'd wished they hadn't even asked. Only in the quiet dimness of the empty church, where she went each evening to practice her music, did she forget her shyness and lay her soul bare. She was a real person then, and *only* then. She found a joy in letting her fingers fly over the keyboard with such perfection, releasing emotions she'd always kept well hidden.

Until that night last summer when Elder Parsons had found her there, alone and vulnerable in the deserted sanctuary. She hadn't known he was anywhere about until he spoke from right behind her, and she had nearly toppled from the piano stool in her fright. He was a big, coarse-looking man with a roaring voice, and she'd always wondered how his tiny sad-faced wife could bear to have him near her. And when she'd seen the leering look in his eyes, she'd cried out in fear.

But he'd just grinned, unconcerned. They both knew that no one would hear, even if she screamed bloody murder. "Wal, yur jest quite tha li'l ole pianer player, ainchas?"

He'd smelled funny, and she'd decided that he must have been drinking. When he reached out a large, hairy hand and brushed it across her flat chest, she had shrunk from his touch involuntarily, but he'd laughed drunkenly and made a lunge for her. She *had* screamed then, but she was powerless against his great size and strength. He'd had his way with her, and then had abruptly left her where she lay, sobbing, near the alter of her father's church.

And she couldn't tell, of course, could *never* tell what this man, who held such a high position with the church, had done to her. Nobody would believe her, anyway, least of all her father, who had always taken great pains not to cross Elder Parsons. For didn't he owe his job to the man? And so her parents had ranted and raved, and then had finally brought her here in deep disgrace. She supposed they would come back for her when the baby had been properly spirited away to someone who wanted it, but she knew without a doubt that she would never be allowed to play the organ in her father's church again.

Charlie looked up quickly, as Crystal whipped the little car smoothly into a parking space and killed the engine. She saw that Sam had parked just down the street, and she crawled from the car, following the others as they gathered on the sidewalk. It occurred to her that she hadn't the faintest idea of what to buy for any of these girls, who had been strangers to her only a few weeks ago. What if she chose dumb things that they didn't want or couldn't use?

And where on earth was she to go? She looked around her at a town that everyone had called small, but which looked enormous to her. Would she ever be able to find the right store, and then get herself back to the car without losing her way?

Without warning, Sara was at her side. "Hey, Charlie!" she said with a big grin. "Wanna' come with me? Let's go say hi to Gretta!"

Charlie stared at her face in the mirror and saw a stranger. She hoped with all her heart that God wouldn't strike her dead for this sudden interest in the way she looked. Hadn't Papa always preached that a woman's beauty was to be on the inside, with no thought for the outward appearance? She'd wondered if it wasn't the same for men, but Papa had never said. And Sara hadn't been concerned in the least with what Papa might think.

She sighed. It seemed she'd done nothing at all but stand in front of her mirror for this whole week since their trip to town for Christmas shopping. Because she and Sara had done much more than just say hi to Gretta, of course. Gretta had taken one look at her awful mop of hair, had swept it up and away from her face, and then had commented what a shame it was to cover those nice eyes. Sara had pointed out a lovely girl in a magazine full of lovely girls, and had asked didn't she like that one's short poufy hair-do, and she'd nodded yes, it was very nice. And before she knew it they had her in a big chair with a plastic apron tied at her neck, and her long, stringy hair was falling to the floor around her.

She'd watched with mixed feelings of wonder and dismay as Gretta had snipped away her protective shroud with confident ease. And then, when Gretta had finished the job to her satisfaction, Sara'd had another suggestion, and they'd ended up piercing her ears as well. And Sara had just happened to have a pair of tiny gold studs right there in her purse which

Gretta had carefully slipped through the new holes in her earlobes. The change in her appearance had been nothing short of astounding, and she'd been nervous about rejoining the other girls. She knew they'd all gather round and stare at her, and she really hated that.

But the shopping had gone well, and Sara had seemed to know all the best stores, leaving her on her own only when they'd each found presents to buy. She'd bought long woolen scarves with matching mittens for each of the girls, thinking they would be appropriate for this part of the country that was always so cold. And when Sara had guided her back to the parked cars with no problem at all, she was surprised to find that the other girls' excited compliments about her hair only made her feel warm and welcomed.

The past week had flown by in a flurry of wrapping and decorating and helping Helen in the kitchen. They'd baked dozens of cookies and made several batches of delicious candies. Ben had scoured the woods until just the right tree had been found, and they had worked till all hours of the night putting on the ornaments and lights and sparkling icicles. The pile of presents beneath the tree had grown and grown, and then Miss Amy's family had started pouring in, and the room was soon crowded with brightly wrapped packages stacked in every available bit of space. It was a Christmas unlike anything she'd ever imagined! When they'd all gathered inside the chapel last night for a Christmas Eve service, she'd sat proudly at the organ and led them all in singing the grand old carols. Someone, she thought it was Sara, had begged Ben for a solo, and his beautiful tenor voice had brought tears to many eyes as he sang *O Holy Night.*

Later, as they hurried back to the house for hot chocolate and cookies, they'd continued singing, this time their childhood favorites like *Up on the Housetop* and *Jingle Bells* and *Rudolph the Red-nosed Reindeer.* It was a glorious night, shared with all manner of strangers who were aunts, uncles and cousins, but who didn't seem like strangers at all by the time it was over.

And now it was Christmas Day. She'd awakened to see huge flakes of snow drifting past her window like soft feathers, and had stood staring at it with wonder. Finally Bette had rushed her downstairs where everyone was gathering in the living room by the tree. The huge pile of gifts had been opened with great excitement, and the mouth-watering aroma of the feast they were about to partake of now drifted up the stairs and reached Charlie as she still stood at her mirror.

Everyone had liked her gifts, she thought happily, as she had liked theirs. There'd been make-up kits for each of them from Bette and photo albums from Jamila, soft fuzzy nightgowns from April and boxes of chocolates from Brenda. Sara had carefully chosen a piece of jewelry that was exactly right for each one of them, and Sam had surprised them all with soft turtleneck tops, pants, and long flared vests from Wichita. They needed something for their special occasions, she said, and while the new outfits would be shared by all and left for the many girls that would come in the future, everyone was delighted to have something new to wear.

Charlie hadn't had the faintest idea how to use the strange powders and blushes and liners in her new make-up kit, but Sara had hovered over her, as usual, dabbing a little of that and brushing on some of this until her skin was soft and glowing. She had chosen the deep green turtleneck with its matching slacks and the creamy beige vest with tiny green leaves scattered over it, because they just matched the emerald colored earrings Sara had given her for Christmas. She reached up her hand, and tentatively touched her fluffy short hair. The tawny shades of her vest brought out its golden highlights, and a touch of green on her eyelids, along with the dark color of her blouse, made her enormous eyes look like a pine forest in the springtime.

A sharp knock at the door made her jump. Bette had gone down ages ago to chatter gaily with new friends that she seemed able to make at the drop of a hat, so Charlie hurried to see who was there. Had she dawdled in front of her mirror, admiring herself with an unholy vanity, while the others waited dinner below?

But it was Sara, looking splendid herself in the black turtleneck and a black vest embroidered with metallic thread of burnished copper.

"Hey, Charlie Brown," Sara said with a slow drawl. "Ya look just like a movie star!"

Charlie fervently hoped that God was busy right then with some more important matter, and wouldn't notice her flush of pride.

Tom sat at the head of the biggest table he had ever seen and surveyed the group around him. He briefly recalled his long-ago dream when he'd seen himself at just such a table as this one, laden with every kind of good food. He let his eyes wander from face to face, and was pleased at the happiness that radiated from each and every one of them. The girls of the house were interspersed with Amy's grandchildren, chattering as happily as if they were all one family. This was exactly what Amy had wanted, he knew, and he smiled with pleasure.

Ben, who sat on his left, commented that he'd never seen so much food in one place in all his life. They exchanged pleasantries for a few moments before Jonathon asked everyone to join hands while he blessed their bountiful feast. Soon everyone was devouring the delicious meal with eagerness.

Tom looked for his own two children and saw that they were seated, one on each side of Crystal, and were apparently vying for her attention. Jenny was speaking avidly about some matter or other, and Crystal answered at the appropriate intervals, but her mind was obviously on the young man at her other elbow. Tom saw the looks that passed between the two of them and wondered if Jim had found the girl of his dreams at last. And wasn't it about time? Here he was, an old man already, and with no grandchildren of his own. And there was Amy, with a whole roomful of them!

His gaze was caught by the oldest of Amy's six grandchildren, Dani's son Josh. Such a good looking young man, his manners reflecting careful training. Tom wondered how Dani had managed all those years alone, and was glad to see the quiet man at her side who obviously adored her. Young Josh had apparently caught the attention of every girl in the room, Tom saw with some amusement. But then the circumstances of his birth had been explained with no embarrassment whatsoever, and he must certainly be living proof of what their own fatherless children might attain.

At the moment, Josh seemed to be telling some long involved story to Charlotte, who sat quietly at his side. Now *there* was a sight for sore eyes! Such a lovely girl, now that she had gotten rid of all that unattractive hair. But so shy and withdrawn. She'd hardly said a word all through dinner, but Josh didn't seem to care as he rambled on about "their ranch" and "his horse Bucky" and on and on. Tom realized that the boy was showing an unusual kindness to the girl at his side by involving her in the wild chatter around them, instead of letting her sit in an uncomfortable silence as she most certainly would have done.

Tom then let his idle gaze travel to the far reaches of the huge table to find Amy. She sat with her daughter Nicki on her left and Sam on her right, and he could see the glow on her face even from that distance. She was absolutely radiant, the "lady of the manor" so to speak, with her family all around her. For she considered them all to be her family, he knew. He thought suddenly of Joyce, and tried to picture her there. But she would never have fit in here, he realized with a start. For although Joyce had been a good mother to their own children, she'd never had that endless capacity for love that included any and all who might have need of it, as Amy did. Amy, the mother hen who extended her wings to any ugly duckling or hurt puppy or stray kitten who might have need of her love and care.

Tom was suddenly irritated by whatever rules of protocol there were that put him at one end of this grand old table and Amy at the other. He wanted to share his thoughts with her and laugh with her and feel her elbow touching his. She turned her eyes to meet his gaze at that moment, as if he had called out to her. Their eyes locked and held, and some unspoken message passed between them. He remembered again the dream that had brought him to this place and time. Amy had been at his side as they sat at *that* table, he was certain. For hadn't she begged him to stay always?

His sudden need for her very nearly sent him, like some lovesick teenager, to rush awkwardly to her side.

Amy thought her heart would burst with joy. Christmas had been all she could have wished for, and more. Huge, floating flakes of snow had fallen all day. She couldn't remember when they'd last had a white Christmas. It always seemed either to snow the week before, and then it was gone, leaving a muddy mess by Christmas time, or else it came during the New Years' celebrations when the highways were already crowded with drunken drivers intent upon killing themselves.

She had always been happiest when surrounded by her children and grandchildren, and was even happier now that she could include "her girls." And there was Ben and Helen and Crystal and Sam and, of course, Tom and his children, all gathered today around the great table. They'd brought in the small table from the kitchen to add to the length of the one in the dining room, for she had been determined that they would all eat together. When Helen had offered to serve them, she'd adamantly refused. They were equals in this house, she'd insisted, and would sit down together and serve themselves as a family should. Even Gretta had joined them for their wonderful feast, and cribs had been brought in for Megan and Noah, who slept peacefully amidst the boisterous gaiety in the room.

This oversized dining room was built with just this sort of thing in mind, she thought with pleasure. She'd caught Tom's eyes upon her earlier, and knew that he, too, shared in her joy. He'd been there for the Christmas Eve festivities, and also this morning as they madly tore open a multitude of gifts, but she'd hardly had a chance to say a word to him. Just that one special moment when the girls had proudly thrust yet another gift into her hands, and she'd seen with surprise that it was addressed to both Tom and herself. She'd beckoned him to her side, and together they'd opened the gift that had melted her heart. It was a large wooden slab with a gold plaque attached to the front, and etched upon it in beautiful script letters was the verse from their sign outside. She'd read the words aloud in the sudden silence of the room.

In You, O Lord, I have taken refuge;
let me never be put to shame... (Psalm 31:1)
from the Refugees

Below, the girls had each signed their names, and Amy knew a moment of such gladness that she had found it impossible to speak. She had looked to Tom, and had felt an overwhelming closeness with him as they shared feelings too deep to be expressed. And he had spoken for both of them when he looked at the girls gathered around them, their shining faces full of pride and happiness. "Thank you very much. This beautiful engraving will hang forever in the front hall, to welcome all who come after you. It is a priceless gift, and one that Amy and I will treasure always."

A wild cheer had gone up from the group, and then Ben had appeared in the doorway with his gift in hand. He'd built a handsome bird feeder from scraps of lumber he'd gathered during the construction of the chapel, fashioning it in the same general design. "I thought we might hang it

168

outside the big window of the chapel, so that the wild creatures can feed, even as we are being fed with blessings from above," Ben had said happily. "If any of you would like to give me a hand later, I'd surely appreciate it."

And so a whole troupe of young people spilled out into the snow-filled day shortly after dinner, rejoicing in the beauty around them and the friendships they'd formed. When they came back inside, flushed from the cold and with mittens wet from a spirited snowball fight, their laughter filled the house with a wondrous joy. And, although it seemed unbelievable to Amy that anyone could possibly eat another bite, they piled plates with cookies and candies and eagerly accepted the mugs of hot chocolate Helen had ready for them.

And now, as she brushed cookie crumbs from the table that she and Helen and her daughters had just cleared, she noticed a sort of lull in the big house. The young people had drifted into the parlor to play some game or another, and most of the others were talking quietly in the living room. And then Tom was there beside her, his hand on her arm.

"Do you suppose we could slip away somewhere and have a few minutes to ourselves?" he asked quietly.

Amy glanced around her and nodded. "Yes, I think we could. I'll just let Sam know, and get my coat."

As they stepped out into the cold silence of the night, Tom took Amy's arm and guided her to his little car. As he settled her into its sleek, comfortable interior, she thought, as she had so many times before, how few men with salaries the size of Tom's would still be driving the same car for three or four years, or would be living in a small apartment when a fine house was easily affordable. She knew that he spent a large portion of his earnings on The Refuge, and that he gave generously to the Shelter for the Homeless as well.

As he slid in beside her, he grinned apologetically. "I really don't have any place to go, but I just wanted to talk to you. I hope you don't mind."

"No, not at all!" she answered truthfully. "I have never known a finer Christmas holiday, but I find I'm a bit weary. It's rather nice to have a moment of quiet."

And so they shared their thoughts and their feelings, about the day that had just passed, about the work they were involved in, about their families. Amy mentioned that she'd seen the way Jim's eyes seemed to follow Crystal's every move, and how Crystal had never strayed far from his side. Tom spoke of Charlie's new loveliness, and yet she still appeared to be afraid of her own shadow, and he wondered if she'd ever be able to face the world without fear. Amy remarked on the fine gift from the girls, and what a surprise it had been!

And then Tom chuckled as he remembered. "From the Refugees! Now that *had* to come from Sara! No one else would have had the wit to dream that up!"

Amy laughed. "Yes, I'm sure it did. And the money for the gift also came from her, unless I miss my guess. She hears from her father regularly now, and I wouldn't doubt there was a bit of green tucked into her Christmas card. But how nice that she chose to spend it on us, and to let the others share in the joy of it!"

"Yes, that girl has really told the story of our work here, from start to finish. She has grown in so many ways. She somehow reminds me of the Apostle Peter—always brash, and so volatile, and forever getting herself into trouble—but such a blessing altogether. We've had many blessings in this first year, haven't we Amy?"

Amy sighed and laid her head back against the soft leather of the seat as Tom drove carefully down the snow-covered road, not into town, she noticed, but through the quiet of the countryside. "Yes, Tom. I don't believe I've ever known greater happiness than the work here has brought to me."

"I understand that the house is full now, and that we have a waiting list! I can hardly believe it, Amy. I often wish I could find an old hotel, or maybe an apartment building somewhere, that I could buy. I would love to expand our operation to give shelter to the homeless and the abused, and employment for the girls to go to from here, as well as for many others that have dire need of it. There is so much to be done!"

Amy gazed at Tom for a long moment, then answered softly, "We can't be all things to all people, Tom. The work we already do is very important."

"I know that's true, but just think what a place like that could have done for Ben, and for Helen. We've managed to give them a good life, but there must be countless others in the same boat. Although, even if the perfect location became available tomorrow, I'm afraid I'd have to walk away from it. I've pretty well put all my savings, and most of my earnings, for that matter, into The Refuge."

"I'm sure that you have, Tom, and I know that God will bless you for it."

Tom looked at her with a smile and laid a hand on one of hers. "He already has!"

Amy turned to face the window in order to hide the flush of warmth that colored her cheeks. But she moved her hand so that she could grasp his, and the two of them rode in companionable silence, holding hands like adolescents in the early stages of infatuation. And when he drove back through the gates of The Refuge a while later, they continued to sit quietly. Lights blazing from every window of the great house announced that the activities of the day were still going strong inside, and the two of them were somehow loathe to leave the warm privacy of the car.

"I believe we've given the girls here a Christmas they won't soon forget," Tom murmured softly, breaking their silence at last. "You've done a wonderful job with everything, as usual."

"Oh, Tom, I was so afraid that bringing my whole family here might prove to be somewhat overwhelming to our girls, and even to you and Jim and Jenny. But it has turned out just grand, don't you think? And that reminds me. Jonathon and Julie are planning a New Year's Eve party at their home for the girls. They've invited Jim and Jenny and, of course, Crystal, who will be leaving us a few days later. They've asked me to come, and I was wondering, would you like to go, too?"

"No."

Amy looked at him with surprise. "No? Oh, I'm sorry... I... I should have known that you might already have other plans..."

"As a matter of fact, I do have other plans. The country club where all the American Trucking VIP's have complimentary memberships is throwing a big bash that night with dinner and dancing—the whole works. I thought I'd like to go—with you."

"Oh." The disappointment was apparent in her voice. And then as his final words registered in her brain, she swiftly raised her head. "*Oh*! Oh, Tom, you're inviting *me*? It sounds marvelous!! Oh, yes, Tom, I'd love to go!"

He saw again the child-like spirit that always filled Amy with such an irrepressible joy. He bent, almost without thinking, and placed a light kiss on her lips. And then the passion that had lain dormant within him for all these long years suddenly flared, and he pulled her close and kissed her with mounting fervor.

When he finally released her, feeling again somewhat like a teenager on his first date, kissing his girl goodnight in the car because there was nowhere else to go, he stared at Amy's flushed face and whispered, "Merry Christmas!"

They made a striking couple as they entered the elite country club at a few minutes after eight on New Year's Eve. Tom had chosen to wear a black suit and tie, which looked very formal and contrasted nicely with his silver gray hair and his deep blue eyes. Amy wore a soft, swirling dress of dove gray satin which glowed in the warm holiday lights and put a rosy blush on her cheeks. They joined a large crowd of well-dressed partygoers and were shown to a small corner table.

They chatted easily over roast duckling with orange sauce, au gratin potatoes and brandied carrots. They lingered over dessert, which was a sinfully rich concoction called Pots de Creme au Chocolat. And then they listened as the band began to play on the other side of the room, near the dance floor.

Tom finally stood and pulled her to her feet. As the soft slow strains of *September Morn* drifted across the dimness of the room, he pulled her into his arms. She wondered if he remembered dancing to the *Theme from Love Story* on that night so many years ago when she had fallen in love with him.

And then he said, as if reading her thoughts, "We haven't danced together since that night in Tulsa when I was invited to my very first sales awards banquet, and we all went out together. Do you remember?"

As if she could forget! "Yes, I remember. Dani and Nicki were so young, and so excited to be included. It was an unusually happy evening for all of us."

Until we got home, at least, she thought wryly, and I realized that I had let myself fall in love with you, a married man with a family of your own.

How she had agonized over it all, promising herself *never*, no matter what, to let him know. And then Joyce had left him and they had divorced, and the years had passed, and still she had never spoken to him of love.

But there was a new light in his eyes when he looked at her now, a sudden need to be at her side that went beyond the work they did together. And so, when they returned to their secluded little table and he asked her quietly if she would be his wife, she nodded, with tears in her eyes, and whispered, "Yes, Tom. I would be honored."

A radiant smile lit his face at her answer, and he reached into his pocket and handed her a tiny black velvet box. When she saw the magnificent ring it contained she could only gasp, "Oh *my*! Oh, Tom, it's beautiful!"

Tom slipped the dazzling diamond onto her finger and lifted her hand to his lips. Then he stood, with boyish urgency, and asked, "Are you ready to go? What do you say we go crash the Gardner's party?"

They arrived at Jonathon and Julie's house at a few minutes before midnight and were welcomed into a brightly lighted room overflowing with music and youthful laughter and unbelievable noise. There were young people everywhere, for Amy's grandchildren had stayed for the event. Jim stood with his arm around Crystal. Jenny rushed to her father's side to give him a hug. Tom lifted his hand and the room grew quiet.

"Amy and I have something to tell you all. She has accepted my proposal, and we plan to be married!"

The young crowd around them gave a rousing cheer, and suddenly their exuberant young voices were joined by a great shout that sounded throughout the neighborhood. The revelry echoed across town and throughout the countryside. Church bells rang out joyously, and the midnight sky was lit with a wild display of fireworks.

The whole world, or so it seemed to Tom and Amy, had joined in the celebration of their love.

The new year brought two new babies in quick succession, both girls. Jamila and April, who had moved into The Refuge on the same day, gave birth within a space of 48 hours. But under such differing circumstances!

Jamila, a child of the streets, who had never known her father and had no more idea about the identity of her own child's father, left her new daughter and returned to her old life immediately. The infant, the questionable product of a life of drugs and alcohol and careless sex, would not be easily adopted. New parents are just naturally cautious when they know so little about a child's background, and realize the possibility of damage from drugs.

But Amy believed that the child was healthy and normal—after all, Jamila had been with them for the past six months and had lived a clean life during that time. But the girl had been found last summer by an early morning jogger in one of Oklahoma City's parks, unconscious from a bad mix of drugs and alcohol, and three months pregnant. The police had taken her to a local hospital, and she had later been released to Social Services, who had referred her to them. It was such a shame, Amy felt, for Jamila had become an attractive young lady, once free of the vices that had overwhelmed her, and given shelter and a healthy diet.

And so they found themselves with yet another infant to care for until adoptive parents could be found. Tom once again lamented the fact that they had no out-reach facility for Jamila to go to, with honest work for her to do. Maybe, just maybe, she could have found some meaning to her life, could have stayed drug-free, possibly even have raised her child herself. Amy listened to his words with sorrow, understanding his helplessness, and his frustration.

But there had been little time for recriminations, for April went into labor almost as Jamila was walking out the door. April came from a highly respected, well-to-do family in Kansas City, and she was surrounded by her parents, as well as the young father and his parents, for the occasion. She emerged from the long hours of labor looking tired, but excited. She would marry her beautiful little daughter's father as soon as the boy graduated from high school in the spring. It was not exactly what the parents of the young couple had hoped for their children, but they would be supportive and loving, and their tiny granddaughter was already adored by all.

The house was full to overflowing, with two new girls—Patsy and Carol—moving immediately into the room just vacated by April and Jamila. April and her new daughter, Amber, were moved down into the nursery wing, and they welcomed Jamila's baby in with them for the time being. Sara continued to care for young Noah, adamantly refusing to place him for adoption until her own child was born and she could make some sort of final plans. If she decided that she couldn't keep both of them, she said, then she would insist upon adopting them out together, to parents who would treat them as siblings.

And so life hurried on, and through it all Charlie grew more and more confused. This world she now lived in was so different in so many ways from her childhood home that she found it hard to compare the two. She listened to Jonathon talk about a God that hardly resembled the God that her own father had always described, and she wondered how they could possibly be one and the same. She had come to The Refuge believing with all her heart that her pregnancy was due to some fault of her own, some unwitting sin that had brought the wrath of God down upon her. But Jonathon said God loved His children, no matter what. So who *was* to blame?

She could scarcely blame Elder Parsons for his actions. For wasn't he a man of God? Surely God had merely used the man as His instrument for her punishment. She had prayed and prayed for God to forgive her for whatever bad thoughts or evil deeds she might have committed, and to *please* spare her child from further retribution. For she already loved the life within her, and felt his stirrings with wonder. She wished she could find the courage to mention all of these confusing feelings to Jonathon, who seemed so warm and understanding.

And finally she did, on a late Sunday afternoon that was dark and damp and cold outside, but warm and cozy in the small chapel she had grown to love. Their Sunday Session was over, and she had lingered at the organ, sorting through her music until the others had gone and she was alone with Jonathon. When he had finished with gathering his things and straightening the chairs that sat to each side of the podium, he had turned to see her there with some surprise.

"Charlie! I hadn't noticed you were still here! You did a fine job with the music, as usual."

She had a sudden moment of panic, remembering another empty church and that other man who had taken advantage of her there. She should have just hurried out with the others!

But Jonathon saw the flash of fear in her eyes, and asked gently, "What is it, Charlie? Would you like to sit down and talk for a few minutes?"

Her shyness nearly overcame her, but she managed a slight nod and moved to the front row bench he had indicated. He sat beside her, leaving a wide space between them, she noticed gratefully, and spoke softly, "Have you been happy here Charlie? You look so pretty with your hair that way, and all the girls seem to like you very much."

She jerked her head up again, thinking he might be saying those things just to give him some sort of advantage over her, but she saw only warmth and kindness in his eyes. She ducked her head and asked with difficulty, "Do... do you think its, uh, wrong to... to *like* the way you look?"

"Of course not, Charlie," Jonathon responded quietly. "God created many beautiful things in our world, which He obviously expected us to enjoy. He made you a lovely young girl and I am sure He looks at you with pride. So why shouldn't you take some pleasure from your appearance also?"

"But... but my father says a woman's beauty should be on the inside..."

"As it should," Jonathon replied. "We all must look to our inner selves first, making sure we are living as we should. But I believe you to be very lovely on the inside, also."

"No! How... how can you think that? I mean, just... just *look* at me!"

Jonathon frowned, confused. "Are you referring to your pregnancy?"

Charlie nodded, refusing to look at him.

"Do you think you are the first to enter into a relationship with a young man that resulted in pregnancy? The Bible tells of many..."

"No!" she said again, sharply, her eyes flashing, two bright spots appearing on her cheeks. "No, I would never have done *that*! There was... there was no young man at all. It was..."

She dropped her eyes once more, aware that she had said more than she had intended. She must never tell anyone what happened on that dreadful day.

Jonathon reached for her hand and felt her flinch as he touched her. And suddenly he knew. "Charlie, did someone take advantage of you— rape you?"

Her eyes jumped to his at his words, and her face went scarlet. "No! I-I mean... I can't tell you..."

"That's fine, Charlie. I don't need to know the details. But if someone forced himself on you, how could that possibly have been your fault?"

She was quiet for several seconds, then slowly shook her head. Jonathon saw her tears as they rolled down her cheeks and into her lap. "I... I don't know. But... but Papa says God punishes us when we're bad..."

"And do you think that God allowed someone to attack you as a punishment for being bad?"

Charlie finally raised tear-filled eyes to his. "Well, He *must* have, don't you think? I... I mean... what else could it be?"

"And the man who forced himself on you, do you think that *he* is bad?"

The girl stared at her hands, clasped tightly in her lap, for some time before she answered. She then spoke so softly that Jonathon had to strain to hear her words. "I... I don't know. I was so scared, and so embarrassed and ashamed. And I had never liked him, but..." Her words trailed off to nothing, then she once again faced him and asked candidly, "Do you think that's why he did it? Maybe God *knew* I didn't like him and was angry with me... And maybe God used him to teach me a lesson or something, I don't know... But... a leader in a church wouldn't be *bad*, would he?"

"Charlie, all of us do bad things sometimes. And even church leaders are tempted by the devil. What this man did to you was *wrong*, Charlie, and it was his wrongdoing, not yours. But God isn't sitting in His heaven just waiting for a chance to bring His vengeance upon us. Jesus already took care of all that by dying on the cross for our sins, and giving us forgiveness. Don't you see, He's already forgiven you for the bad things in your life, and if the man who brought this shame upon you is truly sorry for his actions, and has asked God's forgiveness, then he too has been forgiven. And God wants *you* to forgive this man, as well. Can you do that?"

Charlie nodded. "Sure. I... well, I never really blamed him in the first place. Are you sure it wasn't *my* fault then? That I didn't somehow do somethin' so awful that God *couldn't* forgive me?"

"I'm sure, Charlie," Jonathon answered earnestly. "There is nothing in this world so bad that God can't forgive. All we have to do is ask."

She could only sit and stare at him. If only she could believe his words! But she knew her Papa saw it all so much differently. Was it possible that this God that Jonathon seemed to know so well was really the loving, forgiving Father that everyone here seemed to know about? And Mr. Logan's son, Jim, he'd said that too. That God loved her, even loved her baby. This baby that her Mama and Papa had seemed so ashamed of, but that she couldn't help wanting so bad.

She smiled suddenly. "I hope you're right, cause I want to believe you more 'n *anything*. I just wish someone could make Papa see it the way you do."

"Maybe that's to be your job, Charlie. Maybe God sent you here for that very purpose. For your Papa obviously sees God as a stern, demanding Father, much like the father he has been to you, I'm sure. If your Papa were to be told about the God we believe in, who is a loving, merciful Father, he might become a more forgiving father, himself, don't you think? Why don't you give it a try?"

They walked out into the coldness of the day, and Charlie shivered, as she always did. But inside she felt a strange new warmth. Imagine— her teaching Papa about God! It would never work, of course. Still, she supposed it couldn't hurt to try. Maybe, if she just wrote a nice, friendly letter, and just happened to mention... well, she'd have to give it some thought, she decided happily.

Sam had felt rather foolish sitting with all those young pregnant girls during Lamaze classes these past few weeks, but Sara had begged her to take over as her birth partner after Sunny died, and she hadn't had the heart to say no. But as she worked diligently alongside Sara in the last stages of the girl's labor, she found herself involved in the most awesome adventure of her life. Childless herself, she was now beginning to understand the pain and the effort and the boundless joy of bringing a new life into the world.

And she realized that they call it labor because it truly is! For even *she* was weak with exhaustion and soaked with perspiration by the time that last valiant push put a squalling, red-faced infant into Dr. Cameron's waiting hands. As she looked at Sara's radiant face, wreathed in a great victorious smile, she knew that it mirrored her own. "We did it!" Sam whispered with awe, and couldn't stop the tears that coursed down her cheeks.

"You have a fine baby boy!" Dr. Cameron exclaimed. "Do you want to see him?"

Sam held her breath. Sara had been unable to make a final decision about the fate of this child. But even though she had never had the privilege of holding her own newborn child, Sam knew in her heart that if Sara looked at this baby she would want to hold him. And if she held him, she would never part with him.

"Yes... *yes*! Bring him to me," Sara answered with fierce pride. "I want to hold him."

When they placed the squirming infant in his mother's arms, Sam knew a joy that was as overwhelming as if this girl were her own daughter, the child her own grandchild. And then Sara raised tear-filled eyes to Sam and said in a small, tremulous voice, "Thank you, Sam. Thank you for everything! Would you... would you consider being my baby's godmother, or whatever it is they call it? He will never know his real grandmother, my mother, and, well... would you?"

Sam's heart overflowed with such an abundance of emotion that she thought it would surely break. She nodded with a sob, and gathered the two of them into her arms. "I would be proud and happy to be this young man's granny! And Noah? Can he be part mine, too?"

"Yes!" Sara answered with determination. "They will be brothers forever, and I'm gonna' manage to take care of them both somehow! With your help, of course!"

Sam knew a moment of panic, wondering just what she had gotten herself into. But Amy, who had been waiting at the door, walked in just then with Noah in her arms and laid him in the crook of Sara's one free arm. "Congratulations, Sara!" Amy said with a great smile. "I believe Sunny would be extremely happy with your decision, and *all* of us will help you in any way we can! You have two beautiful baby boys!"

Sara beamed at the babies in her arms. "Sam's gonna' be their granny!" she said with pleasure.

"Sam! A *granny*! Well, she's certainly *old* enough, at least," Amy joked happily, knowing what this would mean to Sam, who had always lamented her unfortunate inability to produce a family of her own.

Sam pushed Amy aside with a regal toss of her head. "I think you'd best leave us alone with our babies," she said with mock irritation. "One flash of light from that rock on your finger could blind them both!"

Amy exploded into laughter. She gave a sly wink at Sara, and then turned to go spread the happy news to the rest of her ever-growing family.

Amy jumped when the phone finally rang. That would be Tom, at last! She grabbed the receiver and spoke quickly, "Hello?"

"Good morning, Amy," came his familiar voice, and she felt the rush of gladness that it always brought. "How are you?"

"Tom! You're finally home! I've missed you so much!"

"Yes," he answered wearily. "I'm finally home. I think I'm getting too old for these extended trips and unending meetings. I've visited nine sales offices in the past two weeks, and before it was over I hardly knew one town from the other! Maybe I'll just retire!"

She grinned, knowing he was only joking. He loved his work, even though it was rather stressful at times. "When did you get in?" she asked.

"It was after midnight. I wanted to call you, but I hated to disturb everyone at that hour. What's been happening?"

"Well, Sara gave birth to a fine young man yesterday morning, and she has decided to keep the child and raise him, along with Noah, as brothers. I'm not sure just how she will do it, but there's money in her family and I believe her father will help her. And guess what! She's asked Sam to be the boys' godmother and Sam's prouder than a peacock! They're calling her granny!"

Tom laughed. "That's just great! Just what Sam's always needed, and good for Sara, too. Sometimes things seem to work themselves out in spite of us, thanks to a loving Father who always knows what's best."

"How true! Tom, have you heard anything from Crystal?"

"Yes. There was a note from her in my stack of mail, evidently sent about the time I left town. She was out of town herself, covering the opening of a new art display in some museum in Tulsa. She's had a promotion since her big break with *Lifestyles* and is now head of the *Oklahoman's* Arts and Leisure section."

"Wonderful! But the story for *Lifestyles*—shouldn't it be out by now?"

"That's what she wanted to tell us. The staff there has decided not to publish her story this month."

"*What*? How terrible! Didn't they like Crystal's article?" Amy asked, aghast.

"Actually they did. They liked it so much, in fact, that they've decided to hold it for a month and feature us on the cover of the March issue! Crystal will be bringing a bundle of magazines as soon as they're off the presses!"

"Oh, my! On the *cover*! Oh, Tom, that's just marvelous! I can't wait to see it!"

Tom laughed. "Yes, it is exciting news. But we may have to hire someone just to open our mail! I have a feeling we are going to be flooded with correspondence, some of it with checks enclosed, I hope! But I have something else I need to talk to you about, Amy."

"You sound serious, all of a sudden. Has something happened?" Amy asked cautiously.

"I had a message on my voice mail when I returned to the office this morning. Social Services in Tulsa has reported a young black woman who is the obvious victim of abuse from her live-in male companion. She gave the doctors the same old song and dance about falling down the stairs at her apartment complex, but she had undoubtedly been the recipient of a brutal beating. She finally confessed that her man had seen her with the white fellow she has recently become involved with, and that he nearly killed her in his anger.

"Amy, this woman is pregnant, probably by the white man she's been seeing. And she's deathly afraid of Jonas Brock, who she's lived with for the past five years, and who is the father of her other two children. She says he beats her regularly, whenever he gets drunk, and that she has tried to leave him several times, but she always goes back—out of fear, she says, but who knows? The older children are with her mother now, and the authorities are looking for Jonas, but they fear for this woman's life if he finds her before they find him.

"Amy, they've asked us to take her until her baby is born in six to eight weeks. They believe that Jonas would never think to look for her here, and that it may be the only place that they can keep her safe. But, as much as I've wanted to get involved in this kind of work, I'm just not sure we're ready. What do you think?"

Amy was silent for a long moment. "How can we say no, Tom? If this girl's life is in danger, we must help if we can, don't you think?"

"I don't know. I'm afraid that by offering our assistance—her name is Maddie, by the way, Maddie Coleman—I might be putting you and the other girls in danger, and I refuse to do that. I've told the authorities in Tulsa that I would let them know by the end of the week when Maddie is to be released from the hospital. Let's do some serious praying, Amy. I believe God will give us the answer we need."

Charlie tossed and turned in her bed, trying to find a comfortable spot. It was getting harder and harder to sleep these days, and seldom did she make it through the night without having to get up and go to the bathroom. She knew that she would be forced out of her bed tonight, too, but she snuggled under the covers for a while longer and just lay there, relishing her newfound happiness.

The letters to Mama and Papa had turned out much better than she could ever have hoped. She'd started out slow, testing every word, carefully skirting any issue that might offend her parents. She'd told them about the Christmas celebration with a mob of relatives coming in from everywhere, but had cautiously omitted any reference to the abundance of gifts under the tree and the lavish feast they'd all enjoyed. Papa would think it all a waste of good money. And she certainly didn't mention anything about a haircut or pierced ears or that cute boy named Josh who had been so nice to her.

In her second letter she had found the courage to tell them that she was playing the organ for their services here, even though she knew Papa would think it disgraceful for a "fallen woman" to be taking an active part in a church service. She told them about Ben, the gardener, and how he had stunned them all with his unbelievable tenor voice, singing like an angel from heaven. And when Sara had had her baby, she had just casually mentioned what a beautiful baby boy he was, and how Sara had named him after her own father, Lance. She told them that Sara had decided to raise her child herself, and not only that, she was taking on little Noah as well.

Charlie knew that her parents expected her to turn her baby immediately over to the adoption agency, and she supposed that she would, when it came right down to it. But it couldn't hurt for Mama and Papa to think about a cute baby boy, named for his grandfather, and being cared for by his own mother. She just couldn't bear to think of never holding this active little mite that was making her nights so uncomfortable now, and was kicking her with such enthusiasm.

And then she'd written about that new girl, Maddie, who had come and had moved into Sara's old room, now that Sara and her babies had gone down to the nursery. She told them that Maddie had come straight from a hospital because she'd been badly hurt in a fall or something, and that they all had rallied around to help take care of her. But she didn't tell them about the special friendship that had sprung up between herself and the black girl, or that if she wasn't down helping Sara with the babies, she was sitting at the end of Maddie's bed, and the two of them were talking together and laughing like silly children.

For she'd recognized the fear in Maddie's eyes, had understood the girl's quiet reticence. And she had been drawn to her in a way that she hadn't quite grasped, but the two of them had somehow forgotten their shyness once they'd gotten acquainted, and they had spent the long winter afternoons sharing confidences and bringing joy to each other. But, of course, Papa would most certainly have disapproved of their friendship. For there was not one thing the two of them had in common, and Maddie would only be considered to be a very bad influence upon herself.

Charlie squirmed restlessly. The pressure on her bladder was becoming hard to ignore. She heard a sound somewhere and wondered if one of the other girls was as wakeful as she. She hoped Maddie was sleeping peacefully tonight. She knew the girl often had nightmares, and wondered for the hundredth time why Maddie had let that man of hers treat her so badly. For she'd known for some time that Maddie had not fallen down any stairs. But Maddie had told her that she just couldn't help lovin' her man, and that even though she'd left him time and again, and was even now pregnant by another guy she'd taken up with, she knew she'd probably end up going back to her Jonas. The whole thing was almost more than Charlie could comprehend. Maddie was hardly older than she herself, yet she had two little ones already and a third one on the way, and had been with at least two men and never married at all! Papa would be horrified!

Charlie grinned broadly in the darkness of her room. She guessed she'd probably shocked her strait-laced parents with her letters, careful as she'd been. But she hadn't even known if her letters had been read, and so she had become more and more straightforward about her life at The Refuge. She never failed to mention her ever-growing faith in a loving, merciful God. And then there had been the letter for her today! The first mail she'd received since she had come here! When the other girls had gotten Christmas cards, she'd had nothing. And when a package arrived, it was always for someone else. When Miss Amy had handed her a letter this afternoon, she'd been speechless with joy. At last, a letter from Mama!

She'd waited as long as she could. She pushed back the covers and rolled awkwardly out of bed. The sudden coolness of the room made her shiver as she started slowly for the door, feeling her way in the dark. Then she turned back and reached for the letter that still lay on her night stand. She would read it again in the bathroom!

Jonas Brock was getting madder by the minute. He'd been wandering the deserted streets of Bartlesville for nearly an hour, and by now hadn't the faintest idea of where he was goin'. This was gonna' be some wild goose chase, he just knew it! But he *had* to find her! No woman of his was gonna' play around on him with some up-town white boy and get away with it! And Mo's sister, who worked nights at the hospital, had been positive Maddie had come here—to a place called The Refuge, she'd said.

When he'd stopped at that little bar earlier and asked about it, they'd said sure, they'd heard of the place. And they'd given him directions, but then he'd stayed around and had a few beers and now his mind was muddled, his eyes bleary. He'd found the Texaco station all right and made a left turn there, and then he'd gone on to the first light and turned right—or was it left? After circling through town a couple of times, he'd finally found the used car lot, but he couldn't for the life of him remember what he was supposed to do next.

He spewed out a long string of expletives. He'd find her if it took him all night! He rubbed a grimy paw across his tired eyes and shivered in the cold car. This was the last time he would borrow a car from Mo—a car with no heater, in the middle of the winter! But he couldn't risk driving his old car, which wasn't much better but at least had a heater that worked. He knew the cops were on his trail, and he had no intentions of gettin' caught 'fore he found Maddie and taught her a good lesson!

It slowly dawned on him that he had left town and was now on a gravel road somewhere. He was about to turn around in disgust when he saw it. The sign said The Refuge and pointed to a grove of trees he could just barely make out ahead. That had to be it! He pulled the car to the side of the road and got out to walk the rest of the way.

He stood for several minutes in the dark roadway, cursing the cold and the tiny sliver of a moon that hardly gave him any light at all. As soon as his eyes adjusted somewhat to the blackness of the night, he began to walk toward the darker splotch that he knew was his destination. He weaved slightly, and then stumbled. He should never have had those last two beers, but the waitress at the bar had been a purty little thing, and had smiled real nice. His breath came in great smoky puffs as he walked quickly down the empty road, and the frigid air slowly began to clear his head.

When he reached the edge of the trees he stopped again and listened intently. No sign of a dog. He tried to make out the general shape of a house that lay nearly hidden in the inky shade of many trees. He would have to move slow, 'cause it was darker than the pits of hell in there!

He inched his way around to the back of the house, following the line of trees. He saw two small cottages then, and stopped to think about it. Was this the home of a security guard or some kind of caretaker? He'd best be mighty careful. He decided to lose himself in the trees behind the cottages and then approach the house from the far side. He saw the sudden blaze of light from a small upstairs window and stopped again, his heart pounding. That would prob'ly be the bathroom, he decided, and he waited to see if it would go off again.

He stood shivering in the shelter of the trees until he could stand it no longer. Maybe they left that light on all night, or somethin'. But he was gonna' freeze in his tracks if he didn't get on with it. He hurried to the south tree line and stayed in the shade until he reached a point even with the back of the house. He was almost to the side wall when he saw the light go off. He'd wait a couple more minutes, till whoever was up and about had returned to bed, and then he'd slip inside that big back porch. The rest would be easy as pie!

He rubbed his frozen hands with glee and smiled for the first time that night.

Ben came awake with a start. He'd heard something. He looked around the dimly lit room and then realized that Molly had growled at some real or imagined threat. She'd been jumpy as an old woman ever since the pups were born, and he spoke gruffly, "Shut up, Molly!"

He had started to turn over and go back to sleep again when Molly rose from her blanket in the corner and moved to the window, jumping up to place her front paws on the sill. She growled again, and he saw the hair rise on the back of her neck.

Alert now, Ben remembered Tom's warning to him. That girl, Maddie. There could be trouble from a man back home. Keep a close eye on things. He got quickly out of bed and joined Molly at the window. He squinted at the void outside and slowly focused on the outline of the house. The yard appeared quiet, but he stood and watched, trembling with the cold and the burden of responsibility that suddenly seemed very real. What if he failed them, and something terrible happened inside while he stood here, uncertain and afraid?

While he watched, Ben saw the upstairs bathroom light come alive, putting a square of yellow on the blackness of the yard a few feet from his window. He frowned. The sudden light ruined what little night vision he had, making the yard an inscrutable void once again. He stood to one side, away from the glare of the light, and slowly focused on the south side of the yard, staring intently for what seemed to be an eternity. Abruptly, the light from the window vanished, and he blinked at the sudden change.

"I can't see a thing out there, Molly! Are you imaginin' things, girl?"

He sighed and was about to return to the warmth of his bed when he saw a black shadow slip past the end of the house and disappear into the deep shade.

He trembled violently and reached for the telephone.

Charlie completely lost track of the time as she let her eyes feast once more on her Mama's words which she knew by heart now.

Dear Charlotte,

We got all your letters. Your Pa refused to look at them, but I think he reads them when I'm not around. I always leave them on the kitchen table where he can't miss them and I found one in the front room last week.

I'm glad you're doing so good. You sound happy. I miss you being here. I think your Pa misses you too but he would never say so. I would have written sooner, but I was afraid he'd find out and be mad.

I'm writing today because I wanted you to know that I'm really glad you've gotten to know a merciful God—the God of my own childhood. I keep Him here in my heart, but I quit talking about Him long ago. Your father was raised so different, and he's a good man, but he looks to a different God than I do. I always wanted to tell you this, but I was afraid you'd ask the wrong questions and your Pa'd make things harder for you. And you, already such a shy little thing.

And Charlotte, I wanted you to know that I never believed you'd go out and do something bad to get pregnant. I don't know what happened, but I'm sure you didn't mean it to happen. I hope you will tell me about it someday.

Let me know when the baby comes and you're ready to come back home. I'll make your favorite plum pie when you get back.

Love,
Mama

P.S. I think maybe your Pa is listening to your words now, more than he ever did mine. He seems different, softer or something.

Charlie sighed with pleasure. It was a letter she would never have expected to get from her Mama. A letter like you might get from a friend or something. All warm and understanding. It felt good to think of Mama as her friend.

And Mama *knew*! All along her Mama'd had this new God deep in her heart. The God that she'd only just now discovered. She was so glad about that! It made her new faith seem more valid, somehow. She felt a special bond between them that she'd never felt before. And Papa was reading her letters, too! Maybe all those hours of scribbling down her thoughts and feelings was making a difference, after all.

Charlie heard a sound somewhere in the house and decided she'd better get back to her room. If anyone found her here in the bathroom reading a letter in the middle of the night, they'd think she'd gone daft. She hurriedly washed her hands and switched off the light as she left the room. The dimly lit hallway felt chilly to her, and she was suddenly anxious to crawl back into her warm bed. She was almost to her bedroom door when she realized she'd left Mama's letter by the sink in the bathroom. She didn't want the others reading her private letter, and so she turned around and headed back down the hall.

There it was, right where she'd left it. As she reached for it, she caught a glimpse of herself in the mirror. Even though there was very little light, she saw blonde hair that was soft and tousled from sleep, and cheeks the exact same shade of pink as her nightgown. She still had trouble believing this new creature was really her. She stared for a few more seconds. Suddenly she was sure she heard someone on the stairs. She grabbed her letter and made for the door.

When she saw him her heart nearly stopped. The two small night lights that were always kept burning in the hallway gave an eerie dimness, and she blinked quickly. He was big and black, and he smelled bad, like he'd been drinking, and she knew immediately that it was Maddie's Jonas. And he was right here in the hallway, heading straight for Maddie's door as if some secret intuition was telling him where she was. Charlie was so scared she thought for a minute she might faint. But she couldn't be weak and silly at a time like this! She'd always wanted to be brave like Esther and Ruth and the other women she'd read about in the Bible, but she'd never quite figured out how to do it.

Jonas took another lurching step down the hall, and Charlie knew she must do *something*, and do it quick. She heard herself give a weak little moan. "Help me! Can you please help me?"

But her voice was so choked and pitiful that Jonas didn't even hear her. She'd have to do better than *that*! "Oooooh! Oh, help me! Are you a doctor? My baby..."

He whirled around and stared at her, astonished.

She took a step in his direction. "*Please*, doctor. Help me! My baby's coming and..."

"Shush!" he whispered in a deep guttural voice, making a slicing motion with his arm as if to cut off her words. "You tryin' to wake tha whole house?"

She moved toward him, smelling his fetid breath, and remembered that same smell on that awful night in Papa's church. She was momentarily afraid she might be sick, but she took a deep breath and persisted. She must not let this man get near Maddie!

She suddenly reached for his arm and grabbed it in both hands. "You've got to help me, doctor!"

"I ain't no doctor, lady!" he snarled. "Now let go 'a my arm, will ya?"

She moaned again, still softly. The last thing she wanted to do was wake Maddie and have her suddenly appear in the hallway. And then she swayed, as if about to faint. She hoped God would forgive her for all this play-acting! Jonas suddenly grabbed her and went down on one knee to keep her from falling. She moaned again and clutched at her swollen belly.

"Shouldn't you be in bed or somethin'?" Jonas whispered hoarsely. He was just easing her into a reclining position on the floor when Sara reached the bottom of the stairway.

For Sara had been feeding both boys—Noah from a bottle she held in one hand and Lance at her breast in the crook of her other arm—when she'd heard strange groaning sounds coming from somewhere in the house. Alarmed, she'd laid the boys in their cribs and rushed out into the dark foyer at the foot of the stairs. As she'd stared at the upper hallway, which made a large u-shaped balcony that looked down upon the foyer, she'd seen a drama being acted out that had halted her, speechless.

What was that huge man doing in their upstairs hallway? And *Charlie!* It sounded like she was moaning and calling him doctor! Had she gone into labor and completely lost her senses? Then Sara remembered overhearing Amy telling Sam about some man the police were looking for—something to do with Maddie. That surely must be him! And it came to her in a flash of understanding that Charlie must *know* it was him, and that she was in the process of very nicely diverting him from Maddie's room at the end of the hall.

Sara jumped as Ben crept up behind her from somewhere in the back of the silent house. At that same moment Amy appeared from the south wing where her rooms were located.

"*Wha...?*" Sara stopped Amy's frightened cry before she had a chance to utter it, waving a hand in warning, then placing a finger to her lips and pointing up to the scene above them. The three of them stood in the shadow of the stairway and watched in horror as a strange man hovered over Charlie's prostrate body. He then stood, disentangling Charlie's vice-like grip from his arm, and once more started for the room at the end of the hall. Ben instinctively made a move for the stairs, but a light at the front window halted him. Help had arrived! He moved quietly to the front door and released the dead bolt.

Suddenly the foyer was alight and filled with uniformed men holding guns. One of them shouted, "Police! Hold it right there, Jonas! You're under arrest!"

Jonas looked wildly around him and found no place to go. Two officers bounded noisily up the staircase, guns trained upon him. Slowly he raised his arms in surrender.

At that moment the door directly behind Jonas flew open, and Bette let out an ear-piercing scream at the scene that met her eyes. The two policemen on the upper landing quickly frisked and cuffed Jonas, and the officer standing in the foyer below addressed Charlie. "Are you all right, young lady?"

Doors opened as Charlie nodded with a sheepish grin. "Yeah, I'm fine. I was just pretendin' so he wouldn't..." She broke off with a nervous giggle as she struggled to her feet. Bette was at her side instantly, to give her a hand.

The men in the hallway holstered their guns and grabbed Jonas by the arms, one on each side. And as they began moving down the staircase, Tom rushed through the front door, a frantic look on his face.

"*Amy*! Are you..."

He was cut off in mid-sentence as the officers reached the foyer with their prisoner and he was forced to step out of their way. They escorted Jonas out the front door into the cold, black night, and the remaining policeman apologized. "Sorry for all the commotion, folks! But we've been looking for Mr. Brock for some time now. He won't be botherin' you again!" And with that, he stepped out the door and closed it behind him.

Tom spoke again, a note of terror in his voice. "Amy, are you all right?" he asked as he moved to her side and put his arms around her protectively. He was disheveled, his clothes mismatched and mussed. Amy couldn't stifle a tiny chuckle. So this was the *real* Tom Logan! Uncombed, unshaved, and totally unconcerned about anything except her welfare. She knew, without a shadow of a doubt, that this was the Tom Logan that she would love for the rest of her days.

"Yes, Tom. I'm fine. All of us are just fine, thanks to Charlie!"

"Let's hear it for Charlie Brown!" Sara shouted, and Ben began to sing.

For she's a jolly good fellow,
For she's a jolly good fellow!

They all raised their voices in a joyful tribute to the flushed and totally embarrassed young lady in their midst. For the first time in a long while, and only for a moment, Charlie wished for her long hair.

Suddenly the door at the end of the hall opened, and everyone stared at a bewildered Maddie, who emerged, rubbing the sleep from her eyes.

"Whas goin' on anyway? Yu'all havin' a party, or *what*?"

There were giggles up and down the corridor as Charlie started toward the girl, moving with that slow waddling gait that is peculiar to very pregnant women. She gave her friend a brief hug and answered softly, "No, honey. The party's over. You go on back to sleep now!"

Tom paced the length of Amy's small office. "I can't believe I allowed all of you to be put in such a dangerous position! That man could have killed someone! What if...?"

"But we're all just fine, Tom!" Sam stated calmly.

"Yes, we are, thanks to Charlie's courageous actions!" echoed Amy. "And not only Charlie, but Sara, who had the foresight to keep us quietly out of the way until the police got here!"

They had gathered today to get their first look at the March issue of *Lifestyles*, which Crystal was bringing to show them. She would be arriving at any minute, but Tom had his mind elsewhere.

"I've just heard about a hotel for sale—the old Grand Hotel downtown which has been vacant for sometime now," Tom was saying. "They're going to tear it down if they don't get a buyer. I'm thinking of looking into it, and at least getting an idea of what the asking price will be. I know I can't afford it, but we would never have had last night's unfortunate little episode if we'd had a place where we could keep a victim of abuse hidden away and protected."

He looked around, as if only just noticing something. "Where's Jonathon? Is he coming today?"

Amy shook her head. "No, he called to say that Julie wasn't feeling well at all, and that he felt he should stay home and watch Daniel. Julie's due date is fast approaching, and..."

She broke off as Crystal burst through the door, with Jim right behind her.

"Crystal! You're here!" Amy exclaimed excitedly. "And *Jim*! We weren't expecting you! What a happy surprise!"

"Well, we have all kinds of good news!" Jim answered with a huge grin. "There's that silly little article, of course, and then there's the fantastic news that Crystal and I have decided to get married!"

Tom finally stopped his pacing, his mouth gaping with surprise. "Married! Now that *is* good news! I've had my eye on this beautiful little Indian princess since the day she first set foot in my office last summer! Congratulations, both of you! And now, let's see if she can put out a half-way decent piece of journalism..."

"Tom, cut that out!" Amy scolded, grabbing the first magazine off the top of Crystal's pile. "Would you look at that..."

The sudden shrill ring of her telephone interrupted her.

"Hello? Yes, just a moment." Amy stepped into the hall outside her office door and called, "Helen, would you tell Sara she has a phone call?"

When she stepped back into the room she joined the others as they gasped in excited surprise at the magnificent front page picture of their old house. Each of them began to read Crystal's warm, comprehensive account of all they were trying so hard to accomplish, and of the great success they were having.

Sam turned to Crystal with a look of wonder in her eyes. "You have managed to capture the very spirit of our work here, Crystal. And the pictures are nothing short of..."

A sharp knock at the door startled them. "Come in," Amy called.

The door opened and Sara stood before them, pale and trembling.

"Sara! What's happened?" Amy asked with concern.

"My Daddy. He... he's had a bad heart attack. They... they're afraid he..."

Tears jumped to the girl's eyes and she looked as if she might crumble in her distress. Sam jumped to her side and put an arm around her waist. "You must go to him, Sara!" she said urgently.

"But the babies! What...?"

"I'll see to the babies," Sam answered firmly. "After all, what's a granny for, if not to take over in an emergency!"

"Yes, Sara," Amy agreed. "We will see to the babies. You just go, and don't worry about a thing!"

"Come on," Sam said, moving with the girl through the open door. "We need to get you a ticket on the first plane, and get your clothes packed, and you need to show me where the babies' things are..." Their voices trailed them down the hallway toward the nursery where two tiny boys slept, unaware of the pain in Sara's heart. How torn she felt!

It was Amy who was now pacing the length of her office. "What dreadful news for Sara! Her heart must be breaking!"

"I wish there was something we could do," Crystal said.

"Yes," Tom agreed. "She's lost one parent already, and she must be petrified with fear at the thought of losing the other! We must pray for her, as well as her father."

"I think a prayer would be in order right now," Jim answered, and reached for Amy's and Crystal's hands. The four of them formed a circle of unity, and Jim asked a quiet prayer for Sara's safety and well-being, and for her father's return to health.

There was a moment of silence, and then Amy turned to Crystal. "Have you set a wedding date yet?"

"We're thinking it will be sometime this summer, maybe late June or July, when Jim's out of school. And what about the two of you?"

Amy looked at Tom with a smile. "We've finally decided on April 25th, if we can work it in around all the new babies!"

"And speaking of babies, I've just heard about a hotel that's for sale," Tom informed Jim and Crystal. "You remember, son, I was talking to you at Christmas time about the possibility of expanding. Do you think you'd have time to go take a look at it with me while you're here?"

Jim glanced at Crystal with a question in his eyes. "I'd like to do that, if we have..."

Another loud knock brought their heads around toward the door as it flew open once more. It was Bette. "Miss Amy, Charlie's in labor!"

Amy tossed her copy of *Lifestyles* on her desk and rushed from the room. And Jim and Crystal burst into laughter at the bewildered look on Tom's face.

He shook his head with baffled amusement. "Well, I guess the meeting's over!" he said with resignation.

Charlie delivered a nine pound four ounce baby boy after 26 hours of cruel labor. Her tiny frame had no business trying to give birth to such a hulking child. There was a time of extreme urgency when the boy's head had finally inched its way into the birth canal but there hadn't been room for his broad shoulders, and they had stuck right there and refused to budge. Dr. Cameron had worked with feverish intensity, for there was no possibility of a Caesarean section at that point in time, what with the head already crowned.

When the good doctor finally forced the reluctant child into the world, the boy gave a lusty yell of protest for the brutal treatment he'd been given. It was at that precise moment that Charlie knew without a doubt that she could never part with this hard-earned prize. After a thorough checking to determine whether or not he'd broken the little one's collar bone in his effort to save the lives of both of them, Dr. Cameron handed the hefty bundle to his new mother with a grunt of satisfaction.

"You've got yourself a football player here, that's for certain!" he said with a tired smile. "This boy's already half grown!"

Charlie looked at her new son with amazement. This was exactly the kind of boisterous, hearty child that her father had always wanted! She would name him Jonathon Abner, after the two men who'd most deeply affected her life. And she would either take him home, with her parent's blessing, or she would go elsewhere. But he was hers, and she had worked far too hard to get him here to ever give him up.

She closed her eyes and said a silent prayer of thanksgiving. And she asked her new-found Father for the strength she knew she was going to need. For, although this fine young man would carry his grandfather's name, she could see that he was the spittin' image of Elder Parsons.

Sara stared at the endless blue of the sky beyond her window with unseeing eyes. A tiny tear trickled slowly down her cheek, and she absent-mindedly brushed it away. She was on her way home—to what? Her father, who might be dying, might even be gone before she arrived there. And left behind were her babies. She felt an aloneness that threatened to overwhelm her.

What would it be like, she wondered, going back home now? Her friends all thought she had gone away to school last fall. She was sure her secret was safe, since no one except her father and Caroline had known the real story—and *they* weren't about to tell! She clenched her jaw with determination. She would have to face Caroline without her father's protection. Protection? She shook her head silently at the thought. Surely she didn't need *protection* from Caroline, did she? The woman was a witch, that was true, but hardly a threat! But, if her father died, what then?

She sighed. She couldn't think about it now. The tall, strong figure of her childhood must not leave her. Daddy, who'd been so proud of her, who'd loved her even when she'd rebelled and defied his authority. She couldn't imagine their house without his booming laughter. And the mills! What would become of them? Would Caroline want to sell them? They couldn't sell them and put all of those loyal men out of work! They just *couldn't*! What would happen to the Marshalls? And *Ross!*

She let her head drop into her hands. She must stop thinking like this! *Her father was not going to die!* He just couldn't—he was too young, *far too young!* Only—let's see—only forty-six! Yes, definitely too young. A strong man like that would beat this thing, would recover and live to hold his grandsons as he had once held her. And he would love them, too. No matter what hateful Caroline might say.

So was she considering taking the boys back to Missoula? She had steadfastly avoided contemplating their future beyond her stay at The Refuge. There was plenty of time to decide, wasn't there? But as the airplane rushed through an endless void of blue, thoughts of home, and of Ross, and of a possible confrontation with him, invaded her mind and settled there, stubbornly refusing to budge.

She remembered the sandy-haired boy that she had walked away from on the night that little Lance was conceived, and wondered if he had changed. Had he fallen in love with some girl he'd met at college? Would he hate her if she told him he had a son? She knew as surely as she drew breath that he would accept his responsibility for the whole thing and insist that he marry her! And, although she'd vowed the day her son was born that she would raise him to know and to love God as Ross would want—as she, herself, wanted—she simply could not face marriage with a man who had been forced into it against his wishes.

And, of course, there was Noah, also. Not just one child to raise and care for, but two! Now that would be enough to douse the enthusiasm of the most strong-hearted of men! An image of Ross, standing beside Rattlesnake Creek, fishing poles and a can of bait lying nearby, with two young boys, one brown-skinned, the other white, on either side of him, their small hands securely clasped in his strong ones, formed in her mind. She couldn't stifle the small smile that played at her lips.

She looked at him with shocked disbelief. The man who lay silent in the hospital bed was a mere shadow of the man she knew as her father. The only sounds in the room were the hum of the various monitors, the constant drip, drip, drip of the liquids that sustained his life, and the hiss of oxygen that eased his tortured breathing. She wanted to scream at the injustice of the whole thing. This man who'd toiled with the best of them in the lumber mills, who'd been strong and healthy and robust—to be brought to *this*! He looked so pale and shrunken—so *old*!

The tears coursed down her cheeks as she reached for his hand. A nurse appeared silently, checked the monitors, wrote something on his chart, and then disappeared as quietly as she had come. Sara felt a sudden need to escape from this awful room. She couldn't help her Daddy. He wasn't even aware of her presence. She turned and dashed from the room, only to find Caroline in the hallway outside.

"The doctor says he has stabilized somewhat," the woman said in a flat monotone. "They hope he will regain consciousness before morning."

Sara stared at her stepmother. Caroline also seemed older somehow, with dark circles under her eyes. There were unmistakable signs of stress in the woman's face, which was understandable, of course. But that hard, unemotional voice! As if Caroline were angry—at *her*? Or maybe just resentful of this interruption in the whirlwind of a gay, socially satisfying lifestyle.

A surge of rage brought bright spots of color to Sara's cheeks. Had it been that constant stream of late night parties, the continual pressure to entertain and to impress and to exceed his political peers that had taken this awful toll on her father's life? Had this woman, whom she'd detested from the moment she'd laid eyes on her, pushed her father beyond his limits and caused his heart to fail? She clenched her fists, but forced herself to remain calm.

"I will stay with him tonight. You go home and get some rest. You must be exhausted," Sara stated with no sign of her inner turmoil.

Caroline nodded. And without another word, she turned and retreated down the corridor and into an elevator. Sara moved slowly back into her father's private room. They'd moved him there from ICU only a short while before she'd arrived, she learned from the nurse who checked his vitals every few minutes. There had been constant improvement. They expected him to regain consciousness soon. She was welcome to rest on the cot in the corner. If she needed anything, just press the red button next to Mr. Franklin's bed.

Sara sighed and settled herself on the narrow, uncomfortable cot. What she needed was a hot shower and a real bed. She needed her father restored to the man he'd been when she'd last seen him. She needed her babies, and her arms ached with that need. She thought again of Ross. He was undoubtedly nearby. Would she see him soon? What if he decided to come and visit her father? What would she say to him? She finally drifted off into a restless sleep.

Sometime later she was startled awake by a flurry of activity in the room. There were excited voices. She saw several white-coated figures hovering over her father's bed and sat up abruptly. What was wrong? The nurse nearest her turned with a smile. "Your father's awake. Would you like to say hello to him?"

Sara scrambled from the narrow cot and moved to her father's side. "Daddy! How are you, Daddy?"

He opened his eyes with some effort and finally focused upon her. "Sara," he whispered softly. "Glad you're here..."

As if exhausted by the effort, her Daddy's eyes closed again. The doctor, who had been watching him closely, turned to Sara and said quietly, "He's doing fine, but he needs lots of rest. He will sleep normally now. And you might as well sleep, too. We'll keep a close watch on him."

Sara returned to her meager bed with a heart filled with gladness. Daddy was going to be okay! She breathed a quick prayer of gratitude and once again closed her eyes. But there was little sleep, and with many interruptions, she found. When the morning sun peeked in through the small window above her cot, she felt the same sluggishness that always followed those nights when the boys vied for her attention, one waking the minute she got the other to sleep.

But her father was obviously better! He managed to let her know, in whispered half-sentences, that he was proud of her decision to keep her child, that he was pleased that she had named him for his "old Granddaddy." He was sorry for his initial reaction to her pregnancy. He asked where was

Caroline and nodded with apparent relief when Sara told him she was at the house, getting some much needed rest.

And Sara was glad that she had been the one to be here when her Daddy awakened. Glad to have had these scattered moments with him alone. Glad that Caroline hadn't felt it her duty to arrive early and "take over." But when the woman still hadn't made an appearance by late morning, Sara began to wonder if she was ever to get a warm bath and some hot food in her stomach. She hadn't eaten since yesterday and had slept very little. And she desperately wanted to call Sam and check on her two sons.

At a few minutes before noon Caroline sailed into the room, refreshed and stunning in a sleek yellow pantsuit, the dark circles gone, or at least artfully hidden beneath her makeup. She had apparently taken time to visit her hairdresser, for she was freshly combed and curled and coifed. "I understand he's been awake," she said with a glance in Sara's direction. She gave a dismissive wave of her hand and added, "Joe's waiting in the car for you. You can go now."

Sara bristled at the woman's authoritative manner, and spoke sharply. "The doctor says he needs to rest. We're not to talk to him unless he wakes on his own."

"I've already spoken with Dr. Preston," Caroline answered with haughty disdain. "Such a nice young man, and so good looking!" She said those last words to the wall above the bed, her back to Sara as though she had totally forgotten her presence. Sara snatched her coat and purse and fled from the room.

Lance Franklin's improvement was amazing, and he soon insisted that he needed no one there overnight. Sara and Caroline took turns keeping him company during the daytime, as neither much liked having the other around. By Saturday Sara was thinking strongly of returning to Oklahoma and her babies. She would wait until Monday. If Daddy continued to improve, she would go.

But Saturday promised to be a beautifully sunny spring day, and Sara wanted nothing more than to saddle her mare and go for a long ride. Caroline would be with Daddy, whenever she got herself out of bed and finished with her lengthy toilette, that is. How she longed for the crisp mountain air, the tangy smell of pine, the feel of leather beneath her, the warm sun on her back. *Home!* She had missed it more than she'd realized.

She hurriedly dressed in faded Levi's and a warm woolen shirt. She pushed her feet into her old riding boots with a sigh of pleasure and grabbed a glass of milk and a hot cherry turnover as she dashed out the back door. The long days confined in a hospital room had taken their toll, and she took a deep breath of cold, clean air. Joe was waiting in the car for her, and she crawled in with a grin, her mouth stuffed with Mary's fresh pastry, her heart filled with joy. It was good to bask in the love and care of Joe and Mary once more. If only she had her babies here, and Daddy was home again and healthy, and Caroline would just disappear into the sunset or something... Oh, well! She'd just have to be satisfied with the day that stretched invitingly before her.

She chattered happily with Joe as they drove out of town toward the Marshall's farm, which, of course, still belonged to Daddy, and seemed more like home to her than that monstrosity in town ever could. She couldn't wait to see Ginger, even if it meant facing Ross again. After all, Daddy had all but sold her mare in his anger last fall, and had only conceded to keeping her when the Marshall's had obligingly agreed to care for her there. And wouldn't it be easier to see Ross for the first time after all these months there, in the company of the other members of his family? What could he say beyond how have you been, and how's your Daddy doing, and how's school going? She must remember that they all thought she'd been away at school. Maybe she should think up some atrocious story to tell, to get them all laughing and to avoid any uncomfortable questions.

Sara drank in the beauty around her, the snowcapped peaks, the early spring flowers, the stalwart beauty of the huge pines. Suddenly the little farm where she'd grown up appeared before them, and quick tears stung her eyes. It looked just wonderful! Sugar, Ross's beloved collie, came bounding out to greet them with a burst of wild barking that brought Becky to the front porch. Sara jumped out of the car as Joe brought it to a stop, hugging the excited dog and waving at Becky.

"Sara!" Becky called happily. She turned and hollered into the open door, "Mom! Sara's here!" She then leaped off the porch and enveloped Sara in a breathless hug.

Martha Marshall was out the door in the next instant and ready with a hug of her own, along with a warm greeting for Joe. "Please, come in! It's so good to see you, Sara, sorry as we all were about your Daddy's poor health. Joe, don't leave yet! I've got fresh eggs in the house that you can take home to Mary!"

It seemed to Sara that she had never been away. The warmth and the love and the goodness of these people was unchanging. But there had been definite improvements to the house and the yard. A freshly painted picket fence enclosed the carefully kept lawn, and the house, also newly painted, Sara noticed, had a look of comfort and luxury that hadn't been there before. The mills were thriving, and, from the look of things, so were the Marshall's. As well they should! Jim Marshall had been made general manager of the entire operation, and was indispensable to her father. She wasn't surprised that he was absent on this Saturday morning, but she wondered where Ross might be.

Finally, she asked, "And where is Ross? Does he have classes on Saturday?"

"No, no. He left early this morning with his fishing pole," his mother answered with a smile. "Thank goodness he didn't ride Ginger, because I'd be willing to bet that's what you have in mind for today!"

Sara nodded, glancing eagerly at the door. Becky noticed, and, grabbing her friend's hand, said "Come on! Let's go see her! She'll be tickled to death and rarin' to go on such a great day!"

Becky had changed, too, Sara saw. From a gangling young girl into a remarkably attractive young lady, dressed in Levi's and a handsome western shirt that were a cut above anything Sara had seen her wear before. But prosperity would never change these people, she realized with a touch of envy, as it had changed herself. She was glad. And she knew that she was disappointed that Ross wasn't here. He must be very grown up, too, she guessed, with only a few weeks left before he would graduate from college.

But her first sight of Ginger chased all other thoughts from her mind. Her mare was grazing in the small pasture behind the barn, the dark chestnut of her well-groomed coat gleaming in the bright sun. Sara saw the horse lift her head at their approach, and then, with a glad nicker of recognition, come galloping toward them.

"Ginger!" Sara cried brokenly. "How are you, girl?" She threw her arms around the mare's long neck and buried her face in warm horse-flesh. "Let's get the saddle! I can't wait a minute longer," Sara said to Becky who stood beside her, grinning broadly.

Once astride, Sara let her mind empty of everything except the beauty around her. The old familiar trails, the grandeur of Squaw Peak, buried at this time of year under an exceptionally heavy blanket of snow, and the riotous chorus of birdsong and chattering chipmunks, all brought memories of her mother sharply into focus. She wondered what Mama would think about little Lance, her first grandchild. And Noah! She hoped Mama knew, for she believed her Mama would be proud of her decision to raise the boys.

It seemed an eternity since she had held those babies! Even though she called every night and Sam assured her that everything was just fine, she longed to be there, to hold them and give them her love. She wished she hadn't had to wean Lance so suddenly, because nothing in her young life had even begun to prepare her for the feeling she'd gotten when he'd first latched onto her and partaken of the gift of her milk. Such sweet pain! And then, barely two weeks later, she'd known the pain of milk-gorged breasts, begging for release. But there'd been no choice in the matter. Nobody had ever promised that life would be fair!

The sound of rushing water came to Sara's ears, and she realized that Ginger, free of any restraint from her rider, was taking them, as she always had, to the banks of Rattlesnake Creek. Sara grinned. "Nothing's changed, has it girl!" she said softly to her mount. She turned her face up to the sun, eyes closed, heart filled with a bittersweet mix of her love for this rugged country and her longing for her children in Oklahoma.

Ginger's sudden nicker brought her sharply to her senses, and then she saw him standing there, fishing pole in hand. It was a moment from the past, the same shock of wheat-colored hair against sun-bronzed skin, the same deep azure eyes that seemed to reflect the blue of the vast Montana sky above them. She stared at him, speechless. He was tall and broad and incredibly handsome. A man. He said her name softly, "Sara."

She felt her body go weak, her heart struggle to stay confined within her chest. Something about the genuine warmth of his smile and the deep tenderness in his eyes, accompanied, as it was, by the rough huskiness in his voice, brought unexpected tears to her eyes. She blinked them back quickly. She was grateful for Ginger's solid bulk beneath her quaking body.

"Hi, Ross," she finally managed in a small, breathless voice.

"I was hoping you'd come home, Sara. How's your Daddy?"

"He... he's feeling much better."

Ross nodded slowly. "Good. We've been prayin' for him. And Dad's been in constant touch with him, of course, since he got to feeling like talking a little. I wanted to go see him myself, but..."

It was Sara's turn to nod. Unable to think of anything else to say, she asked, "You catchin' anything?"

He chuckled softly, and she knew that he, too, was remembering that summer day long ago when she had first happened on to him here.

"When I first laid eyes on you, in this same exact spot, by the way, I thought you were the most beautiful girl in the world. But I was wrong. You're even more beautiful today." He spoke in that same quiet way he'd always had, with simple honesty. She flushed with pleasure, and shook her head.

"The sun must surely have blinded you! I've got dark, ugly circles under my eyes, and my hair..."

"Get down."

His quiet authority held her momentarily suspended, unable to move. Then she swung down to the ground to face him. He covered the space between them with two long strides and pulled her into a strong embrace.

Time and place and all sanity fled in the warmth of his arms. "I've missed you so much, Sara," he whispered. "Why did you leave me?"

She squeezed her eyes tightly shut and searched for an answer. She knew he wasn't questioning the distance that she had put between them, only the separateness, the shutting out. "I... I was so scared... and so embarrassed. I thought you must hate me..."

"Oh, Sara," he groaned with despair. "How could you ever think such a thing?"

She realized that this young man deserved nothing less than the truth, and she reluctantly pulled out of his arms and gazed into his gentle face.

"Ross, I... I didn't go away to school last fall like you think I did. I... I've been in Oklahoma..." She wavered beneath his steady gaze.

But he only nodded, his warm hands on her shoulders, his eyes filled with understanding. "I was sure you weren't at school. But Oklahoma? Why...?"

"I had a baby, Ross. Your baby. *Our* baby. I... I'm so sorry about everything... for how I acted and..."

But he wasn't listening any more. His eyes wide with wonder, he asked, "We have a baby? Oh, Sara! Oh, thank You, God! I was so afraid you might have run away to have an abortion, or something..." His voice broke, and he pulled her back into his arms, rocking her gently.

But she wasn't finished. She knew she must tell him the whole story.

"I almost did have an abortion, Ross. I... I was so scared, and I couldn't bear to tell my Daddy. And... and *Caroline*! She guarded me like a probation officer for the entire summer, as if she suspected I might go and do something stupid and embarrass them totally. Which, of course, was entirely true! I... well, I was on my way to an abortion clinic in Helena when I saw an article lying in the back seat of the taxi I was riding in. It was all about this place called The Refuge in a little town in Oklahoma. It was like... well, *you* would have said that God spoke to me through that article, and I know now that He really did. Anyway, I told everyone I was off for school, but I really went to Oklahoma to have our baby."

"But why didn't you tell me? Let me help you? My family would have been more than glad to do whatever they could..."

Sara winced at the pain in Ross' voice. She'd been bent on sparing him, and of hiding her own shame from him, and she'd ended up hurting him terribly. She wondered if he could ever completely forgive her.

"I know that now, Ross. But I was so afraid that my father's career would be damaged if everyone found out about the pregnancy, and... and you were so upset that night. I was too ashamed to face you... Can you ever forgive me?"

He pulled her tight again, and laughed softly in her ear. "Oh, Sara, you silly little goose! There's nothing to forgive! But tell me everything. Tell me about our child and this place in Oklahoma—*everything!*"

She looked up at him with a broad smile. "Well, you have a son, and his name is Lance Eugene Franklin. He's just beautiful, and he's with his new granny in Oklahoma. Her name is Sam and she has red hair just like mine! The Refuge is a really groovy place where girls like me can go, and they take care of you and teach you about God and about responsibility and everything..."

"Oh, Sara! I'm so glad! But let's get married now, so I can take care of my son and of you..."

"No, Ross!"

His face fell. "No? But... but why *not*? He's my son, *our* son, and he deserves a father, and we could be a real family..."

But she was shaking her head firmly. "Ross, I didn't tell you all of this to force the responsibility of a wife and a son upon you. You haven't even finished school yet, and you have your life and a career to think about. We can't just... just *get married* because of a mistake, a... a foolish *whim* that was my fault, not yours! Marriage should be built on something more than that, on love and respect and mutual trust..."

Her forceful manner wavered at the light she saw in his eyes. He lifted his hands to cup her face in their warmth. "Sara, will you just hush for a minute? I *love* you, Sara! I've known that I wanted you for my wife ever since that day when you found me right here, and I fell hopelessly in love with you. *Please*, tell me that you love me, too, and give me a chance to show you how much I care, and let me be a father to my son!"

"Sons."

"*What?*"

"Sons, as in two. I... I haven't told you about Noah..."

He laughed, a joyous sound that filled their beautiful Montana valley and joined with the crashing turbulence of their wild, madly rushing Rattlesnake Creek. It was the sweetest sound that Sara had ever heard, and she took his hand and led him to the big flat rock that had surely been placed beside this scenic stream by a benevolent God for just this sort of occasion. They sat together on its sun-warmed surface and she told him everything he wanted to know. About Amy and Tom and Jonathon and Sam. About the cheerful Helen, and Ben, who could sing like no one she had ever heard before, and Crystal, who had made them famous. She told him about Sunny, whom she'd loved and lost, and the child that Sunny had poured out her life for. The son that she had vowed to raise as her own, as a brother to baby Lance.

She saw the unmistakable pride and love in his eyes as she spoke. She saw his obvious delight at the prospect of raising not just one son, but two. She heard the intensity in his voice when he begged her to take him back with her, so that he could get acquainted with his new family. And so she told him, her heart bursting with the wonder of it all, what he most wanted to hear.

She told him that she loved him.

Sara fairly floated through the door of her Daddy's room that evening, and then stopped short at what she saw. Her father appeared to have aged at least 20 years since she'd seen him the day before, his face a pale, sickly gray color. She was astounded at the change in him as he lay there asleep. She slipped back through the door and hurried down the corridor to find his nurse.

"What's happened to my father?" she demanded when she found Shirley, who had been his night nurse since the heart attack. Shirley was a sweet-tempered lady and very gentle, and Sara admired her very much.

"I think he is very tired this evening," Shirley said, frowning slightly. "He had company all morning—his attorney, I think they said. But he seemed in good spirits at lunch time, according to Nancy. Mrs. Franklin was here awhile this afternoon and... well, I'm not sure what happened. I... well, I think they may have had some sort of disagreement, or something..."

Sara realized that Shirley was reluctant to discuss any family quarrels that may have taken place. She thanked the woman and slowly returned to her father's room. What could possibly have happened? And why had her father called Ed Jones in to see him? Or maybe Ed just came to visit, she mused. The two men had been friends for many years now.

Her Daddy opened his eyes and smiled weakly as she approached his bedside. Swallowing her fear, Sara greeted him calmly, "Hi, Daddy. How are you feeling?"

"Kinda' tired, I guess," he answered in a low, defeated voice.

"Where's Caroline?" Sara asked cautiously, hoping she wouldn't further upset her father, but intensely concerned about what could have taken place today to make this drastic change in him.

"She's gone." He looked so sad that Sara reached down and planted a kiss on his forehead.

"Gone? She went home already?" she asked in a light, nonchalant tone.

"No. She's gone. Back to Washington."

Sara couldn't hide her astonishment at his words, spoken with obvious pain. She saw a tear slide down one cheek and fought to hide the anger she felt inside. What in the world had that woman done now?

"But... but *why*? Was there an emergency or...?"

Her Daddy slowly shook his head. "No. No emergency. She was... I guess it was my fault. She was very angry... I didn't mean to hurt her feelings..."

His voice trailed off to a weak whisper. Dying as she was to know the truth, Sara could see that reliving the ordeal was tiring him even further. And so she merely said quietly, "I'm sure everything will be okay, Daddy. We'll talk about it later. You need to rest now."

But he shook his head with renewed strength. "No. I want you to know everything. You see... well, I called Ed in to see me this morning. I wanted to make some changes to my will. I... I wanted to make sure you and the babies would be well provided for. I didn't mean to upset Caroline, didn't even think about it..."

Her father looked so agitated and unhappy that Sara quickly interrupted, "Oh, Daddy! You didn't need to change anything! You can give *everything* to Caroline, I don't care! I just want you to get well..."

"No. It's just not right!" he countered with all the strength he could muster. "She... Caroline was a wealthy woman when I married her. She has no need... But you have those little ones to raise..."

"Daddy, you can give every penny to Caroline if it will make her feel better—make *you* feel better! I'll be fine! 'Cause I talked to Ross today. We're gonna' get married, Daddy! Ross will take care of us. We don't need your money, *really*!"

Her Daddy smiled for the first time since she had entered his room. "Oh, baby! I'm so glad... Ross is a fine young man. Yes, he'll take good care of you..."

And then he drifted off to sleep. Sara stood at his bedside, holding his hand, for some time before she finally sat in the chair next to him, watching him closely. He had seemed somewhat relieved as he fell asleep, but still she worried. She didn't like his deathly pallor, and his breathing seemed more labored than before.

When Shirley came in to check on him later, Sara followed her back into the hallway and asked anxiously, "How do you think he is? Should I stay with him tonight?"

"His heartbeat is a little rough, but I think it will settle down as he rests. You go on home and get some sleep. I promise to call you if anything changes."

Daddy was still sleeping at nine o'clock, and she was fighting to keep her own eyes open. It had been a long, emotional day. She decided to call Joe to come and get her. Certainly Daddy would be better in the morning!

The call came a few minutes after midnight. She must come to the hospital immediately. Her father had suffered another massive heart attack. They were trying to reach Mrs. Franklin.

She burst into the room where anxious doctors and nurses were frantically fighting for her father's life. But she knew instinctively that there was no hope. She buried her head in the rumpled sheets and clung to his arm, sobbing hysterically. Joe and Mary stood quietly at the back of the room, tears freely flowing. They were joined shortly by Jim and Ross Marshall. But Caroline was nowhere to be found. Her maid had reported that Mrs. Franklin had attended a party that evening, but that she had not been told where. They would continue calling all her friends...

At a few minutes before one Lance Franklin's tired heart gave up the battle and stopped forever. His daughter was inconsolable. But Ross was there. Somehow, in the midst of the turmoil and the tragedy, Sara came to the realization that Ross would always be there.

～

Tom was pacing the perimeter of his office and talking to God. He had just ended a most unsettling conversation with Amy. Her call had come as he was diving into the huge stack of mail that lay on his desk, a common occurrence since the latest edition of *Lifestyles* had hit the racks. He knew he shouldn't complain, since his incoming mail was just a drop in the bucket compared to the great load that arrived each day at The Refuge. And, once he had separated the private letters from his business correspondence, he found he had a hard time concentrating on the details of his work when there was that other stack of unopened mail sitting there that would undoubtedly interest him far more. The gracious words of encouragement, the personal stories, and, of course, the many kind donations, all were a great source of encouragement to him.

But Amy's troubling news had left him dejected and uncertain. And so he paced, and he questioned, and he pleaded.

Dear God, please help me to a better understanding of what it is You want me to do here. I allowed that poor girl Maddie to come under our care only after I felt sure it was Your will that I do so. And then all that trouble with Jonas—which turned out all right, I admit—but now, after we have managed to see the girl safely through her delivery, Amy tells me she has up and left us in the middle of the night! To go, without a doubt, back to the man who caused such pain and turmoil in her life!

Dear Father, what am I doing wrong? She has turned her back on her new baby daughter, "because Jonas would never accept a white baby in his house," as she put it in the note she left with her child. Both she and Jamila have returned to that old way of life, making our work here seem to be of no consequence at all! Is it all in vain, then...?

He was dimly aware of knocking somewhere...

God, just tell me what to do! That hotel that's right here, and for sale, and, it would seem, the perfect answer for so many of our inadequacies—is that the direction we need to go? And if so, then how? We would need at least a half a million dollars just to get started! We need your help, Lord. We simply can't do this thing alone...

The knocking persisted, and he realized that someone was at his door. Maybe they would just go away...

God, I don't want to seem ungrateful. You have given us so much already! Crystal's story has reached thousands, and the money keeps pouring in. But nothing even close to what we would need! Maybe Amy is right when she tells me that I can't do it all—that there will always be those who need care and spiritual guidance and just a chance to start over. But that hotel, properly run, could provide jobs and food and shelter to so many, and, at the same time, become a prominent downtown facility that the city could benefit from and be proud of! I just know we could make it work, if it is Your will, God. But there are so many unanswered questions...

The knocking had grown progressively louder. Tom looked at his door with a loud sigh. "All right, all *right!*"

He pulled the door open with a frustrated frown darkening his features. And came face to face with Bill Johnson, president of American Trucking Company.

"*Bill!* Come in! I... I'm sorry I was so slow to answer. I'm afraid I was doing some deep soul searching and I..."

"Don't worry about it, Tom. I would have just gone away, but I have something very important I'd like to talk to you about," Bill Johnson responded with a warm smile. The two men had become great friends over their long years in business together. They each tended to seek the other's company for almost any occasion, whether it was a game of golf or a men's fellowship meeting at church.

Bill lifted the copy of *Lifestyles Magazine* that he had carried with him into the room and continued with some excitement, "Tom, I want to congratulate you and Amy! This article about your place is just superb! And well deserved, I might add. I have the highest regard for your efforts there, and that is what I've come here today to talk to you about."

The older man pulled his spectacles off and ran his fingers through his thinning white hair. He was a large man, his younger days as an especially talented college athlete still apparent in his bearing. "Tom, I've just come from a meeting with the other Johnson boys, and we've voted unanimously to make a large donation to your work at The Refuge. And about time, I might add! We should have been helpin' you long ago, God forgive us. We were just wonderin' if there was somethin' special you might be needin'. Maybe a new wing or..."

"Or a hotel!" Tom interrupted with a broad smile.

⁕

Tom talked of nothing but the wonders of "his hotel." It seemed that he and Bill Johnson were always either busily examining every inch of the fine old structure, or closeted in Bill's office, going over all of the details. They were equally excited about their new project, and they came to the mutual agreement that the sale of the hotel should be announced to the public as an acquisition of American Trucking Company, with no mention of any connection to The Refuge.

"That way," as Bill put it, "we can staff it with your young girls, or Ben's homeless friends, or whoever may be in dire need of a job, without any embarrassment to any of them. And I believe we can seal off that top floor for victims of abuse and their families without anyone even suspecting that they are there. A Safe House at the top of a luxurious old hotel! Now who would ever guess at such a thing?"

Bill laughed his great booming laugh, and Tom grinned, as excited as a kid with a new toy. "Yes, I agree. If we tell the world that our private living quarters are to occupy that top floor, which they will, of course, then no one will need to know that half of it is to be converted into small apartments for battered women and their children. And your idea to make the only access to that floor be a private elevator opening into our suite just adds to the safety of this arrangement!"

And so they worked and studied and planned. Every sort of inspector was brought in to determine the extent of the renovation. The building was found to be structurally sound and remarkably solid. They would need to replace the old outside stairwells that were used only for a fire escape, and plans were underway to build a retractable stairway for the private top floor, which, when released in an emergency, would join the steps going to the floors below them. Together, they thought of every eventuality. They would try to retain as much of the original decor as possible, restoring and refurbishing it to become again the luxuriously grand old hotel it had been when it was built in the early forty's. The Grand Hotel of Bartlesville would become The Grand American Hotel.

Amy listened to Tom's incessant chatter with quiet pleasure until Julie went into labor on a cold March night. And then Tom's hotel took a sudden back seat to Jonathon and Julie's brand new baby girl, and he had to be quiet and listen to Amy's excited ravings. He did so amicably, realizing with pride that Miss Amy Elizabeth Gardner would soon become *his* grandchild, as well! Besides, he was so pleased with life at the moment that he would gladly have given Amy the moon if she'd wanted it, and if only he could get his hands on it.

The only splinter in their happiness came when Tom announced his intention of turning the top floor of his wonderful hotel into fine living quarters for the two of them to go to after their wedding. He saw her face fall in that first unguarded moment, but then she rallied with a smile. "Well, yes, that will be nice, I guess. Whatever you think is best, Tom. I... I just assumed we would live here at The Refuge..."

"But there will be so much more space in the hotel, Amy! Here we would be cramped into one room, and with very little privacy. And besides, I could oversee the work at the hotel much more effectively if we lived there, don't you think?"

"Of course, Tom," Amy answered tentatively. "But what about our work here? Who will take care of the girls?"

"I think we can safely leave Sam in charge here, with Helen and Ben to help her. And we'll be close by if she needs us," Tom responded, his mind clearly made up.

And Amy had gone along with his plans, as he knew she would, but he had a moment of doubt every time he remembered her obvious disappointment at his decision. It was true that her lovely little chapel was right there on the grounds, and he knew the pleasure it gave her. But he would see to it that they attended every Sunday Session there. Thus reassured in his own mind, he let the matter rest and poured all of his energy into making the Grand American a prestigious landmark once again.

And then one bright day late in the month, Sara returned, with a tall, good looking stranger at her side. She introduced Ross to all of the ogling girls with great pride, met Sam in the back hallway with a giant hug, and then rushed to find her sons. How they had grown and changed, and how beautiful they were! Sam stood beside Ross, both with tears in their eyes, as they watched Sara gather her babies into her arms with a sob of joy.

Charlie was glad Sara had come back before she had to leave to go home. Everything just seemed to be livelier when the spirited redhead was about, and that boy Ross! Sara had explained that it was Spring Break at his college, and he would be staying for the entire week. She knew all the girls were envious of Sara and her handsome young man, and she had to admit she'd felt a bit of a twinge herself. How wonderful it would be to have someone so nice who wanted to marry you and take care of you forever!

She hurriedly changed her own little Johnny. She was sure Sara was alone with the boys in the room next to hers, and she wanted to have a little chat with her while she had the chance. She knocked softly on Sara's door, then entered at Sara's invitation, with her son in the crook of her arm.

"Charlie Brown! Let me see that boy of yours!" Sara said, beaming.

Charlie flushed proudly as she held her son out to Sara.

Sara welcomed the boy into her arms and said with deep feeling, "You must be so proud of him, Charlie! And I'm proud of you, too, and your decision to keep him. You've become a brave girl since you joined us here!"

"Me? Brave?" Charlie asked, shaking her head in denial.

"But of course! It took a lot of courage to stand up to Jonas that night, and I understand you took charge of Maddie's baby girl until she was adopted out. And now you've defied your parent's wishes by keeping your child! I'd say that's a far cry from the shy little 'fraidy cat you were when you first came here!"

"Well, I haven't faced my Papa yet," Charlie said with some trepidation.

"You'll do just fine. And they're gonna' be plum amazed at how different you look now!"

"Amazed isn't the word!" Charlie agreed with a small laugh. "And it's all your fault, Sara! You've helped me and encouraged me and.."

"Led you astray!" Sara finished with a laugh, squeezing the other girl's arm with fondness. "I'm so glad you came in here today. I've got something I need to talk to you about."

"What's that?" Charlie asked, taking Johnny back into her arms so that Sara could pick up Noah, who had begun to fuss.

"Well, Ross and I have been talkin'..."

"Oh, Sara, he's so *nice*! And *so* good looking," Charlie interrupted with a sparkle in her eye. "And the rest of us are totally jealous!"

Sara laughed with pride. "He is pretty special, isn't he? And he's taken such a fancy to this place, you wouldn't believe! He asked Miss Amy so many questions about The Refuge that she finally sent him off to see Mr. Tom. And that's where he is right now! But, Charlie, he is insisting that we get married right now, this week, in our very own little chapel! Would you play the organ for us, Charlie?"

"Oh, Sara! How *exciting*!" Charlie gushed. "Of course, I'll play for you! Just tell me what and when... Is Ben gonna' sing? What are you gonna' wear? I'm positively *green* with envy..."

Everyone pitched in to help. Sam took them shopping and Amy decorated their beautiful little chapel with early spring wildflowers from their own little forest. Ross ordered airline tickets for his parents and Becky so they could come for the grand occasion. And on a mild evening late in March, Sara walked down the aisle of the candle lit chapel to become Mrs. Ross Marshall. No one was happier at that moment than Ross Marshall, himself.

Two days later Ross joined his family for their flight back to Montana. He begged Sara to go back with him, but she shook her head solemnly. He had a degree to finish and didn't need the distraction of a wife and two children. And besides, she needed to study hard now, so that she could pass her GED before school was out. He must come back for Tom and Amy's wedding, of course, and she promised to take the boys with her to attend his college graduation. And then they must decide where they would live and what they would do. For she was a wealthy woman now, and her father's vast lumber business would soon be hers. The whole world lay beckoning to them, but it would wait for a few more weeks.

And then it was time for Charlie's parents to come. She was so nervous she felt ill. They knew nothing of her decision to keep her child. For that was something she could only tell them face to face, with her son in her arms. What if her father refused to take her home with a child in tow? He could very well make quite a spectacle of himself in front of Miss Amy and all the girls, she knew. She had everything packed and ready, but only when her Papa agreed to give her child a home would she take her things from her room.

She heard the knock at the front door and trembled violently. She heard Miss Amy's call to her and glanced self-consciously at her reflection in the mirror. She wore the stylishly simple green linen sheath she had worn for Sara's wedding, with her tiny emerald colored stones in her ears. A shining cap of blonde hair framed her lovely face, her cheeks softly flushed, her enormous eyes a forest of the darkest green. She smiled shyly at the image she saw, squared her shoulders, and picked up her infant son.

She walked into the front foyer, her head held high, and faced her astonished parents.

"Hello, Mama... Papa. I'd like you to meet my son, Jonathon Abner," she said in a quiet, controlled voice.

They stared at her with undisguised amazement. Her Papa's face turned a deep red. Her Mama lifted trembling hands to her face and then finally found her voice. "Charlotte..! Your *hair*... and th-the baby... we thought... so you didn't give the child..."

"No, Mama. I didn't give up my child for adoption. I couldn't. I love him."

Abner Brown spoke for the first time. "And you expect us to... to just *take* you back... with that... that *brat*?" he spat out at her.

"He's no brat, Papa. He's my son... and *your* grandson. And yes, Papa, I expect you to take us both home with you. Otherwise, we will both go elsewhere. *Because I will not give up my son!*"

Charlie said the words with a quiet finality that gave no room for argument. A sudden cheer rose from the upper hallway, and Sara's voice rang out above the rest, "'*Way to go, Chuck!!*"

Charlie's parents gaped at the group of girls gathered at the top of the stairs. Mrs. Brown stammered faintly, "Ch-*Chuck?*"

Sara sauntered casually down the staircase and said with an impudent grin, "Here, Charlie Brown. Let me hold little Jonathon *Abner* while you get your things!"

She took the baby from Charlie, and then suddenly seemed to change her mind. "Or, better yet, *you* hold him for us, would you Rev. Brown?" she asked sweetly as she thrust the boy into the flustered man's hands. Abner Brown looked wildly at his wife, then back at Sara, but the saucy redhead had turned abruptly away, giving him little choice other than to accept his grandson into unwilling arms.

Sara grinned broadly, winking at Amy who stood quietly to one side, and took Charlie's arm to lead her to her room. Charlie glanced anxiously back over her shoulder at her parents, and then heard her Mama say in a small, excited voice, "Why, I do declare, Abner, I believe the boy has your nose!"

Charlie felt her heart stop with fear. Surely they would notice the square jaw and the high forehead and the black hair that so clearly identified him, in her own eyes, at least, as none other than the son of their own Elder Parsons. But Mama was only beaming with undisguised pride.

For the first time, the Rev. Abner Brown looked at his grandson. Charlie couldn't be sure, but she thought she saw a small smile light his face.

THE WEDDING

Spring came early. The countryside was dotted with bright splashes of vibrant yellows and rich purples and glowing pinks, all nestled in the soft green of new growth. Amy gazed at dew-laden grass touched with golden highlights. She raised her window just enough to get a good whiff of fragrant air, and then reached for her sweater. She just couldn't waste a perfectly gorgeous morning like this one!

She slipped her feet into her old gardening shoes and waded out into the beauty of Ben's immaculately groomed lawn. The chill of early morning air was softened by the sun's warmth. A mockingbird serenaded with joyful notes, soaring above the happy chirping of a multitude of sparrows and robins that flitted about the yard. Amy took a great gulp of the sweetly scented breeze that stirred her hair, and wandered toward the south side of the house which was bordered with a row of heavily budded lilac bushes. She could smell their fragrance already!

How she was going to miss the beauty and peacefulness of this grand old home. She trusted Tom's judgment, and wouldn't even think of interfering with his plans for the hotel, of course, but her heart was here, with these girls whose needs were so great. For who would be there to hug them when they were lonely, to listen to their fears and concerns, to teach them how to diaper a newborn? Sam, and Helen, she chided herself sternly. And they would do the job just fine without her! She would have plenty to keep her busy at their new hotel, caring for struggling mothers and hurting children who were trying to escape from the horrors of abuse.

The sound of a car in the driveway brought a glad smile to her lips. Tom! What was he doing here so early on a Monday morning? She heard the car door slam shut, and he soon appeared from behind the house, walking gingerly through wet grass.

"Good morning, Tom!" Amy called happily. "What brings you here today?"

"Oh, I had a hankerin' to see my best girl," he answered with a crooked grin and a quick kiss. "But what in the world are you doing out here? This is like wading in six inches of water!"

Amy laughed gaily. "It *is* pretty soggy, I guess. But such a beautiful morning! I was just remembering that April 25th is less than two weeks away, and I haven't yet decided how to decorate the chapel for our wedding. Maybe..."

"Our *wedding*?!" Tom responded with feigned surprise. "So *that's* why I have the 25th circled in red! I was wondering..."

Amy chose to ignore his banter and asked thoughtfully, "What do you think about using a mix of white and lavender lilacs in huge white baskets scattered about the sanctuary? They smell just heavenly, and lavender is such a soft, springy color. Don't you think that would be nice?"

"Sounds just fine to me, as long as you don't make me wear a purple tux or something!"

Amy chuckled. "No, I thought I would just let you and Bill Johnson get together and decide what to wear, since he's to be your best man. After all, the two of you could stock a fair sized menswear shop with the clothes you already have! And you both have great taste! Maybe a dark charcoal gray..."

"So let me get this straight. Bill and I can choose any color we want, so long as it's charcoal gray, right?"

Amy sputtered again with laughter. "Something like that, yes. Did you really come over here this morning just to see me?"

"Actually, I came to see Ben," Tom answered, and then added quickly, "but I *do* have something to talk to *you* about first! Do you think we could go inside where it's dry?"

Amy took his arm with a slight shake of her head. "Well, you got yourself out of *that* one pretty slick! Come on, let's go in the house."

She kicked off soaking wet shoes at the front door, and then saw Tom hesitate as he glimpsed the shine of the hardwood floors inside. He bent and removed his shoes also, leaving his expensive black loafers next to her battered old tennis shoes. Amy thought with some amusement that the discarded footwear was a fair facsimile of the two of them—she, the carefree country girl, and he, the highly polished executive. But he padded behind her in his sock feet with no apparent embarrassment.

Once inside Amy's office, Tom came right to the purpose of his visit. "Amy, would you mind terribly if we changed our plans and decided to live here, at The Refuge, instead of at the hotel?"

She stared at him with undisguised amazement. "Mind? *Me?* Well, no... of course not!" she stammered with joy, and then added mischievously, "If you *insist*, that is..."

Tom grinned. "I was pretty sure you would prefer it that way, and ever since young Ross Marshall came to see me that day when he was here I've been thinking about something, and, well, I called him this weekend and we had a long talk. Then he called Sara, and they talked, and he called me back again last night. Amy, I've asked Ross and Sara if they would like to live in the executive suite at the top of the Grand American Hotel and manage the business there. They are very excited about it, but Sara had one stipulation. She has requested that Sam move there, as well!"

"Oh, Tom! I... it's just *perfect*! For *everyone*! Ross spoke of wanting to get into some kind of work similar to ours here—in fact, he could hardly talk about anything else! Is it all settled, then?"

"Almost. I want to have this whole south wing converted into living quarters for us. With Sam moving out, there should be plenty of room. She has agreed to move into your house in town while the renovation is being done, if you don't mind. And can you move your things into one of the rooms in the nursery wing for a while? The work should be done and the area livable by the time we return from our honeymoon trip."

Amy's smile was radiant as she moved into his warm embrace. "I will happily move my things, Tom. What a wonderful surprise! Thank you for understanding my feelings about living here."

Her fervent kiss was all the thanks Tom could ever have asked for.

Ben hung up his telephone with a sigh of relief. It was all settled! And none too soon! He'd heard Tom drive up, and knew he would be knocking at his door in a few moments. Ben couldn't stop grinning.

It was downright amazin' how the blessings had begun to pour in, and almost from the minute he'd vowed to God to devote the rest of his life to serving Him in any way he could. First Crystal had approached him about disclosing a bit about his background in her story for *Lifestyles*—she'd been uncommonly discreet about it, too, bless her heart. But she'd mentioned that he'd sung with a popular gospel quartet until his voice had failed him, and then he'd had to search for work anywhere it became available.

And she'd spoken of how Tom Logan had "rescued" him with a most welcome job as the groundskeeper for The Refuge. And then they had urged him to return to his music, asking him to sing a solo during the dedication ceremony for their newly completed chapel. She'd described the miracle that had restored his wondrous voice, and the great joy that it had brought to him.

And that had been more than enough for Ron Sharp, his best friend and The Churchmen's talented bass singer. Ron had written to Ben immediately upon reading her story, and then the two of them had talked by phone, and one thing had just naturally led to another.

Ben's head jerked up as he saw a shadow pass his window, and heard the light tap at his door. He threw it open with joy.

The girls decided it was time for their inspection of this hotel that was being constantly talked about with such great excitement—"the girls" being Amy and Sam and, of course, Sara, since she was soon to take up residence there. Ross had arrived that very morning for the weekend's wedding ceremony, and there was no keeping *him* a minute longer from visiting his future abode and new responsibility. They enlisted Helen and the girls of the house to baby-sit Lance and Noah, and they all piled into Sam's Cadillac for the trip to town.

Tom and Bill were on hand for the grand tour, of course. They proudly showed off the gracious reception area. Its large circular check-in counter sat beneath a magnificent crystal chandelier hanging from the second story ceiling. A sweeping staircase would welcome guests to the widely curving balcony that overlooked the spacious gathering place below. A huge fieldstone fireplace dominated the room, and comfortable armchairs and sofas would be clustered about in cozy groupings that invited intimate meetings and quiet conversations.

"This is the core of the main floor," Tom explained, "with a large dining room off the back hallway and three smaller shopping areas on each side. They will each open onto the U-shaped walkway that surrounds the central reception foyer. The six smaller shops will be easily accessible to our guests here, as well as to the general public, who may stop in for lunch or dinner in our fine dining hall."

"Do we have the shopping spaces leased out yet?" Amy asked with unbridled interest.

"We are talking to a retired business woman about opening a gift shop in this front space. It's a prime location and she is extremely interested. And we've offered the front space on the north side to Gretta, who will happily open her own beauty shop there as soon as the remodeling is completed," Tom answered proudly. "Sara has suggested we reserve the back corner unit for a child care service, both for our guests and for our employees. We can staff it with our own girls from the house, or others who need work."

"It sounds to me like you've put a lot of thought into this whole operation," Sam offered. "Are the other spots still up for grabs then?"

"Well, Jonathon would like to see a Christian books and videos shop go into one of them, and he is currently negotiating with a couple from church," Bill answered. "The husband lost his job a couple of months ago and they are having a rough time of it right now. We're thinking strongly of offering the space rent-free until they can get on their feet again. And the middle space on the south side is to be the management office. We plan to divide it into two offices—one for you, Sam, and the other for Ross. The private elevator to the top floor will be accessible only from Ross's office."

"Have you set an opening date yet?" Sam asked eagerly.

"We're shooting for June first, with our grand opening celebration sometime during the middle part of July. We should be able to attract some summer visitors who will, hopefully, spread the word about our grand facility," Tom responded with some excitement.

Ross, who had been silently spellbound up until this moment, finally asked with some trepidation, "Are you folks really sure you want to entrust all of this to Sara and me? We're pretty young, and very green, and as excited as I am about the whole thing, I... well, I guess I just want to be sure that *you're* sure about it."

"We're all new to this business, young man," Bill Johnson said with a warm smile. "And Tom and I have agreed that we'd rather have a manager fresh out of school that we're sure we can trust, than a veteran in the business who we don't know. The important thing is the fact that you believe in the work we're trying to do, and you're willing to ask for help whenever you need it."

"And, besides, Bill and I will be just across town if you need us." Tom added.

"And I'll be right next door." said Sam.

"And God is always only a prayer away!" Amy finished with a smile.

Sara reached for Ross's hand and spoke for the first time. "Ross and I were hoping we all could meet together every Monday morning for a short devotional and prayer meeting to start each week. We believe that if we have God's blessing on our work here that nothing but good can come from it, regardless of the problems we may face. Would that be possible, do you think?"

Bill Johnson looked at Ross's beautiful young wife with surprised pleasure. "It's not only possible, my dear, it's absolutely necessary!"

Amy smiled at Tom with wonder, and agreed, "Yes, Sara, you can count on all of us to be here, at least in spirit. Even if Tom and I happen to be in the middle of a crisis of some sort at the house, our prayers will be with you, I promise!"

As she turned to Sam she saw, much to her delight, tears of pride and joy welling in her best friend's eyes.

Amy stood at the small window of her room in the nursery wing and gazed at the glory of the pre-dawn sky. A few thin clouds rested near the horizon, catching the first golden rays of sunlight that promised to peek above the trees at any minute. The morning sky was an artist's palette of crimson and ochre and amethyst, the perfect prelude to this, her wedding day.

Amy thought of other wedding days—her first as the bride of the wildly handsome Jack Gardner when she was so young and so impetuous. And her second to Nick Anderson, a quiet man who had seemed to be the exact opposite of the irresponsible and unreliable Jack, and who had promised to be the father she had so desperately needed for little Jonathon. She sighed aloud. She'd married Jack after a whirlwind romance that had fed her naive imagination with thoughts of glamour and freedom, coming, as she had, from a strict rural upbringing that had allowed very little of either. And then Jack Gardner had abandoned her and their small son, and she'd had to learn to fend for herself. As devastating as it had seemed at the time, it had been one of God's most cherished gifts in her life, bringing her into contact with George and Samantha Sanders—her beloved Sam, the friend of a lifetime!

How complicated and unexpected are life's pathways, she thought with wonder. For she had married Nick Anderson for the stability and security she had never had with Jack, only to learn, much later, of his addiction to alcohol. The few drinks that he had taken during their early years together had seemed so harmless, an escape, really, for this shy man. For he had faced such sorrow when his mother had fallen prey to Alzheimer's and he'd found himself powerless to care for her. And Nick had given Amy the priceless gifts of their daughters, Dani and Nicki. But as the years and the struggles and the disappointments had taken their toll, he had turned away from God and his family, and had sought oblivion in drunkenness.

Tears filled her eyes as she remembered those horror-filled years when Nick had lost his job and they'd been forced to move to Tulsa. The loneliness and fear of that time rushed over her with a wave of anguish—her constant terror for her daughters, the desolation of a loveless marriage, the horror of Nick's infidelity and his abusive behavior toward her and their children. But God had been there always, even though she had failed many times to recognize His guidance and direction.

And through it all she could now see the one shining star, the one sure source of strength that God had provided for her when she had needed it the most—Tom Logan. For hadn't it been her Father's guidance that had led her to American Trucking Company when it became apparent that Nick would no longer be able to provide for his family? And hadn't Tom become her friend, her support, her very sanity during those days when she'd lost Nick to another woman, and then to the tragic accident that had snuffed out his life? Those days when she'd very nearly lost Dani as well?

Amy brought herself back to the present with firm resolve. She must not dwell in an unhappy past on this, of all days! For she understood, finally, that God had taken her down the rocky roads of her life to bring her here, to this place, on this day. She knew that her own struggle against the devastation of her husband's alcoholism, her own pain during that time of uncertainty and confusion when her young daughter Dani gave birth to an illegitimate child, her own fight to keep her faith strong when God seemed so very far away, all had given her a greater tolerance and an increased depth of caring for the girls here at The Refuge.

And today she would become the bride of Tom Logan. For the first time she would marry for that best of all reasons—love. She thought of Julie's words about Jonathon. *He is a man that I can submit to entirely and know that he will never make a decision regarding my life that will hurt me... because he loves me... and because he loves his God.* How true those words, and how wonderful that knowledge!

The sun was now well above the tree tops, smiling from a cloudless sky. Amy heard a baby cry in the next room, then heard Ross' quiet voice as he soothed the restless infant. It mattered not whether the distressed child was the blonde headed, blue-eyed boy that was his own son, or the black-eyed, dark headed boy with almond colored skin that would become his son as soon as the adoption proceedings were completed. He loved them equally, and with an astounding fervor.

Amy smiled as she pulled on her long robe and stepped into matching slippers. She'd dawdled long enough! Her daughters, who had arrived with their families the day before and who were staying at her house in town, would soon be at the door, anxious to help with all those exciting last-minute preparations for the momentous occasion of this day. Charlie and her family had arrived early, also, and she knew that Charlie would be at the chapel later this morning to go over the music with Ben. And Helen was probably picking fresh lilacs for the sanctuary this very minute!

She rushed from the room with a glad heart and a grateful prayer on her lips.

It was a lovely, old fashioned wedding. Amy had insisted upon the traditional vows that had united her parents so many years ago. The ceremony had been simple, yet beautiful. She had chosen a softly gathered silk dress in the lightest shade of lavender, and, because Sam had found it and had pronounced it as being "just perfect", had worn a wide-brimmed white hat that trailed long satin ribbons to a point well below her waist. A lavish bouquet of fresh orchids and white roses added the finishing touches to her stunning ensemble.

Sam, who served as her matron of honor, of course, had chosen an elegant suit of royal purple, and had carried a single white rose bud. And Tom and Bill had looked so handsomely distinguished in their splendid dark gray pin-striped suits and black ties. Amy sighed happily, now that it was over and she was surrounded by all the people that she loved the most. She looked up at the man who stood at her side, and who was now, incredibly, her husband. How in the world had he and Ben managed to give her the surprise of her life today, when she had thought she had every detail planned to perfection?!

And it *had* gone according to plan, with Jonathon's opening remarks, those oft-spoken words that symbolized the traditional wedding ceremony... *Dearly beloved, we are gathered here today...* And then Ben singing *The Lord's Prayer* as only he could, and that beautiful part as they exchanged their rings, which Jonathon had referred to as "their rainbows of promise." She remembered his words. *When we look at a rainbow, we see only a part of it, as is true of all of God's gifts. But from heaven above the rainbow forms a perfect circle of color, and it signifies the promise of God's everlasting love. Likewise, as you exchange these rings today, I ask you to repeat after me your promises of love... With this ring I thee wed...*

Yes, it had all gone exactly as she had planned—until Ben had sung the beautiful *For Always*, and then had remained in place as Charlie continued to play soft background music instead of letting them return to the service. Amy had gaped with undisguised astonishment as three strangers suddenly rose from three widely scattered spots in the sanctuary and moved to the front to join Ben at the microphone. And then they had begun to sing in that wondrous harmony that could only come from her beloved group, The Churchmen. They sang a glorious song that she had never heard before...

To you, I pledge my troth this day,
To love and to cherish all the days of my life.
We'll walk in the shelter of God's precious love
Together, as husband and wife.

We're joined in love by God's Holy Hand,
We two shall become as one.
We offer our praise as humbly we bow
Before God, and Jesus, His Son.

In You, O Lord, we take refuge,
Our rock, our fortress, forever You'll be.
Into Your Hands, O Lord, our God
Our lives we commit to Thee.

Tears welled in her eyes as she remembered the beautiful words that seemed to speak only of them and their life here at The Refuge. She must find Ben and his friends. She wanted to meet them and to thank them. And there he was, coming toward them, surrounded once again by the group that had gained such respect in the field of Gospel music, a tremendous smile spread across his face.

"Tom! Here's Ben!" Amy spoke excitedly, tugging at Tom's arm and interrupting his greeting to a co-worker from American Trucking. She moved into Ben's arms with a glad cry, "Oh, Ben. What a wonderful surprise! *Please,* introduce me to these gentlemen!"

Ben appeared to have added at least two inches to his stature as he stood proudly before them, introducing the original singing group known as The Churchmen. Amy happily shook each man's hand and thanked him for coming and singing for their wedding. And then Ben turned to his three friends and added, "I am proud to introduce to you my boss and his wife, Mr. and Mrs. Tom Logan!"

Amy beamed, and Tom offered a warm greeting to each of them and then congratulated them on a wonderful performance.

"And that song!" Amy exclaimed. "Wherever did you find it?"

"Actually, I wrote it for this very occasion," answered Ron Sharp, who not only sang bass with the group, but who had also written or arranged much of their music. "I happened to read the article about your work here, and noticed that your center was named The Refuge, because of the verses in Psalm 31. I then set out to write a wedding song that would incorporate those verses. It seems to have worked out very well."

"It couldn't have been better," Tom agreed heartily. "And Amy, I believe Ben and the boys have some exciting news to share with us."

Ben swelled with pride. "The boys have asked me to come back and sing with them again, Amy. And I have agreed, under the condition that half of all the proceeds from all recordings and concerts is to go into a special fund. You see, Tom and I have talked a great deal in the last few weeks about a mission for the homeless. We have come to the conclusion that a shelter gives only shelter, which is very important, of course. But I would like to go a step further and offer a rehabilitation program to help these folks break away from the vices and the dependencies that bring most of them to that hopeless state.

"We have drawn up tentative plans for The John Benjamin Smith Rehabilitation Center for the Homeless, to be built here in Bartlesville as soon as funds are available. I figure once a person is living a clean life, he or she is then ready to begin earning a living again. Tom's hotel will be there to offer steady employment. And I have Jonathon's promise to give these folks the spiritual counseling to see them through the whole process. We will give them shelter and food, of course, but we want to do so much more than that. We want to give them hope and self-reliance and the comfort of God's love."

Amy's tears spilled over as she once again threw her arms around the simple, kindly man who had been so much more than just their gardener. "Ben, I can't tell you how proud and happy I am! We will miss you dreadfully, of course, but you must promise to come back and sing for us whenever you're in the area."

"The boys and I have a lot of work to do, but our tentative plans are to hold annual benefit concerts here in Bartlesville each year during the Christmas and the Easter seasons. The proceeds of those concerts will go solely to your work here at The Refuge. How does that sound?" Ben asked happily.

"It sounds perfectly marvelous! And look who's here! Crystal Atoka, who is now head of *The Daily Oklahoman's* Arts and Leisure Section, and soon to be our daughter-in-law. Crystal, these gentlemen are gonna' need some brilliant publicity in the very near future. In case you haven't figured it out by now, this is John Benjamin and The Churchmen!"

∽

Their guests had slowly trailed through the trees and back into the house for cake and punch. The day was impeccable, a light breeze stirring new leaves with a soft, whispering sound, the fragrance of dogwood blossoms and wild roses mingling in the warm afternoon air. It was the kind of lazy spring day that beckoned young and old alike back outside, and several people had carried their slices of wedding cake and cups of fruit punch out onto the wide front verandah to linger there in the late afternoon sunshine.

Amy and Tom moved leisurely through the clusters of their friends and relatives, sometimes together, but more often apart, greeting their guests with warm hugs or hearty handshakes. Amy smiled as she caught sight of Charlie and her parents, and noticed that the Rev. Abner Brown was proudly holding his new grandson. A wide smile warmed his rather austere features into a surprisingly pleasant countenance. She noticed Sara and Ross, each holding a baby, chatting avidly with Crystal and Jim, and then turning to welcome Julie and Jonathon, as they approached the two young couples. Love was certainly in the air today, Amy thought gratefully.

At that moment, she spied Josh, her fine looking young grandson, deliberately making his way to Charlie's side. She saw Charlie's quick blush, then watched as the girl introduced Joshua to her parents. The two young people then drifted toward the front door. Amy watched with fascination as Charlie apparently dominated their conversation, for once in her life, talking animatedly about something or other. How very interesting, Amy mused, as she scanned the group around her for Josh's mother, her oldest daughter, Dani.

She found Dani in the corner, talking quietly with Jerry Snyder, and looking very much in love, herself. The two of them were planning a late May wedding, and Amy thanked the Lord once more for that quiet, sweet-natured man that had finally erased the last of the loneliness and pain from her daughter's eyes. She'd known of the constant struggle in Dani's life during those years following that horrible night when, upon learning of her father's tragic death, she had sought solace in the arms of an unknown serviceman. It had been an unending battle to provide for, and to parent, her young son alone. For Dani had never seriously considered the attentions of any man since that time, Amy knew, until she had met this lonely widower who was trying, also alone, to raise his two young daughters.

Amy moved again, slowly, accepting the congratulations of those who continued to greet her. She let her eyes drift over the room, now searching for Nicki and Mike. She knew that if she located one of them, the other would be close by. For her youngest daughter and her husband had written a very special love story of their own through the years. A tale of strong commitment and unwavering loyalty. It showed in the four well-mannered children they were raising, and in the quiet assurance each always seemed to find in the presence of the other. Spotting them visiting with Sam in the front hallway, she had begun edging in that direction when a tug on her arm stopped her. She looked over her shoulder to find Tom, with an elderly gentleman in tow.

"Amy, I want to introduce you to an old friend of mine, Brother Seth Walters, from Chicago," Tom said eagerly. "He is the minister of the church I attended when I worked up there, and he has traveled all this way to be here today. Seth, this is my wife, Amy."

"I'm so glad to meet you, Brother Walters. Tom has mentioned you many times. How nice of you to come today!" Amy exclaimed.

"Well, I've wanted to see your place firsthand, since Tom and I spent many hours together, talking and praying, as we struggled to understand God's plan for you here. And I must say, I'm mighty pleased with all I've seen. I read both of Miss Atoka's fine articles, of course, and so my visit just serves to confirm what I already felt to be true. And that reminds me, did you happen to help a young lady named Kasaundra Lawrence sometime last fall?"

"Sunny! Why yes... yes we did," Amy stammered, her face showing her obvious distress. "She was here f-for several weeks, but..."

"Did you know Mrs. Lawrence, then?" Tom asked, when Amy floundered, unable to speak of the girl's death.

"Yes, Sunny and Noah attended our church in Chicago. As a matter of fact, I married the two of them. It was such a sad affair, what with Noah's untimely death, and Sunny's pregnancy. She came to me in utter desolation, with no money and no place to go, and, I suspect, very poor health. Such a sweet girl! I referred her to Social Services and recommended The Refuge as a suitable place for her. I've heard nothing since then." The old minister frowned with apparent sorrow.

Tom laid a hand on his friend's arm and said softly, "Seth, we lost her. She died in childbirth. The doctors here diagnosed her as having a congenital heart disease. But she gave birth to a fine son." He looked about the crowded room and found Ross and Sara, who were moving toward the front entrance. He caught Sara's eye and beckoned to them.

As the young couple approached, Tom continued, "Seth, I would like you to meet Ross and Sara Marshall. Sara was a very close friend of Sunny's while the two of them were residents here. And this is Sunny's child, Noah Franklin Lawrence. He will soon be legally adopted by Ross and Sara, and will be raised as a brother to their own son, Lance."

The elderly minister took young Noah into his arms, beaming with pleasure. "I'm so happy to meet you folks. I'm Seth Walters, close friend and minister of the Lawrences. I loved Sunny like my own daughter, and it makes my heart glad to know that her son will be loved and well cared for. May the Lord bless all of you!"

Amy finally found Charlie sitting in the front porch swing, with her baby in her arms. She sat down beside the girl and laid a hand on her arm. "I've been looking for you, Charlie. I wanted to thank you for playing for our wedding, and to give you this small gift from Tom and me. You played beautifully, as usual, and I want you to know that we have missed you sorely since you went home."

"Thank you, Miss Amy," Charlie said with a shy smile. "You didn't need to go and buy a gift for me. I would never have missed playing for your wedding. It was so beautiful... and I'm very happy for you and Mr. Tom."

"How are things going for you Charlie? Have you made any plans for your future?"

"Yes, Miss Amy, I think I have. As a matter of fact, I was just sitting here thinking about a lot of things. It's... well, it's different for me at home, now. Mama and Papa are treatin' me real good and everything, but I feel sorta' out of place there all of a sudden. It's like I've changed, grown up, I guess, but they still treat me like their little girl—and I don't mean to sound stuck up or mean or anything, but when I came here I saw a whole different world..."

Charlie let her thoughts hang in the air between them, as if uncertain of her feelings. Amy slipped an arm around her shoulders and gave her a quick hug. "I felt exactly the same way when I was your age, Charlie. Once I got away from home and started college I felt like my whole existence up until that time had been shut up inside a box, with never even a chance to see anything on the outside. I made some foolish mistakes once I began to explore that world outside my box, but I also began to understand that there were many people who thought and felt and lived much differently than I. It was the first time I ever really saw the world through my own eyes, instead of the eyes of my parents."

Charlie gave her a grateful look and nodded solemnly. "Yeah, I know. I never even realized that people like Sara and Maddie *existed*... And Miss Crystal and Jonathon... *everyone* here taught me so many things. Going home was like going back in time, to a life I don't belong in any more..." Charlie once again paused, as if striving to understand her conflicting emotions. Amy remembered the shy, frightened girl that had come to them last fall and smiled to herself. This young lady had certainly "grown up," as she, herself, had put it. And had grown into such a lovely young woman, with poise and a quiet self-confidence that spoke of new maturity and a strong faith.

Charlie suddenly turned and said with a rush of excited determination, "Miss Amy, Ben has asked me to join The Churchmen as their permanent accompanist. It would mean taking Johnny on the road with us, I know, but all of the group have insisted that he'll be no trouble. And two of the men have wives who travel with them. One of them has a daughter that's near my own age who arranges their travel schedules and overnight accommodations. They would all help take care of my baby when I'm busy practicing or performing. Ben says they'll pay our expenses, and even give me a percentage of the proceeds! And it would give me a chance to see all the places I've never been, and to play the organ for Ben and the others night after night, proclaiming God through our music!" Charlie's eyes reflected her mounting excitement. "Miss Amy, I think I'm gonna' accept their offer! Do you think I can do it?"

"Of course you can do it, my dear! You are a wonderful musician, and you would be in the company of many fine Christian men and women." Amy's smile broadened as she added mischievously, "As Sara would say, *Go for it, Charlie Brown!*"

They returned home in the midst of a blinding thunderstorm. The wedding trip had been brief, but entirely wonderful, Amy thought, as Tom drove his little car carefully on the rain-slickened gravel road toward The Refuge. And it really was home, she reflected, as much as any house had ever been to her, the place her heart longed to be. As relaxing and enjoyable as the past few days in the beautiful Colorado Rockies had been, she was intensely anxious to reach the gates of The Refuge.

A sudden gust of wind rocked Tom's little car, and the driving rain slammed against the windshield with such force that Tom leaned forward in an effort to see the road ahead. It was late, nearly midnight. Turbulent weather throughout the Midwest had delayed their flight to Oklahoma City, and then they'd had the long drive back to Bartlesville, made longer by the storm cells that had cropped up all along the way. It was typical spring weather for Oklahoma, Amy knew, but she shivered from the cold damp wind that managed to invade the little car in spite of closed windows and the heater running full blast.

Lightning flashed across the inky sky and illuminated the row of trees that surrounded their house. The giant cottonwoods and sugar maples swayed and twisted in the vicious wind like frenzied dancers driven by some inner fury. When they finally reached the driveway, Tom pulled the car as closely as possible to the back steps. An umbrella would be useless in that kind of wind and so the two of them jumped from the car and made a wild dash for the shelter of the back porch. It couldn't have taken more than a few seconds, but they were both drenched by the time the back door slammed shut behind them.

The house was dark except for the kitchen. Helen hurried to greet them, the smell of coffee and something fresh from the oven heavy in the air.

"Helen!" Amy gasped with a warm smile. "You should have been in bed hours ago! What smells so *good*?"

"I knew you'd be needin' somethin' hot to warm you up on a night like this. You're both soakin' wet! Let me get some towels, and then, as soon as you've changed into dry clothes, I've got coffee and cinnamon rolls to munch on," Helen fussed. Amy was never so glad to see anyone in her life, and would have grabbed the other woman in a warm embrace if she hadn't been dripping wet.

Later, as they sat around the table in the warm kitchen, Tom asked quietly, "Helen, are you sure you don't want to manage the hotel's food service? These cinnamon rolls are out of this world!"

Helen laughed with pleasure. But she was shaking her head as she answered. "No, Tom. I just don't feel like that's where I belong. Mebbe I'm just kiddin' myself, but I believe I have somethin' to offer the girls here, and I'd really like to just stay put, if you don't mind."

"How are the girls?" Amy asked eagerly.

"Well, Doc Cameron told that new girl Judy Harper today that he's pretty sure he can hear two heartbeats..."

"*Twins!*"

"And we got a call from Social Services in Dallas askin' if we could take in two more girls. I told 'em we might have to hang 'em from the ceilin' if we did, but I'd give you the message and let you call 'em back when you got home..."

"Well, Brenda should deliver any day now..."

"Actually, Brenda has a new daughter, born early this mornin'..."

"*A new baby*—and I wasn't even here to help! Oh, Helen, are they all right?"

"They're fine! Everything's just fine..."

Finally, after Amy had been completely reassured that all was well with her girls, Helen led the two of them to the newly redone south wing. Amy gasped with pleasure. The rooms were lovely. The spacious bedroom was now furnished with the giant old four-poster that had been her grandmother's legacy to her so many years ago, and her comfortable old rocker waited nearby. The new curtains and bedspread were a wedding gift from Sam, Helen said, and were the softest shade of blue.

The adjoining sitting room was an even greater surprise. It was obvious that Sam and Helen had spent many hours making the room comfortable and cozy, with an attractive mix of her things and Tom's. A cheerfully crackling fire had been laid in the brick fireplace, and one lighted lamp in the corner gave the room a soft, romantic glow. After making sure they had everything they needed, Helen said goodnight and left the newlyweds alone.

"Do you need anything from the car?" Tom asked.

"No! Nothing that can't wait until morning. And I certainly don't want to send you back out into that awful storm!"

Another great crash of thunder followed her words, and Amy moved gratefully to the warmth of the fire. Tom took her hand and pulled her down beside him onto the couch that faced the fireplace. "You know, it's on a night like this that you really appreciate having a refuge to go to," he reflected. "A place of warmth, a shelter from the storm."

Amy settled into the strength of his embrace and asked quietly, "Tom, what made you change your mind about living here? Was it just to please me?"

"No, Amy, although pleasing you is very important to me. But it was the letter I got from Seth Walters after Crystal's article in *Lifestyles* was published that started me to thinking about my purpose here, and how far I had strayed from it. You know, we get so caught up in our own plans sometimes that we tend to forget God's plan for us. And, I must confess, that is exactly what I did.

"I've told you a little about the dream I had when I was living in Chicago—the dream that Seth managed to convince me was God's way of revealing His plan for my life. That dream very clearly outlined the work I was to do here, but in my excitement about opening the hotel, I lost direction, intent upon my own devices.

"Amy, the Grand American Hotel is a wonderful mission, but it's not *my* mission. There are others who will gladly and skillfully handle those other projects. Ross and Sara and Bill will see to the hotel, and Ben will proceed with his work for the homeless. But God sent me *here*, to The Refuge, and to you, and to the young women that need our help. It is here that I will stay."

Roanoke Public Library
308 S. Walnut
Roanoke, TX 76262

CPSIA information can be obtained at www.ICGtesting.com
Printed in the USA
LVOW060851120512

281405LV00002B/4/P

9 781462 401390